THE FAIR DEAL

Eve has been brought up at Corderhay Park by her adoptive parents Jack and Antoinette Corderhay, along with her younger half-sister Anne-Marie. As they grow up, Anne-Marie becomes a spoilt, wilful young woman who will stop at nothing to get her own way. During a holiday in Paris, Anne-Marie makes a desperate phone call which results in Eve rushing over to France. What she discovers has life-changing consequences for their family and friends, and especially for Eve herself. It looks as though once again Anne-Marie has taken her happiness with no thought for anyone else.

The Fair Deal

by

Patricia Robins

Magna Large Print Books
Long Preston, North Yorkshire,
BD23 4ND, England.

British Library Cataloguing in Publication Data.

Robins, Patricia
    The fair deal.

        A catalogue record of this book is
        available from the British Library

        ISBN   978-0-7505-2974-7

First published in Great Britain in 1952 by
Hutchinson & Co. (Publishers) Ltd.

Copyright © 1952 by Patricia Robins

Cover illustration © Pavel Libera by arrangement with
britainonview

The moral right of the author has been asserted

Published in Large Print 2009 by arrangement with
Claire Lorrimer

Magna Large Print is an imprint of Library Magna Books Ltd.

Printed and bound in Great Britain by
T.J. (International) Ltd., Cornwall, PL28 8RW

CONTENTS

Book I

CAUSE

CHAPTER 1

Eve looked around the room and said to herself:

'Now what *haven't* I done?'

She was always saying that – to herself! She was so afraid that there might be something she had neglected. She was, of course, far too conscientious, often to her own detriment, and the first to recognize that fact. But she was a girl with a deep, passionate sense of gratitude. Unceasingly she felt grateful to the parents who had been so good to her and who, even after their own child came into the world, had continued to love and cherish her as their own.

There was nothing she would not have done for any one of the Corderhay family. Hers by adoption – like the name. She knew little about her own parents. It was a closed book, never discussed. She was particularly devoted to the quiet, charming man who was her father. Jack Corderhay was popular with everybody, and Conservative Member for the district. One of the old school struggling to keep up appearances on rapidly dwindling means. Spending capital. Determined never to leave Corderhay Park, the home which he had inherited from old Admiral Sir John Corderhay, who had lived here in the days when they kept a staff of eight or nine indoors and six gardeners.

Extravagant, luxurious, amusing days for people like the Corderhays. But not so amusing now with half the great gardens going to rack and ruin, and only one or two faithful 'dailies' from the village of Ashmenster, which was about ten miles from Bournemouth. A series of living-in cooks of all nationalities came and went for some very good reason.

The whole family maintained that the fort was being held only because of Eve. Eve, who helped to turn out the rooms, keep the lovely silver polished, the exquisite china washed, and the flowers arranged with an artist's touch. Eve really loved the place more than did her sister by adoption, Anne-Marie, who was a Corderhay by birth and blood. Sometimes when Jack Corderhay saw Eve's almost desperate efforts to keep things going in the old grand manner, he would laugh and say:

'I think you really *are* my daughter and that the blood of the Corderhays runs in you instead of in that pickle of a daughter of mine!'

This pleased Eve, just as she was pleased when the woman whom she called 'Mother' praised her – congratulated her on the success of a dinner-party, or the way the guest-room was arranged, or the shopping done.

'You are my g-r-eat comfort and help, *chérie*,' she would often say, and clasp Eve to her bosom. One of those emotional embraces which embarrassed even while it pleased the quiet, reserved English girl, who thought Antoinette Corderhay must surely be the most lovable woman in the world.

Antoinette was French. Jack Corderhay had married her during the First World War when he was a young Staff Captain stationed in France. She had been the daughter of a French General. *Petite*, vivacious, with a flair for clothes – that touch of chic which is the heritage of the Frenchwoman. And all the facile charm which she had handed on to her daughter. Anne-Marie definitely favoured the mother's side. Antoinette, strangely enough, had none of the average French-woman's shrewd judgment or aptitude for running a household – or thrift. She had always been madly extravagant, and the people whispered that a good deal of Jack's present financial difficulty was due to the fact that his French wife had always spent money like water and could not get used to the change in the family fortunes. She and Jack were still very happy together, however – the tall Englishman, now grey-haired and in his sixties, was still a lover to the pretty little woman with the touch of silver in her golden hair, and the still perfect, tiny figure. If they ever had differences of opinion it was on the subject of money. Antoinette simply must learn to cut down, but Jack Corderhay was damned if he could see how to make her realize it.

Anne-Marie was as big a spendthrift as her mother, if not worse. Spoilt, of course. Antoinette, from the start, had worshipped the baby which had come so late in life – the Corderhays had been in their early forties when she appeared – nine years after their adoption of Eve. There had once been a son. The first fruit of that marriage soon after the 1918 Armistice. But he had died in an accident at the heartrending age of three. He had been as beautiful as an angel. There was a miniature of him in Antoinette's jewel-box which Eve had seen, but no other photographs. His name was never mentioned. The wound was too deep and the years had not lessened the hurt for the bereaved parents.

'*Never again!*' Antoinette Corderhay had cried after the funeral. It had been in London, where the small boy had run away from a careless nursemaid and been run over. '*Jamais encore!*'

But a few years later they had adopted Eve. Not because they had particularly wanted a child, since the precious little John could never be replaced in their affection, but because Antoinette Corderhay had been ill – some kind of nervous illness which could not be cured by her luxuries at Corderhay Park, her trips to the Continent, or even a world tour. The specialists in London and Paris said that she *needed* a child. Something real and absorbing to occupy her mind and turn the attention from herself.

Then it seemed that at the psychological moment the baby Eve was produced. Her parents had been old friends of the Corderhay family, both victims of an air accident. Jack Corderhay had returned home one day with the infant – and with the English nanny who had been in the General's family in France and who had brought up the '*petite* 'Toinette'.

At first it had been doubtful it would work. Antoinette had turned her face from the small bundle in old Nanny's arms. She had bitterly resented putting a strange child in the nurseries which had once echoed with her own little baby son's laughter. Then she had thawed.

On Eve's tenth birthday – seventeen years ago – she had heard the story of her adoption from her mother's lips.

'One look at you I took, *chérie*, while old Nanny was bathing you. You were a funny little baby with deep blue eyes and dark, silky hair. You had rather a sad look. *Triste*. You have always had it, although we have tried never to let you be sad. But perhaps

13

there is sadness in your nature and it showed on your baby face, so I took you to my heart and from that hour you were the consolation of our lives.'

They had never regretted the adoption. And for Eve it had been wonderful. She could remember only the happiest childhood, even though that latent 'sadness' made itself felt at odd times, deep down within her. Once she knew the truth about her parentage she could well believe that she was not Antoinette's child. Even that gay little Frenchwoman had never been able to interest Eve in frilly frocks and ribbons – or dolls. Eve had never been 'the little doll' Antoinette would have liked and had later found in Anne-Marie, whose arrival had so electrified the family. At first the whispered 'mistake', later the worshipped toy. But Eve had grown into a tall, thin child with smooth, dark hair, a grave little face with thoughtful brows and proud, determined lips. Nobody had ever quite understood her. Least of all Antoinette, who was full of emotion and slashed her feelings about the house like electric sparks. Eve was affectionate, but could not always show it. From the start she seemed to find it difficult to express what she really felt, which condition sprang, really, from an obliterating shyness. Quite naturally, she always put herself in the background and had what her friends called 'an inferiority complex'.

'I'm so ordinary,' she would say. 'I've no looks and no talents. I'm absolutely *ordinary*.'

That was, perhaps, true. There was nothing extraordinary about Eve. She had a moderately good figure, but her nose was a little too straight, she considered, to be lovely. Only when she smiled did she ever approach beauty, because of her dark, glowing eyes and soft, beautifully curved mouth.

Even her disposition was open to criticism from those who did not know her intimately. She was inclined to be moody and a little intolerant. She had set herself a high standard and cherished many ideals. Most of the young men whom she met had fallen short of those ideals, and far short of the man whom she loved as a father. Her shyness made her at times both curt and awkward. She loved to arrange parties for the others – loved especially to do things for Anne-Marie, who was so radiantly beautiful, fascinating to a degree. But Eve herself shrank from parties. She was not by nature gay, and in Anne-Marie's presence she felt positively dull. But there were plenty of things that she did like: books and good music and animals. From babyhood she had adored dogs. She had an old Cairn terrier, now nearly nine and on its last legs. It slept in her room and she could hardly bear it out of her sight, and was highly indignant when Anne-Marie called it a 'smelly old thing'.

For a long time now she had turned a deaf ear to Mrs Corderhay's suggestions that Wumpy should be destroyed. Twice Wumpy had almost died, and Eve had sat up all night nursing him. Nobody in the house had dared to interfere. Eve was like that, sweet and yielding to the family demands as a rule, but at moments so stubborn that nothing could move her from her purpose. The old Cairn, Wumpy, was one of these 'purposes'.

She had never been jealous of Anne-Marie. This was one of the traits her father admired in Eve's nature. Like everybody else, she worshipped at Anne-Marie's shrine and was, indeed, one of her most ardent admirers.

Anne-Marie physically resembled her mother .... was very like the old photographs which Jack Corderhay kept on his dressing-table, taken in Paris in 1914. Diminutive, like a Chelsea figurine, with an exquisite skin. She wore her spun-gold hair close-cropped with curled fringe above her wide-set, violet eyes with their incredibly long lashes. She had her mother's high-pitched, tinkling voice, and her bad memory. Anne-Marie could never remember anything. It was always:

'Eve, darling, where did I leave my blue bag?'
'Eve, I've lost that ticket for the dyer's...'
'Eve, where is my fountain-pen?'

And Eve always knew. In her quiet, unob-trusive fashion she would go round the

16

house after the others had gone out, and tidy up and restore order. Both Mrs Corderhay's and Anne-Marie's bedrooms were generally left in a state of hopeless confusion.

But whereas Antoinette Corderhay had a kindly and lovable nature, Anne-Marie was something of a problem – even to her devoted family. Eve had been brought up with her and, being six years older, had tried to 'mother' her and set something of an example. Even in her early teens she had subconsciously felt that to be necessary with Anne-Marie. But it hadn't always worked.

In the last year or two Eve had been forced to realize that her beautiful young sister was not a good character. Behind her excessive charm and physical attraction she was a mass of egotism. Eve tried to forgive her selfishness on the grounds that the rest of the family was to blame because she had been too indulged.

Jack Corderhay, also, had from time to time seen the red light of warning, but any efforts to discipline his small young daughter were always counteracted by her mother, who would cry:

'She did not mean it, *la pauvre!* She is still so young, *ma petite ange.*'

But Anne-Marie was not a little angel, and who should know it better than Eve? For how often in the nursery and schoolroom days had she tried to cover up some fault of

Anne-Marie's rather than see those limpid, violet eyes fill with tears, and those rose-red lips droop at the corners? Anne-Marie was so sweet when she *was* sweet. One kiss, one hug and all could be forgiven. That was the trouble. Nobody could be cross with her for long. In fact the only time that Eve had ever really lost her temper completely with Anne-Marie had been when she found the younger girl tormenting Wumpy. Then she had slapped Anne-Marie's face and there had been resentment between them for days. But even then Eve had found it in her heart to forgive her when Anne-Marie, shaken with sobs, begged for forgiveness. (Not because she was really sorry that she had hurt Wumpy, but because she could not bear people to be cross with her, and Eve was rather frightening when she was really cross. She became so ice-cold and remote!)

On the whole Eve had felt fairly happy about Anne-Marie until that incident of young David Bardwell.

The Bardwells lived in Ashmenster – retired Army people. David was at Sandhurst. He had taken Anne-Marie to a dance there and had fallen crazily in love with her. Eve was used to the fact that most of the boys who met her sister fell in love with her. Along with her other attractions, she had a seemingly inexhaustible flow of energy, an almost feverish gaiety and a touch of

18

méchantrie inherited from her French mother which seemed to captivate the men even more than her amazing beauty.

David, along with the rest, was captured. He was a quiet, good-looking boy, still young, for he had celebrated his twenty-first birthday on the same day as Anne-Marie. At that time – it had been last summer – he had been continually in her company and it had been rumoured in the village that they might make a match of it. Not that Antoinette thought him good enough for her 'little flower'; he had no money, and she could not envisage Anne-Marie as a good soldier's wife.

Eve watched the affair rather anxiously – feeling very much the 'older sister'. They both seemed so young. But her anxiety was really for David, for whereas Anne-Marie was full of natural guile, David was a simple, trusting young man. He was very good-looking, which had attracted Anne-Marie, but she had often mentioned to Eve that he 'bored her'. And when Eve had suggested that it might be cruel to encourage him to no purpose, Anne-Marie had given a peal of her silver-bell laughter, and said:

'Men can take care of themselves. I never worry about *them.*'

She and David had held their combined coming-of-age dance at Corderhay Park. Anne-Marie, naturally, had been the belle of the ball, with white flowers in her golden hair and a white tulle dress sparkling with silver sequins … an ethereal ballerina floating in the arms of all her partners, flirting outrageously – particularly with David, who looked exceptionally handsome in his 'Blues'.

Later the breath of tragedy had blown like a menacing threat through Corderhay Park. Eve shivered even now when she remembered it. Fortunately there had been very little scandal because all the guests had gone home when young David Bardwell had been found shot in the moonlit grounds of the Park, clasping an hysterical note in his hand, which only the aghast family had read. It accused Anne-Marie of breaking all her promises to him and then throwing him on one side. Which, in fact, she had done, and Eve knew it. She had felt a moment of burning horror of her sister and the overwhelming selfishness and vanity which had led Anne-Marie to be so cruel to the young cadet. She could pity David even while she deplored the weakness of his character that had led him to such drastic action.

Fortunately, David did not die, and his parents had left the district, taking him with them, and soon afterwards emigrated to South Africa. The incident was a closed book. But Eve knew that her father had been badly shaken by it. Antoinette Corderhay had blamed the boy entirely, and called him an hysterical fool. She had exonerated her daughter, both to the girl herself and to David's indignant parents.

This had been bad for Anne-Marie ... to be exonerated. She should have learned her lesson in that awful moment of finding David with the wound which had so nearly ended his life. She had experienced only a fleeting moment of remorse as she knelt beside him on the moonlit lawn, screaming, imploring him to speak to her, while his blood stained her billowing white gown. But it was astonishing how soon she had forgotten it.

With a callousness that had frightened Eve, a month later she had observed:

'Thank goodness David's off to South Africa and *I* shan't be troubled by him any more.'

'Haven't you any pity for him?' Eve had asked.

Anne-Marie, sitting in front of her dressing-table, trying out a new hair-style, shrugged her shoulders and answered:

'No! I think he was stupid. I hate stupid people.'

'But he loved you!' Eve had persisted, hoping to touch some depth ... some real human emotions, in the younger girl. But Anne-Marie had laughed again.

'That sort of love is ridiculous. David and I had some amusing times. But I didn't want to marry him, and he should have accepted his *congé.*'

'Would *you* have done so if you loved some man madly and he led you on, then abandoned you?' Eve asked.

Then Anne-Marie replied unhesitatingly:

'I wouldn't *dream* of loving anybody who didn't love me. Why give your heart for nothing?'

And that was typical of Anne-Marie. She would never give anything for nothing. She would always want a rich reward if she gave anything at all.

She had never tried to conceal this side of her nature from Eve, but she took care not to be quite so outspoken or revealing to her parents. Something of the actress in her responded to the value other people placed on her, and this no doubt accounted for her great popularity, for with each one she became the person they wished her to be. Only with Eve was she herself, and this, possibly, because she knew better than to try to 'pull the wool' over Eve's far too-observant eyes.

So, when David's name was mentioned by either of her parents, Anne-Marie's face became sad, lost, tragic and she would fall silent as if she could not bear to think of the great tragedy that had befallen him … and her.

Inevitably, Antoinette remarked to her husband, that *la petite* was suffering from shock and a quite unnecessary remorse for her part in the affair … she was looking tired, pale, listless and needed a complete change.

Always sympathetic to his wife's wishes and even now, after so many years, unable to refuse her anything she desired, Jack Corderhay agreed to manage the 'complete change' somehow or other. Finances could not be more difficult, he explained patiently, than they were at present, and really they should be economizing further rather than adding to their expenditure, but if 'Toinette would tell him what sum of money was involved, he would do his best.

'I thought, perhaps, a month or two in Paris!' his wife said eagerly. 'After all, *chéri*, our daughter is half French and she has not been to France since she was a tiny child. We had hoped to "finish her off" there, had we not? A few months would not cost so very much, and it is just what she needs. She is very young still, and she needs the gaiety of Paris to forget this unhappy beginning to her womanhood.'

She looked up at her tall husband appealingly and it was with difficulty that he tried to steel himself against the desire to give her whatever she desired.

'My darling, I hate to disappoint you, but a holiday abroad … it is out of the question. You see, we could not give Anne-Marie this advantage unless we gave it to Eve, too. We simply could not afford it.'

'But a month or two, Jack! Surely that

cannot be beyond our means! They could go to a family … just have a small personal allowance … it could be managed somehow … even if I have to cut down myself. I can manage the house on a little less, maybe … cut down my dress allowance … help in every way I can…'

Jack Corderhay drew a deep breath. It was so very difficult for him to refuse his adored little wife anything and she had tried so hard to appreciate this new need for economy. She never complained, and even if her efforts to economize were not very successful, she had done her best … no longer going to the best model houses for her clothes, refusing to permit him to buy her expensive jewellery at Christmas and anniversaries. Maybe there was still some further way in which *he* could cut down his own expenditure and manage this holiday for the girls. For his innate fairness would not permit him to send Anne-Marie without Eve.

The passionate, emotional flood of gratitude from his wife, when he finally agreed to the project, more than made up to him for the fact that his last hunter must be sold, and he quelled his disappointment by telling himself that he was getting too old for hunting, anyway. It was time he gave it up.

Anne-Marie received the news of her impending holiday with a rapture similar to that of her mother. She danced round the house like a butterfly, kissing her mother in a hundred different places, hugging her father and singing in her clear, sweet voice as she rushed along the corridor to Eve's room to tell her the exciting news.

'Isn't it magnificent, Eve, darling?' she cried. 'Paris … just think of it … *Paris!* Oh, Eve, I can't wait till we get there. I shall want to see everything, do everything. Isn't Papa a *darling?*'

But Eve, pale, silent, thoughtful, showed none of Anne-Marie's pleasure in the project. Her first reaction to it was that she did not wish to leave home. She would like to see Paris, to travel, but some other time … some day in the future. Paris in the autumn might be very beautiful, but she could not bear to miss autumn at Corderhay Park. Besides, her mother needed her help and she had only just started to assist her father in keeping the estate accounts … in fact she was replacing as far as possible the bailiff who had had to leave because they could no longer afford his wages.

No one knew better than Eve how short money was getting. Perhaps because his wife was so lacking in understanding of the true position, Jack Corderhay had made Eve his confidante. She had grasped the position instantly with her calm intelligence and offered several helpful suggestions which had led her father to trust her judgment and rely on it. Nowadays he would talk over most of his business affairs with her and Eve knew that he had begun to depend on her. She could not leave him now ... and neither could he afford to let her go. Even if he did not realize this fact, then she did.

Quietly, without announcing her intention to Anne-Marie or her mother, Eve went in search of her father, finding him in his customary place when he was tired or worried ... the big, book-lined library. He looked up at her as she came into the room, a smile lighting up the tired face ... a smile of welcome. For no matter how weary or dispirited he might be, Eve was always welcome. Her quietness soothed him and her unspoken understanding was both restful and sympathetic, and nothing seemed quite so bad when she stood behind his chair with her long, slender fingers on his shoulders, saying:

'We'll find a way round that difficulty, Father. Let's think about it for a moment.'

And she would state the position as she saw it ... clarifying things in his own mind as she spoke and making the most complicated problems seem suddenly clearer by her own clear insight and judgment. And cleverly, she would make it appear that he, rather than she, had thought of the solution, so that he never quite realized to what extent he relied on her. Only Eve knew it, and drew happiness in the knowledge that now, at last, she could repay this man who had been so wonderful a father to her.

'Father, I can't go to Paris!' she said, as she reached her accustomed position behind his chair, her hands resting lightly on the shoulders of his rough tweed shooting-jacket. 'Please don't make me go. I'd really prefer to stay here ... with you.'

He turned to look at her, searching her face for any trace of self-sacrifice that he sensed was there. He knew his Eve better than anyone else and it had occurred to him that something of this kind might happen.

'I wouldn't send Anne-Marie without sending you, too, Eve. You know that. You are both my daughters.'

'I know, Daddy...' Eve said quietly, lapsing into her childhood name for him. 'But I don't want to go. It has nothing to do with money. I'd honestly rather stay here ... with you and Mother.'

Still he was not convinced.

'I want you to go for other reasons, Eve ... to keep an eye on that scatter-brained young sister of yours. The change will do you good, too.'

'Then if you wish me to go, to look after Anne-Marie, of course I'll go, Father. But I'd rather stay. I wouldn't want to miss the autumn here. It's so very beautiful. Even Paris could not make up for Corderhay Park.'

'But Paris...' he argued. 'That is something different ... it should mean so much
to a girl of your age. Not one in a thousand
would miss such an opportunity. Besides, it
would be part of your education. Naturally,
I don't want to force you to go if you don't
wish to do so. Anne-Marie can be placed
under the supervision of some reliable
person ... your mother's sister, no doubt,
would... It is you I am thinking of, child.'

'But, Father, would *you* want to go to Paris
now ... leave Corderhay Park just when
things are so beautiful? Everything is turning golden and brown and the Virginia
creeper on the south wall turning deep red
... and the log fires burning in the evenings
... the smell of the bonfires and the leaves
thick along the drive... I can't explain very
well, but *you* know what I mean, Father,
what it means to *me*.'

He did know, for he felt the same way
himself. It wasn't just the autumn, but every
season seemed to bring some new beauty
and delight to the beautiful old house and
grounds. He never wished to leave it, and
when he had been forced to do so, coming
home meant returning to a beloved ... a
completion of something inside himself. He
had attributed this great love for his home to
traditional emotions, to the fact that for centuries this had been the home of Corderhays
... his father, grandfather, great-grandfather,

back to the time of William the Conqueror. Each had left something of himself in the stone walls, the lovely grounds, added some little personal gift to its beauty ... the yew tree, hundreds of years old now ... the south wing, added in Tudor days ... the silver cups in the saddle room (for all past Corderhays had been great horsemen) ... the ever-lengthening line of portraits in the gallery ... the changing decorations which Antoinette, his wife, had added soon after the end of the First World War when there was still plenty of money to spend ... bathrooms, central heating, fresh gay curtains and carpets and rugs ... bringing new life and beauty to the mellowed loveliness of the years.

He had been born into this world knowing that as the eldest son this house would one day be his. His education and boyhood training had been to this end ... to make him a fit master of this great house. It was in his blood, and his love for it had seemed a natural thing. But Eve's feeling... Eve, who after all was not by birth a Corderhay, who was not even a man, felt as he did – maybe even more intensely than he did – the need to preserve this place.

'Perhaps after all,' he mused, 'it is up-bringing rather than heredity that instils these emotions.' For Anne-Marie, he knew, had only a casual fondness for her home... Anne-Marie, who was a Corderhay – half a

Corderhay, anyway – and yet less of one than Eve. She was in every way her mother's child, and yet while he loved her for this likeness to the woman he so adored, Jack Corderhay sometimes wondered if that likeness was only physical. He sensed rather than saw that Anne-Marie could be selfish, hard, petulant and self-willed, none of which traits were to be found in Antoinette's warm-hearted, passionate nature. Man-like, he had fallen under the spell of Anne-Marie's charm, a charm she never failed to exhibit in her father's presence, and it was only some instinct that made him doubt her – an instinct that could judge after a moment or two the best puppy in a litter, the unreliability in a young mare deceptively hidden behind soft, liquid eyes and gentle mouth.

'It is not always gold that glitters,' he mused, thinking of the girl at his side. Eve was no outward beauty, and yet in her he knew there was only the best – the *very* best.

'We'll say no more about it, my dear,' he said gently. 'I've no doubt your mother will think you're mad and Anne-Marie will be most disappointed, but I shall be glad to have at least one of my daughters left to keep me company.'

He was too fair to say 'my favourite daughter', but he knew at that moment that if he had to part with either he would prefer that it should not be Eve.

CHAPTER 2

Anne-Marie went to Paris alone and life continued much as usual without her at Corderhay Park. For the first few weeks after her departure everyone missed her a great deal, and the large old house seemed strangely empty without her gay laughter and the strains of her fresh young voice singing one of the French folk-songs her mother had taught her, the soft, soothing notes of the piano which she played so effortlessly.

Perhaps Eve missed her most of all, for there was no one to look after ... to 'mother', as she had always mothered Anne-Marie. The days had been filled with odd jobs she would always be doing for Anne-Marie ... a dress to be altered, since Eve was a neat and talented needlewoman; an outing to town to accompany her to a theatre or a film; a small party of friends to cater for; a tennis party; or a little dance in the nursery, where, since they were children, they had always entertained their own friends.

It was not in Anne-Marie's nature to spend a day idly and she thirsted always after entertainment, being unable to amuse herself. Even the gramophone and huge library of records she had accumulated palled after half an hour or so and she would seek out Eve to find her something amusing to do.

But Eve soon managed to adjust herself to doing without Anne-Marie's companionship. Now, while she had time to spare, she settled down to redecorating her mother's, sister's and her own bedrooms. Antoinette had been wanting to get them done for some time, but Jack Corderhay had managed to talk her out of the expense of decorator's bills with promises to get one of the men on the estate to 'do a bit of painting in the house' one wet day.

Knowing her mother's wishes, Eve made the promises facts and supervised the work according to Antoinette's skilful ideas. When the paint and distemper dried, Eve ran up on her sewing-machine new curtains, new frills for the kidney-shaped dressing-tables, a cushion cover for the *chaise-longue* Antoinette insisted upon keeping in her bedroom, where she would often recline with a novel and a box of chocolates, looking like some dainty, Dresden-china figure in a flowing pink *négligé*.

It never occurred to Eve to resent her mother's idleness ... indeed, no one expected Antoinette to be the one to sew and supervise and busy herself with household matters. She was so inefficient at such tasks that everyone, by mutual agreement, preferred to keep her well away from them. Antoinette's job was to be first a decorative companion to her husband, second a mother and thirdly a hostess. Each of these roles she did perfectly and with such pleasure and charm that it was enough she should occupy herself in these ways. Coming in tired from a long day's work, Jack Corderhay wanted nothing more than to find his wife dainty, fresh, ever beautiful, waiting in her most becoming dress or gown to draw him over to the fire that always burned in the cold months in her bedroom, ready to listen to his account of the day's news ... there to delight him as she had always done since the first day he had laid eyes on her. He would not have wanted her to turn into a 'housewife' in the true sense of the word, for none of the past Corderhay ladies had ever had to work and he would have hated to see her doing so, even had she been able.

As a mother, too, she filled the role to perfection. It was Nanny who had scolded, punished, pleaded, cajoled; Antoinette who had soothed, petted, spoiled and loved with all her passionate nature. Disappointments ceased to matter when Antoinette's arms hugged you close, her soft voice with its French accent murmuring soothing words. Worries were halved by the mere act of her sympathy so readily given, and she always found time to listen to tales of their childish upsets. Nanny might do the dosing if someone were ill, but Antoinette made the patient feel better by the mere fact of her presence and her desire to have them well again. As a mother she could always be relied upon for comfort, beauty, love.

And as a hostess Antoinette excelled herself, for here her French blood could come to the fore and she would be gracious and graceful, tactful, amusing, making the least attractive member of any party feel important and welcome, bringing out the best in her guests and never able to enjoy herself until she saw that each one of them were enjoying themselves, too. It was an unceasing disappointment to Jack Corderhay that they had had to entertain less and less as time went by, for he knew Antoinette missed this social side of her life. She seldom complained and when he mentioned it would smooth the lines from his forehead, saying:

'But, *chéri*, I have you to entertain me. What more could any woman want!'

'You were meant for a better life than I can offer you now,' he would reply sadly. But Antoinette, ever optimistic, would say:

'We have had wonderful days together in the past, my darling, and maybe they will come again. Meantime, I have you and Eve and Anne-Marie … what more do I need?'

Perhaps she too missed Anne-Marie, for

when she was home she would spend hours in her mother's room, gossiping, laughing, listening to Antoinette's stories of her life in France and the romantic tales of her maternal grandmother's 'beaux'. It was Antoinette's favourite topic, and Anne-Marie loved to listen to these romances.

At times, hearing their high, silvery laughter, Eve would think of them as two sisters and of herself as the mother. Often it seemed to her that she was born older than her mother would ever be. But she was never jealous, never anything but proud and pleased of the rôle she played in the family. It was her choice that she should be the housekeeper, the one to do the everyday, dull routine jobs. It satisfied something inside her to know that things ran efficiently because she was there to manage them; satisfied her to know that they would manage less well without her and that she was, therefore, of use to them and able to make life better for the people who had chosen her for their daughter out of the kindness of their hearts.

She never forgot the debt she owed her mother and father. But for them she would never have known Corderhay Park, never have had this perfect setting and background that so adequately filled her desire for poetry and beauty in her life. But for them, she might never have had her carefree childhood, never known Antoinette's love, her father's quiet understanding and affection … never, also, had a gay, sweet, pretty sister like Anne-Marie to brighten the dull days with song and laughter.

It appeared, however, that no matter how much the family might be missing Anne-Marie, she had no time to miss them. Her letters were filled with descriptions of gay parties to which she had been invited, of excursions to Montmartre, to Versailles; of the new friends she had made. She had been sent to a family recommended by Antoinette's sister, who normally lived in Paris but was at the moment in America on a long holiday and therefore unable to have her niece to stay at her home.

The family consisted of a Frenchwoman with a daughter a year or two younger than Anne-Marie and a son two years older.

Anne-Marie wrote describing them thus:

Louise is really two years younger than I am, but she looks like a schoolgirl. Her parents make her keep her hair in plaits and she is never allowed to go anywhere without a chaperone. I feel very sorry for her as she can never have much fun always having some aunt or her brother tagging along wherever she goes. She says all French girls of good family are guarded like this if they are to make good marriages and she prophesies that I shall never make 'a good marriage' carrying on as I do. Of course, she is jealous of my freedom really and because I can do my hair and dress how I want and so of course I'm prettier. Madame doesn't approve of my going about on my own, but since you and Papa wrote and told her I was of an age to take care of myself, she hasn't been able to stop me.

Anyway, I do have a chaperone really as Jean takes me nearly everywhere. I think you'd like him. He's studying to be a doctor at the Institut de Médicin and he has heaps of amusing friends. The French boys are a lot more fun than English boys I think. They seem to know just how a girl wants to be treated even though most of them, like Jean, are about my age. Fourteen of us are going on a picnic to the Bois de Boulogne next Sunday.

I'm having a wonderful time and learning French very quickly. I always thought I spoke like a native until I came here and I'm sure, you, Maman, will be pleased with my progress. I am very happy and well and only have one regret … that the time passes so quickly and I have only two months left.

Each succeeding letter spoke of the gay times she was having, of her reluctance to come home at the end of the three months' holiday.

Eve, watching her father's face as he read these letters, noticed the lines of worry creasing his forehead. Knowing him so well, she guessed that he was seeking some way in which he could manage to prolong Anne-Marie's stay. Her hints to be allowed to do so were barely concealed, and Antoinette, passing the letters into her husband's hands, would say:

'She sounds so well, Jack ... so happy. It seems a shame ... well, she must be thankful for this much at least, *la petite!*'

It was Eve who provided the solution and by doing so was ultimately to feel responsible for all the ensuing events. It seemed at the time such an ideal solution and afterwards ... how bitterly she was to regret those words to her father!...

'Suppose Madame would agree to an exchange, Father ... send Louise to us for three months and keep Anne-Marie that much longer. It would cost us nothing to support Louise here ... to take her to London a day or two to see the sights ... she could ride Anne-Marie's pony ... attend the Christmas parties. I'm sure she would enjoy herself after the strict life she appears to lead in Paris. And if Madame is anxious, there is always me to act as a chaperone. After all, I am twenty-seven! That's practically an old maid!'

There was no reason against the idea that Jack Corderhay could find, even had he wished to do so. As it was, he blessed Eve once more for finding the solution. Antoinette was wildly enthusiastic and, strangely enough, Madame wrote also *enchanté* with the idea. Louise, it seemed, was not asked her wishes and Anne-Marie did not need to be asked if she was happy to stay a further three months. Her letters were radiant and once again filled with new plans of parties and dates and young men.

In due course Louise arrived, and being a quiet, sensitive girl, used to a very strict discipline, made little impression on the routine at Corderhay Park. Eve liked the girl and did her best to find suitable entertainments for her, which was easy enough, since everything was new and interesting to her and the freedom from elderly, dull chaperones such a relief. To Louise, Eve seemed just a companion, as Eve had intended it to be, and their few excursions to London sightseeing and to the theatre were pleasant for both of them.

Antoinette made herself charming to the girl who had developed a schoolgirl adoration for her which slightly embarrassed the more reserved Eve and her father but amused and flattered Antoinette.

As the days went by Louise became less shy and reserved, and when Christmas came she was the radiant 'belle of the ball', dancing with several of the young boys who the year before had partnered Anne-Marie. Contrary to expectations, there had been no letter on Christmas morning from Paris, but a telephone call came through during the evening festivities, and the maid who answered it came to Eve with the curious report that it was Miss Anne-Marie asking to speak to her personally and not to fetch her mother or father.

Eve, looking slender and lovely in a flowing pale blue net dance-dress, hurried across the hall to the small study, where she shut the door against the noise of the radio-gramophone and the excited laughter and chatter of the guests. As she lifted the receiver she felt a chill of apprehension steal over her, although there was no reason as yet to cast this shadow on a day so filled until now with happiness and celebrations.

'Hullo! This is Eve Corderhay here. Is that Anne-Marie?'

Anne-Marie's voice, clear and sharp, came over the wire as if she were speaking from the next room.

'Eve! Thank heaven it's you! Eve, you're alone, aren't you? Mummy and Daddy aren't standing by you waiting to speak to me?'

'They don't even know you have tele-phoned,' Eve answered reassuringly but with a sinking heart. Anne-Marie's voice was so nervous, so obviously *distrait*, as Antoinette would have termed it.

'I'll wish them a happy Christmas in a moment. I must speak to you first. Eve … you've got to help me … you've *got* to…'

'Of course I'll do anything I can, Anne-Marie. Tell me what's wrong. You're not ill…?'

'No … at least not exactly. Eve, I just can't give you any details over the phone. You must come to Paris … as soon as you can… I shall go out of my mind if you don't come soon. I need you desperately, Eve. Oh God … if only I could make you understand…!' Her voice trailed away and it sounded to Eve as if Anne-Marie were sobbing. But she could not be sure.

'You are ill, Anne-Marie? Of course I'll come … tomorrow morning on the first boat. Mother and Father will understand and you aren't to worry about a thing–'

'But you mustn't tell Mother or Father!' Anne-Marie broke in. 'Swear to me you won't say anything to them, Eve. Think up some excuse for coming. They mustn't think anything's the matter with me. I'll kill myself if you tell them I've sent for you. Eve, promise me you won't tell them a word?'

Eve bit her lip. This conversation was getting more and more incoherent and only the desperate tone of Anne-Marie's voice convinced her that something was indeed seriously wrong.

'Surely you can tell me what this is all about, Anne-Marie? I won't tell anyone, but if you're ill, Mother should know. Is Madame there? Shall I speak to her?'

Anne-Marie was sobbing in earnest now and Eve felt her heart contract in a sudden rush of affection for the young sister who sounded so bitterly unhappy, lonely and desperate. She could just make out her renewed vehement exhortations not to tell a soul … not Madame, nor anyone in the world.

'But, Anne-Marie, what am I to say to them here? What reason can I give for coming if I don't know what is wrong and I mustn't mention this conversation? It's Boxing Day tomorrow and there's a luncheon party. I shall have to provide a very good reason for wanting to go off so inopportunely.'

'Then come the day after,' came Anne-Marie's voice, a little calmer now as if Eve's common-sensical remarks had soothed her. 'Say you want to come to Paris for the New Year. Father will let you. He said he owed you something to make up for missing these months. Mother won't mind. Just say you want to come and spend New Year with me. You can–'

The cool, distant voice of the operator, speaking in French, broke in to inform Anne-Marie that she had exceeded her six-minute time allotment and must discontinue the call.

'*Mais je veux encore trois minutes!*' Eve heard Anne-Marie's voice. 'Just a few more minutes, *please!*'

Eve could just translate the operator's reply that many others were waiting to wish their friends and families *un bon Noel,* after which words there was a click and only a humming on the line.

Eve stood for a few seconds, waiting in case the call should be reconnected, but it was only to hear the voice of the operator at the local exchange telling her the party had cleared the line and asking if she wished to make a call.

'Yes, yes, I wish to put a call through to Paris,' she cried. 'Is there much delay?'

'I'll find out for you,' the man said. 'Shall I call you back or will you hold on?'

'I'll hold on!' Eve said.

She waited anxiously, glancing every now and again at the door in case her mother or father should come in, and on a sudden impulse slipped across the room and locked the door. Now she could not be disturbed. But this foresight was in vain, for there was a five-hour delay to France and it was already nine o'clock. No doubt Anne-Marie would be in bed and asleep by 2 a.m.

She sat down heavily in one of the tapestry-seated chairs and lit a cigarette, trying to calm her nerves and thoughts before returning to the dance-room and perhaps to the questions of her parents. What was to be made of this call from her young sister? Obviously Anne-Marie was in trouble of some kind … needed help … and badly. There had been no mistaking the sincerity and desperation of her pleas to Eve to come quickly. Eve's first instinct was to obey this call for help, but the secrecy Anne-Marie had imposed on her made things so complicated. How was she to explain this sudden desire to go to Paris when all along she had striven to convince both her parents that she did not wish to go?

Apart from this angle, there was Louise to consider. It had been Eve's job to accompany Louise to all entertainments, and there was a big dance at one of the neighbouring houses on New Year's Eve which was only for young people, and neither Jack Corderhay nor his wife had been invited. They were to attend a quieter evening with other friends. Who would accompany Louise if she was not there?

'Oh, what ought I to do?' Eve asked herself, as her mind whirled in circles. If only she knew what lay in the balance ... knew what was wrong with Anne-Marie ... knew why this secrecy must be maintained. That Anne-Marie was unhappy was only too obvious, and with this knowledge Eve knew she would have no peace of mind until she could go to her sister's assistance. On the other hand, she hated the idea of deceit, and in this case it was going to be so difficult to accomplish her visit without suspicion on the part of her parents. Why ... oh, why had Anne-Marie refused to allow her to confide in their mother and father? It must, indeed, be serious if she wished to keep the 'bad news' from them.

'Maybe it's money!' Eve thought, suddenly seeing the explanation. 'She has got herself into debt, and knowing Father's financial position, cannot bring herself to ask him for an addition to her already generous personal allowance.' This had been paid in French francs by Madame on the arrangement that the equivalent amount in English money be paid weekly to Louise for pocket expenses, so evading the travel currency difficulties.

'If that is all, I can send her some money!' Eve thought with relief, but almost immediately she realized that this was not, after all, so easy. How did one send money to another country in these times? One could not just post a cheque or a postal order! It would undoubtedly mean forms to fill in and endless complications that would hold up its arrival. And Anne-Marie had made it clear that this matter was urgent. Perhaps some man was pressing her for payment ... making things unpleasant for her! It was so like Anne-Marie to overstep her allowance. She had her mother's extravagant tastes and never seemed to be able to budget successfully.

'Thank heaven I have saved a bit for a rainy day!' Eve thought. She had never seemed to need all her dress allowance, for she preferred the simpler, more tailored clothes and dresses that did not go out of fashion. She had often, since she had a stock-size figure, managed to buy clothes in sales and off-the-peg that looked every bit as smart on her as did some of Anne-Marie's hand-sewn frocks from the model house.

At the back of Eve's mind she had thought perhaps one day she might have a better use for her savings than frittering them away on little luxuries. Already she had over a hundred pounds in the bank and deep in her thoughts she had more than trebled this figure so that it might be offered one day to her father at the precise moment when he most needed it. For Eve, at heart, was a romantic and an idealist. It appealed to all that was generous in her nature to know that she had it in her power to repay in this way a little of the great debt she owed her father and mother for making her their child … every bit as much loved and cared for as their real daughter.

Now 'a rainy day' had come, if not quite in the way she had anticipated; by keeping this small scandal of Anne-Marie's from her parents' ears she would save them worry and pain and perhaps disillusionment in their young daughter. It would be Eve's job to see that Anne-Marie took more care in future. Perhaps the shock of finding herself in this position had already taught her a lesson.

'Anne-Marie always called on me to get

her out of scrapes!' Eve told herself with mixed feelings of affection and exasperation. Perhaps it was time she learned to take her punishment instead of having Eve ready to help her avoid it. But in this case … if money difficulties they were, and Eve felt convinced of it now … it meant more to Eve to keep her parents in ignorance of the facts than to start disciplining Anne-Marie.

'I'll have to go over to Paris myself as Anne-Marie suggested,' Eve decided finally. Her return fare would not take so much of that hundred pounds and of the remainder she knew she could take at least thirty-five pounds in foreign currency. This, surely, would cope with whatever debts Anne-Marie had incurred.

It remained only now to find a way to explain to her parents why she wished to go … and to allay their suspicions.

She unlocked the door and went in search of her mother and father, who were waltzing together in the brightly lit ballroom. She stood for a moment watching them, Jack Corderhay so tall and distinguished in his tails, Antoinette so small and fragile and dainty, her head tilted up as she smiled at her husband, one lavender-gloved hand resting on his shoulder, the other held tightly in his.

'They are still so much in love with one another!' Eve thought, with a rush of love and affection for them and a tiny tinge of envy. 'Perhaps one day I, too, shall love and be loved this way!' Then the wistfulness gave way to a strangled emotion that could find no other expression than the sudden rush of tears to her eyes: 'They are such darlings! I love them both so dearly. If I can prevent it, they shall never be unhappy!'

Then, controlling herself, she went to meet them as the waltz ended.

'I've just been talking to Anne-Marie on the telephone,' she said with a smile which bolstered the lie which followed. 'She rang to wish us all a happy Christmas, but I could not find you in time to put her through to you. She was limited to a few minutes only because there are so many people waiting for calls abroad. She was so upset not to have spoken to you.'

'*Ma petite!*' Antoinette cried. 'We will telephone to her now instead.'

'I thought of that, but there is a delay of five hours,' Eve explained, glad that here at least she could speak the truth.

'What a shame!' her father said, linking his arm through Eve's. 'Never mind! I dare say the little baggage is having far too gay a time in Paris to miss us for long. She is at a party, Eve?'

Eve nodded her head, and with an effort forced herself to add:

'She sounded as if she were having a wonderful time. She kept begging me to join her for the New Year Party, as if she didn't know it was quite impossible.'

She did not lift her head to meet the quick gaze she knew her father shot at her, for she had assimilated an envious tone to her voice.

'Then it is to be a gala affair?' Antoinette asked eagerly. 'Ah! Paris. There is nowhere quite like it in the world, is there, *chéri?*'

Jack Corderhay looked at his wife's face and back to Eve's bowed head.

'For the young, I agree, my dear. For the old, too, maybe. I suppose Anne-Marie is surrounded by admiring young men and is the centre of attraction. I'm afraid most of the young men here tonight are really hers and Louise's contemporaries rather than yours, Eve. This was to be your party and I'm afraid it has failed. We don't seem to know many young men of your age. These boys here tonight are all children.'

'I'm having a lovely time, Father,' Eve said quickly, hating to think she had led him to suppose she was envious of Anne-Marie's popularity with the opposite sex. 'Really, I don't mind a bit about the men.'

'But you should, my darling,' Antoinette said tenderly. 'After all, you are only young once. Love is important when you are young. You know, Jack, it is time we found our Eve a husband. We have neglected this duty.'

'The years seem to have gone by so quickly since the end of war,' Jack Corderhay said thoughtfully. 'Let me see ... you are ... twenty-six now, Eve?'

'Twenty-seven, Father; but I haven't any wish to get married yet. I'm quite happy here.' Any other time she would have added: 'and I never want to leave my home ... not even for a day... I'm quite content as I am ... some day perhaps ... but I want to be with you and Mother for a few more years ... at Corderhay Park...'

Instead, remembering Anne-Marie, she murmured:

'It was just that Anne-Marie sounded so ... anxious for me to go. I thought perhaps if it had been possible ... maybe just for a day or two ... for the New Year's party, I mean...' She broke off, unable to bring herself to voice this subterfuge any longer.

But she had said sufficient. In an instant her father was saying:

'My dearest child, of course you shall go. You should have told me sooner that you had changed your mind. We shall manage it somehow ... even if we cannot manage quite the six months...'

'Oh, but Father, I wouldn't want to go for six months ... just for this one party. I haven't really changed my mind at all. I would hate to go more than a day or two. Just to see Anne-Marie ... and for the party. And I don't want any money, Father. I have some of my own. I'd like to pay my own way.'

'That is certainly not to be allowed, *chérie*,' Antoinette broke in, her arm around Eve's shoulders. 'You keep what is your own and this shall be only a little of what Anne-Marie has had as a present.'

'But, Father–' Eve tried to break in, but he silenced her with a determined gesture of his head.

'I greatly appreciate your thoughtfulness, Eve, my dear,' he said gently. 'But, believe me, we are not quite in such desperate straits that we cannot pay our daughter's return passage to Paris. We will say no more about this. It is to be understood that you go ... and you stay for as long as you wish. Some arrangement can be made with Madame if necessary. Louise, I think, would like to remain here a little longer.'

'But I don't want to stay more than a day or two, Father!' Eve repeated. 'Really I don't. I don't! Just for a day; two days ... that is all!'

'We aren't forcing you to remain if you don't wish to,' Jack Corderhay said with a smile. 'So don't look so desperate, Eve. Anyone would think to look at your funny little face that you were asking me to pay a few hundred pounds debt, you look so guilty.'

Eve bit her lip.

'Perhaps I feel guilty!' she whispered. 'What is to happen to Louise? Who will take her to her New Year's Party?'

'That is not your concern, *ma petite*,' Antoinette said firmly. 'You are entitled to as much freedom as Anne-Marie and I will not permit these differences between you. You are getting a complex, my darling, about your duty to us. You have no duty – none other than that of any child to any parent. You will make me regret that I have told you we adopted you if you continue to look at things in this way. Now, do not worry your pretty head about Louise. Nanny shall take her to the party and Jack and I will collect her. That is quite sufficient chaperoning, to my mind, and what Madame does not know will not worry her.'

'Well said, my dear!' said Jack Corderhay. 'Now run along and enjoy yourself, Eve. It is understood that you shall join Anne-Marie for New Year. You may make any arrangements you wish to and I leave the matter entirely in your very capable hands!'

With rare impulsiveness Eve stood on tiptoe and kissed first her father's cheek, then her mother's.

'You're dears!' she whispered. 'And I love you both very much!'

Not trusting herself to speak to them further, she turned and went quickly away to find Louise.

But though she danced, smiled, laughed, joked until the last of the guests had departed, her actions were automatic and she knew her replies were merely mechanical. For at the back of her mind she could not forget that for the first time in her life she had lied to the parents she so adored; that Anne-Marie was in trouble and that she, Eve, could want nothing less than to leave the home she loved so dearly, even for a few days.

Perhaps some sixth sense or instinct warned her that, once separated from it, it might be a very long time indeed before she was to return to her home again.

CHAPTER 3

Three days later Eve arrived in Paris. She had sent Anne-Marie a telegram on Boxing Day morning, advising her that she would arrive some time on the twenty-eighth of December, to which her young sister had replied briefly with the one word 'wonderful'. She had not, of course, let Anne-Marie know the time of her arrival in Paris, for the travel agencies had been closed on Boxing Day and she had been unable even to start planning until the succeeding day.

Her father had paid her passage and given her a ten-pound note for pocket money. She had refused to take the second one her mother had offered her, but had carefully withdrawn as much money as she was permitted by regulations to do from her private banking account. In her mind this small sum was to see Anne-Marie out of whatever difficulties she had incurred.

She travelled alone, therefore, in the Paris taxi to Madame's address, and the thrill of being in France's great exciting capital was greatly dulled for her, since only half her mind could take in what she saw from the window.

'It's the trouble of having a one-track mind!' Eve told herself reproachfully. 'I can't enjoy anything until I know what Anne-Marie needs me for so badly.'

With mixed feelings of relief and anxiety Eve found herself outside the door of Madame Boulanger's *appartement*. Hardly had she touched the bell when the door was flung open and Anne-Marie rushed past her, calling in French to the taxi-driver to wait … that she and the other mademoiselle would need him again immediately.

The driver, only too pleased to have two such beautiful young fares, for he had the Frenchman's eye for, and appreciation of, feminine good looks, obligingly pulled up by the kerb and waited.

'You don't mind, do you, Eve? I must talk to you before anything else!' Anne-Marie cried, and without waiting for Eve's answer, rushed back indoors, to reappear a moment later with her coat flung hastily round her shoulders.

Eve had been tired and cold and looking forward to a warm fire and a nice strong cup of tea, but the quick glimpse she had had of Anne-Marie's white face and enormous, violet-shadowed eyes had put all such thoughts out of her mind. She would ask questions later. Meantime, she would do whatever her young sister required of her.

In the taxi, Anne-Marie ordered the driver to take them to the Hôtel Belle Vue.

'It's quiet there and we can have tea in the lounge without being disturbed,' she explained to Eve. And then, as if she had only just realized that Eve had really come at last, she said on a half-sob of relief: 'Oh, Eve, darling, I'm so thankful to see you. I felt sure you would come. I've been so *desperate!* So utterly alone.'

Eve, hearing the tears in Anne-Marie's voice, felt a renewed shock of apprehension. Not only did Anne-Marie sound unhappy, but she looked ghastly. Her face, usually so rounded and full of colour, was thin and drawn and deathly white. She looked, at this moment, almost the same age as Antoinette, but without her mother's vivacious sparkle.

'You're not to worry any more, Anne-Marie. Whatever has happened, we shall soon put it right!'

'If only I could believe that!' Anne-Marie

whispered, clinging to Eve's hand as if she feared to let it go. 'It's so much worse than you can have imagined, Eve. I'm so frightened ... so terribly afraid.'

Impulsively, Eve put her arms round the trembling shoulders and drew Anne-Marie close to her.

'It can't be as bad as all that, darling,' she said gently. 'Now don't cry ... you won't want people in the hotel staring at you!'

Anne-Marie gave a shaky, tearful laugh, and obediently wiped the tears that had fallen heedlessly from her eyes.

'We're there!' she said as the taxi pulled up. 'Can you pay him, Eve? I – I haven't much money!'

A flood of relief spread through Eve.

'So it was money!' she thought. 'I guessed right. Thank heaven it's nothing worse!'

But ten minutes later, sitting in the almost deserted lounge of the hotel, tea uneaten by either of them, Eve found herself too shocked and horrified to believe what Anne-Marie had just told her.

'It's true, Eve!' she whispered, her gaze averted from her sister's agonized face. 'If only it weren't! But the doctor said there wasn't a doubt. I think he guessed I wasn't married. He – he suggested I might call and see a chemist he knew of in some dingy street in the poorer part of the city... I was too frightened to go at first... I've read books about such places and people... I couldn't believe this was happening to me... Eve, I kept on hoping against hope, and then when another week went by I knew suddenly that it was true ... so I–'

'Anne-Marie, you didn't go – to the chemist the doctor told you about?' Eve broke in, horrified.

The younger girl nodded her head.

'I was so desperate, Eve,' she said in that same dull, lifeless voice in which she had recounted her story. 'He gave me some medicine and a box of pills – told me that if I took them until the end of the month they would bring everything back to normal – but... Oh, Eve, they didn't make any difference! I was terribly sick and dizzy and I felt ghastly, but I didn't mind so much because I kept hoping. But the weeks went by, and just before Christmas I knew they hadn't made any difference. Eve, I'm going to have that baby! What am I going to do? *What am I going to do?*'

It needed every ounce of Eve's intrinsic self-control not to cry out in horror. That Anne-Marie – her own sister – should find herself in this predicament – should have allowed such a thing to happen in the first place! It stunned her into a horrified silence which seemed to have a nightmare quality as the implication struck her mind. Jack and Antoinette would have to be told ... and it would kill them to discover such a thing about their own daughter. If it had been her, Eve, who was not really their daughter, perhaps then they would not have minded so much, but Anne-Marie, their darling … their baby who was so innocent … *la petite ange*–

Eve's mind came to an abrupt halt at this point. With a great effort to keep the horror and shock from her voice, she said as calmly as she could:

'And the – the father, Anne-Marie? You are in love with him, of course? He loves you? Surely since this must be so, you can be married? The baby will not be born for another seven months … it could be early…'

'It's due in six months!' Anne-Marie announced as if she were stating the time of day, her voice was so lifeless, so devoid of any tone. 'And … I can't be married. He – he won't marry me. He's gone!'

'Gone!' Eve cried. 'But where, Anne-Marie? Who is he? What is his name? Doesn't he love you?'

Anne-Marie's voice was barely a whisper.

'He said he loved me … wanted to marry me. It was only because we were going to be married that I… Oh, Eve, don't think too harshly of me! It was only once … just bad luck that this happened. I know you must be shocked, but you're so different from me … so cold and unfeeling. I'm young and attractive and I have French blood in me. I – I loved him so much. I couldn't refuse anything he asked me. You've got to understand.'

'Understand!' Eve thought. Perhaps when she had had time to think about it she might learn to understand how Anne-Marie could do such a thing. It was so contrary to every instinct in herself that at the moment she still found it hard to believe. Antoinette had stressed so many times the importance of innocence ... explained to each of them, when they were old enough, the 'facts of life'. She could remember her mother's voice, saying with gentle wonder: 'Love is a beautiful thing, Eve. You will know when it comes to you. You will want, then, to give yourself to him as he will want to possess you in every way ... the ways that I have just explained to you. This is nature and it is right and beautiful. When you are married, you will understand what I mean, but until then, never try to make yourself believe that second best will be good enough ... will do no harm... You may feel greatly attracted to some man, but without love, this is a base emotion and you would regret terribly that you had not your youth and innocence to offer the right man when finally he comes into your life. And when you are married, you will bear his children and understand the miracle of birth, of nature, that has made men for women and women for men in so perfect a way.'

Eve, the idealist, had listened and understood this desire to keep herself for her one true love.

'But,' she told herself now, 'I have never had any temptation to behave otherwise. I've never been attracted physically to any man. Anne-Marie was in love ... she said so ... believed he loved her ... that he would marry her...'

For the first time since Anne-Marie had spoken Eve felt sympathy flowing from her to her young sister.

'I'm trying to understand, Anne-Marie. But you must tell me more. Who is he? Why can't he marry you? You can trust me, you know. I won't tell anyone else.'

'I do trust you, Eve!' Anne-Marie said eagerly. 'That's why I sent for you. I couldn't bear it if Mother or Father knew. I've got to do something ... get rid of it ... anything. But they mustn't know ... ever.'

'They'll have to know!' Eve thought. 'It's my duty to tell them.' And at the same time something within her recoiled from Anne-Marie's four words ... 'get rid of it.' ... Never that! Whatever else, this wrong would not be added to the others. She could not have meant it. She was merely hysterical...

Anne-Marie, watching the expression on Eve's face, felt that former sympathy being withdrawn and hastily sought to renew it. It would never do if Eve condemned her, refused to help her. Eve was her last hope!

60

'It wasn't a Frenchman … it was an Englishman…' she said quickly. 'He was in Paris on business… I met him at a party … he was crazy about me … said he had fallen in love with me at first sight and that no one else would ever do for him. He was older than me … lots older … thirty-two, I think. His name was Paul … Paul Johnson. He was … very attractive in a queer sort of way. He wasn't like the boys we've met at home. I think, maybe, he hadn't the same background.'

'You mean he wasn't a gentleman?' Eve asked bluntly, for this did not seem the time to prevaricate.

'Well, sort of, but he hadn't been to public school… I think he went to a grammar school and won a scholarship to technical college and went into business. Anyway … I- I fell in love with him. Then … one evening after we'd been dancing … I went back to his hotel with him. He said we would be married next day and … I believed him. Next day we were to meet for lunch to make the wedding arrangements…'

Eve broke in in amazement:

'You mean you were going to be married without telling anyone? Mother? Father? Me? Oh, Anne-Marie…!'

'We were going to elope, Eve. It seemed so romantic and exciting. Paul had overstayed his time in Paris and we were coming back to England together … to tell you … surprise you. But ... he never kept the lunch date, and when I 'phoned his hotel they told me he had gone ... left ... and that there wasn't any forwarding address. I realized then that I hadn't ever known his home address ... the name of his firm ... anything about him. We'd only known each other a fortnight and it had all been so romantic ... so sudden... Can't you understand, Eve? Nothing else seemed to matter very much ... who he was ... where he lived... Of course, I was heart-broken ... desperate. I don't know how I ever got through those days after he left. Then ... when I learned about ... the baby ... I wanted to kill myself. Oh, Eve, what am I going to do? I'm terribly short of money. I had to pay that doctor most of my last month's allowance and the chemist charged me far too much only I was too desperate to argue. *What am I going to do, Eve?*'

Eve took a deep breath. What was to be done? Could this man be traced somehow? A private detective might find him, and yet that would cost a great deal of money, and how could one go about it without her parents knowing? And even if he were found ... with a name like Paul Johnson ... perhaps thousands of them in England (supposing he had returned to England in the first place), maybe he could not be made to marry Anne-Marie. Clearly he did not love her ... had run out on her. Could one force a man to marry a girl just because she was going to have his child? And if he did agree to do so ... would that be the best for Anne-Marie? To spend the rest of her life married to a man who didn't love her?

'Perhaps if he knew about the baby–' she began hesitantly, but Anne-Marie broke in swiftly with:

'I'd never marry him, Eve. Not after the way he treated me. I hate him now ... hate him! I hate the baby, too. Oh, Eve! If this only *was* a nightmare and tomorrow I could wake up and find it wasn't true!'

'Yes! And I wish it, too,' Eve thought, realizing suddenly what a heavy load of responsibility Anne-Marie was putting on her shoulders.

Oh, how could she have done this? How could the pretty, laughing, happy little girl they had all so adored have come down to this sordid, seamy world of horror?

'Because we have always spoiled her,' came the answer. 'It's our fault ... mine, Mother's, Father's. She has always gone her own way ... had whatever she wanted from life irrespective of the cost. This trip to Paris ... if only Father had refused to let her come ... been firm with her, since he could not really afford it.'

'If only I'd never come here in the first place!' Anne-Marie said, as if reading Eve's thoughts.

'Does Madame Boulanger know?' Eve asked.

Anne-Marie shook her head, an expression of horror in her eyes.

'No, no, no! You mustn't tell her, Eve. No one must know. Promise me you'll never tell another soul. I swear I'll try to kill myself ... like David did ... if you tell anyone. I couldn't bear anyone else but you to know.'

'We shall have to tell Father and Mother,' Eve said pityingly. 'They *must* know, Anne-Marie. They will understand ... help you. But we have to tell them.'

'You can't, Eve. I'd die first. Think what it would mean to them ... to Father ... his own daughter. It mightn't have mattered to him so much if it had been *you* ... you're not really a Corderhay ... but it would ruin Father's life. And Mother... Eve, you know they mustn't know. You love them, don't you? You wouldn't break their hearts?'

'Hush! Everyone will hear you, Anne-Marie,' Eve said, as her sister's voice rose hysterically. 'Of course I don't want to have to tell them, but how else can we manage?'

'I could stay here ... in Paris ... another six months–'

'But Father can't afford to let you stay here!' Eve interrupted. 'And what excuse can you give?'

'Then Louise can stay at Corderhay Park! Surely she is enjoying herself? Madame says she sounds so happy. Madame would let her stay. You could write and tell Father I'm so happy here, too, and that Madame would agree. Father would let me stay if you thought it was a good idea.'

It was possible, Eve thought. But she could not leave Anne-Marie alone in Paris to face things by herself. And besides, afterwards, there would be the baby.

'And Madame ... she would guess!' Eve spoke aloud.

Anne-Marie's hands went to her face, covering her eyes as if she could not bear Eve to see the shame in them. Once again pity stirred Eve's heart. Pity for her sister ... and an even greater pity for her mother and father. She would do anything ... anything in the world rather than see them hurt and disillusioned. Anne-Marie might have been cruel to stress the fact that she, Eve, was not a Corderhay, and that if it had been she in such a predicament they would not have minded so much; and yet it was true, Eve thought. If only she could have the baby for Anne-Marie!

'I'll get it adopted!' Anne-Marie broke in on her thoughts. 'I'll only have to hide away for the next six months. Maybe there's still a chance I needn't have it...'

'You'll have it, Anne-Marie!'

Eve's voice was so sharp and angry that the younger girl flinched. Any hope she might have entertained of a speedy solution faded. She might have known Eve would never agree to anything like that. Eve was so strait-laced!

'It can be adopted, then,' she said, covering up her mistake. 'You were adopted, Eve. And you've been happy. The baby wouldn't know any difference.'

'But we would know!' Eve said. 'It would be *your* child, Anne-Marie. You couldn't desert it! Deny it its mother's love.'

'I'll never love it ... never want it!' Anne-Marie cried passionately. 'If you knew how I hated it already!'

'She doesn't know what she is saying,' Eve excused her sister. 'Naturally, in her condition...' Oh God ... this was so much worse than anything she had expected. The paltry sum of thirty-five pounds would never find a way out of this difficulty! At worst, it would barely pay Anne-Marie's confinement.

She did not realize at that moment that already she was trying to find a solution that would evade the necessity to tell her parents. Somehow it was beyond her powers of imagination to envisage hurting and shaming the two people she loved best in the world.

'If only we had some money!' Anne-Marie said. 'Then it would be so easy. We'd leave Madame's and manage on our own until it was all over.'

'So she expects automatically that I will

stay with her,' Eve thought, with a moment's anger which was quickly replaced by that instinctive protective feeling she had always had for Anne-Marie ever since she had been a little girl of six and first seen the tiny new-born baby in her mother's arms.

'You shall help me take care of her, Eve,' Antoinette had said, and Eve had felt a thrill of pride and silently vowed in her childish mind that always ... always she would guard and protect this little bundle of babyhood.

Reluctantly she brought her mind back through the years, and in doing so turned to look at the young girl who had evolved from that tiny golden baby. Anne-Marie's face was turned away from Eve so that only her profile was visible to the older girl; yet this was sufficient to reveal how thin and pale she had become over these last months, how terribly much older she looked ... how different!

'Oh, no, no!' whispered a voice inside Eve's heart. 'This can't have happened to Anne-Marie ... not to my sister ... to our "baby"!'

And yet who knew better than she how surely this was a fact? There could be no doubting the truth behind Anne-Marie's hysterical confession. The younger girl was distraught, afraid, and certainly not at all well.

Desperately, Eve sought for some past knowledge she might have acquired about women who were to become mothers. Wasn't this the time in their lives when they should look most beautiful? She seemed to recall an article she had read in a woman's magazine in which a doctor had declared that motherhood was beneficial to the health ... the natural evolution of the body and therefore in no way to be feared or thought of as an illness. And yet here was Anne-Marie looking like death and so thin that it frightened Eve to look at her. Could this be due to that horrible medicine the chemist had given her that had made her so sick and faint? Or was fear responsible? Because Anne-Marie was afraid ... perhaps not so much of Eve and her opinion, for she knew her older sister too well to think she would lack sympathy and help from this quarter ... but fear of what her parents would say ... of the disgrace ... to them and to herself ... fear of the future?

The future! It had seemed so bright for Anne-Marie such a brief while ago, and now what could it hold for her? None knew better than Eve what high hopes Antoinette and Jack Corderhay had had of marrying their daughter to some well-to-do young man who could afford to give her the luxuries and home equivalent to that in which she had been brought up. Neither of her parents were snobbish in their outlook ... of that Eve had no doubts ... but it was only natural that they did not wish their daughter to lead the difficult role of cook, mother, wife, nanny ...

all rolled into one when she had been trained to none of these things. It had never seemed necessary, for all the Corderhays' friends were as wealthy as themselves and Anne-Marie knew no other young men than the sons of their contemporaries. David ... but it was best not to remember him and Anne-Marie's behaviour ... nor think of what might have been had Anne-Marie been really fond of the boy ... it only made the present situation more difficult to cope with.

'It is not altogether her own fault!' Eve told herself once more. 'We have all spoiled her and I have always tried to help her evade punishments when it would have been better for her to learn to take the blame for her own misdeeds.' So often she had confessed that she had done this or that because it had upset her as a child to see Anne-Marie's pretty little face blotched with ugly tears. Sometimes Nanny had guessed the truth and had warned Eve against taking the blame for others.

'You hurt them more than you help them,' she had said. And now Eve was beginning to see the truth of that adage. Her actions had taught Anne-Marie to evade responsibility and to do whatever should come into her fancy with the fairly safe knowledge that Eve would probably get her out of trouble if she should be found out ... or that she could talk her way out of a punishment with a well-simulated brimming of tears to her eyes … for her mother could no more bear to see her unhappy than could Eve.

'She's sorry now so we'll say no more about it!' How often had Eve heard those words, too!

And now, no doubt, Anne-Marie was sorry, and yet this time one could not 'say no more about it'. The consequences of her actions must not and could not be avoided because they involved someone else … the child.

'I'll get it adopted!' Anne-Marie had said. But this would once again be evading the consequences and at another's expense. At least if this child had to be born into such unhappy circumstances as not having a father … it should have the right to its mother's love … her name … her protection.

Anne-Marie's name … Corderhay! It brought to Eve a terrible feeling of home-sickness and pain. She had always been so proud of that name in the past. Her pride was part of her love and respect for her adoptive father and partly due to a reflection of his own feeling for his ancestors. Since she was a tiny girl her father had told her stories of the great Corderhays of the past … all of whom had been heroes … even the one who had turned highwayman, for, like Robin Hood, he had robbed the rich to help the poor, in times when men, women and children were dying of starvation and privation and many of the great lords and ladies of the day unwilling to give even a particle of charity.

Now, for perhaps the first time in history, shame was to be brought down on that name, and it was almost more than Eve could bear to entertain the thought of her mother's and father's feelings of shock and unutterable dismay.

If this man could only be traced ... persuaded to marry her! Eve thought again, but realized, even as the idea flashed once more across her mind, as a means of escape from disgrace, that she would be sacrificing perhaps the happiness of three people in order to save the family pride.

Anne-Marie had turned to her for advice and for her there was no one to run to. The responsibility of what Anne-Marie did now was hers, since she could not leave her young sister to face this out alone ... indeed, she would be afraid to leave her. She talked wildly of killing herself ... the baby ... and in this present state of mind anything might happen that would seem impossible in the ordinary course of events.

The younger girl, seeing Eve's intent, thoughtful face, did not interrupt her. For in Eve lay her only hope... She trusted Eve to find a way out as she had always found a way out in their childhood days. Somehow Eve would think of something. She could relax a little now that she did not bear her dreadful secret alone. She had shocked Eve … but that would not affect Eve's wish to protect her, of that she was sure. The very fact that she had been deserted by the child's father had ensured that protection. And if Eve knew the truth…

Anne-Marie shuddered involuntarily, for deep in her heart she knew that if Eve realized what had really transpired these last few months, even she would turn and condemn her. For although she had seldom stopped to consider the consequences of her actions, Anne-Marie still knew the difference between right and wrong. And what she had done was wrong … with no two ways about it. But she had never for a moment imagined that she, Anne-Marie, would get found out and have to pay, in this of all ways, the price of her sins.

CHAPTER 4

A month later Eve and Anne-Marie were sitting in front of the tiny electric fire of their living-room. Anne-Marie was reading a French illustrated magazine, her feet curled up beneath her, her hair, which she had recently washed, falling in soft fair curls round her shoulders. She looked terribly young and very pretty, and Eve, studying her young sister, could hardly believe that in little over twenty weeks she was to become a mother. It was hard to believe that this girl was more than seventeen, so childish was her appearance. These four weeks had made a great difference to Anne-Marie. Her face was almost chubby now and a healthy rose colour had brightened her cheeks. Even her eyes, when they were not a mirror to the constant discontent that she was forever voicing, were larger, brighter now that the dark circles beneath them had vanished.

'At least she is well!' Eve told herself, knowing that this fact alone was worth the immense hard work and self-sacrifice she had had to face to bring all this about. She gazed around the little room that served as both sitting-room and dining-room. Beyond, through one of the doors, was the tiny kitchenette, and through the other door their bedroom, with its two small divan beds.

How hard she had had to search for this apartment. With the very minimum amount of money to spare on rent, it'd been no easy matter to find a home for them that was both cheap and clean and not too dreary, as were so many of the rooms she had seen in this cheaper quarter of Paris. In fact had it not been for the help of Denise, one of the girls who was working with Eve, they might never have been so fortunate as to find this flat.

Denise was a girl of Eve's own age, and Eve knew that if it had not been for her friendship and guidance she might never have had the courage to go through with her plans. Since her arrival in Paris she had lost no time in thinking of a way out of Anne-Marie's problems ... and her first decision had been to find a job. Strangely enough, this had not been so difficult, for a kindly agent had suggested that Eve was immensely photogenic and, while not pretty in the strict sense of the word, had a *je ne sais quoi* that might appeal to a French photographer, for Eve's looks were different from the general run of French girls.

In a matter of days a fashion magazine had decided that Eve had just the figure to show off tweeds and commissioned their photographer to try her out. The results were successful and Eve knew that the salary offered her was generous. Since they would require only a limited number of photographs each week, she would have plenty of time for other free-lance work. It was only a matter of days before other jobs were offered her and work as a photographer's model came pouring in. No one could have been more surprised than Eve, who had never imagined that anyone would find her face 'attractive', nor stopped to consider that her figure was perfectly proportioned and her bone structure ideal for photography. She was in every way photogenic and the agent had had the sense and experience to see at a glance what Eve would never have seen in herself.

Through this agency Eve had come in contact with Denise le Brun, a well-established model who was greatly in demand and earned a good deal of money in this way. Denise also modelled clothes for the popular fashion magazine which had given Eve her first chance. It was here that Eve first met her. Denise had none of the English girl's innate shyness and reserve and, having decided with typical impulsiveness that she liked Eve, she had speedily won her friendship and lately her confidence. For Denise, although the same age as Eve, had had a very different upbringing and had been forced, since the age of twelve, to earn her own living. Consequently, she was far more mature and experienced in the ways of the world than was Eve, and a great deal of privation and suffering had given the young French girl a gentle, sympathetic nature where it might, had she been a less likeable character, have made her hard and bitter.

She was a dark, vivid-looking girl, a little shorter than Eve and with more generous curves. She had deep, liquid-brown eyes and a piquant *gamine* face that had helped so much towards her success in the photo-graphic, modelling world. Her childhood had been in the slums of Paris, and but for her desire to escape from the squalor and degradation of the life her mother had planned for her she might now be in some house of ill repute where so many of the young girls in the slums were sent as soon as they were old enough and before they could appreciate the horror of such a life.

Denise had never known her father, but she believed she must have inherited her emotions from him, for she had never been able to accept the life her mother led, and something deep inside her had recoiled from growing up to such a future. At twelve she had run away and got a job in a laundry. From there she had slowly made her way up to this life, and now it was hard to believe her origin and quite impossible that she should ever return to it.

She had confided these details to Eve one afternoon when they were both awaiting the photographer, who for some reason or another had been delayed. Denise had made tea in the studio and, in front of the wood stove, the first intimacy had grown between them. Listening to her story, Eve had compared the suffering of this girl with her own easy life and background and realized again how terribly lucky she had been … how much she owed to her father and mother.

Impulsively, she had told Denise of her own childhood and what had brought her to Paris.

'It is because you hated and despised your mother ... your home ... that you left them, Denise,' she said. 'Can you understand that it is because I love my family and home so much that I made up my mind to leave them, perhaps for ever?'

'I understand that you love them ... yes!' Denise said in her halting English. 'But to take the blame, as you call it, for this young sister ... that seems too much to do. I can understand your wish to help her ... to stay with her until the baby arrives ... but then to send her home and bring up the child yourself ... that I cannot understand!'

'It is because my mother will not miss me as she would miss Anne-Marie ... and it would not hurt her or my father so much if they ever learned the truth,' Eve had tried to explain. 'I am not really a Corderhay ... Anne-Marie is. My father would never get over the shock.'

Denise shook her head, still not fully understanding how anyone could make such a sacrifice. For Eve had told her that it was her intention to send Anne-Marie home soon after the baby was born. She herself would write a letter to her parents telling them she had decided to stay on alone in Paris ... that she wanted to lead her own life and be quite independent; that for this reason she would prefer to cut away from the family altogether.

'It may be hard on them at first, but they

will let me go. Neither of them would stand in my way. Soon they will forget about me and I shall have to try to forget them. Only it will be so hard, Denise. I love them all so much … and Corderhay Park … my home … means more to me than anything else in the world–'

'Except the family honour,' Denise broke in. 'It is very praiseworthy, *chérie,* but is it not also a … how do you call it … a false heroic? This will not be your baby. But you will take on the responsibility. Have you thought what it means? Hard work all your life? Perhaps never to be married … never have children of your own. And to be cut off always from your real home … your parents whom you love … for this girl who, for all that you say is to be pitied, and I agree … is nevertheless not worth a hair of your head.'

'How can you say that, Denise?' Eve had defended her sister. 'You have never met her.'

Denise gave a curious little smile.

'No! But yet you tell me she has agreed to this plan … is willing … eager, to let you make these sacrifices for her. That is selfish, is it not? Cowardly, too. She should have the courage to take the blame for her misdeeds.'

'But she is so young, Denise! And it was not her fault this man walked out on her. Besides, it is more for my parents' sake than for hers. I wish to protect them.'

Denise shrugged her shoulders in a typical

French gesture, indicating all too clearly that she still did not believe Eve was acting for the best; but for all that, this was not her affair and all her sympathies and admiration went out to the English girl for her courage and selflessness.

'At least you will have one friend, *chérie*,' she said, putting her arm affectionately round Eve's shoulders and embracing her ... an action which was strangely comforting to Eve even while its unreservedness embarrassed her.

'Thank you, Denise,' she said. 'I shall need a friend. Already I need help. I must find somewhere to live. We cannot remain at Madame Boulanger's much longer. Anne-Marie is beginning ... soon Madame will notice something. But all the flats I have seen are either too expensive or too dreadful to contemplate! Is there nowhere in Paris where one can find a small flat with a couple of rooms at a reasonable price?'

Denise gave a delightful chuckle.

'In Paris one must know where to go,' she said. 'I have the ideal place ... two thousand francs a week only and I have even my own bathroom. That is almost too reasonable, is it not, for a furnished place?'

'Two thousand francs!' Eve repeated. 'It sounds ghastly!'

But when she worked it out it was only about two pounds a week. Denise, it appeared, had only a bed-sitting-room, but she believed there was a larger flat in the same block becoming vacant shortly. She promised to enquire for Eve, and a day or two later announced that for three thousand francs the ideal place was waiting for them.

'We will go together to see it this afternoon?' she suggested, and Eve eagerly agreed.

At first she was a little disappointed. The furniture was not very attractive and the curtains and chair covers were dingy and the carpet threadbare. What a contrast to the beautiful rooms in Corderhay Park! A contrast, too, to Madame's house where she and Anne-Marie were living.

Seeing her dismay, Denise had taken her to the floor above and shown her her own little flat. Here there were gay check curtains in the windows and a window-box on the little balcony outside where, Denise said proudly, there were bulbs planted for the spring. She had rearranged the existing furniture, added here and there an ornament, a drapery and transformed it beyond recognition.

'It needs only a little money to be spent … material is cheap enough in the market!' she said. *'Et voilà!'*

She had all the Frenchwoman's flare for home-making, and where her taste was instinctively good her upbringing had helped by giving her a practical and economical outlook at the same time.

'If you like it … we shall do your home together,' she suggested shyly. 'Unless, of course, you prefer that Anne-Marie shall help?'

'I would be glad of your help, Denise!' Eve cried gratefully. For Anne-Marie was filled with a deadening apathy nowadays and was sullen and resentful at times, and at others tearful and filled with self-pity and protestations that she was ruining everyone's life and was better dead!

In view of her condition Eve had tried to be patient and take no notice of her young sister's seeming ingratitude, but at times she had felt discouraged herself and wondered if she could control the sharp reproofs that rushed to her lips.

'It will never work!' was Anne-Marie's inevitable reply to any suggestion Eve made. This, in itself, was discouraging when she was trying so desperately hard to plan things the best way possible for the girl. Anne-Marie had not believed she would get a job … had not believed her letter home would convince her father that she was having so good a time she wished to stay … had not believed Eve would ever find a flat for them at a price they could afford. And when Eve had come back to announce success, it had been only to hear some fresh complaint from the girl … that she wasn't feeling well; that she was lonely, bored, depressed ... unhappy.

In view of this despondency Eve had decided it would be best to have their new home looking as nice as possible when Anne-Marie first saw it, for they were going to live here ... to that Eve had quite made up her mind, and nothing Anne-Marie said would deter her from this decision.

Anne-Marie, however, was far too relieved to be away from Madame's observant eyes to have anything but a feeling of immense relief the day they moved into the little flat. In fact, for the first time since she had learned of her condition she was feeling happier and more confident of the future. A letter had come from Antoinette saying how proud they were to learn of Eve's new job, and to think that she was earning sufficient money to set up a little home for them both and be financially independent! She and their father were, however, insistent that they should accept a small personal allowance which she had arranged with Madame Boulanger to give them in francs every month. This was only reasonable, since Louise had to have a little pocket money and meant that they could continue to avoid currency exchanges. Louise was so happy at Corderhay Park that Madame was content for her to remain a few months longer, and it was Antoinette's opinion that there were the beginnings of a romance between Louise and a young man in the neighbourhood, the Honourable Richard Bainborough, whom Anne-Marie may not remember but Eve might recall meeting at a children's party many years ago, when Anne-Marie was still an infant. Madame naturally was pleased at this prospect of a successful marriage with a 'title' and had asked Antoinette to encourage it and given her permission for Louise to remain for as long as it suited the Corderhays.

Naturally, her letter continued, she and their father were missing the girls and Jack Corderhay particularly missed Eve's assistance with his work on the estate, but they both felt that a year in Paris would be a good thing for them, since this was an opportunity which might not arise again in their lives; and they again congratulated Eve on her ability to support herself and her sister. They would like to pay them both a visit, but for the moment finances would not permit it.

This last announcement had relieved Anne-Marie of her moment's anxiety at the thought of a visit from her parents and she had handed the letter to Eve with a sigh of relief. Things were beginning to work out right after all, and if only the next few months would hurry by and she could have the baby and forget all about it, she could begin life again.

For Eve, too, the letter was a relief, but at the same time she felt an acute misery at certain passages in it. Her father was missing her ... needed her help, and she could not be there. It was so typical of both her parents that they should put the happiness of their daughters first and so readily give their blessing to a project which, for all they knew, was motivated by nothing more than a desire to have a good time. They could not ... must not ... know that Eve's wish to remain in Paris was not of her own choice but through circumstances that would break both their hearts to discover. Perhaps it was as well they suspected nothing of the truth, for there could be no happiness or gaiety for either herself or Anne-Marie for a long time to come. Maybe, in the distant future, after Anne-Marie had gone home, the younger girl would learn to forget all this and start life again. But for Eve there would be a living reminder in Anne-Marie's baby, and she did not feel that she could ever be happy again.

If only she were not so homesick for Corderhay Park! Seeing Anne-Marie in the armchair reading on this wet Sunday afternoon, it was so painfully easy to project her mind back to the nursery and past Sunday afternoons at home. She might so easily have been sitting by the nursery fire knitting, as she was doing now, Anne-Marie glancing through a picture book and Nanny somewhere downstairs seeing about nursery tea ... a fresh boiled egg, perhaps, and crumpets

... and a slice of Cook's cherry cake. Soon it would be time to go down to the drawing-room to spend an hour with Mummy and Daddy. Maybe Daddy would read them another chapter of *Treasure Island*, or Mummy sing them one of her favourite songs, accompanying herself on the piano...

A sharp knock on the door jolted Eve's mind back to the present and she could have wept with dismay, so vivid had been that image of past days. But the sight of Denise in the doorway with a large mound of buttered toast and her bright, friendly smile dispelled a little of her unhappiness in a wave of gratitude. Denise was proving such a good friend, and even while Anne-Marie did not appear to like her, nor Denise care much for her sister, Eve found a great relief in the long talks they had and the knowledge that there was someone else in this foreign country who would advise, sympathize and at least try to understand her.

'Your little sister is jealous of me, no?' Denise had remarked on one occasion, her judgment of Anne-Marie shrewd and unbiased by childhood recollections or family ties.

'I'm sure that isn't so!' Eve had defended the younger girl. 'It's just that she isn't feeling well at the moment, Denise. It makes her irritable and difficult. If you had known her as she used to be...'

But somehow Denise felt she would never

have liked Eve's sister. She was spoilt, lazy, selfish and hard, and even while she pitied her present predicament, Denise could find no trait in the younger girl's character that appealed to her. It worried her far more than Eve realized to think that it was for Anne-Marie that Eve was sacrificing so much ... this, and a family pride when the family was not even hers, except by adoption.

Denise stayed for tea, but she left soon afterwards, for she had several admirers and seldom spent an evening at home. When she had departed to get dressed for her party, Anne-Marie turned to Eve with a petulant sigh.

'I wish I were going dancing, Eve. It's so dull staying here in the flat all day. It's all right for you. You have your work to keep you busy. I have nothing.'

For once Eve rounded on her sister with a sharp retort.

'Then if you're bored, you should do more work yourself, Anne-Marie. The doctor says you're fit enough to do housework. It would be a treat for me to come home to a hot meal occasionally and to find the beds made. And even if I do work, it is not for enjoyment, but for you, Anne-Marie, and for your child. Sometimes I too am tired and bored.'

Anne-Marie flushed a deep pink, for it was not often she heard Eve complain and there was every justification for her remarks. She hated housework ... was bad at doing even the few odd tasks Eve had given her ... and she made no effort to help run the place.

'I do so hate that kind of work,' she murmured. 'I'm not used to it, Eve, and you do everything so much better than I do.'

'Well, at least you could do some knitting!' Eve said, her tone softer again, for she could never resist an appeal from Anne-Marie when she sounded repentant. 'There is so much the baby will need.'

Anne-Marie bit her lip. The baby! Always the baby! Eve mentioned it a thousand times a day, while she was doing everything in her power to forget it. This had become almost impossible now that her waist was thickening and there were definite outward signs of its existence. Deep in her heart lay the hope that the child would be born dead. The doctor had told her that any day now it would 'quicken' ... that she would feel its movements within her as it really became alive ... but so far she had felt nothing and she had almost convinced herself that, perhaps after all, those pills she had taken had destroyed the life of the baby and that it would never exist.

She had not dared to mention these hopes to Eve, for she knew only too well how shocked her sister would be. Eve was so terribly conventional ... strait-laced. It was all very well to talk of knitting baby-clothes and buying cots and prams and so on ... but if she could help it she would see that there was never a need for them. Women had miscarriages ... from lifting heavy furniture, doing too much ... falling downstairs. Eve didn't know that if the child did quicken, she intended to do all these things in turn in the hope that she, too, would miscarry. So why knit ... buy ... talk ... about a baby that would never be born?

Perhaps because she refused to believe in the truth, Anne-Marie had found it so easy to give in to Eve's idea that she, Eve, should look after it once it was born and Anne-Marie return to her home as if nothing had happened. She never stopped to consider the effect on Eve because she really believed, deep inside her, that the child would cease to exist and they could go home together. She was not entirely devoid of any good traits in her character, and although she sometimes made fun of Eve's devotion to her home and parents, secretly she admired her for it and knew that for Eve, anyway, this love was very real and deep-seated. She would not, therefore, have found it easy to be the one responsible for separating Eve for ever from her home.

But then, she argued with herself, even if the baby were born alive, it was her wish to have it adopted. That would entail no sacrifices for either of them now that Eve had so cleverly evaded the necessity for telling her parents the truth. If ultimately Eve refused to allow her to put the child in an orphanage, then it would be her own fault if she suffered the consequences. Anne-Marie didn't expect her to keep the child ... so why should Eve take on this duty? It wasn't her baby ... not even her flesh and blood. But one thing was certain. She, Anne-Marie, was not going to be left with the baby for the rest of her life. She was young, pretty, and she had her youth before her. One day she would marry, and if she wanted children she would have them then ... not that she had ever felt any maternal urges.

As to the father of her child ... Anne-Marie resolutely refused to think of him. She had loved him ... passionately and for the first time in her life, with no thought for herself. She had given in to his every wish and could have denied him nothing.

Their *affaire* had been short, wild, stormy, and although Anne-Marie was not to realize it at the present moment, it was the only time in her life when she would love another human being more than she loved herself.

'I hate him ... hate him!' she told herself so often that she believed it true. And now she hardly thought of him at all ... no longer lay in the darkness longing for him to come to her and light the flame of passion anew in her heart. Maybe it was the fact that she bore his child … but for the time being, anyway, desire had left her and she could welcome the solitude of her bed.

Perhaps conscious of the trend of Anne-Marie's thoughts, Eve interrupted them, saying:

'You never talk … of Paul, Anne-Marie! Is it that the thought of him makes you unhappy? If so, then forget I mentioned his name. But I confess I am curious about him. I cannot help thinking that if he learned about the baby he would want to marry you. What sort of man is he? It is so difficult for me to imagine someone whom you could love so … so desperately.'

Anne-Marie gave a quick, hard little laugh.

'Paul Johnson!' she said, as if she were speaking of someone she had known an aeon ago. 'I don't mind talking about him, but as for loving him … *I hope I never see him again.* As a matter of fact, Eve, I think *you* would have liked him. I often thought that when I was with him.'

Eve bit her lip. Did Anne-Marie know so little about her?

'I could never have loved any man who … who could treat a woman as he treated you,' she said. 'To like a man, I would have to respect him.'

'And you couldn't respect a man who desired you?' Anne-Marie said bluntly. She gave another laugh that sounded this time bitter and strangely mature. 'You don't know anything about love, Eve. When you really fall for a man … the way I did … nothing matters in the world but being with him … belonging to him. It's as if they can cast a spell over you. You *want* to do what they want just as much as they do. You think I was seduced, to use a nice Victorian expression, but it isn't true. I gave myself to him willingly.'

She spoke the words defiantly, but still Eve was not convinced. This man was older than Anne-Marie … had known, no doubt, the way to weaken her defences, arouse her instincts so that she was too blinded by the physical side of her emotions to realize what she was doing. The fault was primarily his. Anne-Marie had been innocent and inexperienced when she had left home. This man had had the responsibility of awakening her to womanhood and he had taken advantage of her lack of experience. His, therefore, must be the blame.

'I've got a snapshot of him somewhere,' Anne-Marie was saying. 'Jean took it one afternoon on a picnic in the Bois de Boulogne. I'll fetch it for you.'

Curious, in spite of herself, Eve waited while Anne-Marie searched in her writing-case for several snapshots, which she handed to Eve.

'That one is of Louise and Jean,' she said. 'This one is Paul. The other one is of me on the balcony outside Madame's house.'

It was only a small photograph, and yet so sharply and perfectly focused that the face of the man was minutely clear. He was not particularly handsome, Eve noted, and yet there was something attractive about the face ... the broad forehead above wide-set eyes. The nose was long but straight and the mouth and jaw strong, determined. The hair, brushed smoothly back, looked fair and thick but not in the least effeminate. He looked very English ... clean-cut, honest, dependable.

'Yet he was none of those things!' Eve thought with a sense of shock. 'It shows how one can misjudge appearances. Even I would have trusted this man, and I am more critical than Anne-Marie.'

'He ... doesn't look–' She began awkwardly, but Anne-Marie, guessing her remark, broke in:

'Like the villain of the piece? Perhaps not. But now you may understand why I trusted him. I really believed him when he said he wanted to marry me. And if you'd known him, you'd have believed him, too. He isn't a "flighty" sort at all. He's rather brusque and matter-of-fact ... sort of down to earth ... like his name. Funny sort of name for a man, Paul! It's so short and squat. As a matter-of-fact, I think it suits him, though in fact he's very tall.'

'How can she talk about him so casually?' Eve wondered. 'If I had loved him ... lived with him ... and he had let me down...' But then, Anne-Marie was different. She seemed to have amazing resilience. Already she was talking about the future as if there were no tragedy or difficulty to face in the present. It seemed as if she could forget whatever she did not wish to remember.

Nevertheless, as she went through to the kitchen to prepare supper on the little gas stove Eve decided that the face that had looked at her from that photograph was not one that could easily be forgotten or cast aside. It stayed in her mind and worried her. Unaccountably, she wished now that she had not asked Anne-Marie if she could see it.

In spite of this, she did not throw the photograph away as Anne-Marie suggested. She locked it away at the bottom of her jewel-case, telling herself that perhaps one day it might serve to trace him. For Anne-Marie had been right when she said Eve was 'so conventional', and at the back of her mind Eve continued to hope she might one day bring the baby's parents together for all their sakes, and particularly for Anne-Marie's. For Eve genuinely believed that once the baby was born, Anne-Marie would not willingly be parted from it.

She did not realize that she was judging Anne-Marie on the assumption of her own feelings under such circumstances and that she was never in her life more wrong. She learned the truth five months later when Anne-Marie gave birth to a golden-haired, blue-eyed baby boy, and, lying weak and tearful in the French hospital ward, utterly and adamantly refused even to see her child.

'In a day or two she will feel differently,' Eve thought, as she stared down at the minute bundle of humanity that was not yet a day old. 'When she sees how beautiful he is…'

'We must persuade her to see him … once will be enough!' was the kindly doctor's comment.

'He is the image of his mother!' said the nurse. 'She will not be able to resist him!'

But they did not know Anne-Marie. Only Denise guessed the determination and desperation of the young girl and was right when she said to Eve, the day the baby was born:

'She never believed it would really happen. In her heart she hoped it would be born dead. It was not a fact to her, and if she doesn't see him she can still believe it isn't true. Can't you see that, Eve? Can't you see that she will always take the easy way out by refusing to accept even the facts if she doesn't like them?'

'Anne-Marie is not like that,' Eve had argued. 'You don't know her as I do, Denise.'

'We shall see, *chérie!*' was Denise's philosophical reply.

And Denise, knowing from experience how hard, ruthless and selfish some women could be, had seen beyond the soft, pretty ways of Anne-Marie and judged her right.

CHAPTER 5

Denise sat on the edge of the bed watching Eve bath the baby. Every now and again she would make an amused comment on the way Eve handled the child.

'You have the experience, one sees!' she said, smiling.

Eve pushed a stray wisp of hair off her damp forehead and looked up at Denise as she deftly fastened safety-pins to hold the nappies in position.

'Only theoretical until now!' she admitted. 'I used to watch Nanny dealing with Anne-Marie. You see, I was six when she was born and for me it was like having a real living doll around the place. Sometimes Nanny would let me wash her face or hold her for a moment or two. And once or twice, for a special treat, I was allowed to give her her bottle. I was very proud and happy!'

'And now also you are happy!' Denise said astutely. 'It is your forte, is it not? Your true self, Eve, to be a mother. You have no idea how right you look just at this moment ... a little untidy, yes, but oh, so very becoming! You know, *chérie*, if I were a man and saw you for the first time ... like this ... holding *le petit* in your arms just so ... I should wish to marry you ... baby and all!'

Eve grinned a trifle ruefully as she tested the heat of the baby's bottle against her cheek and, finding it right, put it in the hungry little mouth. It was all very well for Denise to say she was happy. In one sense it was true that she was content ... in a way she had never yet been in her life before. Ever since she had realized that Anne-Marie had no intention of even seeing her baby, far less caring for it, something fundamentally maternal had risen inside her heart. She had felt that Anne-Marie's renunciation of the baby had made the child hers. That it should be adopted was beyond her consideration even for a moment.

He was a beautiful baby from the moment he was born. His complexion had been creamy-white ... no ugly blotched red about him ... and his features perfectly formed. A fluff of golden hair covered the top of his tiny head, and although new-born babies did not actually smile, he was the most contented child, so Sister had said, that they had ever had in the hospital. He seldom, if ever, cried. Sometimes if his feed was a few minutes behind time his little face would crumple and his tiny fists clench and beat the air in protest, but there were no tears. And mostly, when he was not asleep, he lay with his enormous china-blue eyes, fringed with their golden lashes, gazing at the little world around him in incomprehensible satisfaction.

'He has so little to be happy about!' Denise had said on one occasion. 'And yet look, Eve, I think this time he really smiles!'

'We must find a name for him, since Anne-Marie will not talk of doing so,' Eve had said. 'I think perhaps we might call him Anthony ... it is a little like Anne-Marie and Antoinette and he is like them both. Oh, Denise, how can Anne-Marie refuse to look at him! I don't understand it.'

But as soon as Anne-Marie was on her feet and ready to leave the hospital, she informed Eve that she was going home.

'Put the baby in an orphanage, Eve, and come home with me!' she had begged her sister. 'He isn't your responsibility. You must be mad to think of keeping him. Besides, how will you manage when you're at work all day? You won't be able to care for him properly, and what will his future be ... no father and not even his own mother?...'

'That, at least, will not be my fault!' Eve said sharply. 'I shall do my best to replace you, Anne-Marie, and his father.'

Accepting the rebuke, but with indifference, for nothing seemed to matter a great deal to her any more except that soon she would be going home and could forget all this, the younger girl said curiously:

'But *why*, Eve? That's what I don't understand!'

'Perhaps I am not sure of my reasons myself,' Eve had admitted. 'I just know I have to keep him, Anne-Marie. Maybe because he is so very tiny and helpless; perhaps because he is, after all, a Corderhay and I do not think Father would wish any child with Corderhay blood to be brought up by strangers, cast off by his own kith and kin. I'm not sure, but it isn't your worry any more. I've only one thing more to say about him, Anne-Marie, and it is this ... that if ever you let Father or Mother know where I'm living, give them even the smallest hint, I shall tell them the truth ... the whole truth. You see, if I cannot go home, then at least I can endeavour to avoid the unhappiness of a scene with them, and when they learn I am never returning to them I think they will want to find me. Father, at any rate, will not believe I can cut myself away from home and family without a good-bye or a good reason. I don't think I could bear it if he came to beg me to go home. And for this reason I'm warning you. So you see, Anne-Marie, the safety of your secret lies in your own hands. You can trust me to keep silent only if you can trust yourself to do the same. And it won't be easy. They'll ask questions ... lots of them. Just say I'm having such a good time and have grown so used to living my own life that I do not wish to return to my old life. That I'm leaving the flat and you do not know where I am going.'

This much at least was true, for Eve felt her family might trace her all too easily at the address where she had been living with Anne-Marie. At Denise's suggestion she moved into a smaller flat on the same floor as her friend, and at the same time Denise had a word with the landlady, explaining that Eve was going to take care of her sister's child and wished to be known in future as Madame Daudet. The landlady, unlike her equivalent in England, sensed romance, intrigue, and, revelling in it, was only too ready to agree. But it seemed a pity that, in order to accept the thousand-franc note Denise offered her to remain silent on the subject of the two English mademoiselles, she could not tell the neighbours of this *histoire romantique*.

Her curiosity soon waned, however, for there was little excitement or romance in the tiny flat where Eve started a new life with baby Anthony. No handsome young men ever came to visit her and she was never seen to go out ... even in the company of Mademoiselle Denise le Brun, her friend. Indeed, thought the landlady, this was small wonder, for the poor young thing was hard at work all day while she herself minded the baby for five hundred francs a day. And when the girl came home at night, just in time to put the child to bed, she was too tired, poor soul, to do more than get her supper, rest her feet for an hour or two before the baby's ten o'clock bottle, and then sink into bed!

Was she happy? Eve asked herself. Denise had said so; the landlady doubted how she could be, but in a way she was happy … or would be if only she were not so tired and worried. Anthony was nearly five months old now and he seemed to grow so terribly fast. He always needed new clothes, more milk, more time, and she had so little money to buy the things he needed and even less time to spare for him as she tried to fit more work into the day so that she could earn more money. As it was, she only just made out at the end of each week. Several times Denise had offered financial assistance, saying in that frank, friendly way of hers:

'But, Eve, I have more than I need. It goes nowhere that is of use. Let me give you just this little note…'

But Eve would not permit it. She knew that Denise had been thriftily saving for a *dot* … a sum of money which would, according to French custom, assist her in making a far better marriage than she could have done with a non-existent bank balance to offer a prospective husband. Denise had long ago confided that she intended to marry well.

'I have been poor in my childhood ... really poor,' she had told Eve. 'It is something I shall never quite forget ... those years of my life. They shall not happen again. In ten years I shall begin to look older ... work will not be offered me so much ... my figure will thicken ... and then what would happen to me? To end up as my mother did ... never! I shall marry a rich business man and that will be that!'

'But, Denise, what will happen if you fall in love?'

Denise laughed and shrugged her shoulders.

'Who knows, *chérie?* Sometimes I think I shall never find a man to whom I could give my heart. I am like you ... I think ... how you call it ... fussy? Never do I find one that could make me love him enough to wish to be poor with him. So I continue to work and to save my *dot.*'

But Eve, even while she could refuse to accept money from Denise, could not prevent her giving Anthony presents. Every day when she returned from work there was something for him ... a toy, a little coat, a nightdress ... some grapes ... whatever Eve had been thinking he needed but could not afford.

'You say I am his godmother ... well, then

I have some rights, too, is it not?'

And Eve, tearful and grateful, had to give way.

'You've been a wonderful friend to me, Denise,' she told the other girl now as she sat in the nursing-chair gently rubbing the baby's back to bring up the wind. 'But for your companionship and help I don't think I could have lived through these last months. As it is, it has almost been fun. You make everything seem funny ... when the milk boiled over ... when the only dry nappy fell into the bath ... just when I feel like bursting into tears with exasperation, you laugh and say "*Ça ne fais rien*," and somehow, miraculously, it just doesn't seem to matter any more.'

'And you, too, are a good friend,' said Denise seriously. 'Until I knew you, Eve, I did not like the women. I have no girl friends because always I cannot admire them. And I was lonely. Now, when work is over for the day, I look forward to coming back to my little flat because I know that soon it will be time for *le petit* to have his bath, and we shall laugh much together and afterwards make supper and talk. I enjoy this more, I find, than to go to dances and dinner with men I do not very much like. You are like a sister to me, Eve; the sister I never could have had. Sometimes I am sad when I think that it cannot last.'

It was Eve's turn to smile.

'As far as I can see it will last indefinitely,' she said. 'I certainly haven't any prospect of moving away from here; in any case I couldn't afford it. You'll be the first to go, Denise ... when you meet your rich business man!'

'You make the joke about him always, Eve!' Denise protested. 'It is serious what I say.'

'And I'm serious when I say I can't really believe in him. Or should I say believe that you will ever marry a man you don't love?'

'You are true English, Eve!' Denise said with a sigh. 'Always sentimental. As for me, I am not sure there exists this emotion called love.'

'Oh, but yes, it does exist!' Eve cried vehemently. 'If you could have known my father and mother, Denise... Even now ... when they are both quite old, they love one another as deeply and passionately as ever. If you could have seen them as I did ... on Christmas night last year, dancing in one another's arms...'

The words evoked too poignant a memory for Eve to continue. Corderhay Park on Christmas night! What aeons ago it all seemed to be, and yet it was not yet a year. Soon they would be decorating the old house once more with holly and mistletoe and by now, no doubt, Cook had already made the Christmas puddings.

Eve had had news of home, of course, from Anne-Marie, but her letters seldom contained the small domestic details Eve longed so much to hear about. Wumpy, her darling little dog, was still alive, but Anne-Marie had only mentioned him once to say that he was 'disgustingly old and smelly' nowadays but Father had refused to let them have him put to sleep.

I think Father still believes in his heart that you will come home one of these days, Eve [the letter had continued]. *Not that he ever asks me nowadays where you are or if I have heard from you. But then I don't see a great deal of him. He's stuck away in his dreary old study poring over lots of dull-looking ledgers. Mother says he's worried about money, but we still get our allowance. I hope you're managing all right. Are you keeping well?*

But she never enquired after Anthony and already it appeared that she had started to live a full life again. Several times Richard Bainborough's name had been mentioned ... casually, but nevertheless Eve had wondered if this was not the beginning of yet another phase of Anne-Marie's life. She had believed that Richard Bainborough was Louise's companion ... that a romance had begun in this quarter ... but it did not take much imagination to surmise that if Anne-

Marie had set her cap at him, Louise would not stand much of a chance.

Eve never replied to these letters; neither did Anne-Marie expect a letter, since Eve had said she would not write. But for some curious reason the younger girl continued to send Eve short, brief notes from time to time as if she could never quite put out of her mind the reason for Eve's absence from home. She could not guess, of course, how eagerly Eve awaited this news of home and family; nor how easy it was to reduce her to a silent misery by such remarks as she had made about their father. Only Denise knew and understood and would console Eve by saying:

'They let you go, *chérie*, without much of a struggle. How often you hear from them ... once ... twice? ... and then no more. No doubt they are used to the idea now, *hein?* At first it is hard for them to understand, but what can they do? They accept the fact, and when you do not reply to their letters they realize it is all over. Soon they make themselves forget. That is life. Anne-Marie, too ... she forget her baby son and it is now as if he had never existed. I know ... for I, too, can forget what I do not wish to recall of my childhood days. Only sometimes I think of them and then I am sad to remember the little girl I used to be. But never do I wish to return to childhood. It is over … finished … and nearly forgotten.'

That, of course, was the difference. Denise could be glad that the present was so much better than the past. Whereas Eve, no matter how much she loved baby Anthony, could never overcome her homesickness and her longing to be with her adored parents once more.

'And this love you speak of...' Denise broke in on her thoughts, bringing her once more back to the present. 'You think it is so important? That one cannot be happy without it?'

'My mother never believed marriage could be happy without love,' Eve said. 'I can't speak from personal experience, for I have never loved any man in that way. But I feel inside me that my mother is right. And you have fought so hard for your future, Denise. You deserve only the best. That is why I cannot believe you will marry some fat little man just for his money!'

Denise wriggled her nose and her dark eyes sparkled with amusement.

'You make him sound very nasty!' she said. 'But why should he not be beautiful? Your father … he has a lot of money … or once he did have … is it not? Why should I not marry someone like him?'

'Father!' Eve repeated, smiling, for the idea of Jack Corderhay being married to anyone in the world but Antoinette was absurd.

Nevertheless, it was true that he was handsome and she had always been proud to be seen with him.

'I don't think you'd be lucky enough to find someone like Father very easily, Denise,' she said. 'You know, I have a locket in my jewelcase in which there is a miniature of both Father and Mother. Would you like to see?'

'Certainly I should like it. I hear so much of them and will judge for myself if they are so handsome a couple as you say!' Denise said, teasing.

Her hands still full with the baby as he now took the second half of his bottle, Eve told Denise to go herself to the jewel-case. So it was that Denise came across the snapshot of Paul Johnson. After studying the miniature, she said to Eve:

'It is true what you say. They look so nice, your so lovely mother and the tall, handsome Pappa! And the other photograph, Eve ... may I see it, too, or is it private?'

Eve felt a faint blush spread over her cheeks. She had not forgotten the snapshot of Anthony's father and it confused her to remember how often, lately, she had studied the picture, trying to find a likeness to the baby's face, trying to fathom the character of this man whose child she was caring for. Now Denise's remark had made her behave like a lovesick schoolgirl.

'Of course you can look at it!' she said

firmly. 'As a matter of fact, it's Anthony's father. I'd be interested to know what you think of him. You are usually so good at judging characters from faces.'

'It is because I learnt when I was very young to read what lay in a face. Perhaps if kindness was there, it might mean a few *sous* for a loaf of bread … if cruelty in the eyes, then I could avoid a kick or a curse. We children of the … how you call them … slums? … learned to be astute. Now … this man … I will tell you how he is…'

She looked long and closely at the tiny snapshot and, interested in spite of herself in what Denise would have to say, Eve found herself eagerly awaiting the verdict. After all, she told herself, Anthony might grow like his father. It would be as well to know what traits lay in him, good and bad, to counteract or develop.

'It is strange!' Denise said at last. 'But I find it a nice face. Not kind … maybe … it has too much strength and determination for this. Always this man will have his own way … especially with women. But he would not bully. It would be all or nothing with him. But there is something else, too. I think this is the face of someone who have suffered. Like me, a little. It is a *façade* against the world … as if he have the inferior complex and conceal it by bravado. *Certainement*, it is an interesting face.'

'You haven't said outright if it shows more good or bad,' Eve said, smiling.

'Good ... to look at?' Denise asked. 'That is of the own opinion. For me, I think so. It is a very English face. I would say honest. That is perhaps the good that you mean. But mostly, he is a man. This is something I like. He knows what it is he wants from life and he will get it or it is not his fault. I understand a little why your sister do as she does. Perhaps she cannot say no to him.'

'Well, that's quite a character study!' Eve said with a smile. 'And for Anthony's sake, I hope you're right. I gather that you don't think this man is as unpleasant a character as I imagine him to be.'

Denise shrugged her shoulders expressively.

'One is sometimes mistaken, of course. But I find him *sympathique*. This word I do not think you have in English.'

'But I know what you mean by it,' Eve said. And oddly enough, she knew also how Denise felt. She had tried so many times to hate this man, who, after all, had ruined her life and very nearly Anne-Marie's as well ... not to think of his rejection of his son. Always she had ended up with the thought that it was not for her, Eve, to judge him ... she had not known fully the circumstances. Perhaps (she made excuses for him) he had been married and Anne-Marie's beauty had tempted him to a momentary act of unfaithfulness that was foreign to his true nature. Eve knew how devastating Anne-Marie could be when she set her mind to attract someone. And knowing Anne-Marie, it was not hard to believe she might do such a thing. If he *was* married, he would have had no alternative but to go out of her life as quickly as he had come into it.

'Sometimes this life seems so unreal, Denise,' she said suddenly, as she rose to lift the baby into his cot and tuck him up for the night. 'I cannot believe that I am really living it. I keep feeling I shall wake up and it will all just have been a dream!'

Denise lit a cigarette and blew a cloud of smoke into the air.

'This make you happy, Eve, if it were only a dream?' she asked curiously.

Eve bit her lip.

'I'm not sure, Denise. You see, Anthony is real, and so is my love for him. It would be awful to wake up one morning and realize that he had never existed. And you, too ... our friendship ... it's not easy for me to say these things because they sound a bit sentimental and I'm probably far too English to put into words the things that really matter ... it's just that I've grown so very fond of you. I admire you tremendously and I'm so proud to have you for a friend. You're such a good friend, Denise ... in every way. I think

I have never felt quite so close to anyone before, unless it was to my father. You are ... very dear to me. I would not like to wake up and find I had only dreamt you!'

Denise, knowing her friend, did not attempt to embrace her as she might have embraced another French girl. With her usual tact, she said simply:

'Thank you, *chérie*. I, too, am glad that we are friends!'

She did not say how proud of Eve's friendship she was. She kept to herself the great pleasure it gave her to think that the day had come when someone of Eve's great courage and essential goodness really cared for her... Denise le Brun, daughter of a low-class, ill-reputed woman from the slums. For Eve had a gentleness and fastidiousness that proclaimed her background and set her far above Denise, the unfortunate mistake of a drunken moment, brought up to curses and brawls and at the lowest level to which humanity can sink. Denise had dragged herself out from among the dregs into a better world and there were many who, if they knew her origin, would have scorned and no longer acknowledged her. Eve was one of the few people who knew her secret and to whom it seemed to make no difference.

It was this knowledge that made such a deep mark on the French girl's heart ... for it salved her pride and made all her earlier struggles worth while. It had taught her to respect women where before she had only loathed them … taught her, too, to see a beautiful side to life and increased her ambition to grow even further from its sordidness.

Until she met Eve she had believed money alone could help her. Now she was beginning to learn that she needed something else. Money did not make people good … nor kind … nor honest. Eve was poorer even than herself and yet she was all these things. Money, so Eve said, did not always bring happiness … and love never failed to do so. Denise had seen this as she had watched the laughter and content in Eve's eyes when she looked at the baby. She had felt it also inside herself when she gave up a theatre she might have enjoyed because she felt Eve was depressed and would appreciate her company. Her affection for Eve had made her a better person, more unselfish, and by doing so had made her, Denise, happier.

Could it be true, then, she asked herself, that love alone brought happiness? That this successful marriage she had so often dreamed of for her future would not, in the end, bring her true content? Must she lower her standards and live a life without the luxuries she craved in order to find her soul in the loving of one man?

Denise wondered, doubted, questioned, and was no longer sure that she would not mind a life without love if only she had the power of money. She did not know that soon she was to meet a man who would clear those doubts away with one impulsive sweep of his hand.

CHAPTER 6

Edouard Garret entered Denise's life not more than three days after their last conversation about love, which had occupied their thoughts while Eve had bathed Anthony. Their first meeting was one of chance, for Edouard Garret was an artist. His regular model had fallen ill and in desperation he had applied to the agency from whom Denise and Eve received their work. His intention had been to ask to look through the agency files, which consisted mainly of photographs, and try to find a model with a face that would not only be photogenic but paintable ... a vastly different affair.

In the entrance to the agency he had bumped into Denise, who was just off to a job as he had come in. He had taken one look at her, dragged her back upstairs to the office, talked rapidly and volubly to the woman in charge, and departed triumphantly with Denise held securely by the hand.

'It was *fantastique!*' Denise recounted the story to Eve that evening. 'There was I … on my way to an important appointment which must not on any account be broken, so I had been told. Instead of this I find myself being taken to some … how you call it … garret … in the rooftops of Paris. And all day I am there. Three times the telephone he ring and each time I think it is the agency to say I must attend my next appointment. This man … this Edouard … he have arranged to have me for the morning only. But it makes no difference to him when I say I have to go. I sit all day. Never do he say a word … just paint and paint and paint. I am cold … stiff … nearly fainting with hunger, but that make no difference, either. Always he paint and paint until it is tea-time. I know this because it becomes too dark to paint any more…'

She paused for breath and Eve had time to study her friend's brilliant eyes and flushed cheeks. This was a Denise transformed … glowing … radiant … and so overcome with excitement that her usual good English had lapsed into broken English with a French accent. Eve waited until Denise continued.

'Then he stop! I am too stiff to move. I just sit and he stand and stare at me as if he had not been staring all day! I think … now he offer me the cup of coffee… Eve, if you knew only how much I want the cup of hot, strong coffee. I think I die if I do not have it.

But no … no coffee! Still he not say a word. He come … slowly … so slowly towards me and next thing … he kiss me!'

'Oh, Denise!' Eve cried, half laughing, half intrigued. 'It sounds quite incredible … like a film or something!'

'Incroyable … that is the word,' Denise said as she sank down into a chair, only to rise to her feet again and stride up and down the room. 'I think I become unconscious for a little while … maybe not … I don't know. I find myself in his arms. I open my eyes and he ask me what is my name. "Denise le Brun," I tell him. And then with great fortitude, for I do not know what is happening, I say: "I think you are mad … quite mad!" *"C'est vraie!"* he admits it. "I am mad because for the first time in my life I am in love. I have searched the world to find you, Denise le Brun. Tomorrow we shall be married!" And then … then he kiss me again.'

'I don't know what to say!' Eve said confusedly. 'It sounds so unbelievable.'

'Nor do I know what to say,' Denise laughed. 'This man … this Edouard … he leave me then and make a cup of coffee … such wonderful coffee. After we drink it he talk again. Always to say the same thing … that tomorrow I marry him. I say it is impossible … that we do not know each other … that I do not even know his name. And he reply: "One, nothing is impossible ... see, I have found *you* and I once thought that impossible. Two, we have known each other always ... here in our hearts. And three, my name is Edouard Garret and tomorrow you will be Madame Edouard Garret!" Tell me, Eve, what do you say to this man if you were me?'

'Indeed, I really don't know what I would have said!' Eve admitted. 'What is he like, Denise? How old is he? Tell me more about him?'

Denise spread her hands in a vague gesture of dismay.

'How old? I don't know ... thirty, perhaps, or older. He is dark ... I think ... like me ... but I do not know exactly. Somehow it is like he said ... like you once said ... it doesn't seem to matter. You see, Eve, I, too, have fallen in love. It is unbelievable ... still I cannot believe this day has really happened. Tomorrow, maybe, I wake up and find it is not so. But tonight ... after we have supper and I leave him ... he say: "Tomorrow you will come here again. In the morning I will paint you until the light goes. Then we will be married. Is it not so, *mon amour?*" And know it will be so! It is quite ... crazy, *n'est-ce pas?* He do not know even where I live! If I wished it, he might never find me again, and yet he is certain that I will be there tomorrow. And I will go. I cannot help myself.'

'Are you sure you know what you are doing, Denise?' Eve asked anxiously. 'You know practically nothing about him.'

'I will marry him nevertheless,' Denise replied simply. 'To be married is important to a girl, no? More important than anything else. But for him, no! First he wish to paint me. He is inspired, he tell me. All his life he will wish to paint me, for to him I am all women ... every woman that ever lived. This is my future if I marry him. First to be painted, then to be loved.'

'And you really mean to go through with it?' Eve asked. 'What about your plans?'

'My plans?' Denise repeated, as if they were things of the remote past.

'Yes! To marry a rich man. Has this Edouard Garret plenty of money?'

Suddenly Denise started to laugh. Eve watched her anxiously, but gradually the French girl calmed down.

'It is so funny!' she said at last. 'But you know, Eve, I never thought to ask! And even if he is the poorest man in the whole world, it doesn't matter. Not even if he has been to prison! You see, it has happened to me just as you describe it for your father and mother... I have really fallen in love! So nothing else in the whole world is of any account. I will marry him tomorrow.'

If Eve had doubts as to the advisability of

marrying a man only a day after meeting him, Denise appeared to have none. She ceased to be the quiet, thoughtful, practical girl Eve had known and had only one subject of conversation, one name continually on her lips: Edouard Garret.

Bu they did not marry the next day, after all. True to her word, Denise went to the studio first thing in the morning, and true to his word, Edouard painted her until the light began to fade.

'Now we will be married!' he said. But had entirely forgotten the necessity for a special licence.

'If you could have seen his face, Eve!' Denise recounted the event afterwards. 'It was so comical ... even I must laugh. He just never have think of it. So the day after tomorrow we will be married instead. This time it is I who must get the licence and Edouard give me this to pay for it. He does not know what it cost ... nor does he care. Oh, Eve, I am afraid he is rich! Money lies all over the place ... it is quite horrible! It falls out of his pockets and drawers and one comes across a thousand-franc note behind a cushion as easily as you or I might find a handkerchief! He is rich, Eve, and will be more so. I have discovered that he is a very well-known painter. Everyone wants to buy his pictures. People will pay any price for them, it seems.'

Her tone was so tragic that Eve looked at her in amazement, which quickly turned to consternation when Denise burst into a torrent of tears.

'But Denise, that is what you wanted!' she said, her arm around the trembling shoulders.

'I know, that's just the trouble!' Denise sobbed. 'Now I can never prove to him or to you that I do not marry him for his money. I wish that he were poor ... so poor as I used to be. Then I would work for him and save for him and show I do not mind because nothing matters but love.'

Eve smiled tenderly at the girl, who seemed, at this moment, so much younger than herself and so very vulnerable.

'There's nothing to weep about, Denise, dear!' she said softly. 'Don't you remember that you told me you would marry him when you did not even know he was rich? And you do not need to prove it to him because he has no cause to doubt you, since he did not know of your plan to marry a rich man!'

But intense happiness often brings tears and it was all Eve could do to keep Denise calm in the twenty-four hours that remained before her wedding. Tearfully, Denise had insisted that she would not be married without Eve there to hear the ceremony. Radiantly, she informed Eve a few hours later that Edouard had said she could invite anyone she chose and that he was coming himself to meet this English friend that was so dear to his own sweet love.

Frantically, Eve sought to tidy up the flat and get Anthony to bed before Denise's ardent young lover arrived on the scene. Perhaps Denise planned it purposefully, but when they did arrive it was in the middle of the baby's bath and Eve was wearing an apron and her hair falling in tiny curls from the dampness of the steamy bathroom.

'I wish him to see you just so!' Denise said proudly in reply to Eve's reproachful look. 'Is it not true she is beautiful like I say?' She turned to Edouard for confirmation.

'This picture I must paint ... just so soon as I finish my picture of you, *chérie*,' was his reply. Then his lean, handsome face broke into a grin that was purely boyish and he said with great charm: 'I am so happy to meet you, Eve. I may call you this since I do not know your other name? I have been a little jealous of Denise's affections for you, but now I understand. I, also, will be your friend, I hope. It would greatly honour me!'

Now it was Eve's turn to understand how Denise could have been swept so completely off her feet. Not only was the young painter handsome in a dark, rather foreign-looking way, but he was immensely kind and had great charm. His adoration of Denise was as obvious as hers for him, and Eve hoped, in a silent prayer, that this love would grow as they came to know one another better. It was too beautiful and natural a thing ever to be spoilt.

Not the least charming trait in Edouard's character was his great interest in the baby, and his generosity, too, for the following day, in spite of it being his wedding day, Edouard put a substantial cheque in the post, addressing the envelope to Anthony and signing a pencil sketch of him *From your new godfather!*

'We couldn't accept it!' Eve said to Denise when the ceremony was over. 'You must take it back, Denise!'

But Denise would not touch it.

'I understand how you feel … always you manage alone and this is good thing, but even for you I cannot hurt Edouard's feelings. "For *le petit*," he says as he draws the little picture, "my first child" … and he is so proud to think that he is godfather and can do this.'

So began a period of great happiness in Denise's life and at the same time one of extreme loneliness and depression for Eve. Denise came as often as she could to visit them, but Edouard was painting furiously and made almost impossible demands on Denise's time. Even when he was not using her as a model he could not bear to have her out of his sight for long, and Denise could only slip along to the flat for a moment or two at a time. She did this more for Eve's sake, although Eve did not know this, than for her own pleasure. For Denise was so deeply in love that even a moment away from Edouard's side was too great a loss. But she did not forget Eve's friendship nor fail to imagine that Eve might be missing her companionship, and called in whenever she could.

It was not only the loss of Denise's company that was responsible for Eve's depression. A letter from Anne-Marie had come not long after Denise's wedding, saying that she was going to be married at Christmas … to Richard Bainborough.

It may sound a bit rushed to you, but we see no reason to wait and Richard is as keen to make me his wife as I am to marry him. His family have a beautiful home a few miles from Corderhay Park … they bought the Eversham's old home which, of course, you'll remember. Richard's father has a large business over here and also in America and we shall have all the money we need.

Naturally Mummy and Daddy are very thrilled to think I shall be so comfortably off, and that I'm so happy. Richard thinks Father may have to sell Corderhay Park if things go on the way they are at the moment, but Father never speaks of it. He's very silent and down-in-the-dumps these days and Mother is depressed because he is. Frankly I shan't be sorry to leave

*the gloomy atmosphere around here though, of
course, I shall be near at hand to pop in when
they want to see me...*

There were more details about Richard
Bainborough, but no mention of Louise,
and Eve wondered just what had happened
to the French girl. She wondered, too, if
Anne-Marie had told Richard of her adven-
tures in Paris, but, knowing Anne-Marie so
well now, she doubted it.

Most of all, she wondered about her father.
It had drained all the colour from her cheeks
to read that perhaps Corderhay Park might
have to be sold. It just did not seem possible,
and if it were true, or even likely, it was small
wonder that her father was depressed.

'Oh, I wish I were home with them!' she
thought. 'If only I could be there!'

But she had trouble enough of her own.
The landlady had become less eager to take
Anthony during the day, since, owing to her
husband's ill-health, she had been forced to
take on the duties of porter in his place. Now
Eve was not happy leaving the baby in her
care, since she had to answer the door if there
were visitors, and for those few moments
leave Anthony unattended. Eventually
another woman was suggested to take on the
task of baby-minding while Eve was at work,
and she charged nearly double the old
amount, so draining away Eve's resources.

On top of all this Eve had caught a severe cold which had given her streaming eyes and a swollen face, so forcing her to stop work for a day or two. But for Edouard's cheque to the baby she could never have paid her rent at the end of that week.

On Christmas Eve, therefore, it was small wonder that Eve ended the day in tears. She had managed to ward off the worst of her unhappiness until Anthony was in bed and asleep. There had still been one thing to look forward to ... the enjoyment of filling the tiny stocking for his first Christmas.

But it was this that reduced her finally to tears, for as she placed it at the foot of his cot it looked almost empty, so very little was there in it ... a new rattle and a shiny yellow rubber duck from herself ... a little wooden trumpet from the kind-hearted landlady. That was all. Edouard and Denise were away in the South of France on a brief, belated honeymoon (Edouard having suddenly re-membered that a honeymoon was customary after a wedding!), and although they were certain to have many little gifts for the baby and herself, their parcel must have been delayed in the post, for nothing had as yet arrived. In the sitting-room, one solitary Christmas card decorated her mantelpiece ... from the only two friends she had in the world. It was a beautiful pen-and-ink portrait of Anthony beneath which Edouard'd written briefly: *This little angel, for His birthday.*

'Bless you both!' she whispered as she brushed the tears away from her eyes. 'I needed your reminder that I am not quite alone. I have Anthony ... and perhaps God is with me, too.'

She went back to the bedroom for a last look at the sleeping baby, and as she stood there, quite suddenly and frighteningly, the door-bell rang.

The sound was so unexpected that for a moment Eve could not move. She tried to imagine who could be ringing her door-bell at this time of night ... only Denise ... and she was away...

Perhaps a telegram ... that was the answer. Calmed by this thought, she softly closed the bedroom door behind her and went through the little living-room to open the front door. In the flickering gas-light of the hall beyond she saw a tall figure in a heavy top-coat, a soft felt hat pulled down low over the eyes. A thick, heavy muffler was wound round her visitor's throat, and for a moment Eve could not see his face. Then suddenly he took off his hat and looked straight at her and her heart leapt into her throat. There was no retreat ... no way to avoid this meeting. In fact, she could not have moved even had she wished to do so. She gave one meaningless little cry, and as she did so the man held wide his arms.

'Father! Oh, Father!' she cried, and running to him, she buried her face against his coat.

'Eve! At last! At last! Lift your face, my dear! Let me look at you! My darling child ... you mustn't cry. There's nothing to cry about. See ... I've come myself to take you home!'

'Oh, Daddy, Daddy!' she wept, unconsciously using the childish name that still sprang to her lips in moments of stress. 'I've missed you so! I'm so – so glad to see you!'

'Come now, my dear!' he said gently, unclasping her arms from round his neck. 'Let's go inside your little flat and talk, shall we? You know, it's devilish cold out here in this hall!'

She smiled a little then, through her tears, and allowed her father to lead her into the sitting-room. Automatically, she moved across to switch on the electric fire, and as she did so the first shock of her father's unexpected arrival lessened to a degree where she could feel only thankfulness to see him. Hastily, she glanced round the room to see if there were any material signs of Anthony's presence, and silently thanked God that he was safely tucked away in his cot next door.

This was going to be no easy talk with her father. She might have to lie to him ... anything rather than let him discover the truth. She began to wonder suddenly how her father had found her ... whether perhaps Anne-Marie...

'Father, how did you find me?' she asked abruptly, afraid to hear the worst and yet having to know.

'Come and sit down beside me, Eve,' he said gently. 'Then I can talk to you properly... You know, child, I've missed you a great deal. It does my heart good to see your dear little face again!'

'Oh, Father!' Eve whispered as she moved over to the sofa and sat beside him. 'I'm so happy to see you, too. But you don't look well. You've lost weight. You haven't been ill?'

'So you still worry about me?' he asked with a rueful smile. 'I had wondered if perhaps you'd forgotten all of us at home, Eve. You know, we haven't heard from you since Anne-Marie came home.'

Eve looked down at her hands, which were pressed tightly together in her lap.

'I'm sorry!' she murmured. 'I ... thought it better to cut away completely.'

Jack Corderhay made no comment, but there was a strange look of compassion in his eyes which he was glad Eve could not see, for her face was turned away from him. He noticed how thin she was, how tired and pale. Where was the radiance, the happiness, evidence of the good times Anne-Marie had mentioned? Her eyes looked suspiciously as if she might have been crying before he came in, and the thought hurt him deeply. Jack Corderhay was a fair man, just in all his dealings, and he had never made any difference between his two children. Anne-Marie was his own flesh and blood and Eve his adopted child, yet of the two he knew he was fonder ... not of his real daughter but of the girl who sat so silently beside him. She had been the real daughter to him ... loving, sympathetic, longing to help and lacking any trace of the selfishness so evident in his younger daughter.

He faced the truth now even while he felt he ought not to have a preference. His special love for Eve was an emotion he had never shared with Antoinette, who idolized Anne-Marie and could see no harm in her. She had made excuses when young David Bardwell had been let down so badly by Anne-Marie; and lately had found fresh reasons why Anne-Marie should have stolen Richard Bainborough from the quiet, gentle Louise. Louise had been very deeply in love with the boy and it had seemed as if he were suitably interested in her, when Anne-Marie arrived home from Paris and swept Richard from beneath Louise's feet.

'Richard wasn't really interested in Louise ... it was an attack of calf love,' Antoinette had argued. 'He is really serious about "our baby" and she loves him. Louise has not attempted to stand in their way, so why should we?'

Well, they had not done so and Jack Corderhay silently doubted if they could have prevented Anne-Marie from having her own way about this as about everything else she wanted. But he had felt sorry for the young French girl and angry with his daughter for what he looked on as a particularly unpleasant feminine trick. For young Richard was a good match for any girl. He had his fair share of good looks and more money than he knew what to do with … or would have, when his father died. And Eversham Court would be his with sufficient means to keep it, anyway for his lifetime. Small wonder then that Antoinette had been happy for their younger daughter. Had it not been for Louise's obvious distress, Jack Corderhay might have been pleased too, although he sometimes wondered if the boy was not a bit too weak and irresponsible to make a girl of Anne-Marie's wilfulness a good husband. She needed a steadying hand. He doubted if Richard would wield it.

But now he was not thinking of Anne-Marie … only of Eve.

'I was worried about you, my dear, ever since that letter you wrote soon after you got to Paris. I had been so certain that you would be home in the New Year. When you told us you had got a job I began to realize that you weren't coming back to us quite so soon. But I never imagined you intended to break away permanently. I couldn't believe it when you wrote to say you were going to cut yourself off from us completely … it didn't seem to make sense… "She must have a reason," I told myself. "It isn't just pleasure she is seeking." But I couldn't imagine a single thing that would keep you away from your home indefinitely. Was it to be … for ever, Eve?'

Dumbly, Eve nodded.

'I … I can't come home … Daddy. I … wish … that you hadn't come to ask me to go back with you. I tried so hard to prevent this happening.'

'And you nearly succeeded,' her father replied sadly. 'I suspected that Anne-Marie knew your whereabouts, but she always shied away from my questions and I thought then that you might have made her promise not to tell your mother or me. So I didn't try for long to force her to break her word to you. I determined to wait a little while to see if things would work out differently and we should hear from you. Every day I hoped there would be a letter. When summer came I began to doubt that we should see you again, Eve, unless we made the effort. So I wrote to your mother's sister. She was still in America, but she could give me the information I wanted … the name of a French private detective. By autumn this man had begun his search for you, and last month I learned where you were ... and *why* you were here. At first I wanted to catch the next boat train to France. Then I decided to wait until Christmas. It was a year ago that you left us, Eve. I've come today to ask you to return home with me.'

'Father, you can't ask me that. Don't you understand? That detective ... surely he must have told you...'

'About the child?' Jack Corderhay asked calmly. 'Yes, Eve, he did. He could not tell me much about it ... when it was born ... where ... but he knew of its existence.'

'And you mean that ... it makes no difference? You still want me to come home?'

Jack Corderhay looked down at the pale, tragic little face lifted to his.

'My dear, the child is yours, is it not? It is also my first grandchild. Now, don't cry, Eve. I want this to be a happy reunion. And I'm hoping you will let me see the baby. Is it here?'

Mutely, unable to find words for the tears that had gathered in her eyes, Eve stood up and opened the bedroom door. Her father followed her in, and while Eve stood in the doorway he walked over to the cot.

For a long time he stood staring down at the sleeping baby. The child lay with one small fist flung sideways across the blue blanket, his long golden lashes brushing the round rosy cheeks. Something that Jack Corderhay saw in the innocent baby face caused a stab of pain to his heart ... a memory that had withstood the years of Antoinette holding the infant Anne-Marie in her arms and saying: 'Look at her, Jack. Is she not the most beautiful baby in the world?'

Without a word Jack Corderhay raised his head, and walking past Eve into the sitting-room sat down heavily in the armchair. His head was bowed and Eve, closing the bedroom door behind her, saw that his hands were covering his face.

'I'm sorry, Father. I expect you were hoping it wasn't true. I would have given anything in the world to spare you this...'

'Spare me?' her father repeated, looking up at her now with eyes that were suspiciously moist. 'Eve, you have this moment given me reason to believe in myself again ... in my judgment of human nature. Your mother once confided in me that she was afraid that something of this sort had occurred. I couldn't believe it ... not of you, Eve. I knew you too well. Then I thought about it longer and I felt that whatever had happened, even if it were true, it could not be your fault. Some man had tricked you, I told myself. *I had to know the truth.* Now, Eve, I do know the truth. And I feel humble before such a person as you, my very dear child.'

'I ... I don't understand!' Eve whispered.

'Don't you? Have you been too close to the baby to see what I can see in his face? He is like his mother, Eve ... when she was a baby the same age. Perhaps you were too young at the time to remember ... you were only a little girl when Anne-Marie was born. But I remember and I wish ... yes, I wish now that she had never been born.'

In a horrified instant Eve realized that her father had guessed the truth. He had been right when he said she had lived too close to Anthony to notice how like Anne-Marie he was to look at. For her he had developed character and features that were all his own, and she had never for one moment guessed that her father might see a family likeness. If only it had occurred to her, she would somehow have prevented him seeing the child.

So in the end, all her efforts had been in vain ... the suffering and loneliness and sometimes even hunger... She could no longer protect her father from the truth.

'Father, it isn't true!' she cried wildly. 'You mustn't imagine such things. Anne-Marie is going to be married ... let me go away again ... out of your life and hers. We shall be all right. Don't look so unhappy. I can't bear it! Please believe me when I say he *is* mine. He is—'

'You must not lie to me, Eve,' her father broke in gently. 'I *know* that this child is not yours. I think in my heart I never thought it would be. But it just did not occur to me that it might be … Anne-Marie's. It has been quite a shock, Eve … but I am filled with relief, too. You see, Eve, you mean far more to me than Anne-Marie does. Perhaps I have no right to say it, but it is the truth. I have been forced to see lately how selfish and shallow my own daughter has become. Maybe it is not her fault. We have all of us spoilt her. But I did not think even Anne-Marie could have allowed *this* to happen … allowed her own sister to take the blame for her mistakes. She wasn't worth your sacrifices, Eve.'

'But, Father, it wasn't only for her. It was for you and Mother, too. I hoped you need never know the truth. And she didn't *want* me to take the blame. She wanted to have the baby adopted. She tried desperately to prevent me keeping him. You mustn't blame her for what was my choice. It was partly for myself that I wanted it this way. I have always felt so deep a gratitude to you and Mother for … for having me and giving me the wonderful childhood I had. I felt that in this way I could repay a little of my great debt to you. And I love Anthony. He is a wonderful baby … so good, Father … and so sweet! I couldn't have parted with him. The thought that he might have gone into an orphanage horrifies me. I couldn't live without him now, Father. He … it's as if he were really my own.'

'I am not asking you to part with him, Eve. But this life you are leading ... it cannot continue. You are to come home, Eve. My mind is made up. The boy will come, too. Your mother and I will adopt him and no one shall know his origin. He will live with us ... grow up a Corderhay with any advantages we can give him. They won't be many, Eve. I'm afraid we shall not be able to keep Corderhay Park much longer. But we shall always have some sort of home and he will need a family and a proper background. You couldn't give him this alone, Eve.'

'You mean you won't tell anyone else in the world ... whose child he is? Not even Mother? She might feel that Anne-Marie should...'

'It will be our secret, Eve. No doubt people will wonder, but we shall find a way round that. I will not have your reputation ruined through no fault of your own. One day you will marry, Eve, and then, if Antoinette and I are getting a bit old to make good parents any longer, you shall have the boy if you want him. But in the meantime he will be your brother ... and Anne-Marie's.'

Eve sat in silence, thinking over her father's words. It all sounded so easy ... so perfect ... this solution which had never occurred to her even in her dreams ... to be able to go home and yet keep Anthony, too. There must, surely, be a snag...

'Father … suppose … that when Anne-Marie sees him … she wants him back?'

'She renounced him, Eve, so he is no longer her child,' her father said quietly. 'But somehow, I don't think she will want him. She would have first to admit to Richard Bainborough that he was hers, and I doubt somehow if his family would agree to his marrying her if they knew. I don't think Anne-Marie will take that chance. No, you have nothing to worry about, Eve. She cannot prove that he is hers, and after having taken such measures to avoid any scandal I do not think for a moment that she will try to claim him. He will remain your baby, Eve, since you wish it, as far as you and I are concerned. I will take no action for his future without your approval. But in the eyes of the world he will belong to your mother and to me.'

Tears of relief, of happiness, poured down Eve's cheeks. Tenderly, her father wiped them away saying:

'I shall never forgive Anne-Marie for this … not because she had the child, because it may not have been entirely her fault, and I will not judge her on this score, since I don't know the circumstances … but because she has let you take on her responsibility and the blame attached to it. It was a great gesture of yours, Eve, and for the rest of my life I shall admire you for it. For all you are not by blood a

Corderhay, you are more my daughter than Anne-Marie can ever be. I would expose her, if I could … but it would make a parody of the many sacrifices you have made and I know you wouldn't want it. You have too generous a heart for that. You know, Eve, he will be a lucky man who one day makes you his wife, and I shall be the first to tell him so.'

But Eve only shook her head and said, through her tears:

'I don't want to be married, Daddy! I only want to be home again … with you.'

CHAPTER 7

But Eve was not to see her home again for yet another week. Denise and Edouard, returning to Paris on Boxing Day, found her alone, busily packing up her belongings and cleaning and tidying the flat.

'*Le petit!*' Denise cried, staring round the room aghast. '*Nom de Dieu,* Eve, will you tell me what has happened? Where is Anthony? Why are you packing? What has happened?' And turning to her husband, she cried dramatically, 'I told you we ought not to have left her alone, Edouard!'

Eve put her arms round the French girl and gave her an excited hug.

137

'There's nothing to worry about, Denise. I have only good news for you. Except for the one fact that I won't be seeing you so much. But I hope you and Edouard will come and visit us...'

Denise's face shone.

'Edouard, she is to be married! Suddenly, like me, she fall in love! But where is the baby? Eve, will you tell us, *please,* what is happening?'

Over a cup of strong French coffee, which Eve had grown to enjoy and would no doubt miss in England, she told her two friends of her father's visit. She kept nothing back from them, for they already knew all the details of her secret. 'I never stopped to think Father might find a likeness to Anne-Marie,' she ended her story. 'I was so sure he thought Anthony was mine! The detective must have told him so.'

'Nevertheless it is for the good!' Edouard announced judiciously. 'Now you will be able to return to this home you so love, Eve. And Denise and I ... we will miss you and *le petit* a great deal. He has already gone to England? We cannot say *au revoir* to him?'

'My father took him home Christmas morning!' Eve explained. 'I am to go at the end of the week. Father thought it would be better that we should not arrive home together. He will tell my mother and anyone else who enquires that he couldn't find me, but happened to see Anthony in a pram with some children from an orphanage. He will say that because of the child's unusual Corderhay colouring, he decided to adopt it. It may seem a little strange, but I don't think people will ask too many awkward questions. After all, it will not be the first baby they adopted on the spur of the moment. When I return, Father has told me to announce that I lost my job and decided to come home for Anne-Marie's wedding. Father seems to think we shall get away with it. You know I believe he is quite enjoying the conspiracy! But I hated to see Anthony go.'

'I cannot yet believe all you tell me! It is good for you, but *triste* for Edouard and me, like he say,' Denise commented. 'But you will come to visit us, *chérie, n'est-ce pas?* And never forget that we are Anthony's god-parents. That gives us rights, isn't it, to see him now and then?'

'Of course! And you will come and see us, too,' Eve agreed eagerly. 'Father wants to meet you already. He is so grateful to you both for being so good to me. You will always be welcome at home.'

'So it is full of surprises, this life of ours!' Denise said, half laughing, half sadly. 'It will seem very different when you are gone, Eve. Already it is not the same without the little Anthony here. Soon we should put him in his bath at this time, no?'

Eve nodded.

'I miss him, too, Denise. But he went off quite happily. I thought he was going to cry at first, but then Father lifted him up and sat him on his shoulders, and you know how tall Father is! Anthony just gurgled with delight. They went off in a taxi, and the last I saw of them Anthony was pulling Father's moustache. I only hope they reached home without mishap. I told Father that Anthony's only word, "Gobbum", meant he was hungry, so I don't suppose he'll starve. But I doubt if Father can change a nappy!'

'And who look after him at home? He have arrived by now, no?' Denise enquired anxiously.

'Yes, they went by plane. Father changed his return train ticket because he wouldn't face a slow journey back with a baby! I expect Nanny is putting him to bed now, so he'll be all right. You know, Denise, he made a great hit with Father. I could see by Father's face that he was quite enchanted with him. But then, Father always wanted a son, and Anthony's such a glorious little boy!'

'First I will have a little cry because I am sad for me and so happy for you,' Denise announced. 'Then we shall go to celebrate, no?'

'We show Eve a little of our Paris night life!' Edouard agreed. 'To think she has been here nearly a year and has never been out at night! We make up for it now. We see everything. I show you. It will be our … how you say … farewell…'

They did, indeed, give Eve a night out. She had never enjoyed herself more, and the young French friend of Edouard who was nominated her partner for the evening was immensely flattering and undoubtedly attracted to her. It made Eve feel young again and she realized for the first time how much she had had to forgo when she gave her whole self to Anthony and his welfare without a moment's thought or time for herself.

When Edouard and Denise saw her off on the plane, at the end of the week, Eve felt that a phase of her life was coming to an end. Part of her was sad to recognize this, and yet it seemed at the same time as if there were a great load lifted from her shoulders. She felt so young and happy and eager again. Her whole life lay before her, and in the immediate future her wonderful homecoming and her reunion with Anthony … it was really uncanny how much she had missed her darling laughing baby!

But she would miss Denise, too. And she knew that in the many years to come she might never find so loyal and good a friend again.

Just before the plane took off, Denise clasped Eve in a tearful embrace and whispered:

'We have decided to call our first little girl

141

after you, Eve.'

'Denise!' Eve whispered happily. 'Then you plan to start a family soon?'

'It has already begun!' Denise laughed. 'Today the doctor tell me it is so. Edouard is so thrilled and happy. He will not let me make even the coffee … I am the piece of china that might break … until he wish me to sit for him while he paint, then he forget I am to be the mother and keep me sitting all day long until I am so cold and stiff I could weep! He do the picture to send you Eve, so you do not forget us.'

'I could never do that, Denise. And I'm so happy about the baby. Write to me,' Eve had time to say before she was forced to take her seat in the waiting aircraft and the door of the plane shut her two friends from sight.

But she had no room in her heart for anything but happiness when at last the moment came for her to see her home once more. Her father met her at the airport and together they drove along the main roads out of the town and into the country. Gradually the lanes became smaller and now suddenly the car turned off sharply to the right and they passed through the heavy, wrought-iron gates that stood sentinel either side of the sweeping, mile-long drive to Corderhay Park.

Eyes alight with excitement, Eve sat forward in her seat, scanning through the great beech trees for her first view of the lovely old stone house. Corderhay Park! There it was at last … her home … the place she must always love best in the world and which held all those people nearest and dearest to her. Breathlessly she scanned its face and suddenly she could see the great heavy oak door flung wide open and her mother's tiny, neat little figure waving to them with a flutter of white from the raised hand.

Then the car stopped and Eve was running towards her mother, who stood now with her arms held wide, tears in her eyes.

'Eve, *ma petite*, my darling!' Antoinette wept, as she kissed each of Eve's flushed cheeks and drew away from her to look at her. 'Welcome home! Always I knew you would come home to us, and when your father had that letter from you to say you had thrown up your job, we were so very happy … so pleased that at last you would be returning to us.'

'And I'm so glad to be home, Mother!' Eve cried, feeling how inadequately her words described the emotion in her heart. 'I've missed you all so much. I should never have stayed away so long.'

'We have a surprise for you, Eve,' her father's voice spoke behind her as he motioned them to go into the house. 'You must tell her about it, Antoinette.'

'Of course, Eve … the baby. We have a little boy now, that we adopted. Your father found him in Paris when he went to visit you and could not find you. Is it not exciting? I think he was so afraid to come home without our own little adopted baby that he adopted another one so I should not be too disappointed. Your father thinks he has Corderhay features, but I don't see it so much. He is not as pretty as Anne-Marie when she was a baby, but nevertheless he is very sweet. Your father has christened him Anthony and he is your new brother. We'll go first and see him, shall we?'

Nervously, Eve reached for and found her father's hand. Would her mother sense anything unusual in the silence with which she received her story? But Antoinette was so full of happy conversation that there was no need for Eve to make any comment. Her father had done all the talking necessary.

In the nursery old Nanny was giving Anthony his tea. As Eve went with her parents into the room the child turned round in his high chair and through a mouthful of cereal and milk said his one word 'Gobbum!' and held out his arms to Eve.

For a moment Eve hesitated, longing to rush to the child and hug him, but not wishing to betray herself. Her father, seeing her predicament, said quickly:

'Look, Antoinette, Anthony's trying to get a better look at his new sister. Why don't you lift him up and say hello, Eve, if Nanny will permit the breach of discipline?'

Nanny would permit anything for Master Anthony, whose slave she already was. Later Eve was to find she needed to take a firm hand with the little boy if he was not to become too spoilt. Everyone adored him and it was clear, right from that first moment, how attached to Eve he was. He followed her everywhere and would not settle down for the night unless she tucked him in herself.

But now he allowed her to put him back in his chair to finish his tea and her heart glowed at his welcome, at the knowledge that even in a week he had not forgotten her.

'It's … a wonderful surprise, Mother!' she said. 'With a baby in the nursery again it seems more than ever like home!'

Anne-Marie she did not see until later that evening. Antoinette explained that her sister was with her future in-laws and had hoped Eve would forgive her for not being there to welcome her home. Eve had wondered if her absence was intentional and she felt strangely nervous of meeting her sister again and of hearing whatever comments she might have to make about her own arrival home. In a week's time, her mother had told her, at the end of the month, Anne-Marie was to be married to young Richard Bainborough, and Eve could only hope that her attention would be confined to this and that she would not make a 'scene'.

'Anne-Marie seemed very perturbed when I arrived home with the child,' her father told her when they had tea together in his study, Antoinette having gone over to Eversham Court to tea with Richard's mother to discuss wedding plans and bring Anne-Marie home later. 'But she asked no questions except if I had seen you. When I said I had, she dropped her eyes and as soon as she could went out of the room. I think perhaps she guessed this was her baby, but I refused to satisfy her curiosity.'

'And with Anthony himself … how did she behave?' Eve asked anxiously.

'She takes no notice of him whatever. That is to say she pays him as little attention as she dares with your mother always trying to interest them in each other. I think the child may sense Anne-Marie's uneasiness, for whenever she goes near him he starts to cry. Your mother can't understand it and old Nanny had to voice her opinion and said that it would do Miss Anne-Marie good not to be the baby any longer … that she was jealous of the little boy. Of course, there was nothing Anne-Marie could say in self-defence except that their dislike appeared to be mutual. Your mother hasn't got over it yet, since she cannot understand how anyone *could* dislike Anthony!'

'Poor Anne-Marie. I'm sorry for her in lots of ways,' Eve said, and could not alter this feeling of pity even when her father pointed out that she didn't deserve it.

With his usual tact Jack Corderhay left the two girls alone together for a few moments before supper when Anne-Marie returned home. He knew that they would have much to discuss and that this could only be done without his presence.

'So you came home,' was Anne-Marie's first remark as she paced up and down the room, smoking furiously as if this might control her restlessness. To Eve she seemed strangely different, older, harder, more mature, and certainly a bundle of nerves. Was it just her own homecoming with Anthony that had caused this change in the younger girl?

'Father insisted that I should,' she explained simply. 'He found out where I was living from a detective. I couldn't, of course, avoid meeting him because I had no idea he knew where I lived. He came to the flat and I opened the door to him never dreaming that it might be he.'

'I see! I wondered how he'd found you. I thought perhaps you might have written home after all,' Anne-Marie said in a hard, tight little voice.

'I wouldn't have done that, Anne-Marie!' Eve said. 'We each made a promise to the other. I kept my promise, too.'

'Then he doesn't know that ... the baby is

mine?' the younger girl shot the question at Eve.

Eve bit her lip.

'I did not tell him so, Anne-Marie. But he guessed. Anthony is ... very like you. Nothing I could say would make him think otherwise.'

'I can't see the likeness!' Anne-Marie said harshly. 'No one can prove it. If Father tries to ruin my marriage, I'll–'

'Don't go on, Anne-Marie,' Eve broke in quickly. 'Father is not going to tell anyone. He has promised me. You have nothing to be afraid of.'

'Afraid? Of course I'm afraid!' Anne-Marie said nervously. 'Who wouldn't be with that brat around the place a living proof–' She broke off and flung herself down on the floor at Eve's feet, clasping the older girl's knees and sobbing now in so hysterical a way that Eve was much upset by such loss of control. She tried to help Anne-Marie to her feet, saying unhappily:

'Anne-Marie, don't be like this, please! You've nothing to be upset about. You know you can trust me. Have I ever let you down in the past? And Father won't say anything ... even to Mother. He promised me. If anything, people will think Anthony is mine; they have no cause to suspect you. I don't care if they do wonder about me. I wish he were mine, Anne-Marie. He's so utterly adorable.'

148

'He *is* yours!' Anne-Marie wept. 'I've never wanted him. I hate him! I hoped I'd never see him again when I left Paris. I nearly went mad when Father came home with him. Oh, why didn't you let me have him adopted? Eve, I'm so terribly unhappy!'

Gently Eve forced her sister into a chair and lit cigarettes for them both. It distressed her unutterably to see Anne-Marie in this condition. Whatever she had done, it must be awful to suffer to such extent, although as yet Eve could see no reason for her to be afraid.

'Can't you tell me what's wrong, Anne-Marie? Why are you unhappy? I thought everything was going so well for you. You do love this man you're going to marry, don't you?'

'Love him? No!' Anne-Marie said bitterly. 'I shall never love anyone again. I've finished with love for the rest of my life. I know that. That's why I'm marrying Richard. *He* loves *me* so much that he doesn't seem to notice how I feel. And I'm happy enough with him. He can give me everything I've ever wanted. And I am fond of him. Nothing … *nothing* must stop this marriage. Do you understand that, Eve? I'm going to marry him.'

For several moments Eve could not speak, so shocked was she to hear this outburst. Anne-Marie not in love … and yet so determined to marry Richard. Why? What was behind it? Just a wish for security?

'And you think you can be happy ... without love?' She asked the same question that she had once asked Denise.

'I shall be happy ... or die in the attempt,' Anne-Marie said, her voice more controlled now. 'I shall be doing what I most want to do in this world.'

'You sound so ... so strange, Anne-Marie. It's as if you were trying to get your revenge on someone or something for what happened in Paris,' Eve said, frowning.

A curious smile lit up Anne-Marie's face.

'Maybe that is just what I am doing, Eve. But you wouldn't understand. Only I beg you, if you have any affection left for me at all, don't let the truth come out ... not now, just before my wedding. I *can* trust you, I know, but Father...'

'Father won't tell anyone,' Eve said firmly. 'He has promised me and you can rest assured on that point, Anne-Marie. But I can't feel you are being fair to Richard. Are you sure you're doing the right thing? Marriage is for ever, you know. And even if you are sure you can make *him* happy, *you* don't want to make another mistake.'

Anne-Marie stood up, her voice and emotions completely controlled now.

'I'm certain I'm doing what I *must* do ... and I'm not making any mistake,' she said firmly. 'I can manage my own affairs, Eve, and I don't intend to make Richard unhappy by telling him about Paris.'

And with that Eve had to be content.

But she could not forget this outburst. In her own bed, her last thought was of Anne-Marie and her marriage to a man she did not love. Just before she drifted into sleep her sister's behaviour suddenly made sense. Anne-Marie was, in spite of everything, still in love with the man who had ruined her life … Anthony's father.

Eve's dreams were consequently filled with the presence of Paul Johnson, the man she had never met but whose photograph still lay in her jewel-case. The dreams were hopelessly confused as they so often are, and it was not Anne-Marie, but herself speaking to some unseen listener, saying:

'I still love him, I'll always love him – whatever he has done!' She woke with the tears streaming down her face, his name on her lips, and her heart filled with an overwhelming sense of loss which even her returning consciousness could not dispel.

Book II

EFFECT

CHAPTER 8

Jack Corderhay had timed Eve's return very nicely. The house and most of the family friends were so taken up with the coming wedding, which was to be an elaborate affair, that few had time to think much about the little boy he had 'adopted' or busy themselves with questions as to the baby's origin. Their acquaintances accepted it as natural that Eve should arrive home in time for her sister's wedding. No one associated her arrival in connection with the child's when so simple an explanation as the wedding was to hand.

Although the Corderhays had been out of the social world of London for some time, having had neither the money nor the inclination to keep up with garden parties, Ascot, night-clubs and race meetings, the Bainboroughs moved very much in those circles. They had connections at Court and young Richard Bainborough was considered to be a most eligible young man. Many designing mothers of young débutantes had been bitterly disappointed to read of his engagement in *The Times*, the *Tatler* and the *Sketch*, and Anne-Marie was much envied by all her friends.

Because this wedding was of social notoriety, Jack Corderhay had felt it his duty to see that Anne-Marie Corderhay was married with 'all the trimmings'. Indeed, Antoinette would not have permitted it otherwise, and her husband was still sufficiently proud of his name, if not of his daughter, to do no less than his very best.

Only Eve knew how disastrous this was for the family exchequer. Her father had discussed the question with her, but Antoinette did not yet know ... for her husband wished to keep it from her until after the wedding ... that it would drain away the last of his spare capital.

'But surely, Father, a wedding doesn't cost so very much!' Eve had cried, aghast.

'I'm afraid nowadays it does ... this sort of wedding,' her father admitted. 'With the Bainboroughs' friends as well as our own, there will be about five hundred guests. With champagne and eats it cannot be done on less than two pounds a head. Then there has been Anne-Marie's trousseau ... her wedding dress ... and yours as bridesmaid ... apart from flowers for the church and certainly some kind of celebration for the servants and staff. In all, it'll cost me over a thousand pounds, Eve, and that's us finished!'

'But, Father, it's madness to have this sort of wedding if we can't afford it. Surely we

can have a quieter affair? It cannot be necessary. Not if Corderhay Park is at stake!'

Jack Corderhay shook his head.

'Perhaps in many ways it is a stupid thing
to do,' he admitted. 'But it isn't for Anne-
Marie, Eve. It's partly for your mother. She's
so dead set on it, and I haven't got the heart
to disappoint her. She is so thrilled … so
happy … so proud… And there is my own
pride, too. It's a last fling … if you can
understand me … a glove thrown in the face
of misfortune! And in the end it can't make
any difference. You see, Eve, I have known
for some time that I couldn't keep Corderhay Park going. This has merely hastened the
end, and in a way I'm not sorry. It's a pretty
sad feeling waking up each morning and
realizing all over again that it won't be long
before it's the last time. In a way I'll be glad
to get it over.'

'Father … I'm so sorry!' Eve cried, her
arms round his shoulders, for she could
understand so well what this meant to him …
to sell his home … the home of his family for
centuries… 'Isn't there anything we can do?'

'Nothing, I'm afraid. Things are getting
worse, not better. The next budget … well,
it's no use worrying you with details, Eve.
Believe me, my dear, I have tried to find a
way out … I thought of closing up all but a
few rooms, but I just couldn't afford it even
then. The cost of maintenance of the estate,

taxes… Everything is beyond us now. You see, Eve, there's a new rich now … and we're not among them. Our turn is over.'

'But, Father, what shall we do? Where shall we go?'

'I thought we might go and live in the Lodge,' he said. 'You know I've often thought it was a pretty little place, and it's large enough for the four of us and a couple of servants. I shall pension off poor old Nanny. She's really past it and she's spoiling young Anthony. I thought perhaps you…'

'Oh, Father, yes! I'd love to look after him again. I didn't want to say so, but I've been wanting it these last few days. I simply hated watching Nanny bath him at night!'

'Then that's settled. We'll keep Cook, and Jenkins can remain if he chooses as a sort of butler-cum-handyman … do the fires and that sort of thing. That just leaves enough room for us. It won't be so bad, Eve.'

'Of course it won't, Daddy!' Eve said. 'It'll be fun, and really we're lucky. Have you forgotten that I lived in a tiny flat with two rooms? The Lodge is luxury by comparison.'

'I know, my dear, but I haven't forgotten either what Corderhay Park means to you. You love the place as I do. But we'll put a brave face on it, won't we? We shall make it conditional, of course, that whoever buys the house will keep on the outside staff … the grooms and farmers and so on. I cannot have them homeless. If I get the price I hope for, we shall be able to retire quite comfortably and still manage to send young Anthony to public school when the times comes. He's the one to consider now, isn't he? And you, Eve. My two adopted children!'

Eve had promised not to breathe a word of this to her mother, but the thought remained constantly with her as the elaborate preparations continued.

With only two days to go before the wedding, her mother, father and Anne-Marie were all spending the afternoon at Eversham Court discussing final details. Antoinette had wanted Eve to go, too, but she had made some excuse, preferring to stay with young Anthony and write her first long letter to Denise.

She had another reason, also, and that was to keep Louise company. The young French girl had seemed very quiet and left in the background and Eve had not yet had the chance of a private talk with her since her return to England. Once or twice she had caught Louise's eyes on her … a wistful, appealing gaze … that had made Eve wonder. So while Anthony was having his afternoon sleep, she sought the girl out in her room.

She was hardly surprised to find Louise, head buried in the pillow, sobbing as if her heart would break.

'Tell me what is wrong, Louise,' Eve

begged, sitting beside her and stroking the long, dark hair with gentle fingers. 'You can tell me anything, you know. I shall understand.'

Impulsively, the girl turned and clasped Eve's hands, the tears streaming down her face.

'I know, I know. I have so long hoped to talk to someone. It is that I have to go home, Eve. *Maman* has written only today to say so. Next month … Jean will come to fetch me.'

'But, Louise, you have been away from home nearly a year. Surely you are anxious to see your family and home again?'

'Yes, that is true … if it were just for a visit. But it will be for always, Eve, and I shall never see *him* again.'

'Him?' Eve asked gently.

'Richard!' The name came in a husky whisper. 'Oh, Eve, it is wrong, I know, to wish harm to anyone, but I was so happy before Anne-Marie came home. I think Richard was fond of me, and I … I loved him. I still love him and always shall. I feel this way until I die!'

'Louise, one can get over these things in time,' Eve said, although she did not have much hope that this would comfort the girl. 'You are still very young and often one falls in love a second time.'

'Never like this!' Louise cried. 'Now he is to marry Anne-Marie. He seems not to notice

160

me and yet it makes no difference. I can go on living if only I can see him sometimes.'

Eve continued to stroke the girl's soft dark hair and gradually her sobs died down and she became calmer.

'Don't you think perhaps it will be best for you to go home? When Richard is out of sight it will be easier to forget him, and this you must do now, Louise. I'm terribly sorry that it has happened. Believe me, I know how you feel. But you will get over it ... I'm sure of it. And you will be far happier away from these memories!'

Louise gave a deep sigh.

'I wish I could think so. It is wrong, I know, to feel this way about the husband of another woman. And yet *she* did not consider my feelings when she came home and met Richard. I have been so jealous, Eve, and so very unhappy. I don't think I can bear to go to the wedding.'

'Of course you will go!' Eve said. 'You wouldn't want anyone to guess how you felt, would you? You will be smiling and cheerful, and when people look at you it will never occur to them that you are hiding a very real sorrow in your heart. You still have your pride, Louise, haven't you?'

The younger girl flushed.

'Yes, Eve, but I had forgotten about it. I will go and I will be brave ... at least not to show my tears. You are very kind. I shall not have anyone to talk to like this when I go home. *Maman* would not take me seriously. To her I am always the child still.'

'But you will, Louise, dear!' Eve said on a sudden inspiration. 'I am writing to a very dear friend of mine ... a French girl called Denise. She is just married, but before this she knew what it meant to be lonely and unhappy. I shall tell her all about you, and when you go home you will call and see her. I shall tell her, too, that she is to ask Edouard, her husband, to find you a very dashing, handsome young man ... far nicer than Richard. They will see that you have a wonderful time and forget all this!'

'If she is your friend, Eve, then I know I would like her. But I doubt if *Maman* would permit me to go alone with strangers.'

'I think she will permit it, Louise,' Eve replied. 'Tell me, have you heard of a man called Edouard Garret?'

'Edouard Garret ... the painter?' Louise gasped. 'This is not the husband of your friend?'

'Indeed it is!' Eve smiled. 'I believe he is very well known and has many acquaintances among the society your mother would wish you to be in. She can have no objection, surely, to her daughter being seen out with someone of his fame?'

For answer Louise hugged her. Then her face fell.

'But I shall be frightened of so well-known a person,' she said.

'Not when you know him,' Eve replied. 'He and Denise are two of the most natural, charming, simple people in the world, Louise. I'll tell you how they met, shall I?'

And she recounted the romantic story of Denise's meeting with her famous husband, knowing it would touch Louise's romantic young heart. When she left the girl, Louise was smiling once more and had settled down to answer her mother's letter.

Eve had barely begun her own letter to Denise when the old butler knocked on the door of her father's study, saying:

'Beg pardon, Miss Eve, but there's a young gentleman to see you. He's in the hall. He wouldn't go into the drawing-room, just asked me to fetch you.'

'A gentleman to see *me*?' Eve asked. 'Did he give his name?'

'No, he wouldn't do that, either, Miss Eve. It's no one we know, if I may be so bold as to say so. I've never seen him before. But he was quite firm about my fetching you. "It's *Miss* Corderhay I want to see," he said, "and no one else."'

'Very well, I'll go down and see who he is,' Eve said, mystified. 'Thank you, Jenkins!'

She brushed the hair from her forehead and straightened the tweed skirt she was wearing, and with that long, graceful walk that was so typical of all her movements, went unhurriedly along the passage and down the wide staircase. Half way down she paused and stared at the picture in the hall.

Anthony, very much awake and full of life, was perched on the edge of the big balustrade. Holding him with one hand, the stranger was leaning towards the child with his watch held against the baby's ear.

Delighted, Anthony was saying, 'Tick-tick, tick-tick!' and his companion laughed as he tried to make him say: 'Tick-*tock*, Sonny, though I really can't think why. You're quite right, it goes "tick-tick" after all!'

Something in the shape of the head ... in the width of the forehead or the line of the jaw ... struck a chord of memory in Eve's heart. So acute was this feeling of recognition that she felt her heart hammering in strange apprehension. Then quite suddenly the man looked up, perhaps sensing her presence, and she was looking at him full face. Then she knew ... recognized him without a shadow of doubt, and her heart lurched into her mouth. This was the face in the photograph ... the face of Paul Johnson ... Anthony's father.

Unconsciously, Eve ran down the remaining steps and hurriedly lifted Anthony from his perch, holding him tightly in her arms. She could not have explained that strange gesture of maternal possessiveness ... as if she were afraid of the man watching her...

He was looking at her with an expression of surprise coupled with dismay.

'He was quite safe up there, really!' he said. 'Sorry if it gave you a scare!'

Nervously, Eve cleared her throat and tried to find an excuse for her behaviour.

'It wasn't that. It's just that he shouldn't be here. He ought to be in the nursery!' She said the first thing that came into her head. And as if to confirm it, Nanny came hurrying along the passage saying:

'There you are Master Anthony. I couldn't think where he'd got to, Miss Eve. He darts away from me and is up to goodness knows what mischief.'

'Take him up to the nursery, Nanny,' Eve said, and with half her mind she thought: 'Father's right. Nanny's getting too old to cope. Something serious might happen one day. She's so short-sighted.'

As Nanny took the protesting child away Eve turned back to her visitor.

'Sorry to have caused such an upheaval,' he was saying. 'As a matter of fact, I asked that butler chap of yours to find Miss Corderhay. I'd be grateful if you could tell me where she is.'

'He has the most amazing eyes I've ever seen...' Eve thought, as she said automatically:

'I'm Miss Corderhay. What can I do for you?'

He frowned suddenly and for a moment looked like a small boy with a big disappointment.

'But I was so sure this was the place,' he said uncertainly. 'Perhaps I've made a mistake.' He fumbled awkwardly with a parcel which he held under his arm, and drew out a copy of the *Tatler*. Using his knee as a prop, he thumbed quickly through the pages until he came to the place he wanted. Then he turned and showed it to Eve.

Obediently Eve looked at the picture. It was the engagement photograph of Richard Bainborough and Anne-Marie. Underneath was the usual 'The engagement is announced of...' etc., etc.

'That is my sister!' Eve said abruptly.

The man drew a deep breath.

'Then could I see her, please?' he asked impatiently.

Desperately, Eve sought to clear her mind. She had never been more at a loss for words, less in control of her thoughts. All that her mind seemed able to register was how tall and broad-shouldered this man was. He literally towered above her, and she was five feet seven. Had she not still been standing on the bottom step of the staircase she would have had to look sharply up at him. Even now she must raise her head.

'Pull yourself together, Eve!' she told herself. 'This is important. This is Anthony's father … the man Anne-Marie…'

But there her thoughts came to an end.

'Isn't Anne-Marie in?' he was asking, as Eve didn't speak. He looked as if he thought she was half-witted, Eve decided. Really, she must collect her wits.

'No … no! I'm sorry, she's out. But … I think I know who you are. I mean, Anne-Marie has told me about you. Perhaps we could go into the library and you could explain why you're here. I … I see from this' – she pointed to the glossy magazine picture – 'that you know Anne-Marie is to be married the day after tomorrow.'

'That's just why I'm here!' he said, as if at last he was getting somewhere. 'I've got to see her, Miss Corderhay. Look … you're quite right. I ought to explain. Will you lead the way?'

Blindly, Eve walked towards the library, her mind whirling with a hundred questions. Why had he come? What would Anne-Marie say? Did she still love him? Did he still love her? Had he come to try to make her marry him?

In the library, she sat down on one of the leather-studded chairs, and gratefully accepted the cigarette he offered her. Her first words sounded stupid even to her ears as she asked him if he would like tea. He brushed the offer aside, not rudely, but brusquely. Eve irrelevantly remembered Denise's summing-up. 'He's a man who knows what he wants and get it … or it won't be his fault.'

'Unless of course *you'd* like some!' he added quickly, remembering his manners.

Eve shook her head.

'Then I'll get down to business,' he said. 'You know, don't you, that your sister and I were … well, friendly? That I met her over in Paris this time last year?'

Again Eve nodded. How much was he going to tell her? What was his intention? His personality was so overpowering that it seemed to charge the room with electricity. Today the library had none of its quiet, sombre atmosphere. It was truly electric.

'I fell in love with her!' he announced, as if he were saying it was a rainy day. 'I was mad about her, wanted to marry her, and I think she cared about me, too. Then suddenly, without any reason or any warning, she stood me up. It simply didn't make sense in view of our previous meeting. She'd promised to meet me for lunch at the Hôtel Metropole. And she didn't come. I waited over an hour and then went back to my hotel to see if there was a message. I tried once to get her at the place where she lived, but she wasn't there. I realized then that she'd cut our date. Well, I was angry, hurt … and pretty surprised too. And most of all angry. I'd overstayed my time in Paris on her account and I decided to cut off home right away. Of course, I kept hoping she might contact me at my hotel to explain everything … I didn't want to believe it was finished. So I hung around all evening. I rang her once more before I got on to the plane, but they said she still wasn't there. That finally did it. I flew home and tried furiously to put her out of my mind.'

Aghast, Eve had listened to this story. She never doubted its truth. Whatever else this man might be, he was not a dissembler, not dishonest. At last it was beginning to make sense … somehow, somewhere, he and Anne-Marie had missed one another. She had waited, perhaps in one room, he in another… And he had been too proud … too hurt … to make all the moves … and Anne-Marie in her turn believed he had stood her up. What an appalling catastrophe!

'But somehow I couldn't get her out of my mind,' he went on. 'I kept worrying … and wondering. Something somewhere didn't make sense, but I couldn't put my finger on it. Months afterwards I allowed myself to start remembering again, and the more I thought about it the more I began to think I'd acted hastily. I ought to have stayed on, seen her first, heard her explanation. I doubted I'd made sufficient effort to find out what had happened that night and I began to think about going back to Paris to look her up. I didn't feel I could rest till I knew what had happened to her.'

'So he isn't altogether bad!' Eve thought. 'He had a conscience. Denise was right. He felt morally responsible for Anne-Marie and it worried him all along. He never wanted to walk out on her … desert her!'

Never for a single moment did she doubt his story.

'Then suddenly I saw this picture of her in the *Tatler*,' he went on. 'It was last week I found it … an old copy, of course, but I happened to glance through it at the dentist's. I couldn't get away from my firm before … sort of Christmas rush of business … but came down here the very first moment I could. I had to see her before she married this man … just to make sure I was really out of the picture.'

'This is dreadful!' Eve whispered. 'If only you'd tried to find her before! After all, the wedding is in two days' time – the day after tomorrow…'

He leant forward, his face alight with eagerness, his blue eyes fixed intensely on Eve's face.

'Then you think there's still a chance? That she does care for me? Oh, I could kick myself for not making this effort sooner. But I wasn't sure… I didn't know what to think. What had happened?'

'She must have gone to a different hotel or room in it,' Eve said. 'She always thought that you had stood her up!'

'Then she *did* care!' he said, catching hold of Eve's hand and holding it tightly in his as if in this way he was holding a link with Anne-Marie. 'You'll help us, won't you? It isn't too late. She isn't married yet! Lots of engagements have been broken at the last moment!'

Eve bit her lip. This wasn't the time to mention Anthony and yet he figured so largely in the picture. However much Anne-Marie might not like the idea of letting Richard down like this at the last moment, she had her child to consider. And married to his father, she would be able to love her son.

Then only did its repercussions on herself strike Eve. If this man took Anne-Marie *and* Anthony... 'Oh no!' a voice whispered inside her. 'He's my baby.'

'You're going to help us, aren't you?' Paul Johnson was saying. 'I feel I can trust you. It's funny, but you don't look in the least like your sister. Though you're pretty, too, in a different way.'

His voice was so matter-of-fact that Eve could not take offence.

'I'm really not Anne-Marie's real sister!' she said. 'Her parents adopted me as they had no child of their own. Anne-Marie was born six years later.'

'Forgive my curiosity!' he said simply. 'It was none of my business. But Anne-Marie *is* my affair. I must see her.'

'She's with her future in-laws!' Eve said doubtfully. 'My mother and father are there too. I don't see how I can fetch her away without them. Of course they don't know anything about you ... and–' She broke off awkwardly.

'Couldn't you just telephone her? Tell her to make some excuse ... a headache or something ... and come back here? You can explain when she gets here ... or I will.'

'All right!' Eve said weakly. 'I'll telephone her. I ... I wish I knew how she was going to take all this.'

'That's not your worry, it's mine!' Paul Johnson said firmly, with a glance at Eve's anxious face. 'I'm fully aware of the fact that she may have changed her mind about me ... if it was ever made up. I realize, too, that it takes courage to upset a wedding of this sort. It's a society "do", isn't it? But somehow I think I can convince her it's for the best! At least, I shall have a very good try!'

'And he'll succeed, if anyone can!' Eve thought. 'He's the kind of man who will nearly always get what he wants ... by sheer dogged determination ... if nothing else.'

With an effort, for something inside her that foresaw the coming loss to herself forbade the gesture, she held out her hand and clasped his.

'Good luck!' she said. 'I'll do ... everything I can ... to help you.'

'Thanks. You're very nice!' he said inadequately but sincerely, and as Eve walked away towards the phone his compliment gave her heart a comforting glow.

CHAPTER 9

Waiting to meet Anne-Marie at the bottom of the drive, Eve stood huddled against the wrought-iron gateway, her coat wrapped tightly around her to keep out the cold. Anne-Marie was taking longer than she had anticipated to get away from the Bainboroughs and Eve did not doubt that she was taking her time. She had been very irritable on the telephone when Eve rang her asking her to get back as quickly as she could … alone.

'Whatever *for?* Surely it can wait till I come home with Mother?'

'It can't wait, Anne-Marie, and I think you would prefer not to have Mother and Father here.'

There had been an awkward silence, and then Anne-Marie, in a cold, hard little voice, said:

'Oh! Then I suppose it has something to do with Anthony. I thought I made it clear that I don't wish to be in any way responsible for him. He's *your* child, Eve, to all intents and purposes. Just do what you think best for him and stop worrying me!'

Eve curbed her anger and impatience. She had tried to keep her voice calm when she replied:

'It has nothing to do with Anthony himself … only indirectly. Anne-Marie, I'm not just playing the fool. This is deadly serious. I'll meet you at the bottom of the drive and explain. Get here as quickly as you can.'

Another pause and then Anne-Marie's, 'Oh, all right then!' before she rang off.

'But she'll come!' Eve comforted herself as another shiver of cold ran through her. 'And she'll wish she had come sooner when she hears what I have to say.'

She thought of Paul Johnson waiting impatiently in the library. What a restless, overpowering person he seemed to be! There was a tremendous vitality about him that was slightly exhausting afterwards, but not at the time of being with him, for then his personality carried one along with him.

'I wonder just who he is … what he does!' Eve mused. 'He must have some outlet for all that power inside him.'

She visualized his tall, rather heavy build that might have been ungainly if he had not been so well proportioned and so physically fit. This physical well-being was evident all over him. He moved quickly and lightly in spite of his height and weight ... showing perfectly co-ordinated muscles that prevented clumsiness.

'Even his hands,' she thought now, although she had not consciously noticed them in his presence ... 'are big and square and strong ... practical hands ... determined–'

Her thoughts came to an abrupt end as the headlights of the family Rover swung round the last bend of the lane and lit up Eve's hunched, shivering form. There was a sudden screech of brakes as Anne-Marie pulled up by the gate and waited for Eve to jump in beside her.

'I thought you were never coming, Anne-Marie,' she said with an edge of reproach in her voice.

Anne-Marie leant back in the driver's seat and casually lit a cigarette.

'Well, what else did you suppose! I had to make arrangements for Richard to run Mother and Father home later. I said I had a bit of a headache and then of course, Mother wanted to come with me and Father said he'd come along, too. I had a job to persuade them I'd rather go on my own. They all seemed aghast because I wouldn't let Richard bring me back in his car. What is all this about, Eve? I hope you've not brought me back for some stupid–'

'It isn't stupid ... it's very serious, Anne-Marie,' Eve broke in on her sister's rather petulant voice. 'And terribly important. It may give you a bit of a shock, I'm afraid. There's no way I can break it gently.'

Still convinced that Eve was making a mountain out of a mole-hill, Anne-Marie said impatiently:

'Oh, for goodness' sake, out with it, Eve!'

The older girl took a breath. Since Anne-Marie wanted it plainly:

'Paul Johnson's here!' she said.

She had imagined Anne-Marie would be shocked, but had hardly anticipated the extent to which the younger girl now reacted. Her hands flew up to her cheeks, which, even in the dashboard light, appeared to Eve to lose every trace of colour before a swift violet-red rushed into them. Her mouth had fallen open and her eyes were fixed on Eve as if in this way only could she retain her sanity.

'P ... Paul ... J ... Johnson!' she said at last, the name coming from her lips in an incredulous whisper.

To give her time to recover, Eve launched into the story of his arrival. Anne-Marie listened to every word she said, and gradually her hands ceased to tremble and her voice was almost normal when she asked her sister:

'Did ... did you mention ... the child?'

'It wasn't my business to tell him, Anne-Marie. He may have guessed when he saw him in the hall ... but he didn't ask any questions. All he could think or talk about was you!'

Anne-Marie drew a deep breath of relief.

'Thank heaven you didn't say anything, Eve. You see, I don't want him to know ... he mustn't know anything about Anthony ... not yet. It would ... ruin everything ... if he knew.'

Eve gave her sister a puzzled look.

'But surely, Anne-Marie, Anthony must figure so largely in whatever plans you make. Paul's his father. He has a right to know.'

'*You mustn't tell him!*' Anne-Marie cried, her hand clutching Eve's arm and holding it with a vice-like grip as if by doing so she could force the girl to silence. 'Don't you see ... what will happen? *You* say he loves me ... that he wants to marry me ... but how can I be sure ... if he knows about the baby? I'd never be satisfied that he hadn't married me just because of that. Don't you see, Eve?'

Eve understood now. In any case, it was not her life to plan her way. It was Anne-Marie's affair ... and Paul's ... no longer any of her business.

'I don't suppose I'll even see him again,' she murmured. 'And I certainly won't say anything, Anne-Marie. If you don't either, then that's your affair. But somehow, I feel he might want to know.'

'No, I won't tell him ... not until I'm certain that he ... he's in love with me,' Anne-Marie said swiftly. 'I know what I'm doing, Eve. It isn't your business, just as you said. Let me do this my way. Please, Eve!'

'Of course!' Eve said, feeling suddenly deflated and very cold. 'Now don't you think we'd better go up to the house? He ... he'll be very impatient, I'm sure.'

Anne-Marie slipped the car into gear and drove slowly up the drive to the house. No further words passed between the two girls until they parted ways, Eve to go upstairs to her room, Anne-Marie to the library. Then, involuntarily, Eve said:

'Be kind to him, Anne-Marie. I think he loves you very dearly.'

Then the library door opened and Anne-Marie disappeared inside.

Eve walked slowly up the wide staircase, wishing that she could account more reasonably for the acute depression that had settled over her. Unconsciously, her feet took her along to the nursery wing. Nanny was now putting Anthony to bed. The child recognized her instantly and smiled up at her, his baby cheeks rosy from the warm water, his little body fresh and sweet-smelling, his golden hair a mass of damp curls.

'Gobbum!' he said, his eyes crinkling up into laughter.

'Yes, yes, my sweetling!' Nanny murmured

as she fastened the safety-pins on his nappy. 'Nanny will give precious his supper in a moment.' She turned to Eve, saying: 'Would you mind him for a moment, Miss Eve? I forgot to get his milk from Cook before I came up with him. I'm so absent-minded these days, and the baby ... bless his little heart ... is such a handful!'

'Of course I'll take him, Nanny, and I'll give him his milk tonight. You look tired. Why don't you run along and have a few minutes with your feet up before supper?'

Gratefully, the old woman waddled away to her bedroom and Eve went down to the kitchen with Anthony, in his little blue dressing-gown and slippers, in her arms. He was getting quite a big boy and was heavy, even for her, but she loved the feel of him cuddled up against her, his pudgy little arms around her neck.

'Oh, Anthony!' she whispered against his still damp little head. 'How can I bear to lose you?'

But he only snuggled closer to her and Eve bit her lip to prevent the sudden rush of tears from spilling down her cheeks.

As she tucked Anthony into his cot after his supper she heard a car drive away, and stood for a moment listening as the engine grew fainter and finally disappeared altogether into the night.

'He's gone!' she thought. 'I wonder–' But

she broke off quickly. No doubt Anne-Marie would confide in her in due course.

Her sister's confidences came sooner than Eve had anticipated. As she left the baby's room Anne-Marie came flying up the stairs, her eyes searching eagerly for Eve.

'She doesn't look happy!' Eve thought irrelevantly. 'Only worried!'

'Oh, thank goodness I've found you, Eve!' her younger sister said on a note of relief. 'I must talk to you. Let's go to your room.'

In Eve's bedroom, which was also her private sitting-room, Anne-Marie paced the length of the floor and back as she talked. Eve sat in silence on the edge of her bed listening ... hearing and yet not wanting to hear what was said.

'He wants me to elope with him, Eve. He says it's the only way out of my marriage to Richard. It's too late to break it off in the conventional way. After all, the wedding is only the day after tomorrow. I tried to make him agree that the best thing to do was to let me postpone it, but he wouldn't have it that way. He's so terribly determined and he says things have gone wrong for us once and he won't take any chances this time ... that plenty more can go wrong in a day or two. It's tomorrow or nothing ... our elopement, I mean. He simply wouldn't ... take no for an answer.'

'No!' Eve repeated. 'You mean you tried to

tell him you wouldn't marry him?' Her voice was aghast.

'No … of course not!' Anne-Marie said nervously. 'I meant "no" to elopement. I wanted time to think it over, but he refused to go until I'd made up my mind. I knew Father and Mother would be back soon and I was desperate. I … Eve, I've agreed to marry him … tomorrow.'

Eve took a deep breath.

'Then I think you are doing the only thing possible,' she said. 'And the *right* thing, Anne-Marie. It's … best for Anthony … and you couldn't ever be happy with Richard now … now that Paul has come back into your life. In the end it will be best for Richard, too.'

Anne-Marie swung round and walked across to the window, pulling back the curtains and staring out into the blackness of the night. There were no stars … nothing visible beyond the reflection of the room in the panes of glass.

'I'll … have … to tell Richard,' she said slowly and carefully. 'I shall have to tell him … tonight, won't I, Eve? It … I couldn't just leave him a note … casually, could I? I keep thinking about what happened to David…'

Instantly Eve was up and across the room to her sister. It gladdened her heart that Anne-Marie could at this vital moment in her life think of the man she was jilting rather than the man she loved and was going to marry.

'This isn't the same, Anne-Marie. Not if you tell Richard the truth ... all the truth. Maybe when he knows, he will be glad that ... that he's been let off so easily. I don't mean to be critical or nasty when I say that ... but he has rather imagined that you ... well, that–'

'That he was marrying an innocent, un-spoiled little girl?' Anne-Marie said bitterly. 'Oh yes, that's true enough. But I'll have to *tell* him, Eve, not write, won't I?'

Eve nodded.

'It would be fairer ... and better, perhaps,' she agreed.

'Then I'll see him somehow ... tonight,' Anne-Marie announced, her voice firm now as she made her plans. 'I'll tell Mother and Father my headache is better ... that an aspirin put me right ... and that I particularly want to see Richard about the wedding tonight ... that's true, anyway. They'll let me go, won't they?'

'I'm sure they will,' Eve said. 'And if there's any way I can help, Anne-Marie ... please tell me. What about Father and Mother ... when will you tell them?'

Anne-Marie swung round, an expression of dismay written across her face.

'I'd ... forgotten ... them,' she breathed. 'Eve, I can't face them ... not Mother's disappointment ... Father's look ... Eve, you just said you'd help me. You tell them. You'll be so much more tactful, and Father knows you know the truth, anyway. He'll believe you when you say it's the best thing for me to do. He can tell Mother later. He doesn't trust me any more ... he'll think I'm just ... up to something. Eve, you'll do this for me ... for their sakes as much as mine ... won't you ... *won't you?*'

'I can't!' It was on the tip of Eve's tongue, but yet remained unspoken. She would rather anything than have to be the one to see the expression on her father's face ... worse still, on her mother's ... and yet in her heart she knew she could make her father see the reason of it. He had never spoken about Anthony except as a separate entity and yet Eve knew how he must have felt that his first grandchild was not born in wedlock ... that he could never know the truth about his mother ... nor who his father was. When Anne-Marie and Paul were married ... they would move away to a different part of the country, taking Anthony with them, and start life again ... mother, father and child. This was as it should be, and therefore Jack Corderhay would also want it that way. She could, she knew, break the news to him so much better than her less tactful sister...

'All right ... I'll tell him,' she said slowly.

'After I've gone? Not before. Promise me

you won't tell him until I'm gone. I shall slip away before breakfast ... before anyone is up. You'll be able to tell him first thing in the morning. There's nothing he can do about cancelling the wedding arrangements tonight... And besides, it would mean a scene, and I can't face any more. It'll be bad enough ... with Richard. Eve, you'll wait, won't you ... till I'm gone?'

'Yes, I'll wait,' Eve agreed, wondering if this, also, was not yet another proof that Anne-Marie would not face up to her punishment ... that she must always find someone else to do the unpleasant things in life for her ... and take the brunt of them. But at the same time she could feel pity in her heart for her younger sister. Selfish, wilful, spoilt ... all these things she might be, and yet it was true that she would have enough unpleasantness telling Richard the truth. This could be no enviable task for any girl. She could not believe that Richard, weak though he might be, would take this news calmly. He would be shocked, horrified and terribly upset. No young man could feel otherwise when not only did his fiancée break her engagement to him two days before the wedding, but also confessed to having had a child by the man she was running away to.

'I'll tell Father tomorrow,' she repeated. 'After you have gone. And, Anne-Marie ...

I'd like to wish you ... you and Paul ... luck ... for the future, I mean. You'll let us know, of course, after the wedding? And about ... about Anthony?'

'I'll write to you, Eve,' Anne-Marie promised. And suddenly childishly and impulsively she flung her arms round her sister's neck and said:

'Thanks for everything, Eve ... past and present. I'd never have handled ... all this ... without your help. I'm grateful!'

It was a stilted little speech and Eve was not to know its true meaning until the next day. When she recalled those words she suddenly saw what Anne-Marie had meant by them ... and only then realized what she had done.

Anne-Marie, however, knew exactly what she had done and was about to do, and even while she was a little afraid of her actions, she felt at the same time a queer exhilaration which was part conceit, for could anyone else have managed, she asked herself, to think of such a clever way out of her sudden difficulties in so short a time?

When, an hour or two later, she drove herself over to Eversham Court, her face was still flushed by the inner excitement that upheld her and she was conscious of the fact that never had she looked more lovely. The bright pink of her cheeks accentuated the sparkling deep blue of her eyes, and her expression, usually vivacious, was now alive with the emotions that sustained her.

'Will I regret this?' she paused to ask herself as she waited for the manservant to fetch Richard. 'Shall I be sorry some day in the future?'

But somehow future regrets did not seem to matter. This was the way she had planned her life and her revenge for the unhappiness she had suffered, and nothing … no one … should stand in her way.

As Richard Bainborough came into the hall she flung back her head and looked towards him with a brilliant nervous smile.

'Anne-Marie!' he said, moving quickly to her side and taking her hands in his. 'You're the last person I expected to see. I thought you weren't well?'

Anne-Marie put a finger against his lips.

'Hush, Richard! Not so loud!' she whispered. 'I don't want your mother and father to know I'm here. *I must see you* … alone.'

The young man stared at her in surprise. This conspiratorial Anne-Marie was new even to him who imagined he had run the gamut of most of her moods. But he was far too young and inexperienced to know anything of the girl he was to marry other than that which she wished him to see. She had kept guessing far more mature people than he, who were just as uncertain as to what really lay in her character.

Richard Bainborough was a tall, slender young man in his early twenties. He had not long finished his National Service with the Lancers, and since then he had been 'taking it easy' before going into his father's business, which one day he was to run himself. He was a weak, ineffectual young man so devoid of character and personality that he could never withstand the pressure of other people's and became in their presence what they were themselves. At least, he unconsciously endeavoured to do so. To his adoring mother, therefore, he was still the baby she wished to keep him. With his father, he tried to appear interested in politics, current affairs and the business world in general. His father, having no other son to whom he would one day leave his vast wealth and connections, found him sometimes wanting, but always attributed this lack of character to the boy's youth. On this account Richard was never allowed to make a decision of importance for himself but must always first refer it to his father, thereby slowly destroying any initiative or self-confidence his son might possession.

Nevertheless, Richard was not unattractive. There was a certain boyish charm to his face and he had those rather soft, limpid brown eyes that made women sorry for him and anxious to 'mother' him. Nor was he of an unpleasant nature. He had been brought up to strict rules and standards of behaviour and it would simply never have occurred to him to break them. He was, therefore, honest, truthful, upright and certainly morally sound.

Anne-Marie was the first major event of any importance in his life. It had been no difficulty for her to sweep him clean off his feet, for he was all too vulnerable to be proof against her feminine beauty and wiles. In a matter of days she had convinced him, without appearing to do so, that he must have been quite mad ever to think he cared for the quiet, dull little Louise; that there was never yet in the world any girl with so much prettiness and charm as Anne-Marie possessed, and that she loved him as no other woman could ever love him. He lived now in a world of disbelief and amazement that a girl like Anne-Marie could ever love a dull sort of chap like him, Richard Alan Greenby Bainborough.

Delighted, he had perceived his parents' approval of his heart's choice. Anne-Marie was her most sweet, gentle and becoming self with his father and mother, the former thinking that marriage might at least make Richard grow up a little and the latter thinking that dear, pretty little Anne-Marie was the perfect counterpart for her darling boy.

'Two such babes!' she said tenderly several times a day. 'I shall have to keep an eye on them both. They're far too young to be settling down to marriage.'

Yet she approved because with her Anne-Marie was not just Richard's future wife, but also the pretty little daughter that she had once so dearly longed for to complement her handsome boy.

At the moment, however, there was nothing of the little daughter in Anne-Marie Corderhay. Alone with Richard in the privacy of his 'den', she flung herself into his astonished arms and burst into tears.

'Oh, Richard, Richard!' she sobbed. 'Something terrible has happened. I'm so afraid.'

Stroking her head with awkward tenderness, Richard, feeling more than a little afraid himself, asked her to tell him what had so upset her.

'It's us! You and me, Richard. They're trying to separate us!'

He stared at her aghast as she released herself fro his arms and wiped the tears from her eyes.

'Separate us? Who? Why?' he burst out.

'It's my family,' Anne-Marie said in a choked little voice. 'They want to postpone our wedding, Richard!'

'But why? What on earth for? Anne-Marie, do pull yourself together and tell me the facts!'

'I'm trying to tell you … but … it's so awful, Richard I don't know how to say it. I can't bear it if I'm not allowed to marry you. I can't live without you, Richard. Oh what am I going to do?'

As she broke into a fresh flood of tears Richard put his arms around her once more and, looking down into her flushed, tearful face with the brimming, wide-open eyes, knew that nothing and no one could ever take her from him. Perhaps for the first and only time in his life he felt strong enough and certain enough of himself to see that no one did.

'I love you, Anne-Marie, and I'm going to marry you, whatever anyone says. So don't cry any more. Please.'

She leant against him and his heart beat faster at the faint, elusive smell of her perfume do close to his face.

'Oh, Richard! If only I could be sure you meant it! When you hear … what has happened … you may not want to marry me after all!'

'I shall and always will want to marry you … and that's final,' Richard said manfully.

'Then, Richard, we have only one path to take,' Anne-Marie said, watching his face. 'We shall have to run away together … tomorrow.'

'Run away! You mean elope?' And as she nodded her head he stared down at her in dismay. 'But, Anne-Marie, whatever for? The wedding is the day after tomorrow. Why

run away now, of all times? Besides, whatever will Mother and Father say?'

Anne-Marie curbed her impatience.

'That's just it, Richard. It's what they are
going to say that counts so much. You see, if
they ever discover what I learned tonight,
then they wouldn't let me marry me. I'm
sure of it. And anyway, the wedding won't
be the day after tomorrow. Father has
postponed it.'

'Postponed it?' Richard repeated every
word she uttered as if only by doing so
could he be sure he had heard her aright.
'Honestly, Anne-Marie, this doesn't make
sense. Why, only this evening your other and
father were here, talking over the wedding
arrangements. What on earth has happened
since then to make them all change their
minds and for you to be like this?'

Anne-Marie buried her head against his
coat and he had to strain to catch her words.

'I only just found out myself,' she
whispered. 'It's Eve, Richard ... my sister.
You ... you know the little boy Father and
Mother adopted ... or said they had adopted,
from that orphanage in Paris ... well, well–'

'Anne-Marie, you're not trying to tell me
that it's *Eve's* child.'

She raised a stricken face to his and
looked him straight in the eye.

'Even Father can't believe it. But he said
that if it's true, then I can't marry you,

Richard. And *your* mother and father wouldn't want you to marry *me* ... to be associated with such a scandal.'

'*Eve's child!*' Richard said again his whole being shocked and disturbed by the very thought of it. And then, as he felt Anne-Marie's hands on his arms, claiming his attention, he knew that this couldn't make any difference to his loving her. 'After all, Anne-Marie,' he spoke his next thought aloud, 'it isn't even as if Eve were your real sister, is it? And anyway, it's you I want to marry!'

'Oh, Richard, it's kind of you not to stop loving me because of this. I've been so terribly afraid.'

He bent down and kissed her gently on the cheek.

'We shall still be married,' he said again.

'But, Richard, I've been trying to tell you ... Father has postponed the wedding. He says he won't have a Corderhay disgracing the name of Bainborough. Oh, you know how old-fashioned he is, Richard. And your father, too. He says that if this all comes out in public he'd never forgive himself for having deceived your family. He'll probably tell your parents and then they'll try to separate us, too. Don't you see, Richard, what will happen? They'll come between us!'

Richard tried to follow her reasoning and a frown creased his forehead.

'Of course, I do see that your father is jolly

upset about it all,' he said. 'But I just can't see why he shouldn't want you to marry me. It's nothing to do with us. It would be different if I wanted to back out. He's not the injured party … if you know what I mean!'

He felt after he had said it that he might not have been very tactful, but Anne-Marie did not appear to notice the suggestion he had not meant to infer.

'You don't understand, Richard,' she was saying. 'You see, to him Eve is a Corderhay. He's always refused to make any difference between us, and even though I am his real daughter he always treats us the same. This matters just as much to him as if it had been his own flesh and blood. And he's terribly proud, Richard. Perhaps it's because we've got so little nowadays to be proud about.'

'He can always be proud of you!' Richard said gallantly, but Anne-Marie scarcely heard him.

'We've practically no money left, Richard. I think it's even possible we might have to sell Corderhay Park soon. Because of all this, Father's been terribly touchy, and I think if he could he might move away to another part of the country to avoid any scandal. And I should have to go with him. He'd expect me to go, and Mother too. He wouldn't think it fair for me to marry you and perhaps force the scandal on you, too.'

'Yes, I see what you mean!' Richard said

slowly. 'All the same, I don't see why there should be much scandal, Anne-Marie. After all, everyone believed that the boy came from an orphanage. My mater did, anyway, because I heard her telling some friend of the family how sad it was to think of all those homeless, parentless children, and how brave of *your* mother to take on another child so late in life. No one suspects it might have been ... Eve's.'

'But you don't know the facts ... the reasons,' Anne-Marie said desperately. 'Someone came to the house tonight. That's what Eve rang up about and why she wanted me to go home. I pretended to be ill, of course, but it was all to do with this. It ... it may all come to light ... and I can't bear it if it does, Richard. The shame of having our wedding cancelled at the last minute ... and perhaps having to go away.'

Richard took a deep breath and squared his shoulders.

'I couldn't bear it if you went away, Anne-Marie. I said before that I'm going to marry you, and I will. And if elopement is the only way, then we'll just have to elope, that's all. Still ... I can't say I know much about run-away marriages. You leave a lot of notes for people and things, don't you?' he ended vaguely.

His arms were round her now and she pressed against him in a tantalizing proximity. He felt his heart accelerate and knew that he ought not to be displeased with the thought that perhaps he would make her his wife ... in every way ... sooner even than he'd hoped. He was slightly ashamed of the passion he had for her, but it ruled most of his sleeping and waking thoughts.

'Oh, Richard, you're so wonderful to me!' she was saying. 'I know it'll be all right if we do it this way. Father won't have any need to tell your parents because it can't do any good to be heroic and self-sacrificing *after* we're married, can it? Then they might never know. And that'll be better for Eve, too, as well as being nice for us. Besides, Richard, it'll be such fun, won't it? We'll both get up at the crack of dawn and steal out of our houses before anyone is awake and you can pick me up in your car. We could go right away together somewhere ... Paris, perhaps. It's such a lovely romantic place for a honeymoon and we can be married over there. I've got some nice friends over there whom you'd like, Richard ... you know, Louise's family. We'll visit them. And of course we'll send telegrams to our families to say where we are. And, Richard, we can both give as an excuse that we didn't feel we could face the wedding they'd planned for us. After all, they did plan it, didn't they ... for themselves, I mean? No one asked us what we'd like. And I'd much rather be married to you quietly without any fuss … just the two of us alone. Wouldn't you, Richard?'

Having spent the last few months dreading everything that would be required of him during the wedding ceremony and reception, Richard was only too ready to agree with Anne-Marie that this fact alone made an elopement attractive. Nevertheless, as he kissed her goodnight hurriedly at the garden door half an hour later he wished very much that this hadn't *had* to happen. He supposed that it was necessary, although a lot still didn't seem to make sense, but Anne-Marie had convinced him. Nevertheless, he wasn't sure that he felt happy about this unconventional way round their difficulties.

And as he went up to his bedroom to pack some clothes he wished that she hadn't mentioned Louise. It was silly of him, he knew, to feel guilty, because he'd never said anything definite to Louise … never proposed to her or anything like that. All the same, Louise might have said something to her family about those times he'd kissed her … she'd been terribly strictly brought up … and he'd never felt very easy about the way he'd chucked her when Anne-Marie came home. He hadn't even realized he was doing so until he saw her on the night he and Anne-Marie became engaged. Then her pale, sad little face with its reproachful brown eyes had haunted him and he'd felt a bit of a cad. Of course, he'd forgotten her soon afterwards, and when he did remember her again it was with relief that she would soon be going back to France. It was annoying of Anne-Marie, although, of course, she couldn't have known about the way he felt, to remind him just now of Louise.

'Oh, well,' he comforted himself, he'd soon talk Anne-Marie out of going to Paris for a honeymoon. There were other places… Venice for instance, or the South of France. Just the thought of anywhere at all with Anne-Marie was to think of perfection … Anne-Marie … his bride.

Dear Mother [he started to write],

I do not feel I can go through with the big wedding you planned for me and Anne-Marie feels the same. We're running away together, and by the time you read this we shall be on our way to the South of France. I hope you and the Pater will understand and not blame me too much for spoiling your party. In haste now, but I'll write again as soon as we arrived … Monte Carlo, I expect it will be…

Twelve hours later he sat beside Anne-Marie in the large passenger aircraft that carried them along with thirty other people, not to Venice or Monte Carlo, but to Paris, the capital of France.

CHAPTER 10

When Anne-Marie did not appear at breakfast, Eve felt a strange, unaccountable premonition of disaster. She had heard Anne-Marie return from Eversham Court just before midnight, having found herself unable to settle down until she knew her young sister was home. Soon after Anne-Marie's footsteps had died away down the passage she had dropped off into a deep, exhausted sleep and woken only when the breakfast-gong sounded.

'Everyone seems to be oversleeping this morning!' Jack Corderhay remarked, looking at Anne-Marie's empty place at table. 'But it'll do her good to have plenty of rest before all the excitement tomorrow.'

He and Antoinette launched into a discussion of the wedding, which provided their main topic of conversation these days, for Antoinette could think of little else, so much was she looking forward to it. It was a long time since she had entertained on such a scale, and although her tall English husband had not confided in her, she had an intuitive idea as to the worsening of their financial position and felt that this might be the last grand affair they would ever have. The reception was, of course, to be held at Corderhay Park, and today everyone on the staff was to decorate the downstairs rooms with flowers that had been specially ordered from the hothouses of a big nursery near by. Under her skilful direction she felt confident that the very best results would be obtained, and she could scarcely contain her impatience to begin as soon as the lorry arrived with the flowers.

'You'll help me, of course, Eve, *chérie?*' she said to her daughter. 'There is so much to do!'

Dumbly, Eve nodded her head, wondering how she could bring herself so to disappoint her darling, enthusiastic mother. Soon ... perhaps already, she thought with a pang ... Anne-Marie would be gone from the house to meet Paul Johnson, and it would be her, Eves, responsibility to break the news to her father and mother.

'If only they understand and are not too hurt and upset!' she thought as she pushed her half-eaten breakfast away and stood up to leave the room.

'I'll just run up to Anne-Marie's room with a cup of tea!' she excused herself, knowing that she could not bear this suspense any longer. She must know when Anne-Marie was going ... or if she had already gone ... then tell her parents quickly before her mother could start on the floral decorations that would no longer be needed.

Forcing herself to walk slowly, she went up the wide staircase and along the passage to Anne-Marie's room, her heart beating in nervous apprehension. Outside the door she paused a moment, hearing no sound from within and knowing somewhere deep in her heart that Anne-Marie had already gone.

With a great effort she pushed open the door and saw that her instinct had been right. Everything was in appalling disorder. Tissue paper was scattered over the floor and rumpled bed ... cardboard boxes, that had held some of her trousseau clothes, lay empty and discarded on chairs and carpet. Her dressing-table was littered with unwanted make-up, old ribbons, hairpins ... things that she could not want in her new life. She had taken with her only the things that were valuable ... or new.

Slowly, Eve put down the cup of tea on a nearby chair and automatically she started to tidy the room. Her mind seemed to be quite blank and her movements automatic. Warmth, movement, thought, only returned to her when she saw the envelope addressed to her propped on the crumpled pillow.

'This will tell me she has gone away to marry Paul!' she thought. 'By now she may already be with him ... with the man she loves ... Anthony's father. All this ... Mother and Father and me … we don't matter anymore. Nothing matters now that she is with *him.*'

She took the thin folded sheet of paper covered with Anne-Marie's untidy writing and started to read. As she did so the colour flared into her cheeks, quickly to recede until her whole face was deathly white and her hands trembling so much that the words blurred in front of her eyes.

'Oh no, no! It isn't true!' she thought. 'It *can't* be true.'

My dear Eve [she reread the words once more],

When you receive this I shall be on my way to Paris … with Richard. I daresay this will come as a bit of a shock, but I hadn't the nerve to tell you yesterday. I was sure you'd try to stop me. You see, it's Richard I want to marry and whom I'm going to marry. Paul Johnson doesn't mean a thing to me. You wanted me to marry Paul for Anthony's sake, but you don't care about me … about what I feel. Why should I marry someone I don't even like any more just because you didn't want Anthony adopted? I've told you before that he doesn't mean anything at all to me… He's yours … and I'm not making any more sacrifices for him.

I expect Paul will be pretty furious when I don't turn up at the wedding because, of course, I told him I loved him and would marry him to keep him quiet and get him out of the house. He wouldn't take "no" for an answer and so it's his own fault. I told him I wanted time to think it over. So in a way he has only himself to blame if he looks silly waiting for me at the Registrar's Office like we planned. I'll send him a telegram, of course, if I get the time, but we may be on our way to Paris by two o'clock so it might be better if you sent one for me. I don't know where he's staying, but he'll be at the Registrar's Office in Mayburn Road, Chelsea, at two if you feel like warning him it's all off.

I haven't left a note for Mother and Father because you promised you'd tell them for me. Actually, there's no need to tell them about Paul, nor need Mother know about the past. If you just say that Richard and I felt we couldn't face the big wedding ... it's what Richard has told his family in a note for them. I suppose Mother will be disappointed, but after all, it's *my* life and *my* wedding and *my* future, isn't it?

I suppose you'll be annoyed with me, but you should be thankful since there won't be any question now of my taking your precious Anthony away from you. If I hadn't had the courage to do this you'd be feeling pretty fed up today, so think of that when you're calling me all the names under the sun.

I'll write to Mother and Father later, of course, when they're had time to get over the shock!

Your loving sister,
Anne-Marie.

'*It isn't true!* She can't have done this!' Eve said over and over again, and yet deep in her heart she knew that it was true. It was all so clear to her now ... why Anne-Marie had been so ready to rush off to Richard last night. Eve might have known her sister better than to suppose that she could have been anxious to fulfil the unpleasant duty of breaking things off with Richard and confessing the reason for her behaviour. Instead of which her motive had been to get him to elope with her. Richard wouldn't have been hard to persuade. Even on Eve's short acquaintance with him since her return from France, she had noticed how much under Anne-Marie's influence he was. Nevertheless, Eve thought grimly, Anne-Marie must have had to talk hard to persuade him to make such a decision without his parents' knowledge!

His parents! Eve thought desperately. Perhaps by now they would be reading his note and the first thing they would do would be to telephone her parents...

'I must go and tell them ... *now!*' Eve said aloud. And silently she prayed for courage. Father might not mind so much ... but her mother... And what was she going to tell them?... The whole truth ... about Paul ... or just that Anne-Marie had eloped with Richard to avoid the big wedding planned for them?

'Why should Anne-Marie get off scot-free?' she thought angrily. 'It's time she suffered a little of the blame for her actions!'

And yet Eve knew she would shield Anne-Marie again ... she must do so in order to save her parents pain. Her mother knew nothing of Paul Johnson ... nor even that Anthony was Anne-Marie's child. It would hurt her far more to know this than to realize that the wedding she had so looked forward to would have to be cancelled. And her father ... he would be so ashamed of Anne-Marie. It wasn't often that people who had done wrong ... as Anne-Marie had done wrong ... were given a second chance and an opportunity to put things right ... for themselves ... and in this case for Anthony. Even if Anne-Marie was no longer in love with Paul Johnson ... it was her duty to marry him and give her child the home and parents that were his birthright. Instead ... Anne-Marie had shelved her responsibilities again and put her own selfish desires before anyone or anything else. Ruthlessly, she followed her own path, treading on anyone who crossed it. She had not even had the courage or decency to tell Paul Johnson the truth, let alone her, Eve, whom she had tricked into helping her. Instead she would let him wait indefinitely for her at the Registrar's Office until at last he would realize that she wasn't coming after all;

or until the telegram reached him…

Eve pulled up her thoughts sharply. She would think about Paul Johnson later. First she must face her parents.

With her heart in her mouth, Eve turned and closed the bedroom door behind her, shutting away the disorder and untidiness that was so typical of Anne-Marie's life. Head held high, she went back down the staircase to the breakfast-room, and without looking at her mother she turned to Jack Corderhay and said:

'Could I have a word with you, Father? Alone?'

He looked up at her with an anxious glance. The taut tone of her voice had warned him that there was something wrong. A question rose to his lips, but with a quick look at his wife's face he remained silent. If Eve had thought it best for Antoinette to know she would have told them her news outright and not asked to see him alone.

'You will excuse us, my dear?' he asked his wife as he rose to his feet.

Antoinette nodded her head absently.

'You won't be long, Eve? I'm anxious to start as soon as possible on the flowers?'

'I won't be long, Mother!' Eve said gently, and turning, followed her father across the hall into his study, closing the door behind them.

Jack Corderhay seated himself in the

205

leather armchair and unhurriedly lit his pipe, waiting for Eve to speak. He sensed that she was trying to find words to begin and forced himself not to hurry her. A glance at her pale, anxious little face had warned him that whatever news she had was not good news, and in his heart he knew it had to do with Anne-Marie.

'Oh, Father!' Eve said at last, in a voice so full of pain that instinctively he held out his arm and drew her down towards him so that she was half sitting on the wide arm of the chair, half leaning against him, her face buried against his shoulder. 'It's so difficult to tell you. I wish … but you'll have to know sometime … it's … Anne-Marie…'

'She's ill?' her father asked anxiously.

'No, not ill!' Eve murmured. 'But … she's gone, Father … gone away with Richard … to be married.'

'Gone?' he repeated, aghast. 'With Richard? You mean they've eloped?'

Eve nodded her head.

'But, Eve, why? In heaven's name, they were to be married tomorrow! They hadn't long to wait. What on earth possessed them to do such a thing? Why it'll half kill your mother…'

'I know!' Eve whispered. 'That's why I so hate to have to tell you. She's been so excited … so looking forward to all this. I *can't* tell *her*, Father. You must break it to her.'

He drew a deep breath and there were lines on his face that seemed suddenly to age him as he thought of the hurt he must inflict on his Antoinette. He had tried all his life to shield her from hurt and pain. He had never told her the truth about young Anthony. In his heart he had felt disloyal to Eve, for he knew that Antoinette had wondered … maybe still did … if the boy were Eve's child. But he knew that Anne-Marie was *her* favourite … her darling baby … just as Eve was his, and although neither of them showed outwardly their preferences, they held the secret truth in their hearts. He had known what it would do to his wife to discover what Anne-Marie was really like … how egotistical, selfish … hard. So he had kept the truth from her whenever possible and now he could no longer protect her.

'But why? *Why*, Eve?' he asked desperately. 'Anne-Marie *must* have known what this would do to your mother. Doesn't she care?'

'It's … just that … she couldn't face up to the big wedding, Father,' Eve lied frantically. He was so hurt himself … for Antoinette … so puzzled. She had to lie. 'Maybe … her conscience… Mother would have it that she was married in white. Maybe in her heart Anne-Marie felt it would be a sham.'

For a moment her father's eyes closed over the pain in them. It was possible … Eve's reason … and yet he did not affect the immediate issue … that of telling Antoinette her 'party' was off. Everything would have to be cancelled … all the guests informed … the vicar … the staff … the caterers … thought it might be too late to cancel the van of flowers that was due to arrive any moment now…

The thought of all that was to be done confused and upset Jack Corderhay as much as the thought that Anne-Marie had caused all this trouble was irritating him. He had not yet had time to sort out his own reactions to her behaviour, but his first emotion was one of contempt. However much Anne-Marie had wished to avoid a big wedding for reasons of her own, she should have given more thought to the other people who would be affected by the change of plans … to the shock to her mother. Apart from Antoinette's disappointment, it would upset her dreadfully not to be present at Anne-Marie's wedding, and Anne-Marie, if she had thought of her mother's feelings at all, must have known it. As to her conscience … this hardly seemed the time to remember it! When first the engagement had been announced and the first plans for this large wedding discussed, Anne-Marie had been only too eager for the pomp and ceremony and publicity. Memories of her past had not troubled her then when she could so easily, and with so little fuss, have insisted on a quiet wedding. But she had *wanted* a big, important affair and inflamed Antoinette with notions of splendour for Corderhay Park and the family so that his wife, only too pleased and happy at the thought of an elaborate setting and send-off for her daughter's marriage, had come to Jack and begged to be allowed to do it on a large scale if it was within his financial means.

He had been unwilling to make further drastic drains on his already depleted bank balance, but after a night's consideration he had come to the conclusion that this could ultimately make little difference. It could only hurry on the sale of Corderhay Park which could be avoided very little longer, even without the wedding expenses. Why not ... he asked himself, for Antoinette's sake, agree to this last 'fling'? It would be comparative austerity for the rest of their lives, and he understood only too well how hard this would be for his wife, who had been brought up in the height of luxury and who had no idea of what it meant to 'make do'. Nor, for that matter, had he much idea himself, until of late, of trying to make a shilling do the work of a pound. He could bear it for himself. But it was less easy to stand by and see the wife he so adored having to give up her social position, her expensive clothes, her cars and servants one by one ... and now, in the near future, her home...

He turned now to the daughter he had

adopted and whom he loved only second to his wife. The distress on her face touched him deeply, for her suffering was for others … not herself. What a strong, *good* character Eve had! Without being in the least priggish, she seemed to do instinctively those things which were right … have no hankering after the things which were wrong. And she thought always of others before herself. She was without jealousy … without a trace of selfishness in her. How totally different from the child of his blood!

'My dear, don't worry too much about this,' he said as calmly as he could. 'It may all be for the best. At least it will save your poor old father a few precious pounds! We shall just have to hold up our heads and face the implications … or should I say facts? We'll do it together, Eve. With you to stand by me we shall come through this without any serious consequences. No doubt Lord and Lady Bainborough will be disappointed and put out, too. We shall have to get in touch with them.'

But as he spoke these words the telephone shrilled its warning in the hall, and Eve jumped to her feet.

'Suppose it is them?' she said.

'Answer it yourself, Eve. Say I am with your mother but will ring them back as soon as I can. Your mother must know the truth before anything else.'

Obediently, Eve ran out of the room and was in time to lift the receiver from Jenkins's hand.

'It's for Madame,' he said. But Eve nodded to him that she would take the call for her mother and the old butler disappeared back to the servants' hall.

'This is Eve Corderhay here. Who is speaking, please?'

How calm and cool her voice was, and how her heart thundered her true feelings!

'Oh, Eve, this is Lord Bainborough. I must speak to your father or mother at once. It's terribly important ... I don't know if you are aware of what has happened, but–'

'Yes, Lord Bainborough. We have just found Anne-Marie's note. Father is talking to Mother about it at the moment. I'm afraid she will be very upset.'

'Upset!' came the older man's voice. 'It's positively disgraceful, Eve. I'll give that young cub of mine the hiding of his life. His mother's having hysterics and the house is in an uproar. Do you know where they are at this moment? If you do, I'll fetch them back myself. I will not have Richard treating his mother so inconsiderately.'

Patiently, Eve waited until he had vented a little of his anger. Then she said:

'I'm afraid we are too late to stop them, Lord Bainborough. Anne-Marie must have left in the early hours of the morning. I think they will be on their way to Paris by now.'

Slightly subdued by Eve's calmness, Lord Bainborough said more quietly:

'Well, it's done then. Believe me, Eve, I'm sorry for your family, too. We shall all of us look such fools cancelling the wedding at the last minute like this. Who will let all the guests know? My wife isn't in a fit state to talk to anyone and I doubt if your mother will be, either.'

'You've nothing to worry about, Lord Bainborough,' Eve said evenly. 'I expect Mother has a list of the guests and I will telephone them all myself this morning. I've no doubt they will understand. After all, this isn't the first time two young people have run away from so much notoriety.'

'You're not countenancing their actions, I hope, young lady?'

For the first time Eve smiled.

'Indeed not, Lord Bainborough. They should have considered everyone else and, if they felt this way, have said so before. All the same, I'm sure our guests will take it quite well. After all, an elopement is rather romantic, isn't it?'

'Huh! Hadn't looked at it in that light. I suppose in a way it could turn out all right. Nevertheless, they'll be done out of the reception and they won't like it. Dare say the ladies have got new dresses for the occasion and so on.'

'Perhaps the reception could still take place?' Eve suggested on a sudden inspiration. This, after all, was what her mother had so looked forward to ... they could still decorate the house and carry on their entertainment exactly as planned, but omitting the wedding ceremony itself. The toasts to bride and groom could still be made even in their absence.

'That's a capital plan!' Lord Bainborough was saying eagerly. 'I must say that would relieve the situation immensely. But perhaps your father–'

'I'm sure he will agree with me,' Eve broke in. 'Mother has been looking forward to meeting all your friends and introducing you and your wife to ours.'

'Then may I pass this news on to my wife? I think she'll approve of the scheme. It's really a capital solution, young lady. Tell your father I'll ring him again later in the morning, or perhaps we might all meet for lunch and discuss the change of plans.'

'We should be glad if you would lunch with us ... and Lady Bainborough, of course,' Eve lied swiftly, thinking that nothing could be worse than having to arrange a lunch party on top of all this! But good manners still counted for something and it was what her father would have wished.

Having said good-bye to Lord Bainborough, Eve made her way back to the breakfast room. The door was closed and through it Eve could hear her mother and father talking … her mother's voice high-pitched and close to tears. She wondered if she should interrupt them and decided that it might, after all, be best to do so.

Her parents turned to face her as she came into the room, her father's expression serious and distressed, her mother's flushed and tearful. Neither of them spoke.

'I've just been talking to Lord Bainborough,' Eve said awkwardly. 'We both felt that it might be a good idea … if you agree, of course … to carry on with the reception and only cancel the wedding itself. In this way, if we are unable to contact any of the guests, they won't have come this distance for nothing. A car can be at the church to bring people arriving there straight back to the house … and at the same time it will solve the awkwardness of all the wedding presents people have sent. After all, it's customary not to send them if there's no reception, and they would all have to be packed and returned. What do you think, Father … Mother?'

Her father had been watching first Eve's face as she spoke, then his wife's, and it was clear that Antoinette was thrilled by this sudden reprieve. She had been so very stricken when he had told her that the 'party' was off. She was still so young at heart … so thrilled with such simple things, and this wedding had meant as much to her, who set such store by entertaining, as a birthday party to a small child.

He looked at his daughter gratefully.

'I think it's a splendid plan, Eve. That is if your mother agrees?'

'Agree?' Antoinette cried, flinging her arms round his neck impulsively. 'Oh, Jack ... it is wonderful! Of course, I shall be so bitterly disappointed not to be at Anne-Marie's wedding, but if she is happy, that is all I ask ... and that everything is right for our guests ... and Lord and Lady Bainborough. After all, they will be Anne-Marie's father- and mother-in-law and it is important they do not have a grudge against her or Richard. The poor darlings ... I ought to have guessed that it would be the ordeal for them. How selfish of me to make the plans without being certain they, too, wish for the *grande affaire!* An elopement ... it is after all, very romantic, is it not? I think now of those two children, flying together to Paris ... to be married in my own great city. It is where we have our honeymoon, Jack. You recall? How happy we were...'

Quietly, Eve slipped away, knowing that neither of them would notice her going. Their hearts were too taken up with one another to be unhappy or worried. And meantime there was so much for her to do.

As she went upstairs to her mother's

sitting-room, with its white-and-gold writing-desk, to find the list of guests, she felt as if one load, at least, was off her shoulders. There remained now for her another problem to solve ... one which she had not forgotten, but had had no time to consider until now ... Paul Johnson.

Anne-Marie had asked her, Eve, to send a telegram to him, but how could she do such a thing in cold blood? In her mind she could picture vividly the tall, broad-shouldered man who loved Anne-Marie, waiting at the Registrar's Office for his bride to come. She saw in her imagination the telegraph boy arriving with the impersonal orange envelope announcing that she would never come. She felt the impact of his shock on her own heart and saw the stricken look in those strangely forceful blue eyes. What would he do? What could he do but go away again and try to forget? How he'd hate Anne-Marie for hurting him in such a cruel way! How he must suffer in his heart and in his pride! And what of Anthony? Did Paul Johnson suspect the truth? How would he feel if he knew that now he could never claim his child as his own?

'I can't just send him a wire!' Eve whispered aloud. 'It isn't fair! I'll have to go up there myself ... try to break the news gently.'

But what excuse could she give for her departure at a time when there was so much to do? Two o'clock... Anne-Marie had said.

She would have to catch the eleven-thirty train to London at the latest … could not be back before four-thirty. Who would telephone to all the wedding guests …five hundred of them? Who would assist Antoinette with the flowers … the other preparations?

'What am I going to do!' she thought, torn between two duties that seemed to have equal claim on her time. Her hands twisted nervously together as she tried to think of a way in which she could carry out both of them. It was already ten o'clock. She would have little time now except to change and get to the station.

Suddenly a voice called her name… Louise. She had forgotten about Louise. Why had the girl not been at breakfast? She was so quiet and unobtrusive that people were apt to forget her presence in the house.'

Quickly she got to her feet and called Louise into the room. The girl's eyes were red with weeping and Eve looked at her anxiously.

'You know then, Louise?'

'I knew last night!' Louise whispered. 'I awoke when Anne-Marie returned and could not sleep again. Several hours later, I think it must be, I heard her moving about in her room. Then her door opened and I heard someone walking down the passage … softly … in bare feet, I think to myself. So I open my door and there is Anne-Marie with a suitcase in either hand. "Where are you going, Anne-Marie?" I asked her. She gave a funny little smile. "To Richard!" she said. "We are running away together to be married … today!" "But why?" I asked her, for I did not understand. She put down the cases and came over and look at me close to my face. "I don't suppose you do!" she said in such a queer, hard voice. "But I know what I'm doing, and I know, too, that you'd give anything in the world to be in my shoes. Wouldn't you? Wouldn't you?" I was frightened of the look she give me. I do not know why, but at this moment she seem to me to be bad … evil. I … I nodded my head. "You knew I loved him," I said. "But you took him from me!" She laugh, softly, but so cruelly, Eve. "Yes, I knew," she said. "That's why I did it! Now go back to bed … and don't dare tell a soul or I swear I'll kill you." Through her teeth she said these words and I am drenched in cold sweat. I am afraid … really afraid. I think perhaps she is a witch. It seems silly now, but, Eve … at the time, truly I believed she could do me harm. And this morning … I could not come down to break-fast with my eyes so swollen from crying. I know it is silly now to cry. It is all over … with Richard. But I suppose I had hoped until there was no more hope that something might happen … to stop the wedding. After she was gone I knew I could hope no longer.

So I weep for that … that it is really finished.'

'Yes; it is all over now, Louise,' Eve said gently. 'So you must forget all that has happened. I'm sure in your distress last night you imagined Anne-Marie to be … trying to hurt you. Imaginations are queer things, Louise … like the dark hours of the night … they can distort the truth. But that is beside the point. You *must* forget Richard. You will love other people far more worth while.'

As she spoke she wondered if she could ask this girl, who looked so tired and distraught, to help her. Then suddenly she realized that work would be the best thing to keep Louise's mind off herself.

'I need your help, Louise,' she said firmly. 'Do you feel well enough to do something for me?'

'For you I will do anything, Eve,' Louise said fervently. 'Always you have been so kind to me. I am truly your friend, Eve. Tell me what it is I am to do!'

Touched by the girl's obvious devotion, Eve said:

'I'm trusting you, Louise, because no one else must know where I'm going. But I must catch the eleven-thirty train to London. I can't tell you why because it betrays someone else … but I have to go. And now that there is to be no wedding ceremony … only the reception … the guests will have to be told. I shan't be home until tea-time and haven't a chance to do this. Mother won't have time, either. Do you think you can telephone or telegraph everyone for me? There are five hundred guests, but not quite so many phonecalls, as in some cases it is families who make up the numbers.'

'Of course I will do this, Eve. It will give me something to keep my mind from … *them*. Tell me only the names and telephone numbers and I will go to the little telephone room downstairs and begin!'

Thankfully, Eve gave the young girl all the information she required and left her to it. With barely a half hour left to catch her train, she hurried along to her own room to change into a neat black town suit and coat, hurried back down to the servants' hall to tell Jenkins that Lord and Lady Bainborough would be here to lunch, but she would be absent, and found the young gardener who acted sometimes as chauffeur.

'Will you drive me to the station, please, John?' she said. 'I've only five minutes left to catch my train. Do you think we can make it?'

He gave her a friendly grin.

'Might break the speed limit, but I'll do it, miss!' he said.

Exhausted, but triumphant, and underneath it terribly afraid of what she had to do, Eve found herself ten minutes later on the train to London to break the news to Paul.

CHAPTER 11

An hour and a half later Eve reached London. She had had no breakfast, and although even now she was too nervous and upset to be hungry, she forced herself to go to the station buffet and have a cup of tea and a sandwich. Then, with a little less than an hour before the time Anne-Marie had agreed to marry Paul Johnson, she took the Underground station to Gloucester Road. From there she walked to Mayburn Road, excusing her wish to prolong the coming interview by telling herself she needed the exercise!

Inwardly her whole being trembled at the prospect of breaking such news to the man who must even now be waiting the arrival of her sister. If only she had known where he was staying in London ... could have warned him before this moment! Would he be dressed in full wedding regalia or, since it was to be a civil ceremony with no guests, merely in a lounge suit? Would he have a best man? And what did a Registrar's Office look like? Would she find him easily?

Questions poured through her mind unanswered as she turned into Mayburn

Road and scanned the houses on either side. It was a wide, rather dingy street, filled with grey, depressing buildings. She wondered why Paul had chosen this place in the whole of London when there must surely have been more attractive places. Perhaps it was the only one he knew of.

Suddenly a gold-plated sign attracted her attention and with a little indrawn breath she read the words that told her she had come to her destination. The door was open as she looked up and she walked towards it, wondering if she should ring the bell or just walk in. Then she saw the notice telling visitors to go up to the first floor for the Registrar's Office, and obediently she started to climb the stairs.

'I wish I hadn't come!' she thought desperately. 'I wish I'd sent that wire. What on earth made me decide to do this? If only I could disappear!'

But no earth opened to swallow her up, and gathering the remainder of her courage together she forced herself to knock on the closed door. In an instant it swung open, and raising her face she saw Paul's anxious, eager look. She noted irrelevantly that he was, after all, in a lounge suit ... that he looked taller, broader even than she had remembered him ... and that he had taken hold of her ungloved hand in both his own.

'Why, it's Anne-Marie's sister!' she heard

his voice, deep, a little uncertain, but pleased. 'This is really a nice surprise. I hadn't supposed you would be able to come, too.' He paused and looked over her shoulder down the staircase as if expecting Anne-Marie to appear. 'She didn't come with you?' he asked. 'Is she coming on her own in a taxi?'

Eve swallowed, and drawing a deep breath she said:

'I came alone, Mr Johnson... I came to tell you something... Oh, I don't know how to say it. You haven't ... received a telegram?'

His grip on her hands tightened and Eve realized that, within his grasp, her hands were trembling.

'What are you trying to tell me Miss Corderhay?' he asked, his voice low, panicky, violent. 'A wire? Who from? You're not trying to tell me that–'

'She isn't coming!' Eve broke in miserably. 'Oh, I'm so terribly sorry! There was no way I could have let you know sooner. She didn't know where you were staying last night and this was my only chance to see you ... to tell you.'

He released her hands so suddenly that she nearly fell backwards. She had not known how much she was leaning on him for strength. She waited anxiously for him to speak, and when he did not she looked up at him and was deeply shocked by the violence of his expression. For a moment fear of him overcame her pity.

'So that's it!' he said in a low, furious voice. 'I suppose I might have known this would happen. A nice fool she's made of me, I will say! As a matter of fact, I guessed something of the sort, only like a fool I refused to believe my instinct, if you can call it that, because I didn't want to believe it. But I wasn't completely convinced by all her long protestations of undying love and devotion.'

His voice was full of scorn as he jerked out the words. Knowing that he must give vent in some way to his emotions, Eve remained silent and did not once interrupt him.

'Thought she'd fooled me, I suppose. Well, I doubted her story about what happened that day in Paris. It didn't make sense. I *knew* she wasn't in the hotel because I searched every damn' room in the place. She stood me up then and now she's done the same again. It's not often a woman gets the chance to make a fool of me twice, and I won't stand for it, I tell you. Where is she? I'll give her the biggest hiding she ever had! Where is she, I say?'

'In Paris by now!' Eve whispered. 'She eloped last night with Richard Bainborough!'

Her words shook him into a stunned silence. When at last he had realized their import his face suffused with brilliant angry red and his voice became so violent that even the man who was to have performed the ceremony came into the hall to see what was happening.

'Is there anything wrong, sir?' he enquired.

'Wrong?' shouted Paul. 'You silly dunderhead, of course there is! There won't be a wedding now. Do you hear me? So not get out of here and stay out!'

'He's too angry to know how rude he is being,' Eve thought compassionately. She gave the little man a weak smile, and, a little reassured, he disappeared back inside his office. He felt sorry for the young lady he presumed to be the bride. Whatever had happened, he was certain it was not her fault. All the same, Mr Johnson had seemed a nice enough gentleman, plenty of money, and he'd had the room filled with flowers, transforming the rather dreary, depressing little place where he performed so many dreary, depressing little weddings. It was a nice thought and not many other young bridegrooms had done so much for their future brides.

He shrugged his shoulders, knowing that it wasn't his affair ... not so long as they were off the premises by the time the next couple arrived at half past two. He sat back in his chair and listened without much success to the angry voices now raised in the hallway, unfortunately not sufficiently loud for him to detect their words.

'It's a rotten, degenerate way to behave!'

Paul was saying. 'Just what one might have thought of her type. Aristocracy you call yourselves, and yet you're all rotten. When first I met Anne-Marie I thought: "Here's someone different. She's simple, sweet, innocent ... the kind of girl a man would be proud to make his wife." I didn't find out until the other day what kind of home she came from. Then I gave her the benefit of the doubt. "They can't all be rotten," I thought. "There's still some decent ones about." But I was wrong. Upper classes ... the lowest of the low you should call yourselves!'

His voice was full of scorn, but this time he had gone too far. He had muddied the name of Corderhay and included her in his tirade against he old families of the country.

'It's a free country, of course,' she said, her voice icily cold and calm, 'so you're entitled to your socialist outlook. But you'll find out, as they will, that there are lots of decent people among the families belonging to the aristocracy, to use your own word. There are bad ones, too, just the same as there are good and bad in all the other classes. But you're too biased to be able to see it. You're not responsible for what you are saying ... just because Anne-Marie–'

'Your sister, isn't she? Well, I hope you're proud of her behaviour. Hadn't the courage to tell me how she felt last night. Answer that if you can. Why couldn't she say outright that she loved this chap she was engaged to … or that she preferred his money and social position? Is that it? Well, the laugh is on her, I dare say. I may not have much of a social position, because I had to work my way up. Money wasn't dropped into my lap… I worked for it, do you hear … and I've made a success. I'm good for quite a tidy sum and I've taken care to see it's well invested. So that's one laugh on her, isn't it? One against two. And I'll get even for that second one. You'll see! The day will come when I shall find a way to make her pay for this … or that precious family of yours.'

'Will you kindly leave my family out of it?' Eve cried angrily. 'They aren't responsible for what Anne-Marie has done. They are just as upset as you are.'

'Upset! I don't believe it. Marriage to the titled … isn't that what all your crowd think of as the height of attainment? As to character … that doesn't matter. Nor do they care about the moral outlook. Well, your wonderful parents brought their child up to be a pretty weak, unpleasant sort of woman, didn't they? And yet you say they aren't responsible! Perhaps they didn't bring her up … turned her over to a lot of nursemaids. Couldn't be bothered with their own flesh and blood and the hard work of rearing children. Shelve their responsibilities if they can pay someone else to take them on. Huh!'

It took quite a lot to rouse Eve's temper, but once aroused she could be almost as violent as this man before her.

'You!' she gasped. '*You* try to preach to me about morals!' She was so angry that for the moment words failed her.

'And why not?' he asked, his voice now deadly quiet. 'I've never done anything to be ashamed of.'

'Then you lack any sense of decency at all,' Eve said scathingly. 'And I'm sorry that I ever felt sorry for you. I'm glad Anne-Marie turned you down. I don't hold much brief for her, but now I don't think you're any better than she is. I'm sorry I ever came here ... I didn't want to come and I wish to goodness I hadn't. I hope I never have the misfortune to see you again.'

And before he could recover from his surprise she turned and ran down the stairs and out into the street. Mercifully, a taxi came cruising towards her and frantically she hailed it.

'King's Cross!' she told him, and slamming the door shut she buried her face in her hands and burst into tears. As they drove away from the house the driver saw Paul's large figure come running along the path, his arm waving frantically.

'Want to stop for the young man, miss?' he asked, viewing the huddled, weeping figure with bewilderment. Lover's tiff, of course.

'No! Go straight away ... quickly!' Eve said. 'Please! Whatever you do don't stop!'

'Just as you say, miss!' the driver said, accelerating obediently. 'All the same, it might be better to talk it over, don't you think ... if you'll pardon my saying so!' For he had seen that gold plate worded 'Registrar's Office' and hated to think of this young girl in tears on what should have been her wedding day.

'I don't want to talk to him!' Eve found herself replying, as she sought to control herself and her tears. 'He's perfectly horrible! I wish I'd never come, I ... I hate him!'

'They say as how hate is nearest thing to love,' the driver remarked philosophically over his shoulder. 'Shall I just drive around a bit until you feel better, miss?'

'I'll never feel better!' Eve said in a choked little voice. 'I know he was angry, but he had no right to say those things. It wasn't *my* fault!'

'Perhaps it wasn't altogether his,' said the driver, thinking of the young man's arm waving him to stop. 'These misunderstandings, well, I've had them with my missus ... still do sometimes, and we've been married more'n twenty years! Maybe you said some hurtful things, too.'

'I only said what was true!' Eve replied more calmly now.

'Then why not let me drive you back, miss? There's still time to change your mind. A lady's privilege, they say! After all he may not be so ready to forgive you another day.'

'What's so special about this day?' Eve asked, wiping away the last of her tears and trying to hide the traces of them with her powder-puff.

''Tisn't every day you'll be getting married … leastways, I hope not!' the driver said with Cockney humour.

'Married!' Eve said, feeling dangerously near to laughter now and a fresh outbreak of tears. 'I wasn't going to marry him. It was my sister … and she let him down.'

The driver took one hand off the wheel and scratched his head.

'Then what are you crying for?' he asked.

'I … I'm not crying,' Eve said untruthfully. 'And I don't know w … why I am. Why should I care what he says … what he thinks about us? I'll never see him again.'

The driver gave her a quick, knowing look.

'Sounds suspicious to me, miss, if I may say so. If you ask me, it should have been you getting married and not this sister of yours. I'd say you're the one that loves him all right!'

'Love him? Me?' Eve said in a choked little voice. 'That's just nonsense. You don't know … I was sorry for him … but I hate him now. As to marrying him, if he was the last man on earth–'

'You'd marry him if he'd have you!' the

driver broke in. 'I've heard them words before. When a young lady starts talking about him being the "last man on earth", then I knows just how they're really feeling. You see, miss, it's what my missus used to say to me when we had a bust-up in our courting days. "If you was the last man on earth, Jim," she'd say, "I'd never marry you" … and look at us … married twenty years and still as much in love as the day we got spliced.'

'No, it isn't true!' Eve said, but to herself, not to him. 'I couldn't love him … not even if there hadn't been any words between us today. Even if he hadn't said all those horrible things … about us … about Father and Mother … even if he didn't mean all that, I still couldn't love him. Not after what he's done … knowing he's Anthony's father.'

A deep blush spread to her cheeks and hurriedly her hands went up to cover them. The taxi-driver had thought that she, Eve, had been going to marry Paul … a man she scarcely knew … indeed, whom she had met for the first time last night. Yet it had seemed a longer acquaintance. Was this solely because she had known of his existence for over a year … discussed him with Denise … looked so many times at his photograph? Or was there some strange feeling of having known him before … years before … in an-other life, perhaps?

'No, that's fanciful and stupid!' she told

herself quickly. 'We have nothing in common ... nothing. He even despises all that I hold most dear! And he's selfish ... thinking only of himself and his hurt pride and never giving a thought to poor little Anthony, his son.'

His son! His little boy that she had held in her arms, loved and cared for. Had he realized he had a son when he poured those angry words at her just now? Or had Anne-Marie still not told him the truth? It seemed unlikely now that she could have done so. Only last night (how much longer ago it seemed!) she had told Eve she wished to keep it secret from him until after they were married ... so that she could be sure he had not married her for any other reason than that he loved her. Eve had seen her point ... appreciated this reasoning, and now, suddenly remembering those words, she realized that Anne-Marie had fooled her nicely. Paul Johnson did not know about his son last night, because it would not have suited her plans for him to be told. It would only have made him more than ever determined to marry her. And he was a pretty determined person. So Anne-Marie had begged her, Eve, not to mention Anthony *yet*.

She, Eve, might have told him today ... but, of course, it wouldn't matter any longer. Anne-Marie had realized that by the time Eve would see Paul she would herself be in Paris, married to Richard Bainborough.

How clever and subtle and deceitful Anne-Marie had been!

'And supposing I had told him?' Eve's thoughts ran on swiftly. He would have been even more hurt, disgusted, humiliated. It was as well that he didn't know the truth … need never know it now. He would start life over again, be a little bitter perhaps, but in time he would forget. He would have no living record of the past to remind him, As Eve would always have Anthony to remind *her*.

'At least I have the baby,' Eve told herself … 'his child!'

And as the thought passed through her mind she knew the truth. She could deny it to the taxi-driver, deny it to the whole world, but she could not deny it to herself. She did love him … in spite of all that he had done … of what he was … who he was. None of it mattered. She must love him no matter what crime he committed because that love was a part of herself beyond her control. It was a firm, solid fact, and even the knowledge that she could never really respect him, in view of what she knew of his past association with Anne-Marie, made no difference. She would still continue to feel that quickening of her heartbeats when she thought of him … heard his name … looked at Anthony. And for the rest of her life she must regret that Fate had given her this knowledge too late for her to have had a chance to alter their meeting. Perhaps if she had gone to Paris with Anne-Marie the Christmas before last ... but now it couldn't make any difference. Their paths would not cross again, and if they did there would only be enmity between them because of what had already happened.

Love! she thought, as the taxi wound its way through the London traffic, unnoticed by her. How often she had talked of this all-powerful emotion with Denise. Always she had known it existed. But in her mind she had never associated it with pain ... with unhappiness. She had had too idealistic a view of it ... too romantic an outlook. She knew better now. For Denise it might happen as it happened in books, but for her it had to come like this ... filled with bitterness, sorrow, regret and forever unfulfilled. And it had taken a London taxi-driver to see the truth where she had not understood it in herself.

Paul Johnson! How well she knew each line of his face ... each detail of that photograph she still possessed in her jewel-case! Was it possible she had loved him even then ... when first she had declined to throw the snap away? Was that why she had tried to excuse his behaviour to herself, saying that it must have been a misunderstanding with Anne-Marie that had caused him to break his word to her? She knew better now ... knew that Paul had spoken the truth when he said Anne-Marie had purposefully broken that appointment. For some reason of her own she had not wished to see him again ... even though she carried his child ... perhaps because she still hoped she might not have it and did not wish to be forced into marriage with a man she didn't love. Because she didn't love him ... *could not have done so.* She had only been physically attracted to him ... for had she loved him she could have married him; not once but twice had the opportunity occurred, and each time she had rejected it.

'I shall never understand Anne-Marie's motives,' Eve told herself. 'But she doesn't matter any more. Nothing matters now but Mother and Father and Anthony. I must go on living my life for them.'

'King's Cross, miss!' the driver said.

Eve pulled herself together and found the right fare in her handbag. She gave him also a substantial tip.

'You've helped me to understand ... part of what has happened,' she said to him shyly. 'And I'm grateful. You see, you were right only I didn't know it until you said so ... I do love him!'

'Then I hope it will come out right, miss!' he said sincerely. 'The missus and I will say a prayer or two for you. Funny what praying can do ... if you've got faith!'

'I'm afraid even prayers can't make any

difference,' Eve said gently. 'You see, there are circumstances that must always keep us apart. You've been very kind. And thank you!'

'Best of luck, miss, and don't give up hope. This missus and me will pray for you just the same.'

Afraid of the tears that started again to her eyes, Eve waved a hurried farewell and went quickly to the platform where an earlier train than she had hoped to catch was about to leave the station. She was lucky enough to get a carriage to herself and here she settled herself comfortably in a corner and gave herself up once more to her thoughts.

Soon she would be caught up in the whirl of activity that preceded tomorrow's events. She would be caught up again in the inevitability of life, but just for these few hours she could remain suspended in a dream-like trance that had no part on the earth. She could admit her love to herself, discover its effect on her, its causes, and gather her few memories of the man she loved to her heart before she locked them away for ever.

'I wish I could talk to Denise,' she thought. 'I think she might understand what I don't understand myself. I have no reason to feel this way about him ... no cause to love him. My first knowledge of him was unhappy ... my first meeting with him anxious and filled only with thoughts of Anne-Marie ... and today ... today he has revealed only the worst side of his character. He has been rude, bitter, and crude, too, in his tirade against a class of people to which he does not belong. He has betrayed the aggressiveness of someone suffering from an inferiority complex.'

Strangely enough, this realization made him seem suddenly more approachable ... younger. It brought him closer to her because she could begin to understand him better. He was successful now ... he had said so ... was rich, too. But there had been a time when he was neither of these things. Then, perhaps, he had resented the people better off than himself ... boys at school whose parents could afford football boots, pocket-money, extra coaching and other luxuries that no doubt his family had been unable to give him. He had had to work for everything he owned, and because of the hardships he had suffered he had been bitter about those to whom everything had been given.

'He is typical of so many people in this country at the moment,' Eve thought. 'And in a way he is right. There should be ... and nowadays there are ... nearly equal chances for any boy to have the best education. People of wealth like Father are being taxed out of existence. Anthony will go to public school because father will see to this before anything else, but will Anthony's son be as lucky? It'll depend on what Anthony can win for himself in the business world ... for Father won't be able to help him there. Nor shall I be of help to him then! We can only fit him up as best we can to make it possible for him to earn his living as Paul has had to do ... but without the help of his father's experience. I wonder if Paul realizes that had Anthony become his son in the eyes of the world he would inevitably inherit whatever business it is that Paul has built up so successfully.'

Did Paul realize that by giving his son a good start in life ... by leaving the money he had made to him ... he would merely be changing places with the people he despised ... making his son one of them? After all, it took only two generations to change the positions. The rich had become poor, and the poor in their turn become rich! There would always be people like Paul with brains and ability above others, beyond those of others, that would enable him to do better than the man beside him. Was he then to work all his life to secure the things he hadn't had in order to die and leave them to no one ... certainly not to his children? That would be useless, stupid and would destroy the incentive to work. So, granted that he would start his son with advantages, how would he reconcile himself to the idea that he now belonged to the well-to-do?

'Poor Paul!' she thought, with a rueful smile. 'There will be worse problems to face

238

than Anne-Marie ... when the time comes!'

Or perhaps he would not marry ... would not have other sons! Somehow it hurt her to imagine that he would have these things she could never have herself ... because of him. She would never marry now ... never be able to fall in love as she had sometimes dreamed of doing. It was not in her nature to love so lightly that she could dispense with it when she did not wish its presence. And second best would not be good enough. She was too idealistic. Jim and his missus might pray for her, but it must be in vain, for Paul would never love her ... and even if he did ... she could not marry him. There would always be the ghost of Anne-Marie between them ... and Anthony as a living reminder.

Anthony! she thought of the child again. He was growing into such a beautiful little boy ... golden-haired ... blue-eyed, like his mother, but with no trace yet of the man who would never know now was his father. Would he have Anne-Marie's character or would he inherit his father's determination and pride? Perhaps he would be like neither of them, but grow up with a personality and qualities all his own!

'It will be my job to watch over his development,' Eve thought suddenly. 'Nanny will soon be gone and then I shall be the one to administer discipline ... the discipline Anne-Marie never had!' She would have to fight her mother's tendency to spoil him just as she had always spoilt her little daughter. But her father would help ... of that she was certain ... and could any boy have a better example than Jack Corderhay? If only the years were not taking such a toll on him! Lately he had begun to show his sixty years and even while he remained a tall, upright, handsome and distinguished man, his sharpness had blunted and he no longer had his wonderful memory. Lately he had leaned more and more on Eve for help in estate affairs and asked her judgment... By the time Anthony was in his teens her father would be too old to be a companion for him ... too old to understand a boy's quick, fresh young mind.

And Paul ... who should have had the chance to help his son ... would not even know he lived. Only Eve would know ... and remember in the years to come ... that her brief association with him as the one unhappy romantic interlude in her life.

CHAPTER 12

Paul Johnson was driving in his two-seater Triumph coupé up the long drive that would lead him to Corderhay Park. He had not owned the smart grey sports car very long, and something satisfying about its power and neat lines equalled the satisfaction that at this moment in his life filled his being.

It was little over three months since he had been jilted by Anne-Marie Corderhay and sworn to her sister to have his revenge. The chance to get it had occurred far sooner than he had expected, and he was exhilarated by the thought that it was *his* money ... not Richard Bainborough's ... that would buy his revenge just as surely as it had bought him this powerful, beautiful car.

'I wonder if I'll see Anne-Marie ... or her sister!' he thought, as he slowed down a little where the drive had roughened and might send up a stone and spoil the shiny new surface of his coupé. 'And I wonder if either of them will recognize me ... publicly, or pretend that they haven't seen me before.'

He saw suddenly a man in breeches and rough shooting-jacket crossing the grass parkland. He had a gun hooked over one arm and a leather game-bag slung across his back.

'Gamekeeper ... or perhaps the bailiff!' Paul decided, and on a sudden impulse, he pulled the car to a halt and climbed out of the door. No car ever seemed to have a doorway large enough to take his height comfortably, although there was plenty of room inside for his long legs and broad shoulders.

He had decided after all not to go straight to the house. How much more convenient to get the gamekeeper to show him round the estate first and try to pump him for a few details? He would probably get an unbiased view of the place and hear a few of the snags to this great estate he intended to make his own. For it was only natural that the vendor would crack it up to make a good sale.

Paul had already decided to take the place ... whatever it was like. He had never for one moment imagined last time he had gone into the big stone house that one day it would be up for sale ... and that *he* would come to live there. Or if he didn't live there ... at any rate to own it. How nicely Fate had played into his hand ... affording him so neat an opportunity to take his full revenge on the family he so disdained and disliked! Nevertheless, although he would buy it, it would be at the price he felt it was worth ... and he intended to spend this afternoon assessing that worth. Not even for the satisfaction of revenge would he let himself be worsted in a bargain ... certainly not by a Corderhay!

He walked with long, easy strides across to the gamekeeper, who remained still in his tracks once he had noticed Paul's tall figure coming towards him.

'My name is Paul Johnson,' he introduced himself. 'I've come to look over Corderhay Park with a view to buying it. Helton and Sons gave me an order to view.'

'Yes, of course. Good morning! I mean

good afternoon!' the old man said, a little shyly but politely. Paul noted that he had a cultured voice, but this he assumed to be reasonable for a bailiff if not a gamekeeper. 'Perhaps I could show you round?'

'That's what I was hoping!' Paul said quickly. 'I thought I'd like to see the grounds first ... get the feel of the place, if you know what I mean.'

'You're very wise, Mr Johnson,' his companion said. 'The most beautiful view of the house can be had from the south meadow beyond the paddocks. You've come at the best time of the year. Spring seems to bring out all the beauty of the place, if you know what I mean.'

Paul wasn't sure he did know, but he liked the old man, whom he judged to be in his sixties. A friendly, simple likable sort of fellow, he thought.

'You work here?' he asked, as they fell into step and started walking across the parkland.

The old man's blue eyes twinkled.

'Well, in a way, I suppose I do. Been here all my life, of course, and my father before me. Naturally it'll be a great blow to see the house change hands after so many centuries.'

'I understand your loyalty to your employer,' Paul said. 'Nevertheless, I gathered that one of the conditions of sale is that all the family employees on the estate are to be kept on, the cottages to remain their property, and so on. The family moving, therefore, won't affect you personally.'

The old man gave him a queer sideways glance and then his face broke into a mischievous smile.

'Oh, I shall be about the grounds, I dare say! That is if you or whoever takes over the place will permit it. I'm past doing very much now; I'm getting on in years, but I still enjoy a days' shooting. I shall be living at the Lodge, you know. You maybe have noticed it as you turned into the drive. A nice enough little house.'

'I'm afraid I didn't see it,' Paul admitted. 'I was rather anxious to see the big house, so I wasn't paying much attention. I gathered that the Lodge wouldn't be included in the sale.'

'Rather a large number of conditions attached to the sale one way and another,' the old man admitted. 'Still, there are certain obligation on any large estate owner … to see that his retainers are not the sufferers by his own misfortune.'

'That's a very decent gesture,' Paul assented. 'I gather, then, that this Mr Corderhay has been a kind employer?'

Again a smile lit up the blue eyes, but Paul did not see it.

'He has always done his best, and that is all any man can do!' he murmured.

'And his family?' Paul prompted. 'I understand there are two daughters.'

'Indeed, yes! Very attractive girls ... both of them–' He broke off to open the gate into the paddocks, and for the next fifteen minutes was busy showing Paul the stables, saddle room and trophy room.

'I hope, if you buy the place, Mr Johnson, you'll be able to fill the stables again. The last hunter was sold just over a year ago and the stables seem empty without a horse around. You ride of course?'

'Not very well,' Paul admitted. 'I've never had much opportunity to do so. However, I may well take it up. There is good hunting around here?'

Hunting remained the topic of conversation until they reached the south meadow and the old man stopped talking to point across the field to the house. Paul drew a deep breath, for here indeed was beauty. A long, sloping lawn carried the eye up towards the golden-yellow daffodils that were scattered thick as a carpet along the whole length of the big stone house. Looking upwards, Paul noted the perfection of the ancient architecture ... the soft, harmonious colour of the sandstone from which it had been built, the great square slabs of sandstone that made the roof.

A sudden noise, which was too far away for the two watching men to hear, sent a white cloud of pigeons up from the roof to fly around the wide chimney-stacks and settle once more in the sunshine. The whole effect was one of peace and harmony, and for the first time since he had considered buying the property Paul's thoughts went, not in spite but in pity, to the man who had owned all this ... and must leave it.

The older man must have noticed his emotion, for he said softly:

'I see you appreciate my home, young man.'

Paul swung round, his handsome young face flushing a deep red.

'*Your* home! You mean ... *you* are Mr Corderhay?' he gasped.

'Yes. I'm sorry I didn't mention it sooner, but you assumed me to be someone else and some imp of mischief made me keep up the pretence. It was very discourteous of me, I'm afraid. I do apologize.'

'The apology is mine, sir,' Paul said awkwardly, feeling like a small boy covered in shame and confusion.

'Very understandable mistake...' the old man was saying. 'I do look rather a tramp in these clothes. My wife is always telling me I should throw them away. But truth to tell, I'm far too comfortable in them to dream of doing such a thing!'

Now it was the older man who was behaving like a small boy confiding some misdeed, but quite without repentance, and Paul felt his heart warming towards the man he had expected to dislike. His emotions so confused him that he was quite at a loss for words and could think of little else but the fact that this man was treating him as an equal and with great courtesy, and that he had a quiet humour and simplicity that had found instant understanding in his own heart. Paul was not really vindictive by nature, but he suffered from the remnants of an inferiority complex. It was not that he had ever felt inferior in himself, but he knew his background to have placed him very low in the social scale, and while he was never anything but proud of his parents, he had moved into a higher social circle through his success in business, and here he continually felt himself to be at a loss.

Other people did not notice his 'inferiority', for his speech was cultured and his manners always excellent, but they sometimes mistook the resulting aggressiveness and considered him to be a proud, rather hard personality. Proud he certainly was, and knew this fault in himself. An attack on his pride could reduce his otherwise immovable control over his feelings to a childish display of bad temper. For, like a lot of men who kept their emotions under iron control, when his temper was a roused it was violent and not easily calmed.

It was pride, therefore, and not vindictiveness that had brought him here today.

Since the day he was to have been married he had ridden the wave of his bitterness without stopping to think of its real cause. He had sworn to have his revenge on Anne-Marie and her family, because he had believed them to be rotten in every sense of the world. Truth, loyalty, dependability had been qualities he had always tried to cultivate and which he admired in others as much as their strength of character and purpose. They signified to him the real meaning of the words 'a decent fellow'. Anne-Marie's behaviour had shown her to have none of these qualities, and he had blamed her background, because since boyhood he had resented the advantages given to the sons of the rich ... regardless of their worth or ability to appreciate and make the best use of these advantages. Paul had had to work for everything he possessed, and, only human, he had disliked reaching the top to find himself, after years and years of hard work and toil and self-sacrifice, only on the same level as the young men who had possessed all that he had won since birth.

The war had, to a certain extent, done away with these useless resentments, and he had frequently met and made friends with men he had expected to dislike. He had found them to possess great courage and unswerving devotion to duty and he had realized that after all there were good and bad in every class of people. Not all the wealthy titled young men in the country were wasters, drunkards or morally degenerate. On the whole, he had come up against every few of such worthless men during the war years.

But he had not entirely overcome the prejudices which he realized by the time war was over he possessed. He had not known when he met Anne-Marie in Paris, what sort of home she came from, but it would have made no difference to him anyway, since for the first time in his life he had found himself completely under a woman's spell ... a spell which he had wondered sometimes of late was perhaps weaved around him with threads that were purely physical. At any rate he had never yet in his life known a woman who attracted him as did the golden-haired, blue-eyed, sparkling Anne-Marie. He ceased to care in the first hour of their meeting what she was ... who she was. He knew only that he had to make her his wife ... possess that tantalizing slim young body and make it all his own.

It had been a bitter blow indeed when she failed to turn up at their rendezvous. At first he had refused to accept the fact that it was intentional, but in the long hours that followed he slowly realized that she hadn't meant to come, even although she had known he had overstayed his time in Paris purely on her account and that his business might be suffering badly owing to his absence from it in England. When morning came and still she had not troubled to telephone or explain, he faced the truth and his pride flared up in the usual violent temper.

He had flown back to England, determined to forget her in an orgy of hard work, and had nearly succeeded in doing so when he had come upon her photograph in that old *Tatler*. Then he had known that he must see her once again ... at least ... to find out the truth. He had driven down to Corderhay Park with little hope that she would have some explanation to offer him ... that she was still interested in him. When her sister had told him that she believed Anne-Marie to be in love with him, his surprise had been equalled only by the fierce thrill that shot through his body.

As soon as he saw Anne-Marie again he had fallen once more a victim to her physical beauty and charm. Impulsively he had begged her then and there to marry him, and felt her slim, delicate little body stiffening in his arms. It had taken him two hours to talk her round ... to talk her out of marrying the fellow she admitted openly she did not love. He could not understand her sudden withdrawal, but he had not stopped to question it then. Nothing mattered at that moment but that she should agree to marry him ... to meet him in London the following day ... and become his wife.

When at last she had agreed to do so her surrender was complete and she had returned his kisses and embraces with equal passion. Exultantly he had driven back to London, and late though it was, started to make plans for the following day.

In a whirl of excitement and anticipation he had made all the arrangements, sparing nothing for his future bride. At his hotel he accumulated expensive jewellery, presents, clothes, flowers, air tickets to Spain for their honeymoon, sending telegrams and cables as if they were postcards to ensure that everything would move evenly and perfectly.

Exhausted, but triumphant, he had arrived at the Registrar's Office fully an hour before time and settled down to wait, with ever-increasing impatience, for his bride.

It was small wonder, therefore, that when Eve arrived in her place to say Anne-Marie would not be coming after all … that she had married the other fellow instead … he suffered all the effects of acute anticlimax and thoroughly lost his temper. He had not fully regained it until this moment when he found himself talking to Anne-Marie's father.

Paul must have been lost in his thoughts for some time, his eyes still on the big house but unseeingly. The older man did not interrupt those thoughts, but remained quietly looking at the home he must so soon leave … and at the young man who might be its

251

new owner.

Presently Paul turned to him with an apology.

'I'm taking up far too much of your time, sir,' he said, using the deferential title unconsciously.

'Far from it!' Jack Corderhay said pleasantly. 'I think it is good sometimes to reflect a little in silence. Nowadays everyone seems to hustle and bustle and wear themselves out, never finding time for spiritual communion... I don't mean that in its religious sense ... but communion with self, if you understand me. I was always pointing this out to the girls when they were children in that little verse, "What is this life if full of care, We have no time to stand and stare!"'

Paul smiled.

'I'm afraid the tempo of living has increased a bit in the last few years,' he said. 'Perhaps the war accounts for it. We always seemed to hurry over everything in the Services.'

'You were in the Army?' Jack Corderhay asked, as they strode slowly towards the largest of the farmhouses an acre or two distant from the house.

'Commados!' Paul said. 'Don't know why I chose to be in that branch particularly ... probably because there was lots of action and I'm rather an active person.'

'You were decorated?' his companion

252

asked, for he felt certain that this rather unusual young man had courage. It showed in the firm lines of his jaw and the determined expression so often to be glimpsed on his face.

'As a matter of fact, I was. D.S.O. and the M.C. Luck, of course. That I happened to be noticed, I mean. Plenty of other chaps did far better things but hadn't the luck to be seen doing them.'

'Your father must be proud of you, my boy,' Jack Corderhay said thoughtfully, half his mind considering what little John might have done had he lived...

'My father is dead,' Paul was saying. 'My mother, too.' And, not quite certain what made him say such a thing, he added: 'She was a lady's maid. My father worked as a mill-hand for years. Both of them were ambitious ... for me. They wanted me to have a better start in the world than they had had. They felt this was only possible by giving me a better education. So every penny that could be spared was used to send me to a good school. When I was eighteen I had had very nearly the best education a boy can get in this country ... and after that I had to make my own way. It's been a constant source of bitterness to me that when they died I was still not very far up the ladder. I would have liked them to...'

He broke off awkwardly, realizing that he

had been about to boast of his present afflu-
ence to a man who presumably was penni-
less.

Jack Corderhay had been watching Paul
closely and listening to this outburst with
interest. What a dynamic, queer kind of
fellow this was! One would have thought
him to be a gentleman ... in the old sense fo
the word, of course, for nowadays there
weren't supposed to be any! Yet in fact his
breeding had been on the least importance.
But he was proud ... and although Jack
Corderhay felt he was a little twisted somewhere inside himself, he liked and respected
this self-made man. If he had a son ... if
John had lived ... he would have been proud
to think he could make of himself what this
young man had done. And he must have
made a good deal of money if he were
contemplating buying Corderhay Park.

'You know, I hope you do buy the place,'
he said, following his own train of thought.
'I think you deserve it... Corderhay Park, I
mean. And you've got he qualities it takes to
run an estate like this these days. Believe
me, it isn't easy. Taxes are the very devil!
And everything is desperately hard to get.
Masses of forms to fill in every time a
cottage needs a slate or two replaced and all
that sort of thing. Fact is the Government
don't want you to succeed. It takes grit to
withstand their pressure, and I'm too old a

man to fight them any longer.'

'I ... hadn't thought of it ... quite like that...' Paul admitted awkwardly. 'As a matter of fact, I had other reasons ... for wishing to buy the place.' 'Reasons that no longer exist,' he thought in bewilderment.

'Getting married?' Jack Corderhay asked with a smile.

Paul shook his head violently.

'I shall never get married!' he said. 'I don't think a great deal of women, to be frank!'

'That is because you've been unfortunate in your choice so far,' Jack Corderhay said quietly. 'Of course, I'm a little biased in favour of the ladies, I admit. I've been married forty years and am still as much in love with my wife as on the day I married her. She's a very wonderful person. But apart from her there is also my daughter, Eve. I think she has one of the finest natures I know, and yet withal she is one of the most feminine of women ... pretty in a graceful, quiet way, too. Unfortunately, I think she holds the same view about your sex as you do about hers. All the same, she was born to be a wife and mother, and I live my life in daily hope that she will one day meet the right man.'

'All right ... granted so far ... although I don't know much about this Eve and have never met your wife. But what about your other daughter,' Paul said to himself. And aloud:

'You have another daughter, also?'

He regretted the spite behind his remark when he saw his companion's face grow suddenly lined and unhappy.

'Ah, yes, Anne-Marie!' he said. But he would not commit himself to any personal remarks other than to say: 'She's married, you know. She doesn't live at home any more, so we don't see a lot of her.'

'And you don't really like her,' Paul thought. 'You know better than I what she is really like. It's Eve whom you love ... and respect. Yet surely she is the one whom you adopted?'

'I have a little boy, too!' Jack Corderhay said suddenly, a smile lighting up his face instantly making him look ten years younger. 'He's a fine little chap ... almost a year old now. He's not really our own baby, of course. We adopted him ... but we feel already as if he was ours. He's really incredibly advanced for his age ... or at least Eve tell us it is so. But, of course, she idolizes him. Satisfies the maternal instinct in her, I dare say. You know, I'd like you to meet Eve. And the boy. You must come and have tea with us. It's about time for tea and you can see the house afterwards.'

For a moment Paul did not speak because emotion prevented any words he might have said. He knew now all too clearly that he could not go through with this. Blindly, stupidly, he had condemned Anne-Marie's family who in all reasonableness could not be held responsible for her actions. After all, she was a grown woman and not a child. And it was her family … this nice old man and the wife he adored … the strange dark girl he had met whom the old man so respected and loved … the curly, fair-haired little boy who had enchanted him the last time he had come to this house when he had met him at the bottom of the stairs … these innocent people whom he would cause to suffer, not Anne-Marie, who had already left her home.

He drew a deep breath and said quickly while he had the courage:

'I would very much like to have had tea with you, sir, but as a matter of fact I don't feel I should do so. You see, I've already decided not to buy the place. Therefore it would be taking up your time to no purpose.'

Jack Corderhay was looking at him aghast.

'Not buy it? You mean you don't like the estate?' he asked.

'Indeed, no, sir. I think it looks perfectly beautiful. I wouldn't want you to think that. It's just that … that–' He broke off, not knowing how to extricate himself from this appalling position.

'You mean the price?' Jack Corderhay said awkwardly. 'That surely cannot bother you at this stage? I assure you, if I can find the right person to step into my shoes, I shall not quibble about the price. As a matter of fact we have had several very generous offers already, but neither my wife nor myself, nor Eve, could bear the thought of such people living in our home. We turned them down. It may seem a little stupid perhaps, but I have had the feeling for some time that someone would come along whom we should all feel was the "right" person … someone who would appreciate the place and not want to change it too much–'

He broke off, looking at Paul anxiously.

'But I don't see how you can feel that way … about me, sir. You've only known me a matter of hours … and I don't even come from your … your set.' It wasn't what he had meant to say, but the words spilled out without control.

'Perhaps it is because of your … set, as you call it!' Jack Corderhay said thoughtfully. 'I have always admired courage and enter-prise. You may be a Socialist, but you have courage and determination … otherwise you could never have got where you have in the world in such difficult times. You have had to work to get there … now you deserve your reward. I should like to think that Corderhay Park would give you the things you never had as a boy … the background … spiritual completion … and the same great happiness it has always given me.'

'You are very generous, sir!' Paul said, his

blue eyes glowing with a bright light. 'But all the same ... I ... I don't know what I should do if I did live here. Of course I haven't seen the house except from the outside... The details I have of it ... it's very large. And I live alone. It hardly seems right that...'

'My dear boy,' Jack Corderhay said, putting a hand on his shoulder. 'You must forgive me if I'm talking like a father to a son, but I must say this. You will get married ... I'm convinced of it. Then you will raise a family, and believe me, there is no more perfect place for childhood than here at Corderhay Park. You will be able to give your children all those advantages you missed and which in your heart you already wish them to have, just as your father wished them for you and tried to give you as far as he was able. Try to rid your mind of those socialistic ideas you have. You said that you have no right. Of course you have the right. You worked for it and you've earned it. You have far more right in that sense than I have had. Don't let yourself believe that it's wrong for there to be two worlds ... the rich and the poor. Because if they cease to exist men will cease to work. It is only the thought of bettering oneself and giving one's children a better start than one had oneself that keeps a man going ... working ... as he should work. It is the human element that will destroy the present Government. There

259

must be a rich and a poor ... because there will always be men like you who will work harder and better and longer hours than the men beside them ... because they are ambitious. It is ambition that has made our country what it is ... and the fact that we are simple people at heart and don't ask for the impossible. Don't think I'm anti-socialist. As a matter of fact, I think the party have done a lot of good. There shouldn't be slums and unemployment and poverty. I think that State medicine, when it has settled down, will be a wonderful thing if properly controlled and handled. I think too ... or am beginning to think ... that it is wrong for the titled and the rich to receive the position of authority and importance just because their fathers before them held those same rights. I think it is wrong to pass on responsibility regardless of whether a man is fit to have it or not. He should have to prove his worth in fair competition with the next man before they can be his. But a lovely home ... money ... education ... these things a father should be able to give his children because he has worked hard in order to do so.'

'He's right!' Paul thought. 'This man whom I called degenerate and useless and every other foul name I could think of. He's right and decent and fair ... everything that I would like to be. I can respect him ... look up to him ... learn from him ... something

I've never thought to do from a man of his upbringing.'

'My mind is a little confused,' he said at last. 'I'm afraid you've shown me an entirely new outlook on many of the problems that have puzzled me. But it can't alter my reasons for not wishing to buy the place. It hasn't really anything to do with its size or the other excuses I made. I just find that … that I couldn't be happy here.'

Jack Corderhay gave the younger man a look of deep sympathy. It was curious how much he had taken to the fellow … how much, too, the boy seemed to need help. He was a bundle of complexes and apparently none too happy. But its present cause mystified him. No man, seeing his goal in sight, should feel that he would be unhappy there. Unless, of course, he knew he would be out of his depth in such surroundings. But that would not apply to this pleasant, cultured young man at his side. He would settle down all right … grow up with the place…

'Of course, it isn't for me to advise you,' he said. 'I suppose I'm really least qualified to talk, since I can so easily be accused of salesmanship.'

'Don't think I think that!' Paul said quickly. 'I know how you must feel … how you must be hating all this. It must be heartbreaking to have to show a lot of stupid people over your home, knowing that they–'

He broke off, biting his lip, and stared down at his shoes.

'He's sorry for me!' Jack Corderhay thought. 'He doesn't like the idea of taking it away from me.' Such considerations warmed his heart and confirmed that strange bond of understanding he felt was between them.

'Of course I shall hate leaving in many ways,' he said firmly. 'But I've already said that I should only sell to someone I liked and respected. As to going, well, I'm getting old, my boy. I feel that I've earned a rest ... and my wife, too. The Lodge is a very charming little house. It has every comfort and it should be both easy and economical to run. We shall be able to keep our cook and butler, and Eve, also, will be there to help run the little house. There will be a great load off my shoulders and I fancy we shall be able to relax a little in our old age as we could never do at the big house. In some ways I am even looking forward to it. Now ... before we say any more ... let me persuade you to come back to tea. After tea I shall show you the house, and I know you will be forced to reconsider your decision. I shall be most distressed if you will not do me this honour. My wife is away for the day, but my daughter, Eve, is home, and we shall all have tea in the library together.'

Paul drew a deep breath. He could not refuse in face of such courtesy ... and in an

odd way he didn't want to. There was something he had to do ... an apology he must
make to Eve ... to whom he had been so
rude. Whatever the outcome of the house, he
could not leave happily until he had righted
the wrong he had done both to her and to her
father, in thought and words if not deed.

'Very well, sir, I should like to have tea
with you,' he said. 'I appreciate your
invitation, and I should be very pleased to
meet your daughter Eve.'

CHAPTER 13

In the beautiful old library, with its book-
lined walls, Paul sat opposite his host,
listening with only half an ear to the old
gentleman's reminiscences. The butler had
answered the bell which Jack Corderhay had
rung and been instructed to serve tea for
three and to ask Miss Eve to join them.

But it was not of Eve Paul was thinking.
Instead he was searching his heart to
discover why it was that this room ... which
was very familiar, to him in every detail
since here he had waited so impatiently for
Anne-Marie to join him ... evoked no sad or
bitter memories.

'I ought to feel *something!*' he thought

uncertainly. For here it was he had last held Anne-Marie in his arms, heard her sweet, bell-like voice telling him she loved him ... would marry him. Here that he had suffered such agonies of impatience after Eve had gone off to telephone to the girl he loved and whom he had believed loved him.

But, try as he might he could feel nothing but a quiet, mellow peace and a deep sense of pleasure in the gentle, soothing antiquity of the room.

'I really spend more time in this room than anywhere else,' Jack Corderhay's voice broke in on Paul's thoughts and faded away again.

'I too, should spend a great deal of time here,' Paul agreed in his mind. Here a man could come to sort out his problems and relax after the day's work ... escape a little from the hurried tempo of life. In here life stood still.

But he knew a moment later that life never did stand still. It merely gave the impression of doing so, for the door opened suddenly and a tall, dark girl came into the room and moved across towards her father. Her glance passed over Paul and then, recognizing him, she stopped dead and a swift, bright colour rushed to her cheeks. She stood there staring at him as he rose slowly to his feet, wondering whether he should hold out his hand or not.

Jack Corderhay, however, seemed quite unaware of anything unusual in Eve's behaviour. He had given his daughter a welcoming smile and said now, pride evident in the tone of his voice:

'This is my daughter, Eve. Eve, this is Mr Johnson. He is a prospective buyer of Corderhay Park.'

Paul saw the girl give her father a quick, nervous glance and then her eyes came back to his face, the colour draining away from her cheeks, leaving her chalky pale.

'I see,' was all she said, and her voice so low that Paul barely detected her words.

'Mr Johnson is having tea with me and I hope you will join us, Eve,' her father said. 'Come and sit down by me.'

She remained standing, and with her eyes still on Paul she said quietly:

'You really must excuse me, but I have a lot to do. Anthony—'

'Be blowed to the child!' Jack Corderhay broke in, laughing. 'You spend all your time in his company nowadays, Eve, and I'm jealous of the little rascal. Surely you can spare your old father a few minutes?'

Paul noticed instantly how her face changed as her emotions swept away from him and her surprise at finding him here to consideration of her father. She was over at his side now and her voice soft and gentle as she said:

'Of course I'll stay if you feel like that

about it, Father. I hadn't realized I'd been neglecting you.'

'Nonsense! I was teasing you!' Jack Corderhay said. 'All the same we would be glad of your company, my dear. It's always nice to have a pretty woman to pour out the tea, isn't it, my boy?'

'I seldom have that privilege,' Paul said evenly. 'So it would be a welcome change for me to have the pleasure of your company, Miss Corderhay.'

But to his intense irritation she ignored him completely and sat down beside her father, her face turned away from Paul. He had expected her to give him a pretty cold reception. Nevertheless, her silence made him feel strangely boorish and awkward. Acting on a sudden impulse, he said to his host:

'Your daughter and I have met before, Mr Corderhay. I'm afraid I was unpardonably rude to her at our last meeting, so I shall quite understand if she would prefer not to remain in my company!'

'Met before?' Jack Corderhay repeated in a voice of surprise.

Eve looked quickly at Paul and away again.

'We have … mutual friends … in London,' she said quickly.

Her father gave an embarrassed little cough, not quite sure how to extricate himself from his surprising situation.

Paul stepped into the breach.

'I hope your daughter will accept the apology which I owe to her,' he said. 'I'm afraid I have little excuse except to say that I was rather put out by other matters when we met, and I wasn't altogether answerable for my behaviour.'

'Well, that's a fair apology, eh, Eve?' her father said. 'I'm sure you'll accept it, won't you?'

'Yes, Father,' Eve said. And to Paul: 'I quite understand. Let's not say any more about it.'

'This proves her father doesn't know what has been doing on!' Paul thought grimly. 'And Eve doesn't want him to know. I suppose she has been shielding that sister of hers. Funny sort of set-up.'

'Are you … seriously interested in the place?' Eve was asking him, the tone of her voice suggesting that she suspected he might have other motives for being here.

Paul was saved a reply by his host, who broke in, saying:

'That's a leading question, Eve. And a seller must never try to talk a prospective buyer into showing his hand. It's the best way of making sure he doesn't decide to have it!' His blue eyes twinkled. 'Fact is, I'm hoping he will have it, Eve. He's the first person I've *wanted* to live here!'

'That's very good of you, sir!' Paul sincerely. 'But I haven't made up my mind yet…'

'Of course not! You haven't even seen the house. But I know you'll like it. Somehow I'm sure you will feel it's your kind of place. Don't you think I'm right, Eve?' he appealed to his daughter.

Eve bit her lip ... a nervous gesture which Paul did not fail to observe, thinking: 'She doesn't like me. I wonder why? After all, it wasn't my fault her sister didn't marry me. And I have apologized for being a bit rude the last time we met!'

'I imagine what *we* feel doesn't matter, Father,' she said in her slow, quiet voice. 'It depends entirely on what Mr Johnson feels. But since you've asked my opinion, I would suggest that perhaps the house is a little large for ... for a bachelor.'

'That was a sly little dig!' Paul thought, feeling something within him answering the challenge. 'Damned if I'll let her get the better of me in an exchange of words.'

'Eve, that's rather a personal kind of remark to make.' Her father reproved her quickly, surprise in his voice, as if he never expected anything but the height of good manners from his daughter. Paul felt a moment's sympathy with the older man. After all, he didn't know the facts and he'd cracked up this favourite daughter so much, it must be somewhat distressing to have her behaving so peculiarly.

'That's quite all right!' he said smoothly. 'I

am a bachelor and I expect to remain one, but surely that does not prohibit me from having a large house if I wish.'

'Perhaps not?' Eve said. 'It's a free country. But I imagine your political beliefs would not permit such a waste of space. You're are a Socialist, aren't you?'

Paul was saved a reply by the timely entrance of the butler with tea. The three of them remained silent while Eve poured out from the Crown Derby china teapot. Both men noticed the trembling of her hands and wondered at its cause.

'What has upset her?' her father was asking himself. 'I've never known Eve like this before!'

'I suppose she's got good reason to be angry with me!' Paul was considering. 'All the same, I *did* apologize!'

The silence between them might have remained indefinitely had it not been for the precipitate entry of young Anthony and his nanny.

They burst into the room, the child first on all fours, the old woman hurrying after him, wringing her hands.

'Oh, Miss Eve!' she said. 'He would come in here after you. When I tried to take him upstairs he kicked and screamed and made such a to-do I was afraid he might have hysterics. I'm ever so sorry for interrupting you like this.'

'It's all right, Nanny. He can have tea with us,' Jack Corderhay said, as Eve stooped to pick up the child. 'Miss Eve will bring him up to the nursery later.'

As the old woman disappeared he turned to his guest and said:

'I so hope you won't mind, Mr Johnson? I'm afraid the child is a bit too much for the old woman now. She was my wife's nanny, you know, and is really getting on a bit.'

'I'm delighted!' Paul said, for he loved children and the mischievous, curly-headed little fellow had already taken his fancy when last he'd seen him.

As if sensing his approval, Anthony struggled off Eve's lap and, pulling away from her restraining arms, went crabwise across the floor towards Paul, pulled himself up by his trouser-leg and clambered onto his knee.

Delighted, Paul bounced him up and down for a bit, gave him his watch to listen to and brought loud chuckles from the baby's lips.

'You're a fine little chap, aren't you?' Paul said, with a grin. 'Could I give him a lump of sugar, Miss Corderhay?'

'Gobbum … gobbum!' Anthony said.

To Paul's surprise, Eve was smiling when she met his gaze.

'He understands far more than you think!' she said, in a new friendly voice. '"Gobbum" means "eat", you know. I don't suppose one lump will hurt him.'

'She's herself again now!' Jack Corderhay was thinking, with relief. And Paul:

'What a queer mixture this girl is! A minute ago she was haughty and cold … now … well … she's really a pretty girl when she smiles!'

He watched her covertly as the three of them talked to and about the baby, and he noted how her eyes seemed to take on a new depth and light, her cheeks a brighter colour. Even her voice became warm and sweet and strangely attractive to the listener as she proudly described Anthony's latest exploits or something funny or clever that he had done or said.

His glance strayed from her face to the child's, noticing the contrast of her dark colouring to the bright golden fairness of the baby.

'Wonder what seems so familiar about the child's face!' he thought. 'Reminds me of someone … but I can't place whom!'

He forgot the baby once more as Eve's laugh filled the room with brightness, causing him to look quickly back at her face.

'Never really noticed it before … but she's very attractive!' he told himself … and a moment later was wishing that this pleasant little tea-party need not end so soon. But a few minutes after the thought had crossed his mind Eve stood up, lifted the child into her arms, and said:

'I expect you and Father wish to talk business. I'll take Anthony up to the nursery. Good-bye, Mr Johnson. I'll come and have a chat with you, Father, after Anthony's in bed.'

Paul, standing up as courtesy demanded, held out his hand.

'Perhaps we could say *"au revoir"* instead of "good-bye",' he suggested. 'After all, if I come to live here we shall be neighbours!'

But the smile disappeared instantly from her face ... as if she had recalled only now her previous opinion of him, and a dark secret look flashed over it.

'Until our next meeting, then,' she said quickly. And as if to deny the chances of their meeting again she told the baby, 'Say good-bye now, Anthony.'

'Bye-bye!' the child said obediently, waving his podgy little fist in Paul's face.

Then without looking at Paul again, Eve took the child from the room.

'I'm afraid my daughter can't bring herself to welcome any prospective buyer to the house,' Jack Corderhay said regretfully. 'As a matter of fact, Mr Johnson, she is feeling this more even than I am. But then, I've had my day and, as I said before, in lots of ways I shan't be sorry to go. It's different for her. She has her life before her and she has always loved this house ... done her best to keep it going...'

'I understand how distressing it is for her,' Paul said truthfully. 'But if I should come here, I would want her and all your family ... to feel free to come and go as you pleased.'

'That's very generous of you, my boy! I hope you don't live to regret the offer! However, shall we make a move and see the rest of the house before the light goes? I know you must be anxious to see around.'

'I wish I knew whether I was or not!' Paul thought, as he followed the older man out of the room. 'Fact is, I don't know what I want!'

He became even less certain as he went from room to room, each impressing him more deeply than the last with its beauty and charm, and the whole making him more and more certain that Eve was right when she had said it wasn't the house for a bachelor.

'Of course, I could get married!' he thought, with a sudden flash of humour. 'But it's a strange reason to give up my freedom ... just to fill a house that will cost me my life savings and most of my capital! I'm mad ever to have thought of coming here ... selling out those shares ... leaving myself in a pretty vulnerable position if anything goes wrong in the business ... nothing to fall back on ... crazy ... and yet now I've seen it I want it ... more than anything I've ever wanted before ... and for completely different reasons than the ones that brought me here today. The house has cast a spell on me or something

273

silly ... I don't know ... I don't know what to think ... or say–'

'That's all, apart from the servants' quarters, which really won't interest you much,' Jack Corderhay was saying. 'You wouldn't find much difficulty getting domestic help locally. If you decided to come, I could recommend several nice servants ... but that's jumping your fences a little, isn't it? I don't suppose you want to make up your mind in a hurry.'

'I'd like to think about it,' Paul said. 'But not for long. I usually make up my mind about things pretty quickly. Of course, this is not just a business deal ... it's a very big financial move ... and ... well, I'm a bit uncertain. Nevertheless, I'd like to have the facts before me before I go away ... that is if you can spare me a little more time?'

'Of course, my boy! Delighted!' Jack Corderhay said, although he would not enjoy the ensuing discussion of money. He would have left this to the agent had he not been so anxious for this unusual young man to have the place. He was prepared to drop several hundreds, if not a thousand, if he found the right person to take over. It wasn't business, of course, as the agent had said, but nor could the sale of his home ever be considered solely in the light of a business deal. That was why he had to feel inside himself that it was the right person coming here to step into his shoes.

He repeated these thoughts to Eve later that evening when Paul had driven away in his grey coupé. Jack Corderhay was certain that the young man was tempted by the low figure mentioned, and that if he decided to take the place he would not quibble about the price.

'Of course, I dropped quite a bit from my original price,' he admitted to Eve. 'But I really want him to have it, Eve. I can't think why because he's not the sort of person I visualized living here when first we talked it over together. All the same, I think he's a very unusual young man … worked his way up in the world … and determined to get on. I respect the fellow for his courage, initiative and guts. He's a brave young man, too … worked it up from nothing and worth a fortune now.'

'But, Father, what do you *really* know about him?' Eve said desperately, her hands twisting in her lap as they always did when she was nervous or upset. Paul's visit had been a great shock to her. Of all the people in the world whom she might have expected to see, he was not among them.

When first he had come into the room she had been too shaken by surprise even to speak. It was one thing to have someone continually in your thoughts all day and half the night, when you couldn't sleep for thinking about him … quite another to come face to face with the man you loved and hated at the same time.

When she had recovered a little from the first shock of finding herself in the same room with him, she had guessed instantly that his idea of buying the house had sprung from his desire for revenge. He had threatened in London to make them all suffer ... and what more clever way of doing so than by buying their home lock, stock and barrel? But since neither her father nor her mother knew of his existence prior to today, they could not be upset if he, rather than anyone else, bought Corderhay Park. Nor would Anne-Marie care. She was still abroad and none of them had seen her since her elopement with Richard Bainborough. Her letters had been short and scrappy and filled only with mundane activities. So only she, Eve, knew that Paul Johnson was getting his revenge ... and therefore only she could suffer by it. But it didn't lessen the hurt to her or her pride.

But later, when he started to play with Anthony ... with *his* child ... she had found it in her heart to pity him, and to love him again. He had an instinctive way with the little boy, who had undoubtedly taken a big fancy to his father. And Paul's love of children, which showed in his every action, could not have been simulated. It had struck her forcibly how cruel life had been to him in this one sense... Denying him not only possession of his son, but even the knowledge that he had one.

'If only things had been different!' she had found herself thinking. 'But now it can never be. I would not want him to love me ... nor could I ever marry him ... even for Anthony's sake. I should always think of the past ... and neither of us would ever forget that he was Anne-Marie's child ... not ours! If only I could forget him ... forget he ever existed...'

But her inability to do so even in his absence caused her every emotion to turn to fear when he suggested seriously that he might come to live here ... become their closest neighbour. How could she hope to forget him ... when she might see him every day ... hear his car go past the Lodge ... know that when the lights burned in the windows of the house he was here in these rooms?...

'He mustn't come! I cannot go and live at the Lodge if he comes here!' she thought desperately, as she sat listening to her father telling her how anxious he was for Paul to buy the house. What could she say to her father to make him less keen for Paul to live here and yet not reveal the whole truth? He had formed an opinion of Paul that would be entirely reversed if he knew that Paul was responsible for his young daughter's unhappiness, disgrace ... was Anthony's father.

'I know quite a lot about him,' her father

was saying. 'If you mean his private life, then I don't know a great deal, I suppose. But I'm seldom wrong in my judgments of my fellow men, Eve. At my age you can sum up people pretty well if you're interested in them all your life as I have been. Now this young man … he's a decent, hard-working, honest kind of fellow … intelligent, courageous and not without a sense of humour. Fond of children, too, and that's always a good sign… Tell me, Eve, what don't *you* like about him?'

'I didn't say I didn't like him,' Eve said quickly … too quickly. 'But … well, I can't explain why but I don't want him to come and live here. I … just don't agree with you this time, Father … that's all.'

Her father gave her a quick, searching look. She turned her face away from him, but he caught her wrists and turned her round to face him.

'My dear, don't be afraid of *me*,' he said gently. 'I won't probe into your private feelings. But we have always trusted each other in the past, Eve … confided in one another. Ever since you were a little girl you used to tell me things. We've been … very close to one another, haven't we?'

Eve nodded her head, staring at her hands and not trusting herself to speak.

'Only once did you not confide in me, and then neither of us was very happy. Now I don't want to force your confidences, but I'm not blind, Eve. Ever since Anne-Marie ran off with that silly young Bainborough, you've been different. I can't think ... though I've tried often enough ... what there was about Anne-Marie's wedding so to upset you. The reception all went off beautifully and in the end nobody seemed to mind about the wedding. So I ruled that out. But I've nothing to put in its place. I *know* you're unhappy, Eve ... and I don't know why!'

Eve knelt on the thick carpet and leant her head against her father's knee. She longed so much to tell him about her feelings for Paul ... such mixed-up feelings that needed to be sorted out ... but she couldn't do so.

'I ... can't tell you about this, Father,' she said at last. 'I wish I could. But ... it just isn't anything I can talk about!'

'Then it has to do with love!' Jack Corderhay said calmly. 'I thought of that, but until today I couldn't imagine who the young man could be. Now I think I know. But we won't discuss him if you'd prefer not to. All the same, if he's going to be our next-door neighbour, I think I have a right to know a little more. Because if my guess is right, and you do love him, then I won't sell the place to him. Not if he's such a fool that he doesn't return your affections, my dear!'

'Oh, Father!' Eve wept, her tears falling slowly and silently onto her hands. 'How did you know? I didn't think it showed. But it's true. I do love him. It was … he whom I went to see … when I went up to town the day before the reception. I knew then that I loved him. But I could never marry him … even if he cared for me … and he doesn't. He's in love with someone else!'

Gently, her father stroked the dark, silky hair.

'Nobody else would have guessed, Eve,' he said reassuringly. 'I was a bit suspicious ever since he'd mentioned your last meeting. You see, you hadn't told me about it, and I think you would have done so in the ordinary course of events. As to his being in love with another woman, that didn't strike me as being the case. In fact, he told me he wasn't going to get married.'

'Perhaps not,' Eve whispered in a choked little voice. 'But he's still in love with her. I know that's true. He … he proved it today.'

Jack Corderhay sighed.

'I can't quite see how … or when … but I'll take your word for it, Eve. All the same, young men can change heir minds, you know. And living here, seeing you every day … he can't fail to realize how blind he has been not to realize your worth before.'

Eve smiled a little though her tears.

'You're just biased, Father,' she said. 'I'm really very dull and ordinary. But even … even if that did happen … it would only make matters worse. I can't tell you why,

Father, *but I could never marry him*. There would always be … a … a ghost between us.'

'Ghost? You mean something from the past?' her father said. 'But, Eve, what is past *is* past, if you know what I mean. It ought not to affect the future. Surely in time this "ghost" of yours can be exorcized?'

'No!' Eve said swiftly. 'Never! It's … a living ghost, Father. Not really a ghost at all. It will always be living.'

Jack Corderhay scratched his head in bewilderment. Could Eve mean that Paul Johnson was divorced … that he had a wife living … a wife from whom he had been legally released if not in the eyes of the Church? But he couldn't ask Eve … force her confidence. It was enough for the moment that he had learned so much of what had been troubling her. The rest of the story would come in time.

'We'll leave it for now, shall we?' he said. 'But we can't shelve this question of what we're going to do about our buyer.'

Eve smiled and hastily wiped the last tear from her eye.

'That sounded so funny!' she said.

'Well, what are we to do about him? Shall I tell him I've reconsidered it and that it's all off?'

'He'd be terribly annoyed!' Eve said. 'Perhaps he'll settle the problem by not wanting to live here after all. He was … undecided … wasn't he?'

281

'I don't think he had fully made up his mind… Well, we'll leave it like that, shall we? If he does want to go through with it, we'll have to talk this over again. Whatever happens, he shan't come if you don't want him here, Eve. I promise you that!'

'Thank you, Father,' Eve said. 'I'd better go and get ready for dinner now.'

After she had gone Jack Corderhay leant back in his chair and with thoughtless deliberation lit his pipe. It was time for him, too, to go and change out of these old shooting-clothes. All the same … a minute or two to think … to wonder a little about the future … about the surprising revelation that Eve had lost her heart. Unhappily, too.

'But I like her choice, none the less!' he said to himself, shaking his head and puffing out a cloud of smoke. 'Eve's no fool. Her heart's in the right place, I'm certain. He's a decent young fellow, whatever it is that's keeping them apart. Strange I should have taken such a fancy to the boy without knowing she cared. Always felt I'd never consider anyone good enough for my Eve. But I liked the boy … yes, I liked him. Maybe *he'll* tell me about this 'ghost' if I go carefully. Still, early days yet … no need to rush these things. It'll all sort itself out…'

The dinner-gong roused him from his reverie and sent him hurrying up the stairs to change.

CHAPTER 14

A week before Anne-Marie arrived home from France Jack Corderhay had a letter from the housing agent in whose hands he had placed the sale of his estate, saying that a Mr Johnson had put in a definite offer for the property; that, while the price was lower than they had hoped for in the first instance, Mr Johnson was fully prepared to carry out all the conditions of sale and mentioned that the price had been discussed between them. Would Mr Corderhay kindly communicate his wishes in the matter.

'There!' Jack Corderhay said to himself as he read the letter and put it down before him at the breakfast table. 'I felt sure he'd take it!'

'Take what, *chéri?*' asked his wife, glad to see the smile on her husband's face, which she had noticed to be all too serious and thoughtful of late.

'The house, my dear!' her husband said, in a voice of supreme satisfaction.

His wife stared at him in surprise. Was it possible that after all these years she still did not understand the workings of her tall and dignified English husband? She had never doubted that his thoughtful, serious air over the last few weeks was due entirely to his unhappiness at leaving his home. It had been a severe blow to her when he had told her it was necessary, for she had never imagined that their finances were in so serious a state. But all her personal feelings had been as nothing compared with her distress on his account. She would settle down quite well anywhere in the world provided she had her Jack beside her. She would build a new home for them both and be happy in it if only he could be happy away from Corderhay Park. But she had known only too well what it would mean to him … not just to leave Corderhay, but to sell it and know that it had changed hands … gone out of the family which had lived there for century upon century.

Now, to her amazement, he was telling her with a satisfied smile on his face that someone had decided to buy it.

'But, Jack, how can you feel so happy about it?' she asked, a frown creasing her still-beautiful white forehead. 'And who is this buyer? Is it one of those whom I met?'

Her husband took her hand across the table and gave it a friendly little pat.

'No! You were out the day he came,' he said. 'But I did not tell you about him in case he should decide against having the place. You know, Antoinette, this may sound ridiculous to you, but when I met this young man ... he is in his thirties, I would judge ... I had a curious sensation in my heart ... a presentiment, if you prefer to call it that. I felt that here at last was someone whom I should *like* to take the reins from my hands. I cannot explain my reasons ... he is a perfectly ordinary young man in many ways ... exceptional in others, but with nothing outstanding that I could mention to explain why I felt this way. And at the same time that I felt sure about him... I also felt sure *of* him. I *knew* he would come here. Does that all sound very peculiar?'

'A little, I must confess,' his wife said. 'I can see how you have felt this young man to be *sympathique*. You do not have this word in your language, for sympathetic is not quite the same thing. But it means a kind of sympathy between two people they feel from inside themselves even if they do not know the cause. Nevertheless, I do not see how you could be so sure he would want to buy. Did he seem very anxious to do so? Had he good reasons for wanting it? It is a big house ... and expensive to keep going. He must have realized all this. Had he no doubts?'

'He was full of them!' Jack answered with a grin. 'And far from being anxious to buy, he was the contrary ... telling me straight out that he did not wish to have it after all. But there was some inner reason ... something more important to him than not wanting it … that was drawing him here… I don't know what it was but I could hear the uncertainty in his voice. He didn't want it … and yet he had to have it. However … that problem seems to have solved itself for him, since he has definitely offered for the place. The questions now remains … do I accept his offer?'

Antoinette threw up her hands in a typically expressive French gesture.

'I do not understand!' she said. 'You talk in riddles, my very dear Jack! Explain it to me, please. One minute you say happily that you knew he would want the place … that you want him to come here … the next you wonder if you should accept his offer! Is it a bad one?'

'No. We settled the price before he left,' Jack Corderhay said, no longer smiling now, and his face serious and thoughtful. 'But there is a reason, my dear, which I cannot tell you without betraying someone's confidence. I wouldn't wish to do so without her permission.'

'You mean … Eve?' Antoinette asked.

Her husband nodded.

'Naturally, I do not wish to know if she does not wish me to know,' Antoinette said reasonably. 'Nevertheless, I cannot see what *she* can have against this young man coming here. If he is so nice as you say, then perhaps it is a good thing for her? She is not so young any more, and it is time she was married. Would he not be a good husband for her?'

Jack Corderhay smiled across at his wife.

'You French!' he exclaimed. 'Always trying to match-make and start a bit of romanticizing whenever the breath of opportunity occurs!' His face grew more serious again as he added: 'Eve knows him, Antoinette, and she has something against him ... what it is she will not tell me. I can't feel it is very serious because I would say he was a thoroughly decent young fellow in every way. But she's convinced she has cause to dislike him and so I don't feel justified in forcing him on her as a neighbour if she doesn't wish to see him again. After all, if we are to live at the Lodge we shall be very close neighbours. And it is not going to be easy to maintain social relationships in view of our having owned the estate without further reasons for discord. As it is we shall not be human if we don't resent just a little the person who steps into our shoes. He, too, will be a little afraid in case we are criticizing any changes he may make ... how he manages the place. And he is a very proud young man. There would be ample opportunity for heated words if Eve has something against him even before he arrives here.'

'But, Jack, who is this young man? Do I not know him? How is it Eve knows him and we do not?'

'I don't know that myself,' Jack answered truthfully. 'Eve told me only the barest details. I imagine perhaps that she knew him in Paris … or met him there. I can't tell you any more. But I must have a word with her now … get her approval before I write and accept Mr Johnson's offer.'

'Very well, *chéri*. Whatever you do I know it is for the best,' his wife replied, and rising to her feet kissed him lightly on the top of his grey head. 'I have a lot to do this morning… I am checking over the linen with Eve before we start to pack it up. There is far too much, of course, for our future needs. I will sort out what we will not need for the sale. I have already put some by for Anne-Marie for her new home, and I will leave also enough for Eve for her marriage when the day comes. Do not keep her too long, as I shall need her help!'

She disappeared from the room and almost immediately Eve came through the door, and, kissing her father good morning, said:

'Mother said you wanted me, Father.'

'You've had breakfast?' he asked.

'Half an hour ago,' Eve said, sitting down beside him. 'But I'll have another cup of coffee if it's still hot. I'm afraid my year in Paris spoilt my taste for tea.'

'Ah, yes, Paris!' said her father. 'That seems a long time ago now, doesn't it, Eve? You know your mother had a letter from Anne-

Marie this morning saying she would be returning home to Eversham Court next week, and would be coming over to see us. I expect you'll have a lot to talk over with one another.'

'Yes! We shall!' Eve said, in a cool, hard little voice that did not escape her father. What a strange girl this daughter of his had turned out to be! She was nowadays so secretive and ... bottled up ... as if she had a load on her mind which nothing could lighten. Was it just being unhappily in love that was causing her to behave so oddly ... to look so pale and thin ... or was there another reason? If only she would confide in him ... tell him what was worrying her! Could it have anything to do with Anne-Marie? Was she shielding her sister once again?

'I also had a letter this morning,' he said. 'Here ... read it for yourself.'

He watched her as she scanned the lines and saw the dark colour rush into her cheeks ... noticed that her hands were trembling.

'I thought you might be surprised by it ... although I wasn't myself. All the same, Eve, I told you a few weeks ago that I wouldn't accept his offer if you did not wish me to. That still stands. What do you think about it, my dear?'

Eve folded the letter and replaced it in the envelope with slow deliberation. What did she think? How could she think at all when

289

her heart was thudding inside her and her mind consumed with the one thought that he was coming to live here after all ... that she might see him every day ... that he would be living in her home?

'I don't know, Father,' she said desperately. 'I realize that you are anxious to accept his offer. But at the same time you don't know the facts. If you knew what he was really like ... you couldn't wish him to come here ... you couldn't–'

'Why not, Eve?' her father asked sharply. 'What do you know to his disadvantage? Surely I have a right to know it, too? Can't you trust me, Eve? You must know that I would not betray you ... or him ... to anyone. What has he done to make you dislike him and love him at the same time? What is behind all this?'

'I wish I could tell you, Father. I want to tell you ... but it isn't really my secret to tell. Isn't it enough that I say he isn't all he seems? Perhaps what he did ... in the first place ... wasn't his fault. He isn't to blame for what happened subsequently. But nothing *can* bury the past, and if one day you found out the truth ... then you'd regret his living here. I know you would.'

There was a moment's deep silence while each sat lost in separate thought. After a moment or two Jack Corderhay lit a cigarette and said slowly:

'I have always trusted your judgment, Eve. It's never failed me yet. Nevertheless, I cannot accept what you say as a fact since you won't give me a reason. I'm not saying I disbelieve you ... only that I wonder if your judgment of this man is not ... well, shall I say biased? ... by the fact that you are in love with him. I cannot help thinking that your heart is telling you the truth and your mind is making these accusations against him for some unaccountable reasons. If he were really the sort of man I should not wish to sell my house to and have as a neighbour, how can *you* love him, Eve? Respect and love are too interwoven to be separated as you are trying to separate them. Either you don't love him as you think you do ... or else you are misinterpreting what has happened in the past. Which is it, Eve?'

'I don't know, Father,' Eve whispered. 'This is the problem that I've thought and thought about until I'm nearly crazy with thinking. I know I love him ... but I know you are right when you say one *must* respect the person one loves. Yet I cannot respect him in view of what I know. And what I know is a fact. It doesn't make sense, Father, but in this case both things are true.'

Her father took a deep breath.

'I don't know what to say, Eve. I fail to understand all this ... but if you ask me now to refuse his offer ... then I'll do so and we'll say no more about it.'

'You don't want to refuse his offer, do you?' Eve said miserably.

Jack Corderhay shook his head.

'No, Eve. I'll be truthful. I don't want to refuse it. I cannot help feeling that my instincts are right, and my instincts tell me to accept him. But if you ask me not to do so, then I shall have no hard feelings. I shan't blame you in any way ... in fact, we'll both forget him. Is that what you want to do, Eve?'

'It's what I want to do ... but I can't do it!' Eve whispered. 'I think of him all the time ... all day and half the night. If only I could forget, Father!' And if he comes to live here ... it'll be far worse.'

'That doesn't sound like you, Eve,' her father said gently. 'You have never been the kind of person to run away from something that frightens you. I remember once when you were a little girl ... a man came to the house with a Great Dane ... the dog stood higher than you did and you were frightened. I was watching you. You wanted to turn and run out of the room, but instead you walked up to the animal and patted it on the head with your little hand. You were very surprised when it turned round and licked your face ... and you weren't frightened of it after that. You've always had that courage, Eve, to face up to your fears. Aren't you going to look this one in the face, too? Running away won't help you ... or sending him away. And if you really believe that he isn't worth loving, then seeing him as often as you can will help you to find out that you don't really care for him at all. Then you will be free.'

'Could I grow indifferent to him?' Eve was asking herself. 'If I saw him every day ... remembered each time that he had been Anne-Marie's lover ... was Anthony's father ... should I cease to care as I do? Will I find out things about him that I dislike? I know him so little! Perhaps I could discover other things to make me hate him! Perhaps, too, I should find other things to make me love him ... as I did the other day when he played with Anthony!'

'Let him come, then, Father,' she said at last, in a desperate little voice. 'I couldn't feel any worse than I do now! But if things get too bad ... I'd like you to understand if I decided to go away ... if I couldn't face it.'

'Don't you worry about that, Eve, until the time comes. I think everything will turn out all right,' Jack Corderhay said. 'I don't feel in my heart that we shall be making a mistake. Only time will tell. Meantime, try not to worry, Eve. You're so thin it frightens me to look at you. And don't let Mother overwork you. I know when she says she is going to sort the linen with you that it means you will do it while she listens and talks and generally gets in the way!'

Eve gave a half-smile.

'You shouldn't say such things about Mother!' she reproved him. 'Even if it is true!'

After she had left him Jack Corderhay sat on in his chair for a few minutes, wondering and hoping that he wasn't forcing an issue the wrong way. He had told Eve he thought seeing Paul Johnson every day might cure her of loving him … but it wasn't what he really thought … or hoped. Deep in his heart he knew that he wanted her to marry this young man. She would make him such a good wife, and they were a perfect match temperamentally … the boy having the drive, impetuosity, impulsiveness that would be complemented by Eve's quiet, soothing, gentle personality. And what a fine-looking couple they would make… Eve so slim and tall and dark … the boy so fair and strong and virile!

'I'm as bad as Antoinette with my matchmaking!' he thought. 'Must be old age creeping on. All the same, I'd like to see Eve settled down with a child or two of her own. The way she mothers that boy of Anne-Marie's shows her need of them … always was maternal even as a little girl … looking after her sister and her dolls and that dog … even tried to look after her mother and me!'

He got a little stiffly to his feet and went slowly into the library to write his reply to the agent.

I shall be pleased to accept Mr Johnson's offer and leave it to you to draw up the final details of the agreement. I imagine these will take six weeks at least so suggest that we give August 1st as the date of our departure.

I shall be sending you shortly a list of items to be sold at the auction and feel you might like an extra copy to send to Mr Johnson in case he cares to retain any of these articles. He showed a particular interest in my library and may wish to buy the books. In any such case I wish him to have anything he fancies at a lower figure than the reserve price I shall mark on them for the sale.

He ended the letter with a few formal remarks and, sealing it in an envelope walked with it down to the post-box at the end of the drive before he could think things over once more and be tempted to change his mind.

'Of course, you're crazy, Johnson!' Paul's partner said to him as he read the agent's note telling Paul that his offer had been accepted. 'I simply can't understand what made you do it. Don't you realize what it entails? There's still time to back out of it, man. For heaven's sake come to your senses and write and say you've decided against it after all.'

Paul looked across the top of his desk and gave his partner a disarming grin.

'My mind is made up, Jake, and nothing you can say now will change it. So be a good chap and save your breath!'

The other man, shorter, darker and less well turned out than Paul, shook his head in bewilderment.

'I can't keep quiet!' he almost shouted. 'We've been friends as well as partners for fifteen years. You were a boy of twenty and I was very little older when we started this business. We've never made a move, either one of us, that the other hasn't approved. Now I know this is a personal move on your part ... that it doesn't involve business capital. Nevertheless, I know it amounts to practically every penny you have in the bank as well as the shares you are selling. I'd refuse to buy them if I thought it would stop you and if I wasn't sure you'd only sell them on the market. It's utter madness to bankrupt yourself in such a way.'

Paul lit his pipe and puffed away at it for a few moments in silence. Presently he said in a quiet, even tone:

'I'm not bankrupting myself, as you put it, Jake. I've left myself enough spare cash to furnish the place and keep it going for a year at least. Well, we're making money still, aren't we? Business has never been better and our new export drive to the French is bringing us a tidy little sum apart from our regular orders. Our goods are going to be in

296

short supply all over the world for years to come and no one can turn them out as quickly, efficiently or cheaply as we can … in this country, America, or even in Germany. We're safe, Jake, even though that's a dangerous remark to make these days.'

'So I'll grant we're on a good wicket!' his partner said. 'Neither of us dreamed when we started that we'd reach these proportions. Your "flair", if you like to call it that, and my caution have been a sound basis for a partnership. We tone each other down or up as the case requires. But would we have done so well on our own? I doubt it. It's because we put two heads to every decision, and that's the truth, old man. Now you're refusing to listen to an outsider because this concerns your private life … it isn't my business!'

'You know very well I didn't mean it that way when I told you to let me manage this alone,' Paul said placatingly and truthfully. 'I can understand your caution, Jake, but this is just something I've *got* to do. If I don't do it, then all these past fifteen years we've worked together mean nothing to me. This is what I've been working for … it's the pay-off, as they say in American books! We've wanted different things out of life, Jake, and because we wanted them so much we've worked twice as hard and long and well as anyone else. Fifteen years of our lives have gone towards obtaining our ideals and we've spared nothing to get them. Sacrificed everything, too. Neither of us has ever spent money ... every penny went back into the business for the first ten years. No cars, no holidays abroad, no expensive clothing, drinks, parties ... things we would have liked. We lived as simply as we used to do when we couldn't afford to do otherwise. Then five years ago we started to draw out our profits. We could afford to do it and each of us put our cash into the bank against the day we could obtain our ideals. Well, you want to set up those huge Cancer Research Laboratories and hospitals because of something that happened in your past ... because the girl you loved died in terrible pain and poverty before your eyes without you or anyone else being able to lift a finger to help her. This is your way to square up what happened, and it's a fine gesture. My reasons are more mixed ... more selfish. I came from a poor home, but I wasn't allowed to remain uneducated, and therefore be content with my lot. My parents wanted me to take a step up in the world. I don't blame them ... but they sent me to schools where I was always the poorest boy there, always the butt of the other kids' jokes because my clothes were so shabby, my shoes down at heel, my home unfit to ask them to. I could never accept their invitations ... from the few who thought they'd ask me home as a "curiosity" for their well-to-do families.

Everywhere I went it was always the same, and the unfairness of it made me bitter and lonely ... and terribly ambitious. "One day I'll be richer and better dressed and more powerful than the lot of you," I used to brag to keep up my pride. "See if I don't!" Well, now it's coming true ... at least it's true already that I'm richer than most of those boys I was at school with. I can afford to be better dressed, too! As to being powerful, I think managing this business has been all the power I've wanted in life.'

'So you're taking on this estate, going to live there in magnificent solitude at a fantastic expense, to get your own back on the wretched family that have got to go,' Jake stated rather than asked the question.

Paul bit on the stem of his pipe and looked across at his companion.

'It started like that, I'll admit!' he said. 'I was in love with the daughter of the house. I never told you. I met her over in Paris. She turned me down then and that would have been that, but I happened to meet up with her again. Then she agreed to marry me ... and jilted me a second time. I thought then that I'd find some way to get back at her. When her home came on the market I knew I'd found a way. But after I'd met her father ... his other daughter... I changed my mind. They were ... decent people... I liked both of them... I felt sorry for them, too, as they

299

really love that house. But it was too late to change my mind then ... only my reasons changed. You see, Jake, I'd seen the house, and it's very, very beautiful. It's the kind of place I'd always dreamed of having when I was quite a small boy. There's an atmosphere about it, too, that got me. I can't explain it. I just knew I'd have to buy it if I could. In a way I half hoped someone else would snip it from under my nose ... offer a bigger price than I could afford. But here's my answer ... I've got to have it, Jake.'

Jake shook his head and surveyed his friend disbelievingly.

'I've never known you act this way before,' he said. 'All "fey" and peculiar. I'd have said there was a woman in it if you hadn't already told me she was out of the picture. I could have understood you wanting to get your revenge on her, too. But this "having to go", as you put it ... it doesn't add up, Paul.'

'It will ... when you've seen the place, Jake. And I'm hoping you'll be a frequent visitor. It's a darned great mansion and I shall be pretty lonely living there on my own.'

'Mad to contemplate it!' Jake said, more to himself than to Paul, to whom he was very attached. 'Still, I'll visit you all right. I wouldn't want a house to break up our close association after all these years!'

'Nothing could do that, Jake,' Paul said warmly. 'You've been a grand friend to me as well as the best partner a chap could want. We've got a long way to go together still, I hope Jake. I've been thinking … we might make some efforts to get a bit of business from Canada. It's about the only country we don't supply at the moment. What do you think?'

Jake breathed a sigh of relief.

'I think I'm mighty pleased you can still think a bit about the business,' he said. 'I was beginning to fear you'd lost interest. After all, I told myself, he's younger than I am … he hasn't had a holiday since before the war. You know, Paul, you spent your demobilization working! Of course, you had that trip to Paris, but I gathered that wasn't exactly a holiday as it turned out. You know … in many ways a lot of people must think we're quite mad. Here we are, two of the richest business men in this country, and yet what have we got to indicate it? … no chromium-plated office … no yachts … no racehorses or art galleries … we don't even go to the best tailors. We still watch how we spend our pounds and neither of us feel any too safe with a fiver in our pockets! Must be our upbringing, I suppose. Can't get used to having money because we were born so darned poor.'

'Well, I've launched out a bit,' Paul said, with his charming smile. 'What about my Triumph … apart from this house? Perhaps I'm just beginning to *feel* rich! Tell you what,

Jake, let's be devils and go and crack a bottle of bubbly at the nearest club. And while we're at it we'll make an evening of it, too. We'll celebrate our successful partnership and my new home. That'll take a drink or two. How about it?'

Jake gave a sign that was half disbelieving, half amused at this new aspect of his friend's character.

'I think spring has got into your bones!' he said. 'Still, if you really want to go on a binge, I'll keep you company. When men of your temperate habits go berserk, they usually need someone to carry them home. What's the plan of campaign?'

'After the bubbly, dinner … after dinner … a good musical comedy,' Paul said, and then: 'You know, we really need a couple of women to make this a real evening out, Still, I can't think of anyone offhand to ask, can you?'

'You know I don't go in for the fair sex!' Jake laughed.

'No! And nor do I! Shall have to change that if I'm turning into a country squire! However, between you and me, Jake, my one little flutter with a female wasn't too successful, was it? She soon showed what she thought of me! I reckon we'll have a better time without them, Jake. We can get drunk, too, if we choose!'

'Let's go then!' Jake said, standing up and linking his arm in Paul's. But as they walked out of their office together each was lost in his separate thoughts and neither of them concerned with their evening out. Paul's mind was on Corderhay Park, and Jake was thinking:

'He may think he's got over that girl he wanted to marry … and perhaps he has. All the same, he's not finished with women altogether. There'll be another girl … Paul's the marrying sort. He needs a wife … and kids, too. Wonder who he'll finally hitch up with! He'll need someone to look after him when I push off. For I shan't always be here … maybe not for more than a year or two. When he's had time to replenish his bank account I'll sell out to him … wouldn't want the business to go into anyone else's hands. He'll be able to carry on by himself then and I can start to realize my life's ambition, too. Of course, I'll miss Paul when I go … he's been a good friend and a loyal one.'

'To you, Paul,' he said, as the champagne bubbled in the glass he held. 'And to your future happiness at Corderhay Park!'

Paul gave a loud, happy, boyish laugh and drained his glass to the dregs.

CHAPTER 15

'Well, how do I look, Eve?'

Anne-Marie went swiftly towards her sister, who was in her bedroom sitting at her little writing-desk. Eve turned to look at the younger girl, but there was no smile of welcome on her face.

'Very well,' she said, after a pause.

'That's not what I meant!' Anne-Marie said, pirouetting in front of Eve, the expression on her face half defiant, half appealing. 'Don't you see it, Eve? My mink!'

Eve's eyes travelled over the beautiful mink coat which hung in soft silken folds from Anne-Marie's shoulders ... and back to the pretty, questioning little face. It was the same Anne-Marie as had left the house early one morning over three months ago, and yet there was something different about her which Eve could not define.

'It's ... very nice, Anne-Marie,' she said, without any expression in her voice. She was still too cross with Anne-Marie ... too upset about all that had happened at their last meeting ... to give her the welcome she knew her sister wanted from her.

'It was Richard's wedding present to me,'

Anne-Marie said proudly. 'And he has given me some jewellery, too. I'll show it to you when I've unpacked. But, of course, I'm not living here any more, am I? It just shows what habit is! Richard has taken all the luggage home and dropped me off here to see you all. We only flew over this morning.'

'She's talking too fast and without thinking what she is saying,' Eve decided. 'And that means she is trying to cover up her real feelings. Does she feel guilty? Is she afraid I'm going to be cross with her?'

'Really, Eve!' Anne-Marie was saying, the smile wiped off her face and her mouth drooping petulantly. 'You don't seem a bit pleased to see me.'

'Is there any reason why I should be?' Eve asked, in a cold, hard voice. 'You lied to me, Anne-Marie … when you ought to have trusted me. You didn't play the game fairly … with any of us. Why couldn't you have told Paul outright that night that you weren't going to marry him?'

Anne-Marie bit her lip and walked quickly across to the window, her back towards Eve. She had not expected Eve to speak quite so bluntly. How much did she know … had she told Paul … had Paul told her?

'I *was* afraid!' she admitted slowly. 'I thought you'd go for me, Eve … because of the child. I knew you thought I *ought* to marry him. But I couldn't. And I didn't see why I should.'

'She's being honest now, anyway,' Eve thought. 'Is it true that I forced her into telling all those lies ... lies to Paul and to me? Did I make her rush off with Richard like that and disappoint Mother so much?'

'There's something else I couldn't understand, Anne-Marie. You told me that Paul hadn't kept that appointment with you in Paris ... but he did, didn't he? You were the one to break it. I want to know the truth!'

Anne-Marie swung round and faced her sister, her face flushed and anxious.

'Must we go into all that again, Eve? Surely it doesn't matter now? It's all over and done with ... finished. I'm Mrs Richard Bainborough now and one day when his father dies I shall be Lady Bainborough. Why bring Paul Johnson into it? He's gone, hasn't he? We'll neither of us see him again.'

'That's just where you're wrong, Anne-Marie,' Eve said slowly. 'He's coming to live here. He has bought Corderhay Park.'

She had imagined this would come as a surprise to the younger girl, but she was totally unprepared for the shock that was written all over her pretty, transparent face.

'Paul ... here ... it's not true!' she stammered. 'Who let him come? I won't have it, Eve!' Does Father know?'

'Father knows he is buying the place, of course!' Eve said. 'He doesn't know Paul was the man who was responsible for your disgrace ... nor that he's Anthony's father. I dread to think what he'd do if he did find out. As it is, Father likes him. So you see, Anne-Marie, we might as well all know where we stand. Don't you agree?'

'How ... do ... you mean ... where we stand?' Anne-Marie said, searching Eve's face for a clue to her feelings.

'We'll, we'll all be neighbours for one thing. Are you going to mind seeing him every day? And what is he going to say to you when you come face to face, as you'll surely do at parties if not privately? He's a proud man, Anne-Marie, and he swore to have his revenge on you when he learned you had gone off with Richard. I think he's getting his revenge this way. Perhaps he means to carry it even further ... to tell all your friends ... maybe even your husband ... what you meant to each other in Paris.'

Anne-Marie seemed more in control of herself now.

'He wouldn't do that. I'm not afraid of *that*,' she said, more to herself than to Eve.

'Then what are you afraid of?' Eve asked brutally.

'Why should I be afraid of ... anything?' Anne-Marie cried defiantly. 'Why should you think I'm afraid at all? You're just trying to make me miserable, Eve. You want me to suffer because ... because you're jealous. Yes, that's it. You're jealous because there were two men who wanted to marry me and neither of them were interested in you. You've never had anyone in love with you and–'

She broke off as the older girl rose to her feet, her face deathly white and with such an expression on it that Anne-Marie realized at once she had gone too far. Instantly she burst into tears, and slowly Eve went back to her chair.

'I didn't mean that! I don't know what I'm saying. I'm so upset!' Anne-Marie sobbed. 'I never expected you to be like this when I came here today, Eve. You were always so fond of me. I thought you'd be glad to see me. Oh, I'm so unhappy!'

Eve made no move to go to her, but she asked the next question in a softer tone of voice.

'Why are you unhappy, Anne-Marie? I thought you had done exactly what you wanted … got everything you wanted … regardless of anyone else. Now you've got it … you don't want it … is that it?'

'That's not true. I'm glad I married Richard. He gives me anything I want, and he's madly in love with me. It's you that are making me unhappy. You keep going for me and I don't know why … and it's not fair. I'm sorry for what I said … and sorry for all that happened in the past. But it isn't fair to keep reminding me. Why should I suffer all my life for one mistake? Haven't I suffered enough without that?'

'Suffered?' Eve asked. 'How have you suffered, Anne-Marie? You never had to take the blame for anything and you had your own way right up to the end. You didn't even have to face up to the disgrace ... or Father's disapproval ... or Mother's knowledge.'

'But I have suffered ... I have!' Anne-Marie wept. 'You won't understand because you don't know ... but I have suffered ... terribly.'

There was a note of sincerity in the girl's voice that convinced Eve she was speaking the truth. But she still could not seem to find it in her heart to feel the same affection for her younger sister that she had always felt in the past. She had to force herself to feel pity now and to say more gently:

'I'm sorry if you have been unhappy, Anne-Marie. I hope you will be happier in the future. I won't say any more about ... the past ... but I can't answer for what Paul Johnson will do ... or say. But I would advise you not to tempt his violence ... don't try to ... to revive his admiration. It would annoy Richard and I don't think it would stand you very well in his eyes. I also think it would be as well never to give him any suspicion that Anthony is your child ... and his. He doesn't know and I wouldn't like to think what he'd do if he found out. Steer clear of him, Anne-Marie. That's my advice.'

'And not because I'm jealous,' Eve thought grimly. 'Only because I think he might really do her harm if she tried flirting with him, as she might well do to win him over to her side. He'd never forgive her if he knew Anthony was his child ... never! Oh, why did Father have to let him come here? It would be better for all of them if they never saw him again.'

'You'd better wipe your eyes and powder your nose, Anne-Marie,' she said to her sister, 'or Mother and Father will want to know the reason for your tears.'

'You're not ... cross any more?' Anne-Marie asked, like a small child.

'I'm not cross,' Eve said wearily, thinking how strange it was that she should be so immune all of a sudden to Anne-Marie's appeals. In the past she would have pitied, loved, comforted. Now she could only listen and feel nothing left of the bond that had once been between them.

Nevertheless, she could not help but worry a little as to what would be the issue when Paul and Anne-Marie met again. She could not understand how Anne-Marie could be so sure that he would not decide to bring up their past association. It would, after all, be so simple a way to make her suffer as he had told Eve he intended to do. Or had he thought better of that angry promise? He had already apologized to Eve for his rudeness to her. Could he, after all, have decided that he was well out of it, so to speak, and that at heart he had too nice a nature to want to hurt others just because they had hurt him?

Eve wondered a great deal about both her sister and Paul during the weeks that succeeded Anne-Marie's return and preceded his arrival. She was so busy packing, sorting and listing that she had no time to visit Anne-Marie. But her father had been twice to Eversham Court to see her, and he noticed far more in his few visits there than Eve had divined in her brief interview with Anne-Marie on her return.

'I can't feel in my mind that everything is all right with those two young people,' he told Eve one evening when Antoinette was absent. 'I'm certain they aren't happy, Eve.'

'But, Father,' she argued, 'from what you tell me they are having a wonderful time … always out at some party or at the races or up in London for a night out. Anne-Marie has never had so gay a time in her life before.'

'That's just it,' Jack Corderhay said with a sigh. 'She's too gay. It struck me tonight that she can't sit still for a moment … she has to be rushing off somewhere … as if she wanted to distract her mind as well as her body. And it's been going on for nearly six months. I can understand them leading such a life at first … on their honeymoon, perhaps … but surely it's about time they settled down now

311

… to married life, I mean… They can't get to know much about each other when they are always in other people's company. And Richard doesn't look at all well. He has great rings under his eyes and looks as if he needs a holiday from all this holidaying-about!'

Eve smiled.

'I'm sure there's nothing to worry about, Father. Anne-Marie has always been like this at heart. Even as a little girl she couldn't stick at one thing for more than a moment. She is a restless person at heart and a gay one, too. I'm sure she'll sober down after a bit. It's only natural for her to enjoy all the social activities that money can provide for her. As for Richard … well, I presume he'll put a stop to it as soon as he wishes to do so.'

'I'm not so sure,' Jack Corderhay said thoughtfully. 'He's too much under Anne-Marie's thumb … do anything she asks him to please her. It isn't good for her. She's been spoiled enough already.'

'Well, she isn't your problem any more, Father,' Eve said gently. 'We've no right to interfere with her life, have we? Even if we wished to do so. She's a married woman now.'

Jack Corderhay nodded and smiled up at his elder daughter.

'To change the subject,' he said, 'we move next week, don't we? How's everything going?'

'Quite well, I think,' Eve admitted. 'Though the house looks terribly upside-down and empty since those things went to the sale. Only this room looks the same.' And her eyes travelled round the library, where the same books still lined the walls from ceiling to floor.

'Glad he bought the books!' her father said. 'We haven't room for them at the Lodge and I wouldn't have wanted to sell them elsewhere.'

Eve nodded.

'I wonder why he bought the "art gallery" as well,' she said. 'After all, they aren't *his* relatives!'

'I presume because he imagined the gallery would look pretty odd without them,' Jack Corderhay said; and then, impulsively, 'Let's go and take a last look at them, Eve … a sort of farewell…'

She linked her arm in his and together the tall, grey-haired Englishman and his dark, slim daughter went up the wide staircase and sat themselves incongruously … where they had sat so many times in Eve's childhood … on the top step. Their eyes lifted to the wall behind them where they met in turn the immovable glances of all the past Corderhays who had lived in this house.

'The wall behind those heavy gilt frames is quite a different colour,' her father mused. 'Protected from the dust, I suppose. We noticed it when Antoinette added me to the "Rogues' Gallery".'

'Maybe that's why Paul decided to keep them there,' Eve said. And then, with a tiny sigh: 'Oh, Father, it does seem awful to think that the empty place on your right will never be filled ... by a Corderhay, anyway. You're the ... the last of them all.'

'We mustn't grumble!' her father said gently. 'After all, judging by the long line up there we've had a good run, haven't we?'

'Shall we ... play ... our game?' Eve asked hesitantly, referring to a past amusement of her childhood. 'Do you remember, Father ... you were the guide and I was the visitor. I think I'll be the guide tonight ... and I'll start at the end...' She pointed to the picture, that had been painted of Jack Corderhay when he was a soldier in the First World War. He looked many years younger, of course, very handsome and proud as he stood, one hand on the sword that hung at his side, his head proudly erect as he stared down at them.

'Here, ladies and gentlemen,' Eve began, 'you have the ... the last of the Corderhays ... but by no means the least. On the contrary, this gentleman ... who is still living, I'm glad to inform you ... is one of the most distinguished and well-loved Corderhays in this great old family. You see him dressed here in the uniform of Colonel of the Upfordshire Guards. He is swearing the medal that is most prized of all this country's awards to its fighters ... the Victoria Cross. This he won for outstanding bravery during the Battle of the Somme, when–' Her voice broke suddenly, and she turned to her father and buried her face against his shoulder. 'It's so *sad,* Father,' she whispered in a choked little voice. 'I can't bear to think that this time next week we shall be gone ... that we can never play our ... our game again.'

'My dear, you mustn't cry,' her father said tenderly. 'I know how you feel ... and I have the same sentiments. But we mustn't regret what after all is Fate. Perhaps, also, it is Progress. Besides, things cannot stand still ... and we are making a new life for the country. Who knows but in several hundred years' time the Johnsons will have just such an ancestry to be proud of and be just as sorry to go when your great-great-great-grandchildren buy the place back from them when they go broke!'

Eve smiled a little as she wiped the tears from her eyes.

'I wish I had your courage ... and your sense of humour when things don't go well,' she said.

'You have great courage, Eve ... and a sense of humour, too. But at your age one feels things more intensely, perhaps, than at mine. One cannot always smile in the face of disaster ... not when one is alone, and you have put up a very brave front. Let's look to the future, my child ... to your future ... and Anthony's. There will be plenty of worthwhile things to take the place of Corderhay Park. I'm counting on you, you know, to help me keep up your mother's spirits. This move is going to take it out of her. She isn't so young either these days.'

'I know, Father, and I'll do what I can to take the worst of it off her shoulders.'

Her father knew that Eve was already doing this, but he knew also that it was in Eve's nature to pull herself together when an effort was required of her for others. She had not the same will to work for herself. He had wanted to turn her thoughts away from herself and him, and had surely gone the right way about it.

'There's another thing,' he said to distract her. 'I thought we might start our new life at the Lodge with a little entertaining. You remember those nice French friends of yours whom you told me about ... who were so kind to you when you were in Paris?'

'Denise and Edouard?' Eve said. 'I had a letter from Denise last week. She keeps asking me to visit her.'

'Then suppose we ask her and her husband to visit us?' Jack Corderhay suggested. 'We shall have a spare room, and your mother would be delighted to have French people in the house. What do you say, my dear? Would you like to have them over?'

'Oh, I'd love it!' Eve said eagerly, her face alight with new happiness. 'It seems years and years since Denise and I had a long talk about ... well ... all the things girls do talk about! And I'm sure you would like Edouard. He is not a bit like an artist except that he's so absent-minded. He might even paint us a picture of Corderhay Park to hang in the sitting-room.'

'That would be very nice,' her father agreed. 'And at the same time it might provide the answer to Louise. It is nearly a month since her return to France was discussed, but her mother naturally does not wish her to travel alone. She cannot leave Paris and her son is away, so she is to remain here until someone can fetch her. All the same, although I'm very fond of the child, I think she has been with us long enough. She seems anxious to go home now, too. Denise and her husband might take her back with them.'

'Father, that's a splendid idea!' Eve said. 'I'll write to Denise tonight. She's to have a baby this year, you know, and Edouard thinks she needs a long holiday and a change of air. How soon do you think we would be ready for them to come?'

'That's in your hands, Eve,' her father said. 'I imagine, knowing your love of law and order, that you will have the Lodge pretty ship-shape within a day or two of our moving in there. Why not make it the week afterwards? It will prevent us all from that rather unpleasant feeling of anticlimax.'

'I'll write tonight!' Eve cried. 'I've been meaning to suggest they come on a visit, but we've been so upside-down these last few months ... I know Denise will want to come. She was such a wonderful friend to me, Father. I want to repay a little of all she did for me. She was my only regret at leaving Paris.'

'You know, Eve, I've been wanting to ask you something. I never did so at the time because ... well, it couldn't serve any purpose and there would have been nothing I could have done about it, but are you at liberty to tell me ... who ... who was Anthony's father?'

Eve looked at her father in dismay.

'What made you ask, Father? I do know ... but I can't tell you. And it wouldn't do any good now ... would it?'

'No. But I've wondered. I look at the boy sometimes and think about it. He has always looked like Anne-Marie until now, but I think lately he's beginning to change.'

'It's because he's growing up a little,' Eve said quickly. 'His hair is darker ... but I think it will always be fair ... if not the same light golden colour that Anne-Marie and Mother have.'

'Don't let him see any likeness to Paul,' she thought desperately. 'I've looked for it, but apart from his hair darkening I can't see it. It's Paul's colour now ... and his eyes are the same deep blue ... but Anne-Marie has blue eyes, too.'

'Well, it doesn't much matter, I suppose,' Jack Corderhay said. 'I suppose I have begun to slip in my old age ... started living over the past again as old people do. It occurred to me that you might have thought I acted ... well, oddly, at that time. A Victorian father would have insisted on finding the young man in question and forcing him to make an honest woman of his daughter. Or else have given him a sound hiding. But oddly enough I couldn't seem to attach much importance to who was responsible by the time I found out the truth. Nothing much else mattered but that I'd found you and you were coming home again. I was furiously angry ... and hurt ... with Anne-Marie, but you've always been so soft-hearted about the girl that I felt to upbraid Anne-Marie would upset you as well as make your great sacrifice worthless. You had, I know, wished to keep your mother and me ignorant of the truth. Antoinette, of course, has never known it. It was a stupid thing to have done, Eve, in many ways, but I always loved and admired you for the gesture. It did hurt me a little, of course, to think that you felt you had a certain debt to us that you could repay in such a way. Did you never realize, my dear child, that you had no such debt? Your mother and I always loved you dearly and we never once regretted adopting you. You were such a quaint, serious little girl ... always wanting to help and look after the lot of us! In your own sweet little way you had long since cancelled any obligation to us by giving us so much pleasure in your company. And now, more than ever, I bless the day that you came to us. You've always been a great comfort and joy to me, Eve.'

'Oh, Father!' Eve said huskily. 'What a speech!'

'Hum, yes! Getting far too sentimental, aren't we?' he said with a twinkle in his eyes. 'Maudlin ... that's what we both are to-night, Eve. Well, let's ... what do you young things say ... "snap out of it"? We'll go and get a bottle of the best port from the cellar and cheer ourselves up. Though goodness knows what your mother will say when she comes home and finds us both a bit tipsy!'

'All right!' Eve laughed. 'We'll toast each of these gentlemen in turn ... the Admirals and Generals and Lords and Knights ... the whole lot of them! I only hope that when Paul Johnson comes here he appreciates such gallant company ... Father, don't you think he'll be lonely living her all on his own?'

'Possibly,' Jack Corderhay said, as they walked back down the stairs. 'Still, maybe he'll get married one of these days. I'd have said he was the marrying type ... judging from his behaviour with young Anthony. What do you think, Eve?'

But Eve's face was turned away from him and her father could only just glimpse the colour that had rushed to her cheeks.

'I don't know...' she stammered. 'I hadn't thought about ... that. Perhaps he will ... get married, I mean. Anyway, he isn't our concern, is he?'

'No,' her father said with a smile which Eve could not see. 'Not unless we make him our concern, of course. As a matter of fact I rather thought I might keep him company from time to time. After all, he's not only living in my house but he's taken over my cellar! Come to think of it, I'm not sure if we aren't about to drink his port now!'

'Oh, Father!' Eve laughed. 'How awful! Still, he can't grudge us one bottle, can he?'

'Maybe he won't miss it!' Jack Corderhay said mischievously. 'Doubt if he'll go down to the cellar and count them. He might, of course! I judged him to be a pretty methodical sort of fellow. Must be to have done so well in his business.'

'What *is* his business?' Eve asked curiously, in spite of herself.

'Don't know exactly. Turns out something

a lot of people all over the world want. Made quite a packet, I imagine. But he started with nothing, you know ... told me that first afternoon ... though I don't know why ... that his mother was a lady's maid and his father a mill-hand.'

'I didn't know,' Eve said, more to herself than to her father. 'Though I'd been told something of the sort. Somehow you wouldn't think it ... meeting him, I mean.'

'He's come a long way from there,' her father agreed. 'Had a good education, of course, and the determination to get on. I'd be pretty proud of myself if I were him.'

'You ... do ... like him, don't you, Father. Why?'

Jack Corderhay gave his daughter a sidelong glance.

'Can we ever say exactly why we like someone ... or love them for that matter? It's just something you feel about a person because of what they are ... as a complete entity, I mean. I don't think you can say "I like So-and-so because of this and this and this." Another man may have the same qualities and yet one can dislike him. In fact, there are plenty of self-made men knocking around this country now whom I've met and candidly dislike. It's what the man is ... all his faults and emotions and personality and character rolled into one ... that forms the ultimate impression. Then one feels "Yes, I like him!" or "No, I don't think I'll ever care for that fellow." Perhaps love is felt in the same way with a few biological emotions thrown in ... making it a pretty powerful feeling, don't you agree?'

'It's ... dreadful!' Eve said. 'I wish I knew *why* I loved him, Father. Perhaps I should feel better if I knew what it was all about. But it's so hard to reconcile what one feels with what one knows.'

'So we're back to the "ghost" again!' her father said. 'I wish I could solve your problem for you, Eve. But I doubt if thinking about it will make it any clearer. Something will make up your mind for you. Perhaps he will when he falls in love with you!'

'Father, don't say things like that!' Eve said swiftly. 'I don't *want* him to love me. It would only make things worse. I have told you already I could never marry him ... *never!* Besides, he isn't likely to fall in love with me. I'm not his type!'

'Types don't exist in that context!' Jack Corderhay said firmly. 'Why the girls I used to like before I fell in love with your mother were all dark and sultry! I thought I was mad about them until I found out what love really meant. What happened to the dark and sultry girls of the past then? It was golden hair and blue eyes or nothing!'

'Father, please understand that I don't want to be in love with him,' Eve said desperately. 'Nor do I wish him to fall in love with me, and on no account could I marry him ... *ever.*'

'All right, my dear. I'm not trying to make you do anything, you know. All I want is your happiness, but I fully realize that only you can find it for yourself. So let's forget all about him, shall we? And go and find that port?'

'Yes,' Eve agreed, but although she could help her father find the dusty old bottle he was looking for in the dark, cool cellars, she could not forget Paul Johnson with the same ease.

CHAPTER 16

A fortnight later the Corderhays were reasonably comfortably installed at the Lodge, Paul Johnson was extremely uncomfortably installed at the big house, and Denise and Edouard were spending their first day in England.

The family were having tea on the lawn and Denise, recently returned from a short walk up to the big house, was saying:

'You know, I have the great sympathy for that poor young man. Everywhere is disorder and more ... how you say ... moddle

… than my Edouard's studio!'

'You didn't go in?' Eve asked anxiously, looking at Denise's smiling face and thinking absently how beautiful she was. Her future motherhood was becoming to her, and while her figure was ungainly, her face, hair, eyes had all taken on a new loveliness that made it difficult for her adoring young husband to take his gaze from her. Even now he was lying on his stomach, his brown hair curling untidily over his forehead, his tea grown cold while he did a pencil sketch of his wife's profile.

'I did not mean to do so, Eve,' Denise replied to her friend. 'I think that I just tiptoe up to the house and peep inside the window to see where it is my friend, Eve, she have lived. As I am peeping, this young man come through the French window and see me.'

'Oh, Madame, whatever did you do?' Louise asked, for she was somewhat in awe of the stranger who had bought the Park.

'*La la!* What could I do?' Denise laughed. 'I put my hand over my mouth so... I'm sorry, Edouard, I will not move again ... and wait for him to say what he will.'

'And what did he say?' Jack Corderhay asked, with an amused smile on his face.

Denise shrugged her shoulders.

'He is very nice!' she replied in her French accent. 'He look at me for a moment and then he sigh … a big sigh … and he say "I'm afraid there isn't much to look at at the moment … except a damned awful mess!" I apologize, of course, for looking, but he say: "I'm not at all angry with you. As a matter of fact I'm glad of any distraction. I've been trying to hang those curtains, and can I do it so that they look as they should look … no!"'

'Oh dear!' said Antoinette. 'Perhaps we should have gone up and offered our help, Eve!'

Eve did not reply, but Denise went on:

'That is what he need, of course … a woman to help him. But naturally I do not say so. I ask if I can do anything, but he looked at me in the embarrassed English way … see that I am to have the darling baby … and say in the very gruff voice, "Certainly not!" Of course, I laugh and say at least I can advise him. So I go in and show him that he has try to hung them in the wrong window. After that it is easy and he fix them all right. Then the old woman come and ask him if he will have tea in the dining-room. "Good heavens, no!" he reply. "Drink a cup of tea alone in that great banqueting-hall! I'll have all my meals in here until my friend arrives."'

'So he has a lady friend?' Edouard asked jealously. 'I am glad to hear it!'

'Edouard, will you not be so silly boy. What man look at your wife in this con-

326

dition?' Denise laughed. 'But it is not a lady friend … he tell me his business partner come down from town tonight to stay with him. That is not a woman, is it?'

'I doubt it!' Jack Corderhay said. 'Well, what happened next?'

'He ask me to have tea with him, but I must refuse. I am sorry because he is so lonely but I have the husband and friends who wait tea for me here, I explain. He is very sad and I think now how much he like to be here in this nice garden to have tea with us!'

'Well, he can't!' Eve said violently, and then, when all the heads turned to look at her, she flushed and said, more calmly: 'There's enough of us here without any more! Besides, he might as well get used to being alone in the house. He can't always have his meals here!'

'I hope the couple we found for him look after him properly,' Antoinette said anxiously. 'I really feel we ought to see if there is anything we can do for him, Eve. After all, the poor man hasn't a wife to set things straight for him.'

'Nor an efficient girl like Eve,' Jack Corderhay said mischievously, but Eve gave him such a hurt, angry glance that he turned to his wife and said: 'I expect he'll be all right, my dear. He'd no doubt prefer us not to interfere.'

'What is he like, Madame?' Louise asked

curiously, for she had never seen this man whose name she had heard so often of late.

'Oh, he is the *vrai* Englishman!' Denise said, smiling. 'Very big and tall and fair, and he has such handsome blue eyes!'

'It is enough!' Edouard cried, throwing down his pencil and upsetting the cup of cold tea. A closer look at his wife's face reassured him that she was only teasing him and his jealousy gave way to instant good-humour. He mopped up the tea with his handkerchief in spite of Eve's protest that it wouldn't hurt the grass ... and sat down beside his wife, taking her hand in his own without a trace of self-consciousness.

Jack and Antoinette thought the young couple charming ... and so devoted to each other that it brought back memories to each of them of their first years of marriage. Louise, also, was enchanted with her fellow countryman, and Eve watched them with a queer ache in her heart. All around her ... her mother and father ... her friends ... were happily and wonderfully in love. Only for her were things so twisted and wretched.

She thought of Paul alone in the big house and hated him because he could rouse so unconsciously her desire to run up there this very minute to help him. But she could not ... would not do so; if nothing else, pride forbade it. But pride could not prevent her from longing to go.

Later that evening, when she was alone with Denise for a moment or two before supper, she could not stop herself from asking her friend:

'Did you recognize him, Denise? From that photograph?'

Denise nodded her dark head, her eyes on Eve's face.

'I recognize also that you love him, Eve. You cannot deceive me. I know, too, that you are unhappy. Edouard notices this, too. He ask me why you look so pale and thin. I do not tell him what I guess because I think you do not wish others to know what I have guessed. You do love him, don't you, Eve?'

Eve nodded her head.

'But you cannot forget what happen in Paris!' Denise said shrewdly. 'I see how this is so, but, *chérie*, do not let your pride stand between you and your heart's wishes. Once you told me that I must not let my wish for money keep me from love. You were so right, and now I say the same to you. What have happened … it is over now, is it not? Can you not forget it?'

'That was my father's advice,' Eve admitted. 'But how can I forget what happened, Denise? If nothing else, there is Anthony to remind me.'

'But this nice young man do not know Anthony is his child, so you tell me. You cannot blame him that he desert Anne-

Marie when he do not even know she had his child. For the rest … well, most young men have had affairs of one kind or another. My Edouard … he have many loves, but now he settle down and there exists no other woman in the world for him but me. He is the best husband that ever lived!'

'I'm sure of it!' Eve said, smiling. 'But he is the exception that proves the rule, Denise. Perhaps I am too idealistic, but I always hoped that one day I would find someone who…'

'Was quite perfect!' Denise said. 'Pah! That is no man at all, Eve. I know that one does not like to see faults in those one loves and at first perhaps one does not see them. When one is married one discovers them as one's own are discovered. For you I realize it is difficult that you know something to his discredit before even you know what is nice about him. But that you fall in love with him in spite of this … surely you see then that it is the "real" thing for you?'

'It feels real enough!' Eve said, with a rueful smile. 'He haunts me, Denise. I think about him all day and most of the night! Today when you spoke about him at the house all alone, I longed to get up and rush away to him. I *know* I could never love anyone else, but I can't let myself love him, either.'

'You will in time, *chérie!*' Denise said gently. 'Give yourself time, Eve. See him a little bit, talk to him, know what he is really like inside his heart ... then you can judge more easily, is it not? I think he grow to love you, too, since he cannot help to love so nice a girl as you.'

'But I'm dull, ordinary, not even beautiful!' Eve whispered. 'And he will compare me with Anne-Marie and–'

'And realize what a big mistake he make. A pretty face ... that is one thing ... but a kind, good heart, beauty that comes from inside ... that is much, much more. Edouard show me this as he paints. Always he leave the thing I find so pretty. "Look!" he tell me. "And the longer you look the more used to it you get until it is just dull. But this ... this is different ... you must search deeper to find its attraction, and then you discover that it have a 'soul' and after this you cannot forget it or cease to admire it." He is right, I think. Edouard is nearly always right except when he is jealous. This is always his fault. I have just to smile at a man and he think I am changing my mind about *him!* He think, because he love me himself, that every man love me on sight. Even that I carry the baby make no difference! But perhaps in time he learn that there can be no other man for me but him, then he will be perfect.'

'It's wonderful to see you so happy, Denise!' Eve said. 'I have often thought about you and wondered how you and Edouard were getting on. After all, you did marry him without knowing much about him, didn't you?'

'It is true! But never for even a second have I regret that I do this. Sometimes I think that perhaps I might never have met him that first time, and I feel awful just to think about it! But Fate make sure we meet so, is it not? And perhaps also Fate bring Paul to your life the way it have done for a purpose. We shall see!'

While Eve was trying to make up her mind whether to follow Denise's advice and see more of Paul, the matter was taken out of her hands, for Antoinette announced at lunchtime the following day that she had been up to the big house and invited Paul and his friend to dinner.

'They were delighted!' she said. 'Poor boys. I think they cannot have had a good meal since they arrived.'

Eve flew into a panic, which amused Denise, for she had rushed without thinking to her room to search frantically among her clothes for her most becoming dress.

'Oh what can I wear?' she said at last. 'I haven't a single thing that's presentable!'

'This is not so,' Denise laughed. 'But all the same, I think it will be a good idea that you should look very special tonight. I have brought with me by mistake one of my new dresses which I wear only once before the baby make me too big for it! I make you the present of it, for I think it fit you nicely and suit you very well!'

'Oh, I couldn't take it!' Eve said automatically. But Denise swept her refusal aside.

'I have more clothes than I know where to put them,' she said. 'Every time we go down the Champs Elysées Edouard rush into a shop and buy me some new thing. He is very rich, Eve, and this one dress I cannot possibly miss. When you see it you will not refuse.'

It was indeed a lovely frock ... far more beautiful than anything Eve had ever worn. It was a burnt-corn colour made of silk jersey material and cut with deliberate simplicity so that it moulded itself on the wearer's figure. A woman of anything else but perfect proportions could never wear the dress, but on Eve's neat, slender figure it looked a work of art. At the base of the low-cut neckline Denise pinned a large bunch of imitation violets.

'That is all it needs to make it perfect!' she said, standing back to admire her friend. 'Ah, yes, and your hair. Let me comb it for you tonight, Eve ... a little more formally than you wear it now, *hein?*'

Staring at her reflection in the mirror, Eve felt she was looking at a stranger. She knew that she had never worn anything that so became her ... nor which so completely changed her personality. In this dress she appeared *soignée,* sophisticated, self-assured ... all the things she longed to be!

'It's lovely, Denise!' she whispered. 'I wonder what Mother and Father will say when I wear it tonight!'

But Denise knew she was thinking of someone other than her parents and she smiled a little secretively. Paul would notice Eve tonight as a ravishingly beautiful young woman or else Denise would want to know the reason why.

Paul and his friend, Jake, had scarcely been in the house five minutes before Denise, watching him closely, knew that she had no need to doubt the success of her little plan. He never took his eyes off Eve for a second, except when politeness demanded that he should reply to a remark. This done, he would turn once more to look at Eve, as if he could hardly believe his eyes.

'Confound it!' he was thinking. 'What makes her seem so different tonight? I hardly noticed her last time I saw her. I know I thought she didn't compare in looks to her younger sister. How wrong I was!'

And Jake was thinking:

'So there *was* a woman in the picture after all! And what a girl! No wonder old Paul kept her dark! Secretive young devil. He night have told me about her!'

He watched Paul from time to time and felt a moment's qualm on his friend's behalf. It wouldn't do to show a girl quite so obviously how smitten he was. Unless, of course, he was sure of her. From Jake's observation of women, they liked to do a bit of the chasing and not make their conquests too easily. The girl, however, was paying as little attention to Paul as possible and only when his head was turned away from her did Jake notice her regarding him covertly.

'Now what's up with them both?' he asked himself, as they went in to dinner. 'She looks almost afraid of him. But she's interested, and what girl wouldn't be?'

For Jake had a high opinion of his friend … knew Paul to be attractive to women, with his height and breadth and manliness. There was also a certain charm about the thick, very light brown hair that refused to be kept flat and curled boyishly over his head. He knew him to be an interesting fellow, too, full of information no matter what the subject. Yet tonight he hardly spoke a word, except occasionally to Denise, who sat beside him and with whom he seemed more his normal self.

Paul realized that he was not exactly helping his host and hostess to keep the conversation going, but he was too stunned by his emotions to find it easy to marshal his thoughts into any order. He could not get over the surprise of finding himself so bowled over by this quiet, dark girl whom he scarcely knew.

Eve, too, noticed his confusion and felt

rather than saw his eyes on her.

'It's this dress,' she thought. 'It isn't me! Anyway, what do I care what he thinks of me?'

But she did care, and she felt afraid as her heart quickened its beat every time their eyes met. It would only make things more difficult if he was interested in her, and she felt trapped as the net seemed to close around her with every minute they stayed in the same room together. She longed to get up and leave the table and run out into the twilight of the summer evening ... far away from everyone ... *far away from him*. But she was forced by convention to remain in her chair opposite him and try her best to concentrate on the conversation that flowed around her.

She was glad when at last Antoinette rose to indicate that the ladies would leave the room while the men had their port and cigars, and the door at last put a barrier between them.

'I'll run up to see if Anthony's all right!' she excused herself feebly, and was glad that none except perhaps Denise seemed to find anything odd in the reason for her escape.

But she could not remain in the privacy of her room alone for long. She knew as she sat on the bed with her hands against her hot cheeks that she would *have* to go down again and sit out the rest of the evening. If only she could find a chair far from Paul ...

where she wouldn't have to talk to him...!

But Denise put a careful end to this plan. When the men returned to the room to join the ladies for coffee she stood up instantly, vacating her chair beside Eve, saying:

'I really need a little fresh air. Edouard, *chéri*, would you sit with me by the window?'

Eve could cheerfully have murdered her friend at the same moment as Paul was blessing the French girl's tact.

'I've been wanting to speak to you, Miss Corderhay,' he said politely, as he offered Eve a cigarette. 'I wanted to ask you how the little boy had settled down in his new home. Does he like it here?'

'Yes ... very much, thank you,' Eve said, bending her head towards his hand as he held his lighter to her cigarette. She drew away from him quickly and inhaled the smoke, which seemed to steady her nerves.

'I hope you'll bring him up to the house sometimes,' Paul continued. 'I took rather a fancy to the little fellow!'

'He's your son!' Eve felt like saying, and only just refrained from such an hysterical, crazy remark. No wonder Paul liked the child!

'We ... should like to ... come ... sometime!' she stammered.

'Then why not make "sometime" tomorrow?' Paul said quickly. 'I can't guarantee much of a tea, I'm afraid. We're still a little disorganized. But my cook will find something.'

'We shan't eat much,' Eve said, and thought, 'Now I've accepted, and I didn't mean to do so!'

'Then I'll expect you ... about half past three?' Paul said eagerly. 'As a matter of fact I'd appreciate some advice if you feel you could spare me a little time while you're there. I don't seem to have much of a flair for *décor*. I bought a mass of furniture and stuff and had it sent down from London, but now I don't where to put it all. The house looked so charming when I last saw it and it seems a desecration to leave it like it is at the moment!'

'I'd love to come and help straighten things out!' Eve said naturally and eagerly, before she had time to remember that she had resolved not to see him at all, if she could avoid it.

'That's very decent of you,' Paul said. 'Especially as it must ... well, upset you to ... to be out of your home. I hope you and your family won't feel too cut away from it. I'd like you all to come over whenever you feel like it.'

'That's very kind of you, Mr Johnson,' Eve said sincerely.

His blue eyes suddenly lit up with a smile.

'Do you think perhaps we could be informal enough, since we are to be neighbours, to call each other by our Christian names? Mr Johnson sounds so very ... dull!'

'If you wish it,' Eve said, looking down at her hands. But she could not speak his name.

'Then I may call you Eve?' he persisted.

She nodded her head.

'I didn't know there could be a girl like this still left in the world!' Paul was thinking, delighted as much by her shyness as by the progress he felt he was making. 'And to think that she will be living only a few hundred yards away! Ye gods! I'm a lucky chap to be here!'

'How charming your French friend is!' he said conversationally. 'Her husband is a nice chap, too.'

'But very jealous!' Eve warned him with a smile. 'He was quite upset when he heard you had asked Denise into the house!'

'Oh, well, he's French!' Paul said, with a typical Englishman's outlook that all foreigners were a bit odd.

'And an artist, too!' Eve told him. 'He's very well known in Paris and all over France.'

'Paris is a beautiful city,' Paul said thoughtfully. 'But I have rather unhappy memories of it. But then you know about all that, of course. I forget you are Anne-Marie's sister.'

'But I cannot forget you were her lover!' Eve thought, and said:

'Anne-Marie is living only a few miles from here. I expect you will meet from time to time.'

'Possibly,' Paul said shortly. 'But I don't suppose I shall have time for many parties. I'm on a week's leave from business at the moment, but when I go back to work I shan't be home till late evening.'

'It's a long way to travel every day,' Eve said, remembering her last trip to town ... to see him!

'But worth it ... anyway in the summer,' Paul said easily. 'It's so lovely out here in the country ... especially after a stuffy day in London.'

'Then you prefer country life?' Eve asked. Paul nodded his head.

'I haven't had a chance before ever to *live* in the country. I've always been too busy. But I wanted to do so. I hate big cities. They are always so full of people and everything is so hustling and bustling, if you know what I mean.'

'Yes, I do understand,' Eve said. 'I could never live in London, though I did spend a year in Paris. It was such a lovely city ... but ... I wasn't very happy there, either.'

'I wonder what happened to her in Paris!' Paul thought. 'Did she have an unhappy love-affair?'

He felt suddenly wildly jealous of any other men there might have been in her life. Then he was struck dumb for a moment or two by the thought that perhaps there was some man now ... in the present.

'Would you consider it a very personal remark if I asked you if you ... if you're engaged?' he said awkwardly.

Eve looked at him in surprise.

'What made you think that?' she asked him. 'Anyway, I'm not engaged and not likely to be. I ... I don't want to get married. I ... prefer my freedom.'

'What a strange girl she is!' Paul thought. 'She seemed so domesticated last time I met her, and this evening she is quite the opposite ... that was emancipated remark ... if she meant it!'

But he had no further chance for intimate conversation with this girl who so attracted him, as they were dragged back into the general conversation by Antoinette.

Soon after ten o'clock Paul and Jake rose to go, not wishing to overstay their welcome. For a moment Paul held Eve's hand in his as she bade him a formal good night, but at the same time their eyes met and Paul felt, rather than saw, the spark that suddenly glowed in their darkness for an instant before her gaze fell.

The thrill that this visual contact had brought about made his heart sing as he walked up the drive with Jake by his side. He felt as if he could walk for ever like this ... power and energy and exhilaration giving his feet wings as well as his heart. But Jake brought him back to earth when he remarked:

'You're a dark horse, Paul! Why, I really believed you when you told me you "just had to live here", as if there were no more to it than that!'

'What do you mean?' Paul asked truculently, for he still did not feel like talking … even to Jake.

'You know what I mean … that girl, Eve. Don't try and tell me you aren't interested. I was watching you. And she is interested in you, too, though she tries not to show it. Just what is going on, Paul?'

'Blessed if I know!' Paul said, on a sudden burst of laughter. He was so happy because Jake had said Eve was interested in him. He had begun to wonder if he had only imagined that fire in those dark brown eyes of hers. 'Honestly, Jake, old chap, I never even knew she existed. At least, I had met her once before – twice to be exact – but I was rather taken up with her sister at the time and I never even noticed her. Must have been blind, I suppose. I give you my word … until tonight she meant no more to me than … than, well anything!' he ended feebly.

'You must indeed have been blind!' Jake remarked disbelievingly. 'What's she really like, Paul … to talk to? And why isn't she married already? It all seems rather odd to me.'

'She says she doesn't *want* to get married!'

Paul announced cheerfully. 'But lots of girls feel like that ... don't they? I mean, until they meet the right chap!'

'And are you the right chap?' Jake teased his friend.

'Oh, shut up!' Paul said rudely but without rancour. 'Can't a fellow have any privacy in his private life without his business partner poking his nose in when he isn't wanted?'

'All right, all right!' Jake said, laughing. 'I'll keep out of it. I overheard you asking her to tea tomorrow, so I think I shall feel in need of a nice long walk on my own about tea-time.'

'And I quite agree with you!' Paul said forcibly, knowing that his friend would understand and not expect him to play the host when a very attractive young woman was coming to tea. Jake would keep out of the way.

'Gosh, it's a wonderful night!' he said, as they reached the great oak front door. 'And it's a beautiful house, too. I've never seen such lovely country as there is around here, either!'

'You'll be telling me I'm beautiful next!' Jake said, pushing his friend into the house before him. 'You sound like a young man suffering from his first attack of calf-love. For heaven's sake shut up and go to bed!'

Paul grinned happily as he swung the great

door back and pulled the bolt across it.

'Funny if I married her!' he mused. 'She'd have her old home back if I did!'

'Good night, Paul!' Jake said firmly, but he knew that it would be many hours later before Paul climbed the big staircase. He was far too full of excited energy to think of sleep. Midnight was long past when at last, worn out with dreaming, Paul finally made his way to bed.

CHAPTER 17

Eve, too, had neglected her bed until the early hours of the morning, but her dreams were not Paul's happy ones. Overpowering even the heady excitement that the evening had caused was the realization that nothing could come of this affair with Paul.

Standing at her open window, staring into the bright starlit night, she asked herself how she could have permitted Denise so to persuade her from her former intentions. She had firmly resolved to see as little of Paul as possible, and, when circumstances forced them to meet, to keep as much in the background as she could so that there would be no chance of their becoming involved in conversation and perhaps even a friendship which she did not desire.

'Vanity!' she told herself, with a wry smile. 'Pure feminine vanity, I suppose!' For what else explained the thrill of dressing up in an exotic, becoming dress that was bound to attract attention? What else explained the inward gratification because Paul had noticed her ... not just as Anne-Marie's sister but as a woman beautiful and desirable in her own right?

Fear of what this portended should have come afterwards, but when Denise had said, in her quiet, humorous way, *'Chérie,* you have make the big hit, is it not? Your young man could not take the eyes off you all evening!' her betraying heart had thrilled with this confirmation of what she had known for herself. Whenever she had dared to look in Paul's direction it had been to find his eyes on her, slightly shy when their glances met, but with an expression of admiration, interest, and unmistakably challenging in their unspoken question, 'Are you feeling as I do, Eve?'

She could interpret that glance because there was no doubting the thrill of electricity that passed through her own body to his and from his to her whenever their hands touched for an instant or their eyes met.

But what could it avail to have succeeded in attracting him ... if this had been her motive? It would only make things harder for her and hopeless for him, since love could never blossom between them. Above all, she did not wish to let him down as Anne-Marie had done ... give him an even worse opinion of her sex and make him more bitter towards her family and kind. It wasn't fair to him and certainly not sensible from her point of view. She wanted to forget him ... not find more firmly established his place in her heart. Love begets love, and to know that her own emotions were reciprocated would double the size of her burden. She would be reasonable for hurting them both.

'Can any ideal warrant all this pain and uncertainty?' Eve asked the stars. Was she being unreasonable to refuse to contemplate as a husband a man who had once been her sister's lover and whose child her sister had borne? Surely this was an impossible barrier between them! One day he might discover Anthony's real identity ... it might suffice to ruin whatever happiness they would find together, always supposing that *she* could bring herself to forget Anne-Marie. If she told him about Anthony now, would he resent her because she had not told him this sooner while there was still time to make the child legally his own? She had kept silent because at first she had imagined Anne-Marie meant to marry him, later because she feared what he might do to Anne-Marie if he found out ... and now because she feared that he might try to take the child away from her.

'But he wouldn't do that!' she whispered aloud. 'He is a kind person and fond of children. So suppose I do tell him ... and he asked me to marry him to make the child belong to us both. Could I marry him then ... in spite of what I know about his past? Was Father right when he said that the past didn't matter ... that only the present and the future counted?'

Nevertheless, however hard Eve tried to talk herself into feeling free to further this new friendship with Paul, her mind would reject this demand from her heart, saying to her: 'You resolved never to make do with second best. No one is perfect ... but this surely is an episode in a man's life one should not know ... but since you do know ... you could not tolerate. You would never feel the same respect for him that you should feel if you are to love fully. You could never be completely happy ... nor make him completely happy while this memory would lie between you!'

Exhausted by this inner conflict and the evening's excitement, Eve felt she had no resistance left. She wanted peace of mind more than she wanted love ... release from this tortuous swaying between heart and mind ... perfection and imperfection ... right and wrong. Falling into her bed at last, too tired to fight any longer, she decided that tomorrow she would end this nonsense once and for all. She would keep her appointment to have tea with Paul ... but she would go in her oldest, least becoming cotton frock ... she would make it quite clear to him in every way a woman could that she had no interest in him or his feelings and that she wished him to leave her alone.

But the decision was more easily made than kept when the following afternoon Denise stood watching her carelessly powdering her nose and running a comb through her hair as if she were 'about to go to the post rather than to a tête-à-tête', as the French girl described it.

'Oh, you English!' she said, throwing up her hands in horror. 'Have you no vanity at all? Eve, why must you wear *this* dress?'

'Because it's my oldest and plainest!' Eve said truthfully surveying the childish blue-and-white check gingham, which she had had more than seven years!

Denise gave her friend a closer look.

'It is because you wish to discover if he like you last night only because of what you wear?' she asked shrewdly.

Eve shook her head.

'It's because I don't want to attract him, Denise. I'm going to finish off ... whatever started last night. I don't want him to get fond of me or be interested in me, or have anything to do with me. I want to be left alone to *forget* him.'

Denise sighed.

'Very well, if you wish it! But you are blind, my Eve! You cannot fight what is in the heart ... in your heart or in his heart. And if love *has* started to grow in his heart, as I believe, then no frock or hair style or scowls will alter how he feel! In any case,' she added, with a mischievous smile, 'I think this dress rather suit you after all ... it makes you look the very young girl ... out-door girl ... and I think this please him. Last night he have the sophistication and today the *ingénue* ... in one woman he find all women ... *ça va bien!*'

'That's what you think, Denise!' Eve replied crossly. 'Just you wait and see. I shall be so ... so beastly ... he'll never want to ask me to tea again.'

'We shall see!' Denise said philosophically. 'Where is *le petit?* He goes with you, does he not?'

'Yes! And we shall be back early!' Eve said, and shot out of the room before Denise could make any more disconcerting comments.

Paul must have been watching for her, for as soon as Eve and the little boy neared the house he came out through the French windows onto the lawn and walked towards them.

349

Watching his tall figure striding so easily and effortlessly in her direction, Eve felt her heart jolt in nervous excitement and a joy which she could not prevent. Her eyes went to the fair head and she longed to be near enough to see those intense blue eyes of his, while her ears strained to catch his first words.

When they were in front of one another, however, she could not meet his eyes and could tell only from the glad ring in his voice that he was pleased to see her.

She bent her head over Anthony's blond curls, hiding her flushed cheeks.

'Say "Hello",' she encouraged the little boy, but already Anthony had taken this stranger's measure and, seeing the man's pleasant smile, toddled towards him, his arms outstretched in a mute appeal to be lifted into the air.

Delighted, Paul did what was required of him and sat the little boy on his shoulders, where the child crowed in delight at being so high up in the air. He looked down far below him, so it seemed, to Eve and said, 'Eve, Eve!'

Eve was forced to look up and Paul intercepted her glance and held her gaze for a brief instant during which time she knew her cheeks were turning pink and could have kicked herself for her inability to control her blushes … and her weakness. To counteract this lapse from her intended behaviour she said coldly:

'I'm afraid we shan't be able to stay long, Mr Johnson. I feel very guilty as it is for neglecting our guests.'

The disappointment was as much evident in his reply as in his tone of voice, and she felt suddenly miserable. They walked up to the house in silence... Paul lost in thought, Eve wishing that she could think of something, no matter what, to say ... and the child alone of the three happily content with the present situation.

It was Eve's first re-entry into the house which had been her home, but she was hardly aware of the changes in the sitting-room. Paul, anxious for her to feel at home and approve of his furnishings, drew her attention to them, but her answers were mechanical and he did not take long to realize it. Thinking that perhaps this return to her home was responsible for her quietness, he said impulsively:

'Let's have tea in the library, shall we? I don't expect you'll see much difference there. I left it just as your father had it. It's my favourite room.'

But although she replied politely to any remark he might make, he felt that it was not the house that had changed her after all ... she had been shy enough last evening. It went deeper than that and it confused and worried him. Could he, after all, have mistaken that strange bond between them? He was still as certain as ever of her attraction for him ... for she looked incredibly young and sweet today and somehow more like the girl he felt her really to be ... but he was no longer certain of her feelings towards himself. Last evening he had been sure she liked him ... even Jake had thought so.

'You know, last night we decided to use Christian names,' he said tentatively. 'Today you called me Mr Johnson. Does that mean you don't wish me to call you ... Eve?'

It was the second time he had spoken her name, and to its owner it had never sounded more attractive. His way of saying the one short word had been like a caress.

'Of course not ... I mean ... you can call me Eve if you wish. I'll try to ... to remember to call you ... Paul,' she said, wishing that every word she ever spoke to this man did not sound so childish and stupid and confused.

'Then what about some tea, Eve?' he asked her, with his quick disarming grin.

A smile curved her mouth into a sweet, provocative line, and Paul, seeing it, drew in his breath sharply. It was crazy, he knew, and yet Eve had a completely unconsidered way of striking right at the centre of his heart. With one smile she could double the rate of its beating and send the blood coursing through his veins in a mad tumult. No girl he

352

had ever known had just this effect on him. Eve's shyness and quietness also attracted him, seeing the perfect setting for her tall, slender beauty and those strangely passionate dark eyes of hers. If only he could find a way into the thoughts she concealed behind that smooth, white forehead! If only he knew how to bring a smile to her eyes and words from those all-too-silent lips!

'Tell me about yourself, Eve,' he begged her, when tea had been brought in and the little boy was sitting happily by himself in a large leather armchair munching biscuits. 'Tell me what you do all day … what you like … what you want of life … what you think of this world we live in.'

'I don't think my views would interest you. I'm … a very dull person,' Eve said promptly. 'There's nothing interesting to know about me.'

'Everything about you interests me.' He spoke without thinking, and only realized the personal quality of his remark when he saw the colour flooding into her cheeks again.

'Forgive me if that annoyed you,' he said, and then: 'But why should I ask forgiveness for what is the truth? The fact of the matter is, Eve, that I'm not much of a "lady's man". I haven't had a lot to do with women in my life… I've always been too busy. So I'm probably saying and doing all the wrong things. I dare say I make plenty of social blunders, too. But if I feel something strongly … I have to speak of it. I know it doesn't always pay to be outspoken, but somehow with you I feel you will understand. I'd like to think we could always be perfectly honest with one another … not have to waste time beating about the bush.'

'Waste time?' Eve asked desperately, in order to give herself time to think of a reply to his outburst. But she had not succeeded in side-tracking him from his personal vein.

'Yes. Time is precious when … when you discover something about life that you didn't know existed. You can't wait to know more … to learn every detail … to go on to wherever it is the new discovery is leading you. Do you understand what I mean? I felt ever since last evening like an explorer. You're such a … strange person, Eve. I don't really know anything about you at all. I don't know what you think about when you sit so quietly. But I want to know. I … I like you a great deal. I hope that you will come to like me a little, too.'

'This isn't happening. He hasn't said those things. I'm just dreaming it all!' Eve told herself as she sought frantically to escape the issue he was forcing on her. What could she say to him?

'I know we haven't known each other very long,' Paul continued, seeing the tight expression of her mouth. 'Don't think I'm …

well, that I act like this every time I meet a girl. I don't ... I so rarely meet a girl that I'd care to see again. Last night I felt that if I didn't see you today I couldn't go on living! Does this all sound quite crazy to you? It must do. It does to me, too! I'm not sure what it's all about. Have I annoyed you?'

He sounded so young ... so uncertain, excited, perplexed all at once, that Eve felt suddenly sorry for him. She could understand how he felt, for she had felt the same way herself ... but she wanted less than ever now to be responsible for hurting him.

'I'm not annoyed,' she said gently. 'But it does all seem a ... a little strange, doesn't it? I mean ... you don't know anything about me ... nor I about you. Maybe we just feel that we would like each other if we got to know one another better.'

'*Would* ... *if?*' Paul echoed sharply. 'Don't you mean *when?* We *are* going to see a lot of one another, aren't we?'

His tone was so anxious that Eve felt her heart sink.

'I ... I suppose we'll see each other ... from time to time,' she said awkwardly. 'I hope ... we'll be friends. That's ... what you meant ... wasn't it?'

Paul gave a curious little laugh.

'I don't think I know quite what I meant,' he said. 'But I do know I was hoping for ... for something a little different. I suppose it's all a question of how one divines "friend-ship". Jake has been my friend for fifteen years and I have the deepest affection and regard for him ... but this wouldn't be the same feeling I ... I have for you. Nor would I want only from you what Jake gives me. It's really the difference between men and women ... I mean, do *you* think men and women can be friends ... platonic friends?'

Eve shivered, although the room was warm. She wished that Anthony would cause a diversion, for the conversation seemed to have grown far too personal and too near an issue she didn't wish to face quite yet. But the child was never quieter or more content to amuse himself.

'No ... I don't think it is possible ... except where the man and the girl in question are each in love with someone else.'

'Then you don't think ... *we* could be platonic friends?' Paul took the plunge and said what he meant to say without trim-mings.

'All right!' Eve told herself. 'He wants to have it out today. And I wanted to finish things for good and all. We'll face it now.'

'No ... I don't,' she said, looking straight at him and seeing by the widening of his eyes that he was pleased with her reply. 'You see, I believe one always knows ... when one meets someone ... whether one likes them or not ... seriously, I mean. What I'm trying to say is … that for my part, anyway, I know the first time I meet a man whether he … could mean anything to me … anything special, that is. If it isn't there … then the friendship dies off … either from lack of interest on either side … or because it isn't fair to continue a one-sided affair. But if it is there … then to me that is instant recognition, and then I think one must face up to what one wants of the future. It's really a question of one's ideals … principles … and so on. I believe it would be impossible to have a … a platonic … friendship with anyone one … recognized in this way … as meaning something special… So one has to make up one's mind what one wants to do about it.'

Paul was leaning forward in his chair, listening intently to every word she said. There was a look of happiness on his face which was centred in the very core of his being. Though hesitantly and falteringly, she had shown to him what he had been feeling all along. The 'attraction' was possibly biological in the first instance, but it could mean more … it could grow to mean more. That's why she had said 'when it's there, one must face up to what one wants to do about it'. In other words, he had to sort out in his mind whether he wanted to settle down and get married, and therefore do everything in his power to find out if one loved also with the mind as well as the body … whether such feelings as he discovered in himself were reciprocated. If not, then the friendship was best ended right away, for platonic friendships couldn't exist where that kind of affection remained on one side only. Since he was not the type of man to be interested any more merely in an attraction of the senses (which he knew now his so-called love of Anne-Marie had been), nor Eve the kind of girl to play around with love … it left only two alternatives … to love her enough to marry her, if she would have him, or cease to see her.

'But I already love her!' he thought with a deep inner recognition of the truth. 'I want to marry her … to make her my wife. I know already that everything she is … thinks, feels … must be good and right and decent … for she is all these things. I know she is sweet and beautiful and kind… I know she loves children and that they love her. I *feel* that she is right for me in every way. But could I make her happy? I know so little of her interests in life … does she like reading, plays, music? Does she dance, ride, play tennis? How old is she? When is her birthday?… Oh, what a wealth of information I need to discover about her!'

'I want to be honest with you, Eve … about us,' he said slowly and thoughtfully. 'I realize how unusual it must be for two people to be talking like this only the fourth time of meeting, and the first two times so unfortunate!

But I feel in my heart that it is important that we should be frank. If I am annoying you ... if you would rather I changed the conversation altogether ... please say so.'

'It must come some time!' Eve thought. 'Why not now? Then everything we feel will be out for better or worse and he will know that there is no hope for us. At least I shall have the comfort of knowing he had begun to care for me as I already love him.'

'What do you wish to say?' she asked, her voice so low that he could barely catch her words.

He was looking now into her eyes, as if he could read in them how his words affected her.

'I think I love you, Eve,' he said. 'Maybe it isn't flattering to say only "think", but love, as I believe it can, and does, exist ... must incorporate all the senses, and I know so little of you yet. What I know already, I love. That is the truth, and to hear myself speaking these words amazes me, for I did not think that I could ever feel this way about anyone. I am not from your world, Eve, and our backgrounds must be very far apart, but I have grown into your world and dare to hope that perhaps you would accept me as a part of it. All my life I have worked hard and my reason for doing so, as I once told your father, has been to earn money so that I could buy the things I wanted and never had as a child. Now, suddenly, miraculously, but also rather frighteningly, I realize that there is something more I want ... happiness and love, which are things money cannot buy. But I will work as hard as ever I have done in my life yet to achieve these two things ... one being dependent on the other, as I now realize. It would help me to know that perhaps you might one day grow to care a little for me ... to consider that our futures might be inextricably bound together ... that there was even a spark of hope for me ... with you.'

'Hope! All the hope you would ever need if my love is all you ask for, but you will want more than that if you really love *me*, you will want me to marry you, and this I cannot do.'

She looked up and met the full concentration of his blue eyes and for a moment her heart weakened her resolve. She hesitated for a brief instant, an intense longing throughout her being tempting her to give way and admit that she loved him ... could never love anyone else ... that even though she knew so little of him she was prepared to marry him if he wanted to make her his wife.

The words were on the tip of her tongue when, for the first time since they had begun their conversation, the child interrupted them, coming on unsteady plump little legs to Eve's knee and saying:

'Eve! Eve!' his little curly head tilted on

one side as he tried to divert her attention to himself.

'Anthony!' she whispered. For a moment she had nearly forgotten his existence. For a moment she had weakened, but the child's voice and his little hands pulling at her skirts had brought back reason.

Paul, watching her closely, saw the sudden stiffening of her limbs, the sudden pallor of her cheeks and queer, instinctive closing of her eyes as if she were shutting him out of her life. In that moment he felt that she had become a different person. He had *felt* her earlier response as he talked … had seen the faint colour stealing into her cheeks, seen the bright, responsive light in her eyes, and he had *known* … felt so positive that he was not alone in his love … that she *did* care for him. What had altered the situation that one moment had seemed so hopeful, the next so devoid of hope? Surely not a little child—

Paul's mind came to a sudden abrupt halt. The child! He had never thought much about little Anthony except to admire the little fellow and to think him an intelligent, attractive baby. He recalled now that Jack Corderhay had told him he had adopted the baby in Paris… Paris, where only a few children had this little boy's blond English fairness… Paris, where Eve had spent a year, and so unhappily! *Was it possible that this was* her *child?* She acted as if it was …

361

loved it as any mother might love her own flesh and blood... Eve's child... *Eve's*...

For a moment his mind ceased to function properly, and he could only stare at the little boy and the young woman holding him against her breast, her dark eyes smiling reassuringly into the baby's blue ones.

Thoughts began to race through his brain at double speed. Jack Corderhay's devotion to his adopted daughter ... so devoted that he brought her child back to his home and adopted it, too... Eve so devoted to the father who had stood by her in her trouble... Eve's maternal, quiet, thoughtful ways ... that tragic, unsettled, unhappy look he had glimpsed once or twice in her eyes... Could it be true? And if it were true ... would it make any difference? Could he stop himself now from falling any deeper in love with her? How was he to judge the extent of his emotions when he had never been in love before? He had forced the issue between them by turning the conversation into the channels it had taken. He had already asked her if she might care for him. Could he go back on that question? *Did he want to go back on it?*

If only he had time ... time to think ... to sort out his emotions. Suppose now Eve were to say to him: 'I love you, but this is my child... I cannot be parted from him ... if you want me you must take him, too.'

'*I'd still want her...*' he thought violently. 'I would admire her for standing by the child. Another woman might have left the baby on someone's doorstep! But this girl, the girl I love ... has courage. She showed that courage when she came in person to tell me her sister wasn't going to marry me after all. Surely Eve couldn't have been to blame for what has transpired. Some man has let her down ... made promises he couldn't, or wouldn't, keep...

'But I should be jealous of that other man...' Paul thought suddenly. 'The girl I married I would want to belong to me alone ... and she must have loved him or else she would not have borne his child ... perhaps still loves him. Could I bear this ghost between us?

'Perhaps I only imagine all this... I've no concrete reason to believe the child is hers. Perhaps after all I'm a bit over-wrought and have let my imagination run away with me. In a moment she will prove that it isn't so ... couldn't be so. Already the silence between us has been too prolonged.'

Eve, too, realized that she *must* speak ... and there could be no pretence ... no half measures. He had been honest with her, and now she must be honest with him. It was the least ... the only thing she could do for him.

'Paul,' she said in a whisper, using his Christian name unconsciously for the first

363

time. 'I'm so sorry … so sorry … for both of us … but I couldn't … there couldn't be any future for us. You see … there would be a barrier between us … no matter how much we love each other. I'll admit it, I do love you… No, don't move, don't say anything. I love you … but I can never marry you even if you were to ask me, because…' she drew the child closer to her … 'because there is no undoing what is already done.'

CHAPTER 18

Anne-Marie was bored. Richard had started work again in his father's firm after a lapse of nearly six months, and although he was allowed to arrive and leave his office more or less when he pleased, even the minimum of hours, together with his travelling time, necessitated his leaving Anne-Marie alone for long stretches.

'I've got to do *some* work, darling!' he had explained, anxiously watching for and hoping that her lips would not pout at him as they had so often done of late. 'Father had another talk with me last night and said he thought it was time I settled down again. After all, we have rather been hitting the high spots, haven't we?'

There had been no reply from Anne-Marie and he had continued, desperately trying to make her see that it was not his *wish* to leave her but his duty:

'We can't go on spending money at this rate and let Father keep us. I'm a junior partner in the firm and I've got to earn my salary some way or another.'

'And what am *I* going to do while you are away?' Anne-Marie had rounded on him, her blue eyes angry and her mouth a thin, hard line.

He had put out a hand to touch her, but she flung away from him saying: 'Well, what am I to do all day? I shall be bored stiff!'

He looked at her helplessly. Even after six months of married life he still knew so little of this young wife of his. They had been gay enough together, and she had seemed content, but he had never felt that he held the key to her heart or to her thoughts. He had had so little previous physical experience that he had not fully understood the real reason for her excessive, continuous demands on him. Happily he had assumed that her passion matched his own without a glimpse of the true nature of her feeling when she lay by his side. Only Anne-Marie knew that she was trying to forget another man ... a ghost from the past ... trying to recapture the thrill and completeness of that union with the man she had loved.

She didn't love Richard ... at times she even hated him, but he did not know this. He only guessed vaguely that she was disappointed in her married life ... not when they were going to parties and dances and entertaining ... but when they were alone together. These times were so seldom that his fears that his marriage was not turning out very successfully only struck him occasionally, and because he was still so deeply in love with the young girl he had married he quickly put such fears out of his mind and found excuses for the irritability and hard-heartedness, the petulance and sarcasm which she kept entirely for their occasional solitary moments. Otherwise, in public, she was the Anne-Marie he had known before their marriage ... the sweet, smiling young girl who deferred to his opinion ... made him feel her protector ... assuring him with a thousand intimate little looks, caresses and gestures that there was no other man on earth for her.

His friends congratulated him over and over again, and he had drawn comfort from their envy and approbation, telling himself that if outsiders noticed how much Anne-Marie loved him, then he was indeed stupid to worry that she was growing tired of him already. He continued to give way to her whenever he could, being rewarded by her smiles and the way she would lean against him, saying, 'Oh, Richard, you are a darling!' The sparkle returning to her blue eyes, the lilt to her voice, as she began again the eager anticipatory planning. His own desire for an evening at home was willingly sacrificed to such ends.

But over this question of work he could no longer give way to her. His father was pressing him on the one side and his conscience also. He must go back to the office and not delay doing so any longer. He had expected Anne-Marie to be cross, disappointed ... but at the same time he had hoped that she would see the obvious logic of his having to work. She could not expect him to stay around home having a good time and living on his capital and his father's generous allowance. Anne-Marie was extravagant, and while he grudged her nothing, he knew that they couldn't continue to lead this expensive existence indefinitely. He wanted to follow as quickly as possible now in his father's footsteps and make enough money for his wife to have everything she wanted.

'Can't you answer me, Richard?' she was saying in that irritated voice he dreaded to hear.

'Surely there are lots of things you can do?' he suggested hesitantly. 'Mother always seems to find amusements ... bridge parties and At Homes and–'

'Bridge parties... At Homes!' Anne-Marie

broke in scathingly. 'A lot of stuffy old women gossiping together. I should hate it. And I can't go out to interesting things on my own. I hate being on my own and you know it. Besides, I wanted to go to the races at Ballie Park on Tuesday!'

'Can't you ask one of your women friends to go with you?' Richard tried again.

'Women friends!' Anne-Marie repeated scornfully. 'I don't know anyone I like enough to go out with for a whole day. It isn't fair, Richard! You might at least have considered my feelings enough to put off your silly old work until after Tuesday, at least!'

For once Richard remained adamant. It took all his self-control and what remained of his will to say:

'I'm sorry, darling, but I promised Father last night I would start work on Monday. I'd forgotten about the races, but surely you *can* find someone to go with. What about Eve?'

'Oh, Eve's as dull as ditch-water these days!' Anne-Marie said, but there was a note of thought in her voice. After all, Eve would be better than going alone ... or staying home all day. 'She's tied to that brat!' she added, in case Richard should think she had given way too easily.

'Well, Mother said they had French friends staying with them,' Richard replied. 'Perhaps one of them would mind the child!'

'I'd forgotten about the Garrets,' Anne-

Marie said truthfully. 'Oh, well, if you have to go and leave me, Richard, I suppose I'll have to put up with Eve, but it's a jolly poor alternative to the party we'd arranged.'

She had not bothered to disillusion him when he took her words as a personal compliment to himself. After all, what was the use of upsetting him? It didn't get her anywhere and there'd only have to be a reconciliation scene later. She allowed him to kiss her cheek and then pushing him gently aside disappeared into her bedroom to change for dinner.

When Tuesday came Anne-Marie knew that she could not face another day at home with Richard's mother. Lady Bainborough was kind enough but she talked far too much and too long about her darling boy ... extolling Richard to the high heavens and trying to get Anne-Marie to do the same.

Eve's company would be better than another such day, and although she had seen her mother often, since she was frequently at Eversham Court, Anne-Marie had not seen her father for some weeks, and she felt she would like to see him ... just to satisfy herself that he was not too lonely and unhappy at the Lodge. She had a secret love and admiration for her father which she admitted to no one and only occasionally to herself, for she was jealous of the fact that he preferred Eve to herself ... although he tried not to show it

... and because she knew in her heart that she could never be his 'darling baby girl' again after what had happened in Paris.

Driving down the narrow lanes that led to Corderhay Park, Anne-Marie considered that she had had a poor deal from life. Whatever she had done that was wrong ... surely nothing could warrant the unhappiness and discontent that so haunted her since that unhappy affair. She had lied and tricked her way out of the situation, and fairly successfully, but not without some nasty moments ... for instance, when Paul Johnson turned up again, and she might still be in danger of having her secret disclosed by him. She had got away with most things with most people, but she could not get away from the truth herself ... that she was more unhappy than she had ever believed possible and that her marriage ... made from her desire for revenge ... had given her little real satisfaction in that quarter.

Her thoughts came to an abrupt halt as the village taxi, driving the opposite way up the lane, nearly collided headlong with her car at the Park gates.

The driver jumped out at once and came to the window to apologize to Anne-Marie, although the fault had been more hers than his.

'I'm ever so sorry, Miss Corderhay... I mean Mrs Bainborough,' he said. 'This road is usually so quiet one's apt to speed up a bit.'

'That's all right, Tom,' Anne-Marie said generously, for she rather liked the young boy who had always adored her from a respectful distance from the days when his father had driven the local cab. 'Are you going up to the big house?'

'No, miss … ma'am! I've a young French gentleman for the Lodge. I understand he's come to collect Ma'm'selle Boulanger to take her back to France.'

'Fetch Louise!' Anne-Marie said, the colour rushing to her face. Surely Tom's passenger couldn't be … couldn't be…

Slowly, deliberately, her heart thudding in her breast, Anne-Marie got out of her car and walked over to the taxi. As she stepped up to it Louise's brother Jean put his head out of the window. The expression on his face was almost comical when he recognized her … a mixture of dismay and acute surprise.

'*Toi!*' he said, his own tongue coming naturally to his lips, so surprised was he. '*Je n'ai jamais pensé que…*'

'I didn't expect to see you, either,' Anne-Marie said, her cool voice belying the unutterable confusion of her heart. 'Tom tells me you have come to collect Louise.'

He nodded, his eyes leaving her face and staring down at his hands. Anne-Marie waited for him to speak, but as he did not do so she said:

'Perhaps we could have a word with one another first, Jean. I think you owe it to me!' Her voice was filled with sarcasm, which he heard only too clearly.

'But of course!' he said, with forced lightness. 'Not here I think?'

'No,' Anne-Marie agreed. 'There's a summer-house in the Lodge garden. Suppose you pay off Tom and I'll park the car. Then we can walk there together. I'd prefer to see you alone.'

The young Frenchman had no alternative but to do as she asked. Politeness demanded it if nothing else. Nevertheless, as he did her bidding and followed her through the empty garden he felt furious with Fate for tumbling him into this awkward position. He had known, of course, that Anne-Marie was living near the Corderhays ... Louise had written such details from time to time ... but he had supposed that if he came to collect his sister ... as his mother had insisted ... without warning ... he would avoid seeing Anne-Marie. After all, it was the merest chance that she should be with her family the few hours that he would be with them waiting while Louise packed.

Irritated, but helpless, he walked beside her into the wooden summer-house, hoping against hope that someone would see them from the Lodge windows and interrupt them before the discussion she demanded should become too awkward.

No one seemed to have noticed them, however, and Anne-Marie, having made sure they were alone, turned to him and said:

'Well, Jean. Why did you not answer my letters?'

He lit a cigarette with studied carelessness, conscious of her eyes on him but unwilling to meet her gaze.

Anne-Marie was indeed studying her companion. This was Jean ... Jean, whom she had loved as she had loved no other man ... nor ever could ... Jean, for whom she had suffered and would suffer all her life ... the same dark hair swept back with meticulous care from the high, intelligent forehead ... same dark, almond-shaped eyes, but with so different an expression in them now ... the same slight, perfectly proportioned figure that must have been created to excite ... to attract ... to love...

Memories of the past flooded through her, breaking down her self-control.

'Jean, aren't you pleased to see me?' she begged of him, her voice suddenly soft and pleading. 'I couldn't believe it just now... I longed so often to meet you suddenly and unexpectedly ... like this ... dreamed that you would put your arms around me as you used to do ... hold me close and tell me that you still loved me ... that you *had* answered my letters ... that you could not have

deserted me so cruelly.'

But this was not, after all, the same impetuous young boy she had known nearly two years ago. This was an older, more assured, more experienced Jean ... a young man who could look around anxiously to ensure that no one could overhear them where in the past he had acted without thought ... except for her.

'Really, Anne-Marie ... of course I am pleased to see you,' he said rapidly in his own tongue, for he had heard that sudden loosening of control in her voice and knew that this might turn out to be even worse than he feared. Hysterical women ... well...

'Then you do care ... you still love me...?' Anne-Marie said with renewed hope that sent the colour flaming into her cheeks. 'It's true that you wrote after all ... that your letters went astray: Jean, tell me ... don't keep me in suspense. *Tell me what happened!*'

She was clutching his arms now, gazing up into his face. Gently but firmly he loosened the grip of her fingers. Instantly her face became taut and desperate and before he had time to speak she said:

'Then it isn't true after all. I might have known ... but I was fool enough to hope. I've always had that hope until now, Jean. Did you know that I tried to see you when I was in Paris ... on my honeymoon? Shocking ... wasn't it? Even more shocking, perhaps, if I tell you that *you* were one of two reasons I married my husband. He had money and money could get me back to Paris ... to you. And I married also from revenge ... my husband was your sister's boy-friend ... she was in love with him, and I think he might have married her. But I took him from under her nose ... to spite not her but you, Jean ... because of the way you had treated me. Do you hear me? I've ruined your sister's life for her to make you suffer for ruining mine!'

Her voice had risen a note or two higher and Jean looked desperately out of the doorway, searching for some means of escape ... or a sign that someone was coming. But the garden remained deserted and the house, too, seemed empty. Would no one come to extricate him from this unhappy state of affairs?

'Surely it can do no good now to go over what is past!' he said. 'You are married now and ... and I am about to be married. We must both forget what happened ... so long ago.'

'Forget!' Anne-Marie said violently. 'Oh, *you* may forget perhaps ... perhaps you had succeeded in doing so until I reminded you today. But it is not so simple for me. I love you, Jean, and I believed that you loved me. I thought my life had come to an end when you told me you had to visit those relations of yours for a whole month! How little did I know what unhappiness meant! How little did I realize at that moment that I wouldn't see you again until now. At first you wrote … then when I learned for certain I was to have a baby … *your child, Jean* … I asked you to telephone me. I waited and waited and decided my wire had gone astray. I wrote, telling you the whole truth, and you didn't reply. At first I thought something prevented you replying to me … but gradually I began to understand … you weren't going to reply. You were frightened … you'd stopped loving me … you were backing out because I was to have a baby. You were afraid of the disgrace … of what your mother would say…'

She was crying now, her sobs stemming the words that had poured from her lips. Jean surveyed her with anxiety.

'Please, Anne-Marie, control yourself,' he begged her. 'We do not wish everyone to know of this, do we? I can explain, if you will only listen to me quietly.'

She raised her face, wet with tears, to his.

'I'll listen, Jean,' she said. 'I *want* to hear what happened. For so long I wondered and wondered … now I must know the truth.'

'I had your letters, of course,' the young Frenchman told her, avoiding the searching look from her blue eyes. 'But I will be honest with you, Anne-Marie. I had gone not to visit relations, but the girl to whom my mother wished to affiance me. As you know, in France marriages are often arranged for conveniences in this way. This girl was very wealthy and it was essential that I should marry money ... and quickly. These affairs had already been discussed between our parents, and it was understood that she would have a very large *dot*. I was to meet her during this month, and if we approved of each other and the settlement, then I was to marry her. I told you when ... when our love-affair began ... Anne-Marie, that we could never be married ... that I must one day marry a rich girl.'

'But I didn't believe you!' Anne-Marie said desperately. 'I thought you loved me, Jean. I thought that after a little while you would grow to care more about me ... than money ... that you would run away with me.'

'This was madness to feel so,' Jean said more gently. 'I had my family to consider, and this must always come first. My father's business was in a very serious state since the war. It was up to me to set it right. This has nothing to do with love. But I was fond of you, Anne-Marie ... very fond of you. I cared too much for my peace of mind. I felt, too, that you were beginning to grow too fond of me. After all, we must soon end the association if I was to be married, I told myself. Perhaps it is kindest to do this before things get worse.'

'Kindness!' Anne-Marie whispered. 'Nothing could have been more cruel!'

'I did not think so,' Jean replied truthfully. 'I knew I must go away for a month, so what better time than this when we do not have to see one another in the same house … every day … every night? So when I am gone I did not answer your letters. When you told me about the child … naturally I did not believe it was true. We had made certain this could not happen. So I thought that you were a little upset and were trying this way to … to see I returned quickly to Paris. Then your letters stopped and I heard from my mother that your sister, Eve, had arrived in Paris and that you were leaving our house to share an apartment together. I thought then that you, too, have realized it is better not to continue as we were doing and have taken this wise step to go away from my home. I returned there after I knew you had left.'

'And my telephone calls?' Anne-Marie asked. 'Didn't you realize how many times I rang up for you? You were always out … or *were you*, Jean?'

'Not always,' he confessed truthfully. 'But I thought that you were a little lonely, and it is human nature not to give up anything one has enjoyed too easily … that occasionally one weakens. I told myself I am the one to be strong for us both, and this was hard for me, too, you know.'

Anne-Marie had listened in silence, but now her face had taken on a new expression of hope and her voice was almost joyous as she said:

'Then if you had known that the child really existed, Jean? How would you have felt then?'

He shrugged his shoulders in a typically French gesture.

'Ah, that would have been different, of course,' he said. 'But it is impossible to imagine such a hypothetical case, is it not?'

'But it was true, Jean!' Anne-Marie said, in a voice of such conviction that he looked at her in horror.

'This I cannot believe!' he said at last.

'Nevertheless, it is true!' Anne-Marie repeated. 'That was the reason I left your mother's house. That was the reason Eve came over to Paris ... you thought it was impossible, Jean ... but it happened all the same. Your child was born in Paris over a year ago!'

She knew then by the expression of horror on his face that he had not believed her letters. If only she had forced him to see her again ... how different things might have been! Even now ... it might not be too late.

'The child is here,' she said quickly. 'My father adopted him and he lives here, with my family. No one except Eve knows that he is mine ... and yours, Jean ... yes, yours, too.

He is your son and you cannot desert him now, you know. It is not too late. We can still run away together and my husband will have to divorce me. We'll be able to start again, Jean, together!'

'No! No! No! This cannot be!' Jean said, pushing her away from him with a gesture of horror. 'I have come to fetch Louise back to France because I am to be married next week. Nothing can stop my wedding, Anne-Marie. Nothing *must* stop it. I do not very much love the girl I am to marry, but it is all arranged and it is settled already in writing between our families. I am sorry about the child ... sorry that I could not help you when you needed help. I would have done anything then .. sent money to you ... seen you through until it was born ... but there is nothing I can do now.'

'There is, Jean, there is!' Anne-Marie shouted. 'You can't leave me again ... not now you know the truth. If you don't care about me ... at least you must care about the child... I'll show him to you... When you've seen him you'll have to claim him as your own. He is yours, Jean, and he's your responsibility. Why should I have to face all the blame and disgrace alone? You owe him your name, if nothing else. You owe it to me to marry me!'

She was shouting and crying at the same time and nothing the Frenchman could do could restrain or calm her. He sought desperately for words, but everything he said only made her more hysterical.

'I'll kill myself if you leave me again!' she was saying. 'I'll commit suicide and leave a note telling everyone the truth. I'll kill the child ... and you, too. Yes, I will, I will, I will–'

'Will what, Anne-Marie?'

It was Eve's voice, calm in spite of the concern she had felt as she walked towards the uproar coming from the summer-house. She hoped that no one else had heard these strange voices and would come down as she had done to enquire their origin. Seeing Anne-Marie in a state bordering on collapse had surprised her almost as much as the sight of this strange young man with her. He came towards her now, saying quickly:

'Can't you do anything, mademoiselle? She is hysterical! I cannot calm her!'

'Don't listen to him. He's a devil ... a cruel devil!' Anne-Marie cried, throwing herself on Eve. 'He's ruined my life and I'm going to kill him ... kill myself!'

Reluctantly, but knowing she had no alternative, Eve slapped the younger girl hard across the cheek, and instantly her body collapsed onto the ground and was shaken by deep, heart-rending sobs. Eve knelt by her and with real pity in her heart said:

'Try to control yourself, Anne-Marie! I'll help you if you'll tell me sensibly what has happened. It's Eve, darling. Tell me about it.'

The soothing voice she had used so often when they were children had an effect on Anne-Marie, who said between gasps:

'Don't let him go, Eve. I'll die if he goes away. Don't let him go!'

'He won't go yet,' Eve said soothingly, trying to understand what this was all about. 'Look, Anne-Marie, why don't you go to my room and lie down for a little bit? I promise you he won't go while you're away. You won't go, will you, Mr–'

'I am Louise's brother, Jean,' he said quietly, glad that this strange, dark young woman had taken charge of a situation that was completely beyond his control. This was Anne-Marie's sister and she already knew the truth ... it could do no harm that she had been the one to interrupt them so opportunely. 'I will do whatever you wish!'

'There, he has said he'll stay. Now come with me to the house. No one will see us. Father and Mother have taken Edouard to see the church. Denise is lying down, so we shan't be seen. Take my arm, there's a good girl.'

Slowly, she guided the still sobbing girl through the door out into the sunshine that blazed from a cloudless sky. Anne-Marie never spoke until she was lying on Eve's bed ... her face swollen and distorted from weeping ... her head throbbing so much that even the two aspirin Eve had given her did nothing to relieve it. As Eve turned to go back to Jean, Anne-Marie said:

'He's Anthony's father, Eve. Don't let him go!'

An instant's stunned incredulity flashed across Eve's face before she closed the door behind her. In a trance she walked down the stairs and stood in the cool hall, her back against the front door as if her legs could no longer support her.

Jean ... Louise's brother ... Anthony's father! Could it be true? Was this the truth at last, coming from Anne-Marie's lips when she was too broken, too exhausted to lie any longer? ... Jean ... not Paul ... not Paul ... not Paul...

'I'll have to go and talk to Jean,' she told herself, but her legs made no move to obey her will. 'He'll wonder what I'm doing. I shall have to go ... to ask him ... to find out if its true ... *he* and not Paul ... not Paul!'

Her face deathly white, her fingers clenched into the palms of her hands, Eve finally walked slowly out of the house and back across the sun-drenched lawn to the man who awaited her coming in the summer-house.

CHAPTER 19

As she seated herself on the wicker garden chair opposite the young Frenchman Eve appeared cool and completely in control of the situation ... an appearance belying her real feelings. But she had no wish to betray her personal emotions to a stranger.

'I feel I am entitled to an explanation,' she was saying, as she accepted the cigarette he offered to her. 'You might not consider that this concerns me in any way, but as I "adopted" Anne-Marie's little boy when he was born in Paris and have cared for him ever since, this, to my mind, means that I have a right to know the truth about him.'

'That is understandable,' Jean Boulanger agreed politely. 'I have no wish to deceive anyone, for I cannot feel that I am wholly to blame for what has occurred even if I am partly responsible. May I tell you the whole story ... from the beginning?'

Eve nodded her head and the young Frenchman leaned forward and began to speak with a forthrightness and conviction that convinced his listener that he spoke the truth.

'When Anne-Marie first came to our

home I became very much infatuated with her. We are thrown much in one another's company because my mother desired I should chaperone your young sister whenever possible. She did not feel happy to allow so young a *demoiselle* to go around Paris by herself ... even when her parents wrote to say this was in order. I do not pretend that I was displeased with the idea! Your ... sister ... was a very attractive young woman. Naturally, perhaps, she was pleased and flattered by my very obvious admiration. In time she began to feel for me as I did for her. We were very young ... and only human. I am happy, but at the same time a little worried because my mother and father have begun to discuss a marriage for me. I have explained already to Anne-Marie how in France this can happen and I realize now that it is very different in England. Well, we become very ... how do you say ... *intime* ... but not in any way of which anyone could disapprove. I naturally do not expect anything but the highest moral behaviour from a young girl who comes from the same society as my sister. These things are not permitted for well-brought-up young ladies and I respect these rules of my society. But it becomes more difficult every day. Anne-Marie tells me that she is very much in love with me. I am honest with her and tell her that marriage is out of the question, although I love her, too, because of my family's arrangements to marry me to this French girl who brings the large *dot*.'

He paused for a moment, looking unhappy and slightly embarrassed. Eve waited for him to continue, which he did immediately he had lit another cigarette.

'Of course, I understand now that I ought not to have told Anne-Marie I loved her, but this was true in one meaning of the word ... I was nearly out of my mind with attraction for her, and had she been from a rich family I would have been only too happy to marry her. Each time we bid each other good night it became harder to part, and one night, when all the family is asleep, there is a tap on my bedroom door and Anne-Marie enters. This is not what I would tell to anyone ... you understand? But you wish to know everything!'

'You needn't tell me any more than you consider necessary,' Eve put in quickly. He nodded his head.

'This is how it all began. She told me that she loved me and that it did not matter if I could not marry her if we only could belong to each other. I told her straight away that although I longed to do as she wished, perhaps even more ardently than she, it could not be, since she came from a nice family and this was against my upbringing as much as it must be against hers. Then ... then she tells me that she has already had a love-affair … she mentions two different young men, and I am much surprised. I begin to wonder if in England things are different from in France. In the end of the war the Americans are in Paris and we all see that they behave differently than we do. I think this is also true of the English. But although I am very weakened in my will, still I tell myself it must not be. She is a guest under my roof and this alone makes it impossible.'

'I see,' Eve whispered, wishing that she could discredit what Louise's brother told her, but knowing all the time that he was speaking the truth.

'Of course, Anne-Marie is very angry and we quarrel. We are both unhappy. Next day she will not speak to me and I am miserable. That evening we were to have gone to a party together, but she tells me she is not going … that she has the date with an Englishman with whom she dine. I am consumed with the jealousy and I decide to follow her. That night when he bring her home, he kiss her. I am furious and tell myself Anne-Marie does not love me. But all night I lie awake and think of this and next day I am ready to believe that she only go with this Englishman to make me jealous. I pretend I do not notice. This day she go to lunch with him and again dancing with him in the evening. She smile and laugh into his eyes, and he holds her close as they dance and I do not know what to think! I see them leave in a taxi and I go home, but not to sleep. It is very, very early morning when she come in. I have stayed awake until I hear her bedroom door shut. Next day I tell her she must come to dinner and dance with me. She refuse and say she have an appointment with the Englishman, who love her very much and who know how to appreciate her! Well, what have I to think? I imagine now that he will have what I refuse, and I tell myself I am very stupid. I tell her that she belong to no one else but me, and after a long quarrel which end in each other's arms, she agree to break this date and come with me. That night she come to my bedroom and we become lovers.'

'Only a Frenchman could state such a thing so matter-of-factly!' Eve thought, with an hysterical desire to laugh even while his story upset and revolted her. That Anne-Marie ... her sister, could behave so ... so terribly. And yet she must have loved him ... she still loved him, judging by what had happened half an hour ago.

'For a little while we are very happy,' Jean continued. 'But always I feel we do the wrong thing. I tell her so, but she now love me more than ever, and I realize that it is not fair to her that we should continue. All the time she talk about me marrying her and seem not to hear when I tell her again that this is impossible. I see now that she hope always I fall so deep in love I cannot live without her. But this is not so. She love me more than I love her, and I think it is best for everyone that this arrangement stop. The opportunity arise for me to go away … my mother wish me to visit my fiancée of the future in the country. I tell Anne-Marie that I have to go to visit the relations, and this way she is not hurt. I am to go for a month, and during this time, I tell myself, we will cease our relationship. I have not the courage to tell her to her face, but I am determined to write when I am gone.'

'And did you write and tell her it was finished between you?' Eve asked.

Jean shook his head.

'I have the passionate letter from her the day after I arrive,' he said slowly. 'I think I must break the news gently, and I reply to say that I shall be away a long time and think it is best if she try to forget me … that she may even have gone home to England by the time I am back, and so we must both remember our happy times and I hope we may always be friends if ever we meet again. But in reply to this I have a wire saying to telephone her to Paris. I realize that she will not let me go so easily and I think it best not to telephone. Next day I receive another letter … this is dreadful letter saying she will love me always and that I must not leave her … that she will never be able to forget me and that she cannot believe I no longer love her … that she has the permission to stay in Paris three more months and we *shall* meet again. She say also at the end of this letter that she think she is to have a baby.'

He turned away from Eve and went across to the doorway to gaze out into the sunshine.

'I did not believe this was true. I felt confident that it *could not be so,* and so I tell myself she write this only to make a chain to hold me to her. I do not wish to be unkind, but I feel it best not to reply to this letter. There is nothing I can say that will not hurt her. So I remain silent. Another letter come … more frantic than the first, saying she has been to the doctor and is certain now that she have the baby. She implore me to write … to get back to Paris … not to leave her alone.'

He turned back to Eve and held out his hands appealingly.

'I implore you to believe me, for I swear that this is true by *le nom de Dieu,*' he said on a low, persuasive note. '*I did not imagine for one solitary moment that she speak the truth.* If I had known that it *was* true I would have gone to her. I would have done everything I could to help her. I will not tell you the untruth … that I might have married her. I do not think I would have done this. My marriage had been definitely arranged and my family were dependent on me to go through with it. It was to affect my father's business in no small way and it would have served to no purpose to marry Anne-Marie. My family would most certainly have cut me off and I would have lost my position in my father's firm. I had had no training other than to prepare to run this business and I was very young. I would have had no money with which to assist Anne-Marie ... or the child. We should all have starved. This I think about now, but at the time, naturally, I have no such thoughts, for I did not believe what was in Anne-Marie's letter.'

'Don't you think the least you could have done would have been to make sure?' Eve asked quietly.

Jean bit his lip.

'Yes, I see now that I was too casual ... too anxious to avoid an unpleasant and unhappy meeting for us both. I do not like the scenes, and women ... well, I was afraid, and for this I am responsible. But I hear suddenly from my mother that you have arrived in Paris and that you are to share the *appartement* with your sister. I take immediately the view that Anne-Marie have realized at last that everything is finished between us and have accepted this fact ... that she has done the wise thing and left my home, where we could not avoid meeting. I am very much relieved that she have decided to be sensible and I am more than ever certain that she do not have this baby she have only imagined. That is all, I think, that there is to tell you. I returned to Paris soon after Anne-Marie have left my home. I heard that Anne-Marie have telephoned to enquire for me. I think that she is perhaps lonely and have made this call in a weak moment ... after all, it is not easy to give up such an association, and I, too, had many weak moments when I would have wished to see her again. So I am strong for us both, I think, and I do not ring her as she ask. I have one more letter from her begging me to go and see her at this *appartement* she share with you ... telling me she cannot come to see me ... but that if I ever cared for her at all, I will go to her. I again refuse to go, as I think this is best in the end, even although I really want to see her, to make our association end more happily perhaps ... at least to assure myself she is not too unhappy. But this is weakness and I overcome it. I never reply, and after a little while I begin to think no more about her. I heard many months later that she was back in England and married, and I am happy for her. I never thought we should meet again ... under such circumstances.'

'And you...?' Eve asked. 'You, too, are married?'

'Not yet,' Jean said. 'My wedding was delayed through the ill health of my fiancée, but I am to be married in Paris next week. Already my father has arranged certain business affairs on the strength of this marriage settlement of which I have spoken, and it would ruin him completely if I were not to go through with it now. It is, in fact, a legal document we have signed and already part of my future wealth is committed elsewhere. This may sound very cold-blooded if you do not know of this French custom, but I assure you it is very often done in our society. My future wife is of peasant stock and her family wish her to marry someone with the noble French name. I have to marry where there is money. Each of us and our families find what they want in this wedding. I am not in love with my future wife, but I am fond of her, and I shall be a good husband to her. But I cannot possibly break off this marriage ... even although I now know that I have a ... a son.'

'Then ... you don't love Anne-Marie?' Eve said slowly.

'That is a thing of the past,' Jean said bluntly. 'We were both very young. I would not wish her to be unhappy or to suffer because of me, and naturally I'll do anything you suggest for the child. But this is the most I can do. It would only spoil the life of many, many people if I marry Anne-Marie, and in any case I cannot do this in the eyes of my Church. I am a Roman

Catholic and Anne-Marie would have to be divorced by her husband. It is quite out of the question, for so many different reasons.'

'I see that,' Eve agreed, for clearly it could not right any of the wrongs or undo any of the mistakes for Jean to marry Anne-Marie now. Certainly it would not make for her happiness, since Jean no longer cared about her. She had only herself to blame for what had happened, and yet now Eve could truly pity her in spite of her wrongdoings. She had given everything to the man she loved … staked everything in a bid for his love … and lost everything … happiness … honour … peace of mind. Even his child had brought her no happiness.

'Tell me, please, what I may do for the boy,' Jean was saying. 'I am shortly to be rich … I would like to arrange with you–'

'No!' Eve broke in sharply. 'We don't wish for any financial assistance from anyone. My father has adopted Anthony as his child and Anne-Marie is in no way committed by … by your child. Her husband does not even know that she is the baby's mother. Only father and I know, and only I know that you … you are his father. Anne-Marie has no love for the child, and it would be better for us all, I think, if you forgot what has been said today … forgot that he *was* yours. We all love him here and he is happy. There is nothing for you to concern yourself about on that score.'

'You are very kind,' Jean said. 'I realize that you must hate me for what I have done to your sister ... for the unhappiness I have caused so unwillingly. I will not inflict my presence on you any longer than necessary. I am come to fetch Louise and as soon as she can pack I am ready to go.'

'Perhaps ... that ... would ... be ... best,' Eve said slowly but without rancour. It was true that she could never like this young man, however blameless in some ways he had been. After all, inadvertently though it may have been, he had caused untold misery and suffering for so many people ... Anne-Marie, her father, herself ... perhaps to Richard, too ... and to Louise, his own sister. Nearly ... very nearly ... he had been responsible for ruining her own chance of ultimate happiness.

Paul ... she could remember him again now and realize for the first time how shamefully she had misjudged him. Anne-Marie had put the blame on his shoulders for some ulterior reason of her own ... perhaps because she felt Eve might think she could be taken in by an older man, where with a young French boy...

'But that doesn't matter now,' she thought. 'Nothing matters except that Paul isn't Anthony's father after all. Nothing can stand between us now. Oh, Paul ... Paul–'

'Will you, perhaps, tell my sister that I am here?' Jean broke in on the silence.

'Yes. I'll tell her,' Eve said. 'I must also go to Anne-Marie and tell her that you are leaving. I promised her that I would not let you depart without her seeing you again, but I cannot feel that it will do anyone any good. While Louise is packing I'll try to talk her into seeing it ... this way. How will you get to the station?'

'I came in a taxi,' Jean replied. 'Anne-Marie sent him back to the village, but if I could telephone...'

'I'll do it. You say here,' Eve said quickly. 'It might be as well in case Anne-Marie hears your voice and ... and my parents and friends have returned...'

'I quite understand,' Jean said, with a formal little bow. 'I also am anxious to avoid a further scene.'

'I'll do ... what I can...' Eve said, as she rose to go. But it was not for his sake ... nor for her own ... but because she wished to avoid her mother and father discovering the whole sordid truth.

Anne-Marie was calmer when Eve reached the bedroom, but she was still crying silently, the tears pouring down her cheeks and soaking into the pillow.

She looked round quickly as Eve went into the room and asked huskily:

'He hasn't gone, Eve?'

Eve sat down on the edge of the bed and looked at the pathetic sight of the younger girl's face. Tears had completely removed any trace of beauty and she looked ten years older than Eve instead of six years younger. Acute misery clouded the once sparkling blue eyes and the clear, bell-like voice that had sung around the house so happily was dead and lifeless.

'No, but he will be leaving soon,' Eve said gently. 'I have told Louise to pack as quickly as she can. I hope they will both be gone before Mother and Father and our friends return. No, don't say anything yet, Anne-Marie. I want to do the talking for a little while. You see, Jean has told me the whole story, and although I'm not going to discuss it with you now ... or ever ... I want you to realize that I know the truth ... all of it. You must also realize that you have no claim at all on Jean. You are a married woman, Anne-Marie, and you have made certain vows to Richard. You could break these vows and do one more wrong thing ... but Jean could never marry you, even if he wished to do so. His Church doesn't recognize divorce. So when you married Richard ... was it to revenge yourself on Jean through his sister? ... you made a final end to any hope of a future with the man you loved. I know you loved him ... that you still do, and I'm sorry for you ... really sorry in spite of everything you have done ... the lies you have told me ... but I'm not trying to preach to you now ... only to explain that it *is* all over ... yes, Anne-Marie ... completely finished ... for ever. You can see Jean again if you wish, but it can do no good, and if I were you I would have too much self-respect to wish a man who had once admired me to see me as you are now are.'

The younger girl was sobbing uncontrollably now, her face buried in the pillow. She made no move to contradict Eve.

'You must let him go, Anne-Marie. Believe me, it is best for us all ... and even if you have never before considered Mother and Father before yourself, this time you must do so. I would not answer for Father's behaviour if he learned what I have learned today. I won't tell him ... nor Mother ... for their sakes, Anne-Marie ... and you, also, will have to sacrifice that last moment with Jean for the same reason. Grant me this and I will consider that anything I have done in the past for you is squared off ... forgotten. We'll start afresh together as if this had never happened, and I will try to help you to be happy with Richard.'

She waited a moment, but still the younger girl did not speak.

'Richard loves you, you know, Anne-Marie,' she said. 'I would feel, if I were in your shoes, that it was a great consolation to be loved by someone at a moment when I had lost a love. He is your future and he believes in you. He knows nothing of all this and need never know the kind of person you have been if you can only be your other self with him always. You can be so sweet … Anne-Marie … so lovable and generous and kind. That is the Anne-Marie we all loved so much and feared we had lost. Won't you come back to us … let us help you forget all this unhappiness and bitterness and start again?'

'Oh, Eve … I want to forget … I want to forget!' Anne-Marie cried, turning to Eve now and finding the older girl's arms waiting to enfold her. 'I've been so wretched … so unhappy. I never meant to lie … I was afraid … I told you Paul Johnson was Anthony's father because I didn't want you to find out I'd been having an affair with Jean. I didn't think you'd understand. I never imagined I'd meet Paul again. I was terrified when I did that he would tell you Anthony *couldn't* have been his child. I had to get him out of the house quickly and it was the only way I could think of doing it. I didn't mean to hurt him. I didn't really mean to hurt Richard when I married him … it *was* to spite Louise … or rather Jean because she was his sister. I hated him and loved him, and I wanted to hurt him as he'd hurt me. That's why I never wanted the baby. I would always hate it because of the man who was his father. It wasn't because I didn't like Anthony himself. I'm not really hard, Eve … or wicked. I didn't mean it to happen…'

'No, none of us mean these things to happen,' Eve said gently, as she stroked Anne-Marie's hair. 'But you should have trusted me, Anne-Marie, and not lied to me. I wouldn't have let you face it all alone. You must have known that.'

'But I wasn't sure!' Anne-Marie wept. 'You've always been so good, Eve. I didn't think you'd understand how I could … could have behaved in such a way. You'd never been in love…'

'Perhaps that's true,' Eve admitted. 'I never fully understood before how powerful an emotion love could be. Anyway, it's all over now and we must try to forget it. Start again with Richard, and I'm sure you will find a new happiness with him. If … if you would … would really like it … Father and I would let you … you have Anthony…'

The younger girl would never quite understand what this offer meant to Eve, but she was not going to force this sacrifice upon her sister.

'No … no! I don't want him!' she said. 'He'd only remind me of Jean … I never wish to see him again … ever … or have anything to do with him.'

Eve tried not to show the relief on her face.

'You will have other children one day, Anne-Marie,' she said, 'and you will feel differently about them because their father, too, will love and want them. I'm sure Richard would be a good father. And to have this common interest might bring you closer together. Now I'll have to leave you, Anne-Marie. I hear Louise calling me. But I'll come back, and when you feel better I'll drive you home. Will you be all right if I go away for a few minutes?'

'Yes, I'll be all right,' Anne-Marie said, and with an attempt at a smile she said: 'You've *always* been kind to me, Eve. I've hated us not being friends. It's almost worth … worth having to have a day alike this … to know that … that you still mind about me.'

'If course I do,' Eve said, as she bent to kiss the girl's flushed cheek. 'You're my sister, Anne-Marie, and even when I haven't felt like it I've known I could never stand by for long and see you unhappy without doing anything about it.'

'You're so good to me,' Anne-Marie repeated, in a quiet, sleepy voice. 'So … so … good…' and her eyes closed as the aspirin at last took effect and she fell asleep.

Eve tiptoed silently out of the room and went to find Louise.

CHAPTER 20

Six weeks later Eve was putting the last few touches to the beautiful clothes she was to wear the following day. Denise lay comfortably on top of the bed, resting her legs as the doctor had advised her to do whenever possible. Edouard had returned three weeks ago to Paris, and although she hated this parting from him, she knew that he was right when he told her that Paris in midsummer could be very tiring and the mild English sunshine and complete rest from all domestic worries were what she needed more than anything before her baby was born.

Another reason she had wished to stay was because she wanted so much to attend Eve's wedding, and it would be stupid to make the journey twice in so short a time. Edouard was managing very well on his own, although he was miserable without her, and tomorrow morning he was flying over for the wedding ceremony and she was to return home with him. Seats had been reserved for them both on the same plane that Paul and Eve were taking for the first stage of their honeymoon in Italy.

Eve's face was radiant as she packed.

Denise, watching her, knew that everything had at last come right for her friend as it had done for her. But occasionally Eve's smooth, white forehead would crease into a frown until at last Denise asked her:

'What is worrying you, *chérie?*'

'It's Paul,' Eve admitted; and seeing the French girl's horrified expression she added, with a smile: 'No, I'm not being beset by last-minute doubts, you silly! It's just that he's gone to London tonight for a stag party with Jake and won't be coming home again until tomorrow morning. Suppose he's late...'

'But, Eve, you are not to be married until twelve o'clock! There will be plenty of time. Besides, I do not think your nice Englishman is the type to be late for his wedding ... even if he have to drive down tonight!'

'That's just it,' Eve said, with a sigh. 'Suppose he has an accident? I mean, if he's been on a party and...'

Denise laughed outright.

'Will you stop this at once, Eve! You know your Paul is quite old enough to take care of himself and he is certainly not stupid! Nor is this best man of his, Jake... He will see that your Paul arrives here all in one piece.'

Eve sighed and sat down on the bed beside Denise, her face dreamy and full of contentment.

'It's just that I'm so happy, Denise!' she

said. 'I can't believe it is all coming true! Something is sure to happen.'

'That is just the nonsense of a bride the day before her wedding!' Denise declared. 'You will marry your Paul tomorrow and I shall be there to see you ... at least, I hope very much I shall fit into your little church. Really I am so large now I begin to wonder if I do not have the twins!'

Eve joined in Denise's laughter.

'I'm so glad you've been able to stay for my wedding!' she said warmly. 'You're being here means so much to me, Denise.'

'And to me, too,' Denise replied. 'You were the only guest at my wedding, and I do not forget what this mean to me!'

'You know, I can't dislike Paris any more,' Eve mused. 'Once the very name of your city brought unhappy thoughts. Now I shall always love it for bringing into my life two such wonderful people ... Paul and yourself. Because if it hadn't been for what happened in Paris ... I might never have met Paul at all.'

'It is Fate!' Denise said firmly. 'I believe this now as I have the same experience myself. Suppose Edouard had not come to that agency just as I leave? It would have been so easy to miss each other? *Non,* this does not bear thinking about.'

'Life is wonderful, isn't it!' Eve said ecstatically. 'I'm so terribly lucky, Denise ...

that someone like Paul should love me so much!'

'Nonsense!' was her friend's reply. 'You deserve all of it, Eve. *Certainement* he should love you to distraction!'

'I don't know about "to distraction" but he really does *truly* love me, Denise!' Eve said seriously. 'I've never told anyone about this, but I'd like to tell you. It proves to me how much he cares ... and I shall never feel worthy of it.'

'Tell me, then. I would like to hear,' Denise prompted her.

'Well, you remember the day Anthony and I went to tea with Paul?' Eve asked. 'I didn't really want to go but I had to do so. I'd made up my mind it was to finish everything between us. I was going to be terribly strong-minded... Of course, it didn't work out that way. He started talking to me and I realized that he was already fond of me ... perhaps even falling in love with me. I wanted him to do so ... more than anything in the world, and yet I knew it would only make things harder for me to end it all. But I was weak enough to listen to him ... he asked me ... if there was any hope ... for us, I mean.'

'Just that?' Denise broke in.

Eve smiled.

'I think perhaps the English aren't quite so impetuous as the French,' she said. 'When we fall in love ... at first sight ... if you call it that … we are too cautious to admit it even to ourselves. We are certainly too reserved to show it. There are few Englishmen, I think, who could behave as your Edouard did … met you one afternoon and proposed to you the same evening! It is very romantic … just as your wedding two days later was romantic, but we English prefer to be sure of ourselves first … and of the other person. Perhaps we don't like to make fools of ourselves, and it might make a man feel foolish to declare himself passionately in love and then have the girl turn round and tell him she never heard anything so absurd!'

'It is true!' Denise admitted. 'You are not an impulsive race. You have the sentiments … but you do not show them.'

'Well, Paul wasn't prepared to reveal how he felt. I don't think he knew altogether, anyway. He was trying to find out if I felt the same way. And, of course, I did, but I couldn't say so. I felt I couldn't give him hope if there was none, and how could I marry him when I knew what I did about the past?'

'The past was finished!' Denise suggested. 'Could you not have forgotten?'

'But Anne-Marie was my sister,' Eve tried to explain. 'Anthony was there … in the present. I think if it had just been an affair with some strange girl I had never known … no child to remind me constantly … I don't know. I just felt there would always be this barrier between us. Perhaps I was wrong. Perhaps in time I should have had to give way. I very nearly did weaken. Do you despise me for calling it that, Denise?'

'I do not despise you at all, *chérie!*' Denise said. 'I think I understand a little what the battle for you meant. You have had always the very high ideals and you live up to them. It is only natural that you expect others, too, to have these standards and you find it hard to respect them if they have not. Nevertheless, I do not think you would have let this stand between you eventually.'

'I'd like to think not,' Eve said. 'You see, it makes me feel unworthy of him. But let me go on with my story and you'll see why I said that. Paul had noticed that I was listening to him with my heart and he hoped, I think, that I would say I felt we should definitely see more of one another as he suggested ... in fact, that I realized there was something between us. He was right, too. Then Anthony came to me to climb on my knee and suddenly I felt I must tell him the truth ... that I could not marry him because I knew what he had done with my sister and because Anthony was *his* child.'

'You would have told him then?'

'I meant to,' Eve said. 'But I didn't. I just said that I felt there would always be a barrier between us... Anthony. Now I must explain how the misunderstanding occurred. You see, he'd felt I was going to admit that I, too, cared, then suddenly when the child drew my attention I told him that there must always be a memory of the past between us ... the baby. He had not thought about Anthony much before, but suddenly he began to wonder. He did not know, of course, that Anthony was Anne-Marie's child. He certainly did not imagine it was his, since he had only taken Anne-Marie out once or twice and their "love-affair" had consisted of no more than a few kisses! All he knew was that my father had adopted Anthony in Paris. He remembered then that I had told him once I had been very un-happy in Paris and this made him think–'

'That Anthony was your baby!' Denise cried. 'Oh no, Eve! This is indeed an incred-ible story!'

'But true!' Eve broke in. 'It's quite under-standable. I'd always behaved as if Anthony were mine ... in fact I feel he is mine! Paul had noticed how devoted to the child I was and how I kept him with me whenever possible. It answered all his doubts and he felt that I was confirming it when I told him Anthony must come between us and our happiness.'

'And did you not explain the truth?'

'I was about to tell him then that Anthony was Anne-Marie's child ... and his. I had asked him to let me explain. But he refused to allow me to do so. He said ... I can remember his words: "No, not now, Eve. Let's not talk about it any more for the moment. I'd ... like a little time ... to think..." Of course, I imagined that he had begun to guess what I believed to be the truth. So as soon as I could I brought Anthony away. I felt Paul would get in touch with me again ... would want to know the details. But two days went by and I neither saw nor heard from him. The third day Jean came here and *I* learned the truth. I was about to go up to the house that evening after I'd taken Anne-Marie home, when Paul rang up and asked me to go up to coffee.'

'I remember!' Denise said. 'You wouldn't eat any supper you were to excited!'

'Yes! I knew I had to tell him everything ... even that I loved him, and I was quite ready to risk making a fool of myself if he didn't love me. After all, we'd only met four times. But I didn't care. I had to tell him.'

'So it all came right?' Denise finished. But Eve shook her head.

'Not at first. When I arrived there he took me into the library and sat me down in father's old chair. When I started to speak he told me he wished first to say something to me. Oh, Denise, I was terribly surprised when he started explaining, but I was so happy, too. He told me that although he knew now that Anthony was my child, he had thought about it and felt that it couldn't make any difference to his loving me; that he'd tried to talk himself out of falling in love with me, but it was no use. He did love me, crazy as it must seem on so short an acquaintance, and that if I'd marry him he'd give the child his name and love Anthony as much as if he were his own son.'

'This, indeed, is love!' Denise cried, delighted with such proof that the English could fall just as madly in love as the French.

'I was laughing and crying both at once in the end!' Eve said. 'I was so surprised, Denise … and so happy that he loved me enough to want me even if Anthony had been mine! Later … after he had kissed me … I told him everything … and then it all seemed like a bad dream. It wasn't real any more … only the present was real and his arms around me.'

'It was so also with me,' Denise said. 'Since I am married to Edouard I forget my unhappy childhood. It seems also not real. Tell me, *chérie*, what will happen to *le pauvre petit* now?'

'Anthony? We're going to adopt him legally!' Eve said with a thrill in her voice. 'Louise's brother, Jean, doesn't wish to make any claim … even if he were entitled to do so, which he isn't. And Anne-Marie is only too willing. When we return from our honeymoon we shall go to court and Anthony's original birth certificate will be destroyed ... and he will be re-registered under our name ... Anthony Johnson. It sounds nice, doesn't it, Denise?'

'And does Eve Johnson!' Denise said.

'Anthony will live with us at Corderhay Park,' Eve went on. 'I wish Father and Mother would come back with me. Paul wants them to live there as much as I do, but Father says he really prefers it here and he and Mother can spend their old age in peace! I really think Father likes this little house. He's happy for another reason, too. He knows that when Anthony comes to us there will be a Corderhay living under the old roof once more; and Paul told Father that no matter how many sons we have of our own, he's going to leave Corderhay Park to Anthony when we die!'

'Do not let us speak of death at such a time!' Denise said, laughing. 'Nevertheless, it is nice that your father, too, should be happy. This make your mother happy, too. Listen, Eve ... I think I hear her voice!'

It was indeed Antoinette, calling Eve to the telephone.

'It's Paul, my darling!' she said, with a warm smile.

Eve's heart doubled its beat and the colour rushed to her face. How thrilling it was to hear his name spoken ... to know that in a moment she would hear his voice! She ran downstairs to the sitting-room and her mother closed the door behind her as she lifted the receiver.

'It's Eve,' she said, suddenly shy.

Paul's voice came deep and resonant through the wires, bringing him into the same room with her. She closed her eyes and leant against the table.

'Gosh, I'm missing you!' he said boyishly. 'I'm not enjoying this party at all. Are you alone, Eve?'

'Quite alone, darling,' she said softly.

'Then tell me you love me. It's nearly twelve hours since I heard you say it!'

'Oh, Paul, of course I do. More than anything in the whole world!'

'I'm such a deuced lucky chap!' came his disbelieving voice. 'I'm frightened in case tomorrow doesn't happen!'

She laughed then, her voice as joyous as it was sure.

'I was frightened, too, but it will happen, darling. This time tomorrow...'

'...we shall be in Paris...' He finished the sentence for her. 'Oh, Eve, my darling, sweet, adorable, wonderful Eve. I love you so much and I just don't seem able to say it!'

'You're doing fine, darling!' Eve said, smiling. 'Paul ... I'm missing you, too!'

She heard him swearing softly and harmlessly.

'Confound all these silly superstitions!' he

said angrily. 'I suppose I shan't be allowed to see you in the morning, either?'

'Only when I get to the church,' she said ruefully.

'I'll live until then,' came his voice. 'It'll be hard, my dearest, but it is so well worth living for ... my beautiful Eve with her dark hair covered with a snow-white veil, walking slowly towards me up the aisle ... and when I take your hand in mine it will be for always, Eve. You've no ... no doubts?'

'Not a single, solitary one, Paul,' she said, her voice ringing clear and sure.

'Nor I,' Paul said. 'Now Jake's calling me and I shall have to go. I just had to ring you and say good night. Until tomorrow, my dear little wife-to-be!'

'Until tomorrow, Paul!' she repeated after him, and with a smile that even Mona Lisa couldn't rival she gently put the receiver on its hook.

The publishers hope that this book has given you enjoyable reading. Large Print Books are especially designed to be as easy to see and hold as possible. If you wish a complete list of our books please ask at your local library or write directly to:

Magna Large Print Books
Magna House, Long Preston,
Skipton, North Yorkshire.
BD23 4ND

This Large Print Book, for people
who cannot read normal print,
is published under the auspices of

THE ULVERSCROFT FOUNDATION